THE RECKONING

THE RECKONING

The Knowing Saga Book Three

NINIE HAMMON

STERLING & STONE

The Devil went down to Georgia, lookin' for a soul to steal.

Charlie Daniels

Chapter One

Billy Ray Hawkins was drunk, but not nearly drunk enough. He would be, though. Oh my yes, he surely would for a fact. He'd get so drunk he couldn't feel himself risin' into the air without nothing pickin' him up, couldn't see the shadow of the...something...the creature that lived inside the skin of Chapman Whitworth.

He sat now on the floor, curled up against the wall in a boxcar nobody believed existed buried under a meadow in Caverna County, Kentucky. Sat there among twelve million dollars' worth of gold bars as pure as the ones the army was guarding in Fort Knox sixty miles away. It was stacked along shelves he'd built with concrete blocks and two-by-twelves. When he'd brought the first one down here —what? Thirty years ago?—he'd imagined that the shiny brick of gold had a pleasant odor. Imagined he could smell it. Not flowery or nothing like that, but fresh, like warm grass, maybe, or a woman's skin after she'd had a bath. Now, he knew it didn't smell. The whole boxcar was full of it and he could smell nothing at all but his own sweat. And even with his nose still swollen where the Suit-and-Tie-

Man had kicked him in the face, he could smell the reek of fear in his sweat.

Looking down, he realized he was clutching the bottle of Heaven Hill whiskey to his chest, had his arms wrapped around it the way a man'd hold onto a piece of driftwood in a flood. He tried to release his grip on it, but couldn't quite get himself to let it go. He put it to his lips with trembling hands, instead, and took a long gulp, feeling the fiery liquid burn his throat all the way down to his belly. It didn't warm him, though. The chill he felt didn't have nothing to do with the temperature outside or the whiskey inside. He was cold down in the core of his soul.

Continuing to shiver as the whiskey's warmth began to spread out into his limbs, he longed for the oblivion that didn't come. In fact, getting drunk almost made it worse because as he lost control over himself, he wasn't able to pull his mind back away from what had happened that afternoon in the office with wood-paneled walls and floor-to-ceiling windows looking out over the skyline of Cincinnati. The Man's fancy office. He'd taken to calling Chapman Whitworth that—The Man—so he wouldn't even have to say his name.

Billy Ray'd got all dressed up to go there. Went into Bradford's Ridge and bought himself a suit and tie and white shirt. The coat covered up the full sleeves of tattoos that decorated both arms, but wasn't no way to hide the teardrop tattoo under his left eye. Still, Billy Ray hadn't looked like no rube when he stepped up to the receptionist and asked all polite if she'd tell Chapman Whitworth he was here—that Whitworth was expecting him.

He'd had it planned out in his head what he was gonna say, how he was gonna demand an agreement that spelled out 'xactly what he was paying for. It'd all been too vague, with Whitworth calling him—calling Billy Ray Hawkins, can you beat that!—and sayin' he wanted to meet private. Billy Ray'd known soon's he walked into that motel room there was something "different" about the man. He'd told Billy Ray he'd "heard" Billy Ray had a considerable stash of money and wanted to know could they partner up. Billy Ray'd done what he always done, of course, denied that he had any money, poo-pooed the "myths" about him having a boxcar full of treasure.

But Whitworth'd just smiled a funny kind of smile and went on like Billy Ray'd never said nothing. He told Billy Ray matter-of-fact as "pass the salt" how he was gonna become the most powerful man in the world. But ambition was expensive, he'd said: what he intended to do would cost way more than the salary of a federal prosecutor. That was where Billy Ray'd come in. In exchange for Billy Ray's help, Whitworth had promised to grant him "whatever your heart desires."

When Billy Ray allowed as how he already had enough money to buy whatever he wanted, Whitworth said he'd give Billy Ray what all his money couldn't buy him.

"I'll set you free, Billy Ray," he'd said, in that voice that got inside your head and done funny things in there. "A full pardon. No parole. No parole officer. No restrictions about where you can go and what you can do. You can build a dope empire with no fear of repercussions. You can do absolutely anything you want. You'll be totally above the law."

And Billy Ray'd liked that part a lot and the next thing you know he was saying yes and they was shaking hands on it. They was partners. It wasn't until he left, until he wasn't listening to Whitworth's voice anymore, that the doubts flooded in. Shoot, he didn't even know what it was he'd agreed to pay for!

But he had agreed. And Billy Ray Hawkins always kept his word.

So he'd called Whitworth up, said they needed to talk. He was determined to set some things straight. He intended to demand...

But he'd never got around to the demandin' part.

Whitworth—The Man—had somehow...picked him up in the air and threw him against the wall. He'd stood looking down at Billy Ray and said he was gonna use Billy Ray's gold "to buy an army." Said he needed an army to start a war.

Then an outline had formed around Whitworth, a kind of blood-colored glow that became a shadow stretching all the way up to the ceiling. It was a shadow Billy Ray had seen before and it stopped his heart in his chest and froze the blood in his veins. When the shadow spread out big black bat wings, Billy Ray's bladder had let go and he'd wet himself.

Billy Ray shook his head violently from side to side to fling the image of that shadow out of his mind. But it bloomed up huge as one of them 3-D movie monsters you see with them colored glasses on. He turned the bottle of Heaven Hill up and took two more big gulps of whiskey, hands shaking so bad he spilled down the front of his shirt more than he drank. That shadow hadn't been no movie monster. It'd been real. It looked like...go on, say it...some kind of demon.

Another memory flashed, a bright comet on the black sky of his mind, and lit his whole being with red light.

He shook his head again, but slowly this time, in pleading denial. Please, no. Don't. Please.

~

ANDI BURKE STOOD at the top of the stairs and called down.

"Daddy, I can't find Ossy."

Ossy, short for Curiosity, was the little girl's big calico. He didn't get the name because curiosity killed the cat. He was dubbed Curiosity because he was a he, a male calico. Only one in every three thousand calicos was male. That unique quality was one reason Daniel and Emily had picked the scrawny kitten at the animal shelter and brought it home to Andi.

Daniel came to the foot of the stairs and looked up at his ten-year-old daughter. Her resemblance to her mother took his breath away.

"Ossie's MIA?"

The quizzical look on her freckled face—Emily always said Andi'd been dusted with cinnamon—melted his heart.

"MIA—missing in action."

Though Ossy was strictly forbidden to set so much as a single paw on the furniture, Daniel and Emily had always known that Andi slipped him into her bed every night to sleep cuddled up next to her. Daniel was grateful for the comfort Ossy provided the child after her mother's death. He knew the little girl had cried herself to sleep in the cat's fur night after night for weeks, so he still silently kept the cat's secret.

"Remember what I told you—the difference between cats and dogs?"

Andi's grin planted dimples in both cheeks. "Dogs have owners," she quoted. "Cats have staff."

"Which means he'll honor us with his presence again when it suits him." There was a flap on the bottom of the back door that allowed the cat to go out and, well, cat around whenever it pleased him.

"But as soon as the sun goes down, he curls up on the

window seat in my room. When I go to bed, he—" She caught herself before she let it slip. "He doesn't like to go out at night."

"I'm sure he'll be waiting for you when we get home from Theresa's. Grab a jacket; it's chilly outside."

Daniel refused to allow himself to worry about the cat. He had bigger fish to fry. Way bigger fish to fry.

CONVERSATIONS WERE MUTED, or seemed so to Theresa Washington. Like somebody'd turned down the volume on a radio and you could hear voices but couldn't make out the words they was saying.

It was 'cause she was tired, that was all. Bone weary in a way that didn't have nothin' to do with her new status as a card-carryin' member of the AARP. They was all tired.

Theresa looked at the two men seated side by side on the sofa, not talking much, mostly staring sightlessly into the cold coffee in their cups. She seen on their faces the same gray shadow of weariness she knew Daniel and Jack seen on hers. All of them was beat up. Well, except for Jeff Kendrick. He hadn't been taking hits right and left like the rest of them had. But if he hung around, he'd get hammered, too.

Crock was talkin' to Andi, a child who watched the goings-on of monstrous beings the same way other children watched Barney the purple dinosaur. You could tell he liked Andi. Maybe she put him in mind of his own daughters. Both were grown now and lived on the other side of the country. They were the only family he had after his divorce years ago. Crock wasn't his real name, of course. He was Charles Crocker, a police officer like Jack— a major, Jack's boss in the Harrelton, Ohio, Metro Police

Department, in fact. He'd come out of the past couple of weeks pretty much unscathed—at least from what you could see on the outside. But you couldn't find out about demons and angels and all the rest of it 'thout sufferin' that nobody could see, permanent injuries that wouldn't never heal.

It was gonna get worse, too. Way worse. And them already so beat up and tired they looked like they'd walked in here off a battlefield. Which, of course, they had. They'd come here to talk about it. Theresa had to prepare 'em, best as she could, for what was a-comin'. Right now, she couldn't find the strength to get at it.

Why'd you give this to us to do, Lord? We just a ragtag handful of ordinary folks and you 'xpect us to stand up to the prince of evil?

A brown mutt padded up to her and pressed its cold nose into her leg. Little rascal, not no good for nothin'. She'd never expected as she stood in the rain untying his leash from a clothesline pole the day of Miss Minnie's and Mr. Gerald's memorial service that she would become so attached to the furry critter—or that Becca would. Surprisin' how much company a thing on four legs could be when you woke up alone and lonesome in the midnight dark.

She scratched Biscuit under the chin and he plopped down at her feet.

Theresa made an effort to square her shoulders. Then draped a look of confidence across her face like a surgeon's mask—not that she was foolin' anybody.

"We got to decide how we gone stop Chapman Whitworth." She tossed the words out into the room and the murmur of quiet voices ceased.

"Just like that, you're going to keep a man from running for president." It wasn't a question. Jeff

7

Kendrick already knew the answer or he wouldn't be here.

Theresa liked Jeff. Wasn't no particular reason to—well, except the fact that he'd kept Billy Ray Hawkins from killing her and Becca. There was that. But she'd liked him even before he'd kicked Billy Ray in the face. Jeff was a drop-dead handsome rascal. Bishop woulda said he was "full of piss and vinegar." He was irreverent and cocky, but somehow managed to pull it off without being obnoxious—though she saw Daniel shoot Jeff a look of bitter hostility as soon as he spoke. She had to find out what it was them two had against each other.

"You know Whitworth's going to come after us now," Daniel said. "He used us to get him the publicity he needed, but he doesn't need us anymore."

Daniel started to say more, then looked at Andi intent on her game of rock, paper, scissors with Crock.

"Andi, honey," he said, "how about we go in the den and I'll put on Cartoon Network."

"I'm too old for cartoons," she replied. "That's for little kids."

Theresa stifled a smile. "You can watch Princess Bride on Netflix," she said and saw the little girl light up.

"I know all the dialogue—every word," Andi said. "I like to say it along with them."

The child started toward the den, then stopped in the middle of the room, staring out the wide picture window into the darkness beyond.

"Oh," she said. It was an awed whisper. "It's so…beautiful!"

Everyone in the room turned to look out the window into the night, but there was nothing to see. Beyond the puddle of light from a streetlight at the curb, the view from the living room window was as black as a raven's feather.

The full moon was shrouded by thin gray clouds that scuttled past overhead, sharp as butcher knives slicing open the sky.

"What do you see out there, child, that we can't see?" Theresa heard the scared in her own voice. Andi had the knowing strong, like Bishop and Becca. All three of 'em could see demons.

"Lights," Andi said. "Like fireflies. No, not like fireflies, like…" She looked at her father. "You know that picture on the wall in the dentist's office—a highway at night, only all the cars' headlights are blurred streams of light." He nodded. "Out there in the yard, it looks like that. Only the light's not smeared together. It's more like a streak of glitter hanging in the air, lit up and glowing."

Theresa and the others strained to see it beyond the window in the dark yard. They looked hard as they could but only saw their own worried faces mirrored in the glass.

"One…two…three…four—there are too many to count, and they're all different colors." Andi dashed into the hallway and looked out the window by the door. "They're here, too," she called out, then ran into the den at the back of the house. When she returned, she said, "There are circles of light going around and around the house."

"That's the light from angels," said a soft voice, and everyone turned to see Becca standing in the doorway leading into the kitchen. She'd been serving coffee and soft drinks, so quiet it was easy to forget she was there.

"What are they doing out there?" Jeff asked, and Theresa could hear the unease in his voice.

"I 'spect the angels is out there to keep the demons away," Theresa said. Jeff looked like he'd bit into a worm in an apple.

"The only people who can see demons is folks with the

knowing—like Becca and Andi and Bishop," she told him, knowing he wasn't likely gone believe a word of her explanation. "And the only time they can see 'em is when the demons is possessin' somebody. But the spirit world is full of demons that ain't possessin' nobody and them demons is as invisible as angels. They could be right here in this room same as we are and we wouldn't see 'em, so if we was to come up with some plan to beat Chapman Whitworth, it wouldn't be no secret. The efreet would know what the plan was soon's we made it."

Crock visibly relaxed. "So the angels will keep the demons away from us, protect—"

"Sometimes they will and sometimes they won't. You got to understand, this here's a war. We know who's gone win it in the end, but 'tween now and then they's battles going on in the spirit world all the time that we can't see. Sometimes the angels win and sometimes they don't. The angel in the Old Testament who come to your namesake, Daniel, fought demons for three weeks trying to get there. The Archangel Michael had to rescue him."

She paused. "Angels fight demons in the spirit world…" She looked pointedly from one person to the other all the way around the room. "But when the demons is here in our world—in human bodies they hijacked— God uses people to fight 'em."

"How about you go watch Princess Bride," Daniel said and started to shoo Andi out of the room.

"You just want me to leave because you don't want me to hear what you're saying."

"A very wise person"—Daniel looked at Theresa— "once told me that there are some things in life you're better off not knowing."

When Daniel returned, he got right to the point. "There's no reason now for Whitworth not to—"

"Kill us," Jack finished for him, his voice flat.

Jack was a big black man, a police sergeant—though right now he was on suspension because he was being investigated by the Bureau of Alcohol, Tobacco and Firearms about a nursing home fire he might or might not have set in 1985. He had a stern face, more rugged than handsome. Smiles usually looked kinda uncomfortable there.

"You mean use a hit man like Bosko, the guy who killed Minnie and Gerald Cohen?" Jeff said. She could see he believed that part. What he could see with his own eyes, he believed. She was reasonably certain he didn't believe any of the rest of it.

"Or a black widow spider," Jack said and cast a sympathetic glance at Daniel, who stiffened but said nothing. "We need to keep in mind that demons can control animals."

Theresa nodded.

"Or he could get creative," Daniel said, "and drop a piano on our heads."

"Could he…it…do that?" Crock asked. "With a piano, I mean, could he—?"

"I ain't sure 'xactly what all an efreet can and can't do," Theresa said.

"That's what I've been trying to find out." Becca's voice was soft but strong. Only the hint of a tremble in it. She looked at the door to the hallway that led to Bishop's study crammed with demonology texts and tomes he'd been gathering up for half a century from all over the world. "I've been studying, searching, trying to figure out what Bishop knew."

Theresa wanted to jump up and run over there and throw her arms 'round Becca, tell her how proud she was! Becca'd been the most beat-up by the first encounter with the efreet when she, Jack and Daniel were twelve years old. It had shattered her, and she had spent the twenty-six years since then on the run—from demons both real and imagined. But she was getting better, maybe healing up —finally.

"So you think this…thing's going to try to kill you?" Jeff said. There was no derision in his voice, but no belief either.

"What's stopping it?" Jack said.

Theresa smiled a little. "It's like I said before, '…the devil you know…'"

"I'm not tracking," Jeff said.

"That ole demon knows who we are and where we at. He can keep an eye on us, try to stay a step ahead of us. But if he kills us off, he knows God'll just send somebody else after him—somebody maybe he don't know and ain't expectin'. God coulda already done that. We might not be the only ones tryin' to keep this demon from becoming president."

"You think there are others?" Crock asked. Theresa could hear hope in his voice.

"There ain't no way to know, but if you're askin' my opinion, I'd say not." She watched the light of hope in his eyes gutter out. "We been give this to do. Us, right here in this room."

"Why you?" Jeff asked, gesturing around the room. She knew part of the reason he didn't believe in the reality of what was going on was 'cause they was all such ordinary people. Sort of a random grab from a Walmart parking lot. "Is there something you can do…some special, oh, I don't know, some ability you have that qualifies you—?"

"To be demon-slayers, you mean? You askin' if we got superpowers, X-ray vision, maybe, or somethin' like that?" Theresa chuckled mirthlessly. "This ain't no comic book,

Jeff. This is real life. Real life's always been a war 'tween good and evil. In times past, people seen it better'n we do, though. Smartest thing the devil ever done was to trick folks into believing he don't even exist."

"Are you saying there was a time once when everybody could see demons?" Jeff asked.

"Now, why would the Apostle Paul a'had to warn them folks in Ephesus 'bout demons if they could see the creatures walkin' up and down the produce aisle in the grocery store? What I'm sayin' is folks usta believe in demons. They seen what demons did, even if they couldn't see what done it. You can't see the wind, neither, but you know it's there when it blows the roof off your house."

Jeff didn't say nothing, but Theresa could tell he wanted to. He was keepin' his mouth shut to be polite, didn't want to make fun of an old woman's fairy tales and superstitions.

She shook her head. "We think we got all the answers now, so when somethin' happens we don't understand, we say it's just 'cause we ain't figured out the natural explanation yet. But some things ain't got no natural explanation 'cause they ain't natural. They's forces at work we can't see that live to destroy, that hate 'cause hate's what they's made of." She sighed. "But we're waaaaay too educated to believe they is such a thing as pure evil."

Jack's voice was soft and he looked at Jeff when he spoke. "I hear you, pal. I'm on your side. Everybody in this room except you and me has bought into a gigantic group delusion. I absolutely, one hundred percent do not believe any of this." He looked away from Jeff and murmured the rest with his head bowed. "But whether I believe it or not, it's still true. Ever since the day I watched a flatline on a heart monitor start making little mountains and valleys again, I've been trying to wedge truth into the shape of my personal belief system. It doesn't fit." He lifted his head then; his gaze bored into Jeff's eyes. "I've seen it. I didn't ask to, didn't want to, but..." He drew a breath. "When you've seen it, you understand that the people who're delusional are the ones who don't believe."

Jeff didn't have nothing to say to that, looked to be so shaken he couldn't a'talked if he'd wanted to. The room grew quiet and still.

Chapter Two

Today was the most important day in twenty-six-year-old Ricky Harrison's life. He had been planning it, dreaming about it, almost couldn't remember a time when he wasn't getting ready for the Big Surprise at the Mall of America.

He was so excited he could barely make himself walk slowly. It was like the excitement was going to burst out of him. But he did walk slowly. Yes, sir, he did. He did exactly what Mr. Nemo had told him, just like he'd showed him. Down the sidewalk—without looking back at the van! Mr. Nemo had said not to look back at the van because there were security cameras you couldn't see, and if they recorded Ricky looking back at the van, that would spoil the surprise.

Ricky wanted to look back, though, to see how proud Mr. Nemo must be of him, but Mr. Nemo wouldn't be proud of him if he looked back, so he didn't. He looked forward at the big red-white-and-blue star on the sign above the south entrance to the Mall of America. And he thought about the Big Surprise he carried. Just thinking about it made his stomach feel all funny—almost like being scared, but good scared, not like the scared he'd felt the day he met Mr. Nemo.

He had been bad scared that day when his bus broke down and he didn't know what to do. He never got frightened when he knew what to do. And he always knew what to do—except that time.

On Mondays, Wednesdays and Fridays Ricky got on the number nine bus at the stop on the corner of the streets that bordered CALADS. Waited in the shade under the big sign in front of the building that said Care and Assisted Living for Adults with Down Syndrome. And then he got off at Magnolia Street in front of Anderson's Supermarket where it was his job to bring in the shopping baskets out of the parking lot and line them up in neat rows inside. On Tuesdays and Thursdays in the summertime, he got on the number twenty-two bus going in the other direction and got off at Hadley's Nursery, where he watered plants and sometimes they even let him plant flowers in little green plastic containers to sell.

He knew how to get back on the buses, too, and ride them home to CALADS. But he didn't know what to do when the bus stopped and didn't take him all the way. The motor of the bus had made a funny sound and then stopped running, and the bus driver had tried to start it a whole bunch of times, but it wouldn't start. The bus driver had cursed a lot and had gotten out and stood in front of the bus with the hood up, saying awful words real loud, and then the other people on the bus had brushed past where Ricky was sitting to get off the bus and find another way home. But Ricky didn't know any other way home. Mrs. Shewmaker had told him what to do if he ever got lost, but Ricky was so scared he couldn't remember what she'd said. He tried to remember and thought as hard as he could as tears streamed down his cheeks.

Then Mr. Nemo had gotten on the bus and asked if Ricky needed a ride, and Ricky had been so upset he could only nod, and then they both got into Mr. Nemo's van and Mr. Nemo had taken him to Center Street, a block from the front gate of CALADS. He told Ricky not to tell anybody about riding home in the van because there was probably some rule about not getting into a car with strangers.

So Ricky hadn't told anybody.

The next time he got on the bus, Mr. Nemo was riding the bus, too! And he was there every day after that, in the morning and in the afternoon. And he'd sat with Ricky and said he wanted to be Ricky's friend. Ricky had never had a real grownup man friend, and Mr. Nemo said there was probably a rule against that at CALADS, too, so he would have to be Ricky's "secret friend." Ricky had never had a secret, either, and having one had made his belly feel funny, but good funny.

And then came the day that Mr. Nemo said Ricky should tell a fib, only a little one, at the supermarket— that he didn't feel good and needed to go back to CALADS. But Ricky didn't go back to CALADS. Mr. Nemo took him to the Nickelodeon Universe at the Mall of America.

When Ricky thought about that day, his whole head filled up with so many things he couldn't think about them all at one time. He met SpongeBob SquarePants and Plankton and Dora and rode the carnival rides. Mr. Nemo bought him ice cream and popcorn and cotton candy. Then he dropped Ricky off at the bus stop right before the one at CALADS so Ricky could get on the bus and get back off there.

It was their secret, of course. Such a wonderful secret that Ricky wanted to tell his friend Robert or Mrs. Shewmaker. But he couldn't. He had lied, so he couldn't tell anybody.

Ricky had sneaked away from work to go with Mr. Nemo to the Nickelodeon Universe two more times. Both times, Mr. Nemo said he was sad that he couldn't take Ricky there during the Universe of Light Show that was held every night. He'd told Ricky all about it, though—the music and smoke and puddles of spotlights on the floor and the crowd of children who chased the moving lights and danced to the music. Ricky wanted to see the Universe of Light Show more than he'd ever wanted anything in his whole life.

And right now, in a few more minutes, he would be there. He wouldn't just see it, though. Mr. Nemo had arranged it so Ricky Harrison would be the star of the whole show! Sure, he was going to get into a lot of trouble for sneaking out of CALADS. But Ricky didn't care. It'd be worth it when he sprang the Big Surprise!

He walked slow and steady—that was what Mr. Nemo had said, "slow and steady." He wore a big yellow SpongeBob SquarePants backpack that Mr. Nemo had given him while they were in the back of the van. It had an extra strap that fit around his chest and fastened in the back. When Mr. Nemo pulled it tight, it was uncomfortable and the pack was heavier than Ricky had thought it'd be. But Mr. Nemo had explained that even though one little yellow canary didn't weigh much at all, a whole backpack full of them weighed a lot! He said it was a good thing Ricky had big strong muscles so he could carry such a heavy backpack. When Mr. Nemo'd said that, Ricky had stood up straight and pretended the pack didn't weigh anything at all.

As Ricky got to the south entrance door, a young

mother with two children stepped out and held it open for him.

"Don't leave now," he told her. "You'll miss the Big Surprise." But she acted like she didn't even hear him and kept walking. Ricky hated it when people acted like they didn't see him or hear him, like he wasn't even there at all. But every eye would be on him tonight. In fact, Mr. Nemo had promised him that after he pulled the string on the Big Surprise in the backpack, everyone in the whole country would be talking about Ricky Harrison.

THERESA LOOKED AT JEFF KENDRICK. "You want to know what qualifies us here in this room to fight this evil. But the thing is we ain't qualified, none of us. God ain't looking for qualified. He's looking for willing."

She paused and took a deep breath. "And Mr. Chapman Whitworth knows we been tasked to do this and that we've took it on and I 'spect ain't nothin' he won't do to us now, short of killin' us. What's done happened ain't peanuts compared to what's comin'." She stopped when the memory of the strip search at the Cincinnati Jail bloomed bright and real.

No, can't think about that, about the wailing and the stink.

Her words hung in the air until Daniel spoke.

"We made a mistake before. We went after Chapman Whitworth. This time, we have to go after it, the efreet. We have to find it and—"

"Send it back to hell where it come from," Theresa finished for him.

"Perform an exorcism?" Crock asked. "The Catholic

Church has been doing that for centuries—they're experts. Can't we just ask—?"

"This ain't no exorcism. We ain't gonna kick the demon out of Chapman Whitworth—we gotta drive it back out of this world. A ruler of demons has been summoned from the darkest pit—" She lifted her hand and waved off the questions she could see coming. "I don't know how it got summoned. Bishop knew all that kind of thing, but I don't. All's I know is it's our job to 'un-summon' it."

She looked at Becca. "If you, child, can figure out how we go 'bout doin' that." She nodded in the direction of Bishop's office. "The answer's in there somewhere. Among his books and papers. He found it and we got to find it, too."

"You're going after this...thing...and you don't even know how to fight it?" Jeff asked. She didn't hear no skepticism now, though, not after what Jack'd said.

"It ain't like you can Google 'efreet' and find out all about it. Ain't nobody ever whipped out their cell phone and snapped a picture of one. Demons is as different as people. There ain't no cookie-cutter description that'll cover them all. Some of them's smart and some's dumb as a sack of doorknobs. Some's strong and powerful and others is wimpy. This here one, an efreet, is a king—a ruler. He's smart—smarter than we are."

"If your husband knew how to destroy it, why didn't he tell you?"

"He might have...if I hadn't been so tore up I wouldn't listen. That was right after we lost Isaac and I wasn't fit for nothin'. But most times Bishop didn't talk about none of that stuff, what he was readin' and figurin' out. When I'd ask, he'd get this awful look on his face and say what he was diggin' into was foul. He wasn't gonna bring that stinkin' filth out beyond that door and pollute our lives with it. You know how they say, 'What happens in Vegas stays in Vegas.' Well, what happened in that room stayed in there, too."

"Then why don't we take shifts and systematically go through every scrap of paper in that room, piece by piece," Crock suggested. "With six of us, it shouldn't take—"

Theresa barked out something like a laugh. "Even if they was sixty of us, it wouldn't be no short job. My Bishop, he was…a pack rat. Most of what's in there is books—the kind you can't order off Amazon. Scrolls and such. But they's other stuff, too. That bulletin board by the door's got Post-it notes on it dating back to the Carter administration, layered one on top of the other." She sighed as the memory of his smiling face faded from her mind. "But wouldn't none of us see the answer"—she looked pointedly at Jack—"even if it was written in purple in Hebrew."

"Destroying a Monster for Dummies," Daniel mumbled.

"Don't try this at home," Jack followed.

"He come down to dinner that day, the day he figured it out, just picked at his food, couldn't eat. Said he'd unraveled the mystery, but said 'mystery' like he was making fun of it and kind of grinned. He got real quiet then, said the doin' of it was gonna take everything there was in him.

"I asked him what he was gone have to do, what words he was gone have to say or what ritual from them books he was gone have to perform. He patted my arm and told me it wasn't so complicated he'd need instructions. Then he said, 'Just 'cause it ain't some complex, involved thing don't mean it'll be easy. Some of the simplest things in life is the hardest to do.'"

Theresa turned toward Becca.

"Her and Andi—they got the knowing like Bishop did. Without that, you ain't gone see whatever it was Bishop seen."

She turned back to the others. "Bishop had a plan to get rid of that monster, but you children went on ahead without him."

Jack and Daniel exchanged a look; Becca kept her eyes down.

"So where is it? This demon thing?" Crock asked.

"Somewhere in the thousands of miles of caves under Caverna County, Kentucky," Daniel said. "Now, if one of us could just remember where."

Jeff was incredulous. "You ran across a demon when you were twelve years old and you forgot where you left it? Like losing your bicycle or a pair of mittens?"

Rage washed over Daniel's face like white fire. When he spoke, he ground out the words through clenched teeth. "We didn't misplace it! That whole summer was wiped out of our minds."

"Wasn't the efreet done the wipin', though," Theresa said. "They ain't got the power to control the minds of them that walks with the Light." She stopped, then muttered under her breath, "Mess with their minds, yes--make 'em see things ain't really there, maybe. But not control. Likely your own mind done the erasing. Or God did."

"It doesn't matter why we don't know where it is," Jack said, irritated. "There are four people who do know. One of them is Chapman Whitworth. The other three are possessed children in Bradford's Ridge."

Theresa saw that Jeff was struggling, belief and unbelief warring inside him. She figured the seed of belief Jack's words earlier had planted would likely get choked out in the end. It was that way with most people.

"So we go find those kids and start asking questions, shake some trees and see what falls out." Now that there was something to do, a bit of life and energy returned to Jack's voice.

"You got any time off coming?" he asked Crock.

"Only about twenty-five years of vacations I never took," Crock said.

"Then we'll go—"

"Count me in," Daniel said. "And we need Becca to see the demons."

"Becca can't drop what she's doin' here and go runnin' off after that efreet," Theresa said. "She's got to figure out what to do once we find it."

He thought a moment, then added reluctantly, "Andi, then. I'll have to take her out of school."

"They's some things that's more important than learnin' the multiplication tables."

"How does day after tomorrow sound?" Jack asked.

Daniel and Crock nodded.

"There may be something I can do," Jeff said, and all eyes turned to him. "So we're clear on this, I don't...all this about demons and—"

"You ain't convinced," Theresa said. "We get that. So what's your point?"

"I am convinced that for some reason Chapman Whitworth is out to get you. I've seen evidence you can hold in your hand that he played some part in the murder of Gerald and Minerva Cohen. Not enough proof to charge him, but..." He paused, and when he spoke again, she could hear the ring of cold steel in his voice. "I'd like to help you take him out."

"Why?" Crock asked. He cocked his head to the side. "It's been my experience people don't usually poke a stick at a junkyard dog unless they've got a pretty good reason. What's yours?"

Jeff studiously did not look at Daniel, but Daniel's eyes were boring holes into Jeff.

"The man has hurt innocent people who…didn't deserve to die."

He was talkin' about Miss Minnie and Mr. Gerald, of course—but that didn't explain the look that flashed across Daniel's face when he said it.

"I may still number among the 'deluded masses,' but I might be able to come up with a card or two I could play in Chapman Whitworth's game."

"Such as?" Jack asked.

"Let's just say I know a guy who knows a guy…who has something on Whitworth—at least he claimed to years ago. Blackmail material or so he said. I have no idea what it is, or if it's anything at all, but I'm going to go hopping down that rabbit trail to find out."

"You need to understand—when you in, you in," Theresa told Jeff. "Once the cow's been milked, there's no squirting the cream back up the udder. If I's you, I'd count the cost 'fore I decided to get on Chapman Whitworth's bad side."

"If what you say is true, that's the only side he has."

Jeff was the last person to leave Theresa's house that night. He'd been the first to arrive, so his car in her driveway was blocked in by all the others. After kissing her lightly on the cheek and thanking her for her hospitality, he turned to go, but she caught him in mid-stride.

"You ever gone tell me what it is raises the hackles on Daniel's neck anytime you're around?"

He turned back, his face a mask she couldn't read. "That day in my office, I told you there were some things I wasn't willing to share—remember? That's one of them."

He started for the door again then paused and turned slowly back to face her again. "No…you'll just ask Daniel. It'll be harder for him to…" He stopped. Regrouped. Then looked full into her eyes and said it, flat out. "What Daniel Burke has against me is that I was having an affair with his wife before she di—before one of Chapman Whitworth's henchmen butchered her."

Theresa actually gasped. Full out loud. And her hand flew to her mouth. "Daniel's Emily?" She saw on his face that her reaction upset him, but there was no hiding it.

"I loved her." You could hear the anguish of loss in his voice and see it on his face. "It wasn't just…I loved Emily Burke more than I've ever—"

He stopped abruptly, turned on his heel and walked with purpose out the door—not slamming it, but closing it firmly behind him.

Chapter Three

Billy Ray's pleading didn't do no good. The memory come for him anyway. He didn't have no say. It pulled him down into water circling a drain, emptying into a pipe as cold as a tomb. He put up a fight, but it was too strong, the current was too swift, and he was too drunk. With one final silent scream, Billy Ray Hawkins was dragged into a hole in the black depths of his mind where the memory could feast on him, where it could eat him alive.

Billy Ray and three of the men who worked with him sit on the outcrop of white limestone with their feet dangling in the Three Forks River, popping the tops on one beer after another, telling lies 'bout women and fantasizing what they're gonna do with their share of the dope money. They'd taken off early that afternoon, it being Billy Ray's birthday, and bought four cases of beer to drink at Milkstone—after they run off the teenage boys who was swimmin' in the pool behind the rocks, and chased away the couples makin' out in the nearby cave entrance.

With half a dozen brews under his belt, Billy Ray gets

up to relieve himself, then goes back to his truck to fetch the fifth of Maker's Mark whisky. He'd bought it as a birthday present for himself and had purposed to drink the whole thing tonight!

But he won't have the bottle all to himself if he takes it back down to the river. Four men'd make quick work of a fifth. So he turns instead toward the huge cave entrance— a hundred feet tall and probably twice as wide—on the hillside and considers the rockfall that plugs it like a cork. He spies a rock outcrop on the top of that tumble of boulders that'd make a dandy place to watch the sunset and drink his whisky in peace. Already several sheets to the wind, Billy Ray's climb to the top of the boulder pile is no easy matter. But once there, he's rewarded with the view he was expecting—a ridge of low clouds, painted pink and golden by the setting sun, outlines the green mountains to the west.

His viewing spot has one drawback, though. It's hot up here! It was near ninety while they was working and it doesn't feel like it's cooled off at all since. Billy Ray's about to climb back down and stick his feet in the water with the others when he notices there's a crack in the rock wall of the hillside behind a big boulder at the top of the rockfall. It's a cave entrance. And one thing you can count on—it might be a hundred fifty in the shade or snowing or raining like a big dog, but down in a cave it's always fifty-seven degrees. The trick is to go deep enough in the cave to get to the cool air without going so deep you get lost and can't find your way back out.

But he'll be fine. He has a small flashlight on the keychain in his pocket to light up the cave floor in front of him so he don't trip over nothing. And he'll stay close to the cave entrance so he can make his way back to it.

He follows the small puddle of light at his feet about

fifty yards or so down into the cave and finds a flat rock to sit on that feels gloriously cool. He makes himself comfortable, leans back against an equally cool cave wall facing the jagged crack of light in the cave opening and turns off his flashlight. The dark is smooth, cool and comforting. He always has liked the dark—'cept when he's with his Becca and then he leaves the bedside lamp on so he can see. He opens up the bottle, ripping off the red wax seal, and takes two huge gulps.

Whew! Fine whiskey like that would warm you up if you was sitting on an iceberg. The liquid goes down smooth and it isn't long before his face is numb and his fingers clumsy. He spills a little whisky on the front of his T-shirt, and when he reaches to wipe it off, he brushes the amulet that hangs from a gold chain around his neck—the amulet he'd stole out of the back of one of the campers where them carneys lived who come to town every summer with their rigged games and rickety old carnival rides. Though he can't see it in the dark, his fingers trace its familiar shape and he recalls scooping blood off the floor and dripping it into the little stoppered vial inside the amulet, drip, drip, drip until the vial was full.

He suddenly laughs out loud, hears his laughter echo and laughs harder because it seems like a whole crowd of people are laughing with him, rejoicing with him that there is one less nigger to pollute the planet thanks to Billy Ray Hawkins! Payback. Bishop Washington took his self-respect —offering to help Billy Ray's white family when they come on hard times, pushing Billy Ray's mama away like the big buck done. So Billy Ray took Bishop Washington's son. A fair trade. He cut the boy's body up with a chain saw, drove to a spot south of Cincinnati and threw the pieces into the Ohio River. They'd never find a trace of that boy.

And after that, he always made it a point to seek out

Bishop or his fat wife, Theresa, in a crowd, like at the Kentucky Derby festival or the county fair. Or sidle up to one of 'em picking out toothpaste in the grocery store. He'd get as close as he could and laugh so hard inside he could barely keep it in—here they was standing three feet away from all that was left of their only son and they didn't know it!

By the time his butt gets sore sitting on the rock, Billy Ray has drunk half the bottle of whiskey on top of six beers and has a satisfying buzz in his head. He stands unsteadily and flips on his flashlight to light up the floor so he don't trip over nothing on his way back to the cave entrance. But there is no light where he thought the cave entrance should be. He turns around in a full circle, looking for the jagged beam of sunlight from the crack in the rock, but can find it nowhere.

Then he gets it.

"You idiot," he says aloud, his words slurred. "There ain't no light 'cause the sun's gone down."

Looks like he's going to have to spend the night in the cave and wait for dawn to light up the entrance. He sits back down heavily, clicks off the flashlight, lifts the bottle to his lips and gulps down another swig.

He wakes up in the dark, not certain where he is. He ain't home in his own bed, that's for sure, feels like he's been lyin' on a rock. He reaches down and discovers he has, indeed, been sleepin' on a rock. Then he remembers the cave and decides he don't want to spend the rest of the night here. That cave entrance ain't but a little way away. He's gonna get in his truck and go home!

Flipping on the flashlight, he staggers off in the direction of the cave entrance, clutching the near empty bottle of Maker's. He doesn't find the cave entrance right away, but it's around here somewhere. It doesn't really dawn on him that he's in trouble until he staggers out into a huge cavern. He feels the open air all around him and shines the light upward, but the light doesn't reach the ceiling. Or the walls. Even drunk as he is, he's certain he did not come through this cavern on his way from the crack behind the boulder to the flat rock where he woke up!

He is lost.

The realization sobers him a little. But only a little. He has downed almost the whole bottle of whiskey in—how long? How long has he been in here? Too long. He shivers, turns the bottle up and takes the last swallows in big gulps, then tosses the empty bottle out into the darkness. It hits the floor, rolls, and then clunks up against something solid. Billy Ray shines his light in that direction and he can see... what is it?

All by itself in the center of the cavern is a pile of rocks about four feet tall with a large flat rock stretched across the top to form something like a table. He lurches unsteadily toward it. When he points the flashlight down so he don't trip, he sees lines drawn on the cave floor in black chalk. The lines appear to form a big circle. He steps inside it to trace the other lines that cross and recross the circle, but he can't make out the shape those lines form.

But if there's chalk marks on the floor and stacked-up rocks, that means people come here. He's not down in one of them caves that goes on for miles and never ends. There's another entrance nearby—probably in one of the walls of this very cavern—and he just can't see it. He shines his flashlight out in front of him toward a cavern wall and staggers toward it, looking for an opening.

But he should have kept the light pointed at his feet because he trips, sprawls on his face on the floor of the cave and feels a sharp pain in his chest. He gets to his knees, stumbles to his feet and shines the light on the front of his shirt, where he finds a sliver of glass stabbing through it into his skin. His amulet is broken! As he watches helplessly, Isaac Washington's blood begins to leak out of it.

No! He tries to catch the blood in his palm, but it is no use. The boy's blood runs down the side of Billy Ray's hand and a drop of it makes a big red splotch in the dust on the floor of the cave.

The cavern is suddenly filled with such a blinding red light that Billy Ray lurches away from it, stumbles backward and falls again, landing on his butt just outside the black chalk circle on the floor.

What the—?

It smells like something's on fire, charred, and the light he sees with his eyes squeezed almost shut flickers like flames. A rumbling roar, the sound of a rockslide, shakes the whole cavern and then the light dims around him. Like he is in a shadow. Like something is blocking the light. Something huge.

He lifts his head and opens his eyes. At first, he sees only a black shape in silhouette against an impossible wall of flames that stretches all the way to the ceiling of the cavern. Then the shape moves aside so the flames light it up.

Billy Ray screams, shrieks, wails in utter terror with such ferocity it rips out his throat, sending a spray of bloody spittle into the air. He scoots backward on his butt away from the creature, sucks in a breath and screams again. This time, only blood, no sound, comes out his lips because his first scream was so fierce it shredded his vocal cords. He's screaming in his head, though. Oh, my yes, he is screaming in a high-pitched wail that sounds like an animal, a rabbit maybe, run over by a threshing machine.

A creature fifty feet tall has risen out of a lake of fire, a monster too hideous to fit inside a human head. It looks down at Billy Ray, leans toward him, and Billy Ray hears another sound—but not with his ears. It's a sound like cloth ripping. What is ripping is Billy Ray's mind. It is tearing apart, the gash running down the middle, leaving frayed edges behind it. And then the image of the creature fills his head, leaving no room for any other thought or feeling or memory.

Suddenly, he feels himself running, carried along by his own legs. He does not recall willing them to lift him off the floor or commanding them to flee from the red horror in the cavern. Still, he finds himself racing down a dark corridor lit from behind with a red glow, the roar of a beast bouncing off the walls, echoing and multiplying. Then all is black.

When he wakes, Billy Ray is lying in cool darkness, but a shaft of bright light streams down from above about thirty yards ahead of him. He opens one eye, then sits bolt upright and starts to scream, but the only sound that comes out is a barking cough. So terrified he is instantly sick, he vomits beer and whisky and bile out in heaving gasps that go on and on until he is too weak to move. As he lies panting on the floor of the cave, he becomes aware of wet pants and the stink of urine. He has soiled himself.

He slowly comes to understand that he is in an underground cave that has a hole in the roof. From above, it's a sinkhole in some farmer's field. The dirt and rocks that collapsed into the cave where he is lying form a slope he can scramble out of as soon as he can stand.

And as for what he saw...he didn't see nothing. Not a thing. Lying panting beside a pile of his own vomit, Billy Ray Hawkins manages to stitch back together the rip in his mind. The stitches are halting and knotted. They will not hold well or for long. Eventually, they will completely unravel. But until they do, he will remain sane.

Billy Ray woke up on the floor of the boxcar with his mouth tasting like a pig wallow and a sledgehammer banging away inside his skull. He staggered to his feet, swayed and grabbed hold of the shelf rack that held his gold bars, the gold he was gonna have to give The Man. That was when he noticed it. His pants was wet. He had… no, couldn't be. He hadn't never got so drunk he couldn't hold his water. Well, actually he had once. On his twenty-ninth birthday, he'd woke up with—

He felt the percussion in his throbbing temples. A banging clank in his mind shook his whole body when he banged the door shut in the face of those memories and leaned back against it, trembling.

AS RICKY STEPPED through the south entrance of the Mall of America, a voice rang out from the speakers: "The Universe of Light Show, a nine-minute interactive light experience, will start at seven thirty in front of the Nickelodeon Universe. The show is visible from all four levels of the mall."

The mall was crowded. As people moved back away from the area where the light show would be held, Ricky made his way forward. He bumped into a little girl in a pink dress having her picture taken beside a gigantic Dora Doll. He bent to help her up, but the little girl's mother grabbed her arm and glared at Ricky like he'd done something bad. That happened to him a lot, and to the other residents of CALADS. They talked about it over dinner sometimes, about how some people turned away from them and didn't want to be near them or touch them.

"People are afraid of something 'different,'" Mrs. Shewmaker always said. "Don't be mad at them for it. Just smile at them." So Ricky smiled at the little girl's mother, but she scooped the child up into her arms and didn't smile back.

Ricky had never been in the Mall of America without Mr. Nemo beside him. But he knew what to do and where to go, and Ricky was never scared so long as he knew what to do.

A mist-like fog began to appear on both sides of the space on the floor where the show would take place. Then the music started. Ricky loved music, especially music like this with a strong rhythm. The lights blinked on and off with the melody, like the music was making the light happen by being so loud and forceful.

The music changed. It was creepy, then happy, fast and then slow. Beams of blue, green and pink light stabbed down from the ceiling in rhythm with the music. Ricky was so awestruck by the sight of it that for a few minutes he completely forgot what he'd come here to do.

Children raced around through the fog, trying to catch the moving lights. They'd jump into one of the light circles that looked like a flower's petals on the floor, and then the circle would move and they'd have to find another one. There were big kids almost as tall as Ricky, and little ones who couldn't even walk, just toddling around holding onto the hand of an older sister or brother. The floor quickly became so jammed with children it was hard to move. Ricky had been standing up front and was carried out onto the floor with the wave of children as soon as the music began. And for a little while he chased lights with them, laughing, hurrying from one colored circle on the floor to another.

Then he remembered what he'd come to do, so he stopped running.

He stood very still in the middle of the crowd of laughing children. Wait until they saw the little yellow birds! Mr. Nemo had shown Ricky a couple of them, and the back-pack on Ricky's back was full of them. When he pulled the string dangling over his shoulder from the pack, it would open up and all those birds would fly out into the lights. It would be the most amazing thing any of them had ever seen, little yellow birds and bright blue and red and purple lights.

Ricky's face was wreathed in a happy smile of anticipation as he yanked with all his strength on the cord.

The explosion that followed turned Ricky Harrison's whole upper body into a fine red mist. What was left of him was flung in every direction, dismembered body parts joining the hail of other pieces of children now pelting the crowd and the walls and windows of the surrounding stores.

Sitting in a dark blue van near the south entrance to the Mall of America, strategically parked to be out of view of the pole-mounted security cameras beside the doors, was Sebastian Nemo. Or Alexander Stone or James Carlisle or any of a dozen other names depending on the passport he happened to be using.

He looked at his watch. Fifteen minutes. That was plenty of time. Had the idiot tried to take off the back-pack, maybe, and figured out the strap around his chest was locked in the back? Had he panicked, gone running to a mall guard and—?

A sudden roar ate up the world. The percussion blew out both sets of glass doors under the red-white-and-blue

Mall of America sign with a mighty fist of sound that rocked Sebastian's van.

He smiled. He could hear screaming from inside the building as he lifted the burner cell phone from his pocket, flipped open the lid and made a call. Someone picked up after the first ring, but said nothing.

"It's done," Sebastian said. He was tempted to add, "I just broke a bottle of champagne across the bow of Operation Maelstrom." But he didn't.

Chapter Four

As soon as Daniel pulled his car into the garage, Andi leapt out and ran inside looking for Ossy. She wandered through the house, checking every room, even stood in the dark on the back deck, calling his name. Nothing.

"Looks like Ossy's going to miss tonight's bedtime story," Daniel said, trying to sound cheery. He was actually beginning to fear something had happened to the cat.

Though they'd gotten home late, they still went through the whole routine. Andi took a quick shower and washed her hair. Daniel dried it as she sat on the bathroom vanity that was the right height so she could hold her head down and let her hair fall free.

Andi had shown him all this, of course. It was how Emily had done it.

Then he read her a story she could easily have read herself and she knelt with him beside her bed and said her prayers. They'd been a rote godblessmommy, godblessdaddy, godblessalltheanimalsintheworld litany before Andi had been shot and...died, flatlined—Daniel still couldn't get his arms around exactly what had happened in the hospital the night Jack walked back into his life.

Now, as Andi unconsciously fingered her mother's cross that always hung around her neck, she just talked to God. Daniel hadn't "just talked to God" in a very long time.

With Andi trussed up snug in bed, Daniel went into the living room and turned on the television set—some talking-head show—just for the noise. He stepped out onto the deck, closed the patio doors behind him and began to furiously attack the deck furniture. He pounded his fists relentlessly into the cushions on the wicker couch, again and again, kicked a cushion across the deck and tossed others around until he was panting and the deck looked like a trailer house struck by a tornado.

Then he sank down onto the cushionless swing, put his head in his hands and tried to cry. But he couldn't cry for Emily because he was so furious at her that if she'd been standing there, he would have screamed in her face: "How could you? How could you and Jeff Kendrick have…?"

It took all his strength to hold onto his temper whenever he was in the same room with the man. Daniel had almost started swinging at Kendrick's sarcastic remark about "losing" the demon and ached to smash his fist into that pretty-boy face again.

The ferocity of his emotion shocked him. He hated Jeff Kendrick. He had never hated anybody—no, not even Chapman Whitworth—the way he hated Jeff.

And he wasn't supposed to feel like that. He was a minister, a man of God and he wasn't supposed to…

Daniel was suddenly very tired. He got up slowly and walked into the house, leaving the cushion mess behind him. As he closed the patio doors, the talking head on the television was babbling about the upcoming primary elections. The turmoil, set loose by the accidental death—

Daniel knew it was murder—of Senator Thomas LaHayne, had unleashed a teeming horde of also-rans who had quickly sorted themselves out into four front-runners. Chapman Whitworth was one of them, a dark horse. He had burst on the national scene out of nowhere—thanks to the efforts of the useful idiots who had handed him the publicity he needed—and was gaining ground on the novelty factor of his candidacy alone. People were drawn to the "underdog" campaign. And then, of course, there was his voice.

The race was a dead heat at the moment with no clear front-runner.

Daniel was reaching for the remote to kill the show when the newscaster seamlessly transferred the program to a live broadcast from Minnesota. Terrorists had set off a bomb in a group of children in the Mall of America in Minneapolis. Daniel groaned.

THERESA SHOULD HAVE GONE to bed, but wasn't no way she was gone sleep—not after what Jeff had told her as he was leaving. He and Emily Burke was having an affair. Poor Daniel! Theresa didn't know Emily hardly at all. Other than the time at the hospital the day after Andi got shot—the day after Bishop died!—Theresa'd only spoke polite to the woman a couple of times when she'd come to school for somethin' Andi was doin'. She was a looker, that one was. A knockout. Not surprising a player like Jeff Kendrick was attracted to her. Poor Daniel was grieving her death and her unfaithfulness, all tied up together at one time. And Jeff had said he'd loved her. Judging from the look on his face, maybe he had.

She shook her head and sighed audibly. When folks

started breakin' promises they'd made before God, wasn't no limit to the pain and sufferin' they was pulling down on they heads!

She'd ought to haul herself up out of this soft, comfortable chair now, go to the kitchen to set out food and water for Biscuit and then…Yeah, then what? Get into bed, close her eyes and watch the freak show she'd been viewing almost every night since…she tried but couldn't even remember how long it'd been? Shoot, she couldn't hardly remember nothin', tired as she was from lack of sleep. The dreams had started after she'd spent the night in jail. In jail!

She had dreamed of being locked in a cage with demons, and the reek of it, the putrid rotting-corpse stench, woke her. She'd lain there trembling so violently Biscuit had sensed something was wrong and jumped up on the bed to snuggle in beside her. The comforting—though not pleasant, by no means—smell of his doggie breath had slowly eased the other stink out of her mind.

Now, it'd got to where she'd rather go to the dentist for a root canal than step through dreams into that cold, otherworldly fog swirling in eddies all around her. They was creatures in the fog, shapes twisted and distorted, circling her like jackals closing in on a wounded prey. When she'd try to get away, she'd feel wet, sticky fingers clutch her arm or dry claws scrape across her neck, and hear the demons' grumbling roars—or their high, hysterical laughter. Eventually, she'd lurch awake, screamin'. If Becca heard her, she'd come runnin', put her arms around Theresa and hold tight until she stopped trembling. Becca didn't never ask Theresa what was wrong. She didn't have to.

So Theresa sat in Bishop's chair a while longer, reluctant to face the monsters in the fog/smoke place and equally reluctant to take a white pill that'd make it all go away. She'd finally broke down and got a prescription for sleeping pills. The only time she ever slept well and deep anymore was when one of them little white pills worked its magic. She'd close her eyes in the dark and wake up fresh in the morning without remembering a thing in between. Trouble was, sometimes there was things in between you'd might ought to remember. Becca once found her sittin' at the kitchen table zombielike at two o'clock in the morning. Apparently, sleepwalking was a pretty common side effect of the drug.

Becca didn't like Theresa wandering around the house in the middle of the night and was afraid she might fall down the stairs. So whenever she took one of the pills, Theresa locked her bedroom door. Then she put one of the two skeleton keys that opened it in her underwear drawer and left the other on a hook outside in the hall beside the door. She figured she'd have to be genuinely awake to find the key among her multi-X size panties— and if she wasn't, the act of looking would wake her up. Still, she rarely took a pill, gutted it out most nights, waking in the gray dawn in sweat-soaked sheets with a scream on her lips, almost as tired as she'd been when she went to bed.

Theresa picked up the remote off the table beside Bishop's chair and used it to flip on the television. Anything to put off actually going to sleep. She liked CSI, but it wasn't on. It'd been replaced by a special news program about a terrorist attack at the Mall of America in Minnesota.

~

ONLY WHEN HE felt the drops of liquid strike his shirt did Jack realize his hands were shaking. He set the wineglass carefully on the counter. But he moved no closer to the television he'd turned on, didn't go into the living room and sit on the couch in front of it. He was nailed to the spot with his back to the sink in the kitchen, staring across the width of the room at the images on the screen.

Terrorist attack.

Jack had become quite proficient at banishing thoughts and memories and images he didn't want to deal with. Had a way of slamming the door in their faces and leaning with his back against it as their angry fists beat on the other side. He paid for that, of course. Paid for clamping his emotions down until he either couldn't or wouldn't feel much of anything for anybody. He'd paid for it with loneliness and the little-kid-with-his-nose-against-the-window-pane sense of always being on the outside looking in.

But the trigger of lights and smoke and fire and chaos on the screen was so powerful it slammed into the door and knocked it off the hinges, washing all the old images into his mind along with the new ones forming in front of him.

Lyla.

I don't want to burn to death, Jack.

The red dress falling through the smoke. Holding hands with a man in a black suit. He had died with Lyla that day. Oh, how Jack had wanted to be that man.

"...exact number of casualties is still unclear," said a man with a microphone who had an image behind him of bright lights, smoke and carnage. "Right now the number of confirmed dead stands at seventeen—all of them children. The injured, at least two dozen of them, have been taken to Children's Minnesota Minneapolis Hospital, and an additional eleven have been taken to Abbott North-western Hospital. We don't yet know the extent of their injuries."

Jack reached out a trembling hand and picked up the remote he'd set on the counter. He punched a button and saw a newscaster with the same background behind him. He punched another button and saw the same scene.

The third button filled the screen with the image of Chapman Whitworth. Then Jack couldn't punch the fourth button.

"Tonight the nation weeps with the devastated parents in Minneapolis. Across America, we stand as one. Tonight, all of us are Minnesotans."

His voice was the sound of gentle fingers on velvet, smooth and flawless and melodious. His chiseled face with the burn scar snaking up his cheek like a piece of red barbed wire bore the right look of shock and sorrow and concern, coupled with a barely repressed anger and steely resolve.

"Whoever you are out there," he said, staring straight into the camera, "know this. The fiery sword of retribution hangs heavy in our hands. We are a nation of law. Justice will be swift and sure. We will track you down. We will find you. And you will suffer for the cowardly, heinous deed you have done here today."

Jack finally found the strength to push the mute button and the voice vanished. With it vanished the almost hypnotic spell that held Jack breathless in its grip. Without sound, it was possible to see that Chapman Whitworth was ordinary. The voice was the source of his charisma.

Words scrolled across the bottom of the screen. Jack had pushed some button somewhere that he couldn't find anymore that set up the word scroll and he was embarrassed to call a repairman to come to the house for something like that. Andi would probably know how to fix it. Where was a ten-year-old when you needed one?

He was hardly aware of crossing the kitchen and

sinking down on the arm of the chair that sat beside the doorway. Why had they stuck a microphone in Chapman Whit—?

But he knew why. Whitworth had become a media darling as soon as he'd tricked Jack, Theresa and Daniel into opposing his supreme court nomination. Daniel had derisively dubbed the three of them Whitworth's Useful Idiots. The media doted on him, and Jack could come up with several explanations for that, none of which he liked. It didn't seem far-fetched to imagine that the national media in the United States was riddled with people controlled by evil forces. Not far-fetched at all. The words on the bottom of the screen said Whitworth had been the keynote speaker at the Minnesota Bar Association in Minneapolis that evening, so he was the first "national figure" reporters could get to. How convenient.

With the sound muted, Jack was able to switch the channel away from Whitworth and learned from the other networks that the explosion had occurred while he and the others were gathered in Theresa's living room, talking about stopping another evil. But maybe it was the same evil. Perhaps evil was evil. It didn't matter much what container you put it in, you could still smell the stink.

Nobody knew—at least, nobody was saying yet—what terrorist group was responsible for the attack on the mall. There were, after all, a wide assortment of usual suspects out there to choose from. But clearly Whitworth was convinced it was domestic terrorism, likely pulled off by the isolationist group in Montana—Jack couldn't remember the name—that had announced in a YouTube video their goal to create chaos that would bring the nation to its knees.

The group had sprung up almost overnight after FBI and Bureau of Alcohol, Tobacco, Firearms and Explosives agents had raided a survivalist encampment. It hadn't degenerated into anything like Waco. In fact, it ended more or less peacefully after the leader of the movement gave the obligatory paranoid spiel about the evils of government and then put a pistol to his temple and blew his own brains out.

Apparently, that act had been like puffing on the fuzzy white head of a dandelion. The seeds flew up into the air and came to earth in half a dozen locations that sprouted into enclaves of the Freedom Nation—that was what they called it—who were constantly rattling their sabers and threatening violence. But as far as Jack knew, they were all hat and no cattle. They'd never actually made good on any of their threats, and in his book, the ragtag troop of losers were the least likely to have pulled off something like this.

Jack's money was on the big dog. Al-Qaida. Or maybe the terrorist group called ISIS, a new species of nutcase that had evolved while the US was pulling troops out of Iraq.

He watched the coverage for a few more minutes in silence, then flipped off the television and sat in the quiet of his living room. Theresa had called it, had said the world would grow darker and darker as it spun toward the end. Jack shook his head wearily, yearning with a physical pain for normal. No demons and fiery lakes, just an average, garden-variety existence. But when you were living in occupied territory, you didn't get a say.

Chapter Five

Andi hadn't wanted to go. She liked school and never wanted to miss. But the most important reason she didn't want to go was Ossy. Daddy called him the MIA cat, but she had forgotten what the letters stood for. All she knew was that she hadn't seen him since before they went to Miss Theresa's house Wednesday evening, day before yesterday. Even though Daddy kept saying the cat was fine, she was beginning to get really worried.

Daddy had left big bowls of food and water for him in the laundry room and said Ossy'd be snoozing on Andi's window seat when they returned. She hoped so.

She got in the backseat behind Uncle Jack, and before she scooted over to the other side to sit behind Daddy, she caught a whiff of Uncle Jack's Old Spice aftershave. He wore it every day. Daddy wore different kinds, but Uncle Jack always wore the same one. She could imagine the bottle all by itself in his medicine cabinet. Major Crocker got in behind Uncle Jack and immediately challenged her to a game of rock, paper, scissors.

"When I was a little boy, my mother was so overprotective she only let me play rock, paper," he said.

Daddy and Uncle Jack laughed, but Andi didn't understand what was funny about that.

Then the two men in the front started talking about politics—nominations and conventions and things she didn't understand. She caught the name Chapman Whitworth, though—it gave her chills—when Uncle Jack said he and all the other candidates would be speaking on Monday at the Better Day Society dinner in Lancaster. Lancaster was the place you passed by when you took the paddleboat cruise on the Star of Cincinnati—the place where all the rich people lived in gigantic riverfront houses.

"The Better Day Society gets points for having a sense of humor, at least," Daddy said. "I gave the invocation at the dinner a couple of years ago. The community service awards they give to individuals are plaques, but the plaque they give every year to some business for being a good corporate neighbor is attached to a gold-plated manhole cover."

"Seriously?" Uncle Jack asked.

Daddy nodded. "The last Monday in October falls on the thirty-first this year," Daddy said. "So the dinner's going to be a Halloween costume ball."

"They ought to ask all the candidates to dress as monsters. Whitworth wouldn't have to buy an outfit."

Andi spotted a herd of cattle as they passed a field.

"Daddy, why are some of the cows spotted and others solid black? Are there solid white ones and they marry solid black ones and their babies are the spotted ones?"

"If it worked like that, honey, Uncle Jack could marry a white woman and they'd have spotted babies."

Andi giggled at that thought.

"I'd like to be a spotted person," she said. "But not

boring black and white spots. I'd want purple and orange ones."

She played a game on her iPad, then leaned her head against the window, nodded off and slept for a while. When she woke, she bit her tongue before she asked, "Are we there yet?" She didn't want to sound like some annoying little kid in a TV show. She saw a sign up ahead that proclaimed "Welcome to Caverna County, Kentucky," so it couldn't be far, but she wasn't sure how long she could wait.

"Can we stop soon? I need to go to the bath—" But she didn't finish her sentence. They had rounded a curve in the winding road past the sign, into a valley between mountains that looked like they'd been splattered with yellow and red and gold paint. But the autumn colors weren't what she was staring at.

"It's only a little farther now. Can you wait—? What is it, Andi? What's wrong?"

Uncle Jack had been looking at her with his rearview mirror and Daddy turned around in his seat.

"Andi, what's the matter?" Daddy asked.

Andi didn't know how to tell them what was wrong because she wasn't sure herself. She stared at it, trying to figure out what it was. Was it fog? No, fog was a light gray; this was black. Couldn't be a storm, either, because storm clouds were up high in the sky, and besides, this darkness wasn't coming from the sky down, it was going from the ground up. Smoke, then, from a fire. Not one fire, though—a whole bunch of them. Streams of smoke were rising into the air all around to form a puddle of darkness that hung over the valley between the mountains and spread out in all directions. It was moving, swirling slowly around like those satellite pictures of hurricanes.

"Andi...?" She could hear the concern in Uncle Jack's voice.

They rounded another bend and Andi saw the place where one of the smoke streams was coming from. There was a hole in the mountain next to a huge white rock that stuck out into a river. Even though the hole was plugged up by rocks, black something flowed out of it and rose into the sky. But it wasn't smoke. It was just...dark.

"There!" she managed to sputter and pointed at the rock as they passed by it. Then she turned around in her seat to look back at it.

"Milkstone?" her father said.

"What's—" Major Crocker began.

"It's a big rock in the river that forms a pool where teenagers drink and party—at least they used to," Uncle Jack said.

When Andi turned back around to face front, she spotted where another black stream rose from behind a stand of trees on the other side of the road, and another lifting up from the mountain farther down.

"There's dark...smoke or a cloud or...there's black in the sky," she said, understanding now that this was like the demons she could see and other people couldn't.

The car had reached the outer edge of the black cloud and Andi cringed away from the window as they passed into the gloom. It grew darker all around her and she suddenly felt frightened for no reason at all.

"I don't see anything," Major Crocker said. "Describe it to me."

But that was the thing—she didn't know the words to describe what she saw or explain how it made her feel. As they traveled deeper into the growing shadow, Andi tried to see what it was, exactly. But it wasn't anything at all. Just "not light." Dark and gloomy. And scary.

"It's like…you know, in a dark room you turn on just one lamp and it lights everything around it, but not the whole room."

Uncle Jack nodded his head but kept his eyes on the road.

"This is the opposite. It's like you're in a bright room and someone turns on a lamp only what comes out of the lamp is darkness. It doesn't make the whole room dark, but around the lamp…"

That didn't make sense, so she tried again.

"It's like shadows are flowing up from holes in the ground into the sky. The dark is hanging there in a puddle, getting thicker and thicker, blotting out the sun."

Daddy's voice was soft, and he and Uncle Jack exchanged a look that frightened her almost as much as the sky because the two of them looked scared, too.

"She sees darkness coming out of the caves," Daddy said.

JACK PARKED in a tight space between two pickup trucks in front of the Caverna County Courthouse on Main Street in Bradford's Ridge, Kentucky. They had an appointment to talk to Caverna County Sheriff Hezekiah Lincoln—the man who had told Jack about the strange occurrences in the county and about the children he thought might be responsible for them.

It was late on a busy Friday afternoon—which was court day, from the look of it, so a steady stream of mangy-looking people climbed the wide concrete steps to the big metal doors on the front of the building. They joined farmers paying taxes, teenagers paying speeding tickets and the ladies who gathered in the Home Extension

Agent's office on the top floor of the building to quilt, knit and gossip.

Daniel and Jack got out of the car. Crock got out of the backseat on Jack's side, but Andi sat still for a moment, like maybe she was reluctant to step out into darkness that only she could see. Daniel opened her door from the outside and she sat for a moment, then edged out of the car.

Jack was looking right at her, shaking his head, or he wouldn't have seen it happen. The cat came out of nowhere. It streaked into Jack's field of vision from the right, dashing across the street toward the back of his car. And Andi.

The cat's hackles were raised, its ears flattened and its teeth bared in a vicious snarl. It never broke stride, just launched itself into the air in an impossible leap that struck Andi in the chest, knocking her backward into her opened car door. The cat clung to her pink sweater with the claws on its hind feet and left paw while it swiped at her face with the claws on the right. Andi shrieked and Jack reached out to shove Crock, who hadn't seen it, out of the way so he could get to her. But a big farmer in bib overalls got there first. Likely the owner of the pickup truck they were parked beside, he was standing by the truck, waiting for Andi and Daniel to close their doors so he could open his and get in. The man took two steps, reached out huge hands and grabbed the animal, yanking it off Andi's chest.

"What in the Sam Hill—?" he sputtered.

The cat writhed and twisted, turning so it could claw at the man's arms. When it sank its sharp fangs into a knuckle on his left hand, the farmer responded instinctively—slamming the cat down as hard as he could on the trunk of the car. It clung to him still until he smashed his right fist in a hammer blow downward, crushing the cat's head against the metal of the trunk. The animal went limp, but was still twitching when he flung it off his arm onto the street behind the car, where a foot wearing lace-up shoes stomped it hard. The foot was Crock's. The animal lay still then, sprawled on its back, blood streaming out of its mouth, nose and ears.

That was the first good look Jack got of the animal, and when he saw it clearly, he felt bile rise into the back of his throat. It was Andi's cat, Ossy. No doubt about it. Though it was muddy and bunged up, with cockleburs clinging to its coat and a scabbed-over hunk missing from its right ear, it was definitely Ossy. The patch of black fur around his right eye like the Victrola bulldog and the two perfectly white feet and legs like he was wearing gym socks —it was Ossy all right.

How did Ossy get here?

Andi had recognized him, too, and was clinging to her father, crying, "Ossy! Ossy!" as she sobbed, blood seeping from the scratches gouged into her cheek. Daniel peeled her off and held her out at arm's length, inspecting, making sure there weren't injuries he couldn't see.

"Anybody got a handkerchief?" Daniel asked the crowd that had by that time gathered around the back of the car. "Any kind of cloth I can—?"

A portly woman produced a handful of tissues out of her purse, leaned toward Andi and began to wipe gently at her face with them.

"That cat attacked the little girl, come up out of nowhere," the woman said to nobody in particular.

"Are you all right?" Jack asked the farmer, who was holding his injured hand and arm to his body.

"Do I look all right?" the man said. "That thing just leapt on her—?"

"Wouldja look at that!" exclaimed a voice out of the crowd. "That's a male calico."

"There's no such thing as a male calico cat," said someone else.

"Well, I'm looking at one," said the first voice. "See for yourself."

It was clear the cat sprawled on its back on the asphalt was both male and a calico.

"Well, then that's what was wrong with it. A male calico cat'd have to be so screwed up inside, it'd go crazy," said the first voice.

"That cat's rabid," said another voice. "I seen a rabid fox do that once, come running out of the woods all crazy like, run in circles then tore into one of my pigs. I had to shoot it."

"The fox?" asked the man next to him.

"The fox and the pig—couldn't even eat the meat. You folks is gonna have to get rabies shots or those bites'll kill you."

Jack knew the cat wasn't rabid. It wasn't disease that had driven the animal to violence.

Someone had gone to get the sheriff, or he had heard the ruckus and came to investigate. A stocky man, broad and thick, he pushed through the crowd, trailing two deputies behind him.

"Rabid cat attacked that little girl, Linc," came a voice out of the crowd. "But Joe Prather got him good."

The sheriff surveyed the situation and Jack suspected he picked up on everything that'd happened and maybe even had some inkling what it all meant. Behind the affable, hound-dog face was a keen mind Jack respected. Any man smart enough to realize he didn't have all the answers was on an intellectual level way above the average person.

"Go get a sack," the sheriff said to one of the deputies

who'd come out of the courthouse with him. "We need to send this cat off to the state lab to get it tested."

He looked into Jack's eyes when he spoke next. "Wouldn't want these folks to go through rabies shots if they don't have to, if maybe there was some other reason this cat acted like it did."

~

JACK AND CROCK sat in Sheriff Lincoln's cluttered office, in straight-backed chairs beside filing cabinets drooling paperwork onto the floor. Andi was perched on the edge of the sheriff's desk while Daniel applied Band-Aids to her face. When they finally got the child calmed down, it was clear the farmer, Joe Prather, had taken the brunt of the cat's fury. Andy had scratches down her left cheek—painful, but only scratches. It could have been a lot worse.

"You want to tell me what that was all about out there?" the sheriff said.

"That was Andi's cat, Ossy," Jack said, his voice flat.

"Ossy?"

"For Curiosity...a male calico," Daniel said.

"You brought your cat down here and it attacked—?"

"We didn't bring it."

"If you didn't, who did?"

"From the look of it, I don't imagine anybody did," Crock said. He reached into his shirt pocket and pulled out a small vial filled with cinnamon toothpicks and popped one into his mouth, wallowing it from side to side as he spoke. "You see what a mess it was—mud and stickers, the pads on its front paws were worn down and bleeding."

Its front paws—the ones wearing white gym socks.

"Are you telling me that cat walked all the way here

from Cincinnati?" the sheriff said. "Even as the crow flies, that's more'n a hundred miles."

"Might have hitched a ride on something for a time," Crock said. "But yeah, I figure it walked most of the way."

"Are you sure that's your cat?" the sheriff asked Andi.

"Uh-huh." Andi sounded small and terribly sad. "My sweet Ossy. And I saw it, too. Like a bug, had legs all up and down its sides, but it was slimy, sticky-looking like the trails a snail leaves on the sidewalk."

The sheriff opened his mouth, then closed it again and said nothing.

"It was on the cat's back, riding it, with claws all stuck in…" She shuddered.

"What I can't figure is why," Daniel said. "Ossy didn't have to walk a hundred miles to attack Andi. He slept in the bed with her every night."

Andi shot him a surprised glance and Daniel looked like he'd "let the cat out of the bag" about something.

"Maybe he did have to," Jack said. "Remember the bright lights at Theresa's. Andi might have been… protected in Cincinnati."

"But not here?"

"Maybe it's too dark here." Jack shrugged and ended the speculation with a curt, "It's over now. We'll keep a better eye out from now on."

"There are others out there—everywhere, all around," Andi said in a hollow whisper. "It's dark here and I can almost see them, but when I turn to look, they slink back into the shadows."

Daniel plastered a smile on his face like putting on a stick-on name tag. "How about I buy you a milkshake— any flavor you want." The enthusiasm in his voice rang as hollow as an empty oil drum. "There's a drugstore across the street with an old-fashioned soda fountain…"

He looked a question at the sheriff.

"It's still there," the sheriff said, his good cheer as forced as Daniel's. "And they're open until seven thirty. They make the best milkshakes you ever tasted."

Andi looked like she'd rather eat paint than drink a milkshake right then, but she obediently hopped down off the desk, took Daniel's hand and the two left the office.

As soon as they were alone, Lincoln fired the question. "What did that little girl mean when she said she could see a slimy thing on the cat?"

Jack shot Crock a glance.

"As the newest member of this traveling spook show, let me tell you something," Crock said. "It really is true there are some things in life you are better off not knowing."

"As a charter member," Jack said, "I can testify that the 'normal world,' where you don't see the Wizard of Oz behind the curtain, pulling levers and pushing buttons, is a way better place to live."

Lincoln looked from Jack to Crock, his face thoughtful. "But the trouble with that thinking is it ignores reality— even if it's a reality most people can't see. And it doesn't square up with Scripture."

Jack and Crock exchanged a look.

"I'm not a particularly religious man, but I was raised a good Pentecostal boy and I know who's the prince of this world. That's what this is all about, isn't it?"

Jack slowly nodded.

"Let's hear it, then."

"I'll give you the Reader's Digest Condensed version," Jack said. "A demon, a powerful one called an efreet, was somehow summoned into the world here in Caverna County. It's somewhere down in the caves. We found it when we were kids and got rid of it somehow, but those memories are gone. Now, it has come back. We have to find it again and send it back where it came from."

Jack held up his hand before the sheriff could respond. "Don't ask. I have no idea how we do that, but I'm taking this on faith that there is a way and we'll figure out what it is when the time comes. But we can't do anything until we find the efreet."

"You know it's in the caves, but you don't know where?" the sheriff asked.

"Can we take a time-out here?" Crock said. "Jack has said there are miles and miles of caves under this county, but surely they've been explored—at least some of them—over the years. Isn't there a map somewhere—?"

"No map," the sheriff said. "It's like a honeycomb under our feet. There's not just one level, but layers and layers, going down nobody knows how far."

"And it changes," Jack said. "They're limestone caves formed by underground rivers. The water's still dissolving the rock. This whole county is riddled with sinkholes where some poor farmer's south forty collapsed ten feet or fifty feet when a cave roof below it gave way."

"Folks know the caves are there and maybe have ventured a few hundred yards down into the nearest one of them. Teenage boys, mostly."

"So this efreet could be anywhere," Crock said.

"Three little kids here in Bradford's Ridge know where," Jack said.

"And they know because…?"

"Because they're possessed by demons," Jack said. The sheriff flinched, like he'd taken an invisible blow. "You have to be in the presence of the efreet for that to happen."

"And you want to talk to them, see if you can get them to tell you where it is?" Lincoln asked.

"Eventually, yes, but they won't willingly tell me anything. The demons that control them are smarter than that. I want to find out where they live. They're kids. They can't get in a car and drive thirty miles across the county to keep an appointment with a monster. Wherever this thing is, it's some place those kids could get to on their own. Somewhere Daniel and Becca and I could have ridden to on our bikes. That's where we need to start. Do you have a big map of the county?"

When Daniel returned with Andi and chocolate milk-shakes for Jack, Crock and the sheriff an hour later, they were in the basement file room of the courthouse. A large map of Caverna County marked up with Magic Markers was spread out on a table.

"Making any progress?" Daniel asked.

"I guess you could call it progress," Jack said. "We've excluded all these areas." He pointed to large sections of the map.

"But we've included all these," Crock said, indicating equally large areas encircled in black lines.

Jack explained that two of the children were cousins with family members scattered all over the county. One's parents were divorced—two homes, two locations.

"Those kids could have been in a cave in any one of a dozen places—all of which would have been accessible to you and Becca and me on our bikes."

"So you're saying…?"

"We need more information. Which means"—he glanced at Crock—"we're going to have to exercise our interrogation skills on three small children whose bodies have been taken over by evil."

"Goody," Crock said.

The sheriff said he'd try to get the children to his office in the morning. As they were filing out, the sheriff touched

Jack's arm. When Jack turned, it was clear the sheriff didn't want to say what he was about to say.

"When y'all are talking to the locals, you might want to let the others ask the questions," he said.

Jack had no idea what he meant.

"My deputies have figured out who you are. Word spreads fast in a small town."

Jack felt a wrecking ball slam into his belly and he was left so breathless it was a moment before he could speak.

"Twin Oaks," he said. It wasn't a question.

The sheriff nodded. "Lots of people in this county lost relatives in that fire," he said. "They won't take kindly to a man under suspicion for setting it."

Jack could see in Sheriff Lincoln's eyes the same thing he'd seen in the eyes of the officers he served with in Cincinnati. They all wanted him to deny the charge that he'd taken gasoline into the nursing home minutes before it burst into flame. They'd believe him if he said so, even though there was a security camera video that proved it. But he had to disappoint the sheriff, as he had his fellow officers. He couldn't say he didn't do it because maybe he did.

Jack turned wordlessly and left.

Chapter Six

Sebastian Nemo knew the crowd started to gather outside the restaurant by four o'clock. It wasn't like people camped out on the sidewalk or anything, but after the Daily Meal listed the Desert Dolphin seafood restaurant as one of the ten best restaurants in America, it was suddenly easier to get tickets to the Masters than to get a table in the quaint little restaurant—the key word being little. And a table with a majestic view of the Superstition Mountains east of Mesa and saguaro cacti marching across the sand—well, you better show up by four or you didn't have a chance.

Sebastian had taken up his spot outside the door in the shade on the east side of the building at three—the hottest part of the day, a sweltering ninety-one degrees. But it would begin to cool off now and it wouldn't be too long before he could luxuriate—for half an hour at least—in the air-conditioned interior of the restaurant that would be front-page news in every newspaper in America tomorrow morning.

As expected, the place would be jammed, with a huge waiting list standing outside.

What was it Casey Stengel said once—"Nobody goes there anymore, it's too crowded." Sebastian chuckled.

He hoped he'd be able to enjoy his meal before he had to depart. He was hungry and the menu sounded scrumptious. Duck and pork rillettes, terrines, sausages and pickles all made in-house. A raw bar—which he'd have to forgo because the chair couldn't conveniently access it. He'd measured all the passageways, knew exactly where he could "drive" and where he couldn't. It wouldn't do to get hung up in there.

The doors opened promptly at six. The management didn't want the crowd to have to wait outside in the desert heat a second longer than necessary. Sebastian rolled along behind the maître d'. The building was shaped like a wagon wheel, with the kitchen and bathrooms in the center and aisles fanning out from it to ever-widening table groupings. The choice spots, obviously, were on the outside of the ring that on two sides offered a view of the mountains and desert.

The subdued clack and clatter of silverware on china and the gentle rumbling of conversations all around him covered the whirring sound of the mechanism when Sebastian switched it on. He punched the timer on his watch as he summoned the waiter to order dessert—which he would not, unfortunately, get to sample.

When there were exactly seven minutes left on the timer, he made his way to the men's room in the center of the wheel hub of the restaurant. It had doors opening from two different sides of the building. That was why Sebastian had selected it. He motored into the handicapped stall and waited until the room emptied. Then he rose from the chair and turned his suit jacket inside out, changing the dark blue blazer into a pale yellow one. He put on sunglasses and affixed a reasonably natural-looking toupee to his bald scalp. Stepping out of the stall, he pulled a wire instrument from his pocket and inserted it between the door and the jamb of the stall, using it to hook the door catch and slide it into place. Now, the door was locked from the inside. He pocketed the wire and strode purposefully out the door on the opposite side of the bathroom from the one where he had entered.

This part was where it got a little dicey. Sebastian had to find the right—why, there she was, seated on the aisle two tables from the door! He approached the older woman, who was wearing too much makeup and a dress suited for someone twenty years younger and thirty pounds lighter. She was seated with an older couple engaged in an animated conversation. Perfect!

As he passed her chair, he dropped to one knee and picked up the napkin he had palmed.

"Excuse me," he said. "Did you drop this?"

She looked around, spotted her own napkin in her lap and replied, "No. Mine's right here, thanks."

He smiled his widest, most winning smile and then shoved a hypodermic needle he'd carried in his suit pocket into her ample belly—below the level of the tablecloth so it was unseen. She only looked startled and had no time even to speak before the spasms struck her. She went totally rigid, then flopped out of the chair onto the floor in what appeared to be a grand mal seizure. He stepped back into the crowd that quickly gathered around her, moved nonchalantly to join a group of patrons who were leaving, seeming to be one of them as they walked past the distracted hostess and out the door.

Sebastian moved purposefully, not rushing, to his blue van and got inside. He drove slowly down the street to the end of the block, watching the digital readout count down to zero.

Then the world rumbled as if a volcano had erupted nearby. The Desert Dolphin Restaurant belched a fireball into the sky and the concussive force of the explosion rocked cars in the parking lot. Sebastian lifted the cell phone from his pocket, flipped the top, punched "call" on the number he'd already dialed and spoke to the silence that answered the phone.

"Done." He hung up and drove away while debris was still falling out of the sky. When he turned onto the expressway, he tossed the phone out the window.

BISCUIT WAS SPOILED. Must be Miss Minnie and Mr. Gerald had give that dog whatever he wanted 'cause when Theresa didn't, the poor thing took on like he was dyin'.

If Becca hadn't complained about it, Theresa might have let it go. But when Becca said she had little red bites all over her legs, Theresa knew it was long past time to admit that she did, too. Biscuit had fleas. So Theresa took him to the dog groomer in town and left him for the day— got him washed in that special soap, all fluffed up and smellin' good.

She spent that whole day cleaning the house, vacuuming and emptying the bag outside like the instructions Becca found on the Internet said you was supposed to do when you got fleas in the house. She'd put bay leaves against the baseboards, too, and water in flat pans beside where Biscuit snoozed on the floor in her bedroom and in Becca's so's any stragglers would jump in and drown. It was a lot of work, but the only really hard part was convincing Biscuit he had to sleep in the garage that night. She didn't pick Biscuit up at the groomer's until late afternoon and he wasn't a bit thrilled to be left in the garage when she got home.

"I'm gone take me one of them pills tonight," Theresa told Becca right after they'd got the supper dishes cleared away. "I'm so 'xausted I can't think and I need me one good night's sleep. I'm going to bed early, might not even wait 'til it's good dark outside."

"You go to bed and I'll snuggle up in my girl cave with a mindless novel." Almost completely soundproof—Becca said it was "silent as King Tut's Tomb"—the basement apartment where she was staying had been Bishop's favorite place to read, too.

Theresa set out dishes of food and water for the forlorn mutt in the garage before she went upstairs to get ready for bed. He'd been acting queer for the past couple of days, come to think of it, sniffin' around and whinin', and wouldn't let Theresa out of his sight. But soon's he'd figured out she was gone make him sleep on that quilt she'd spread out on the concrete garage floor, he started to take on somethin' fierce—whinin' and barkin', runnin' around in circles and growling.

Theresa didn't know what to make of it. But she'd puzzle it out tomorrow after a good night's sleep. She put on her comfortable white cotton nightgown she'd once told Bishop had been designed by Omar the Tent-maker, locked the door and dropped the key in among her undies, stirring them around so's she'd have to be full awake to find it.

The setting sun was painting darkening shadows on the yard outside her window when she sat down on the side of the bed with the tiny white pill in her dark palm. It was so little she put it in her mouth and swallowed, didn't even need water to wash it down. Then she stretched out between the sheets, knowing it wouldn't take the pill more than a couple of minutes to whisk her away into tender darkness.

So she let her mind go, let herself think about Isaac. She savored the memories of her boy, kept each one in a frame by itself in a special room in her heart. But she didn't go in that room often. Couldn't. Bein' in there with the presence of him all around—it hurt so bad she could feel her whole being split open like a watermelon with the crack running ahead of the knife and everything inside pink and bare and fragile. His face bloomed in her mind; she smiled and began to nod off, expectin' that when she opened her eyes, the sun'd be shining on a new day. It wasn't.

She come awake—didn't know what roused her—and was instantly aware of the stink. Not as thick and nause-ating as it often was, the smell was still unmistakable—a horrible olfactory stew of rotting flesh, excrement and filth. And the sound of screaming and wailing. She looked at the clock on the bedside table, where the red letters said it wasn't even eight o'clock.

The streetlight on the corner shone through the white sheer curtains, so the room wasn't completely dark. She could see them, little eyes that almost glowed, staring at her from the foot of the bed. Frustration welled up in her chest. She'd took a pill! She wasn't s'posed to be having nightmares, smelling that stink and seeing monsters! Would she never get another good night's sleep?

There was movement on the floor, scurrying like, and she watched one small dark shape, then another and another clamber with ease up the wooden frame of the footboard. The shapes sat motionless then; all she could see was them shiny bright eyes.

She shuddered at the sight even though she understood that what she was seeing wasn't really there, that it was only a dream. She believed that right up until the dream bit her.

When razor-edged teeth sank deep into the side of her foot, the pain shocked her alert. It was real.

Rats.

Then they swarmed up off the floor onto the bed and were all over her and she began to scream.

She kicked at the reeking brown creature that had buried fangs in her foot, then thrashed around on the bed in horror, struggling to sit up—to get them off her—swatting at them, knocking them away, shrieking a high, thin wail of pain and horror.

She could feel their tiny clawed feet as they ran up her body, hear their little squeaking sounds. One bit her on the hand as she tried to knock it away, and it held on, dangling there as she slapped at the other rats' swarming over the bed.

One was in her face. She could smell the horror stink and feel his whiskers on her cheek before he sank his fangs into the side of her neck. She batted at him with her left hand and with the right that had a rat dangling off it. She felt a stab of agony in her thigh, another on her belly. Wiggling, screaming and sobbing, she shoved at the creatures biting her, fighting to get out of the bed so she could run away.

But she was so tangled up in the sheets that when she swung her legs over the side of the bed to stand, the covers went with them, and instead of standing, she stumbled and crashed to the floor, landing on top of a solid carpet of writhing rodents. She got to her knees, with rats biting her in a dozen places, and crawled toward the door, her hands and knees smashing rats as she went. She was conscious of screams, sounds unlike any she'd ever heard, but was only vaguely aware they were coming from her own throat. She made it to the door, reached up, got hold of the knob and turned it.

Locked.

Becca was in the basement, couldn't hear her cries.

Biscuit was locked in the garage.

And Theresa was locked in a room with rats eating her alive.

IN THE LAUNDRY room next to the garage door, Becca was down on her knees with a squirt bottle full of bleach, attacking the mildewed floor drain with a vengeance.

Since Bishop's death, Theresa had let things go. It was obvious in little ways. She might once have been a meticulous housekeeper, but after the loss of the big man who had been her lifelong soulmate, things had started to slide and Theresa either didn't notice or noticed and didn't care.

So Becca had quietly stepped in and taken up the slack. Nothing obvious. She'd mop the kitchen floor before Theresa came downstairs in the morning. She'd dust and clean toilets while Theresa was gone to her weekly Bible study. Over time, she'd gotten the place more or less shipshape. Then Theresa'd come home this morning and started cleaning the house like a buzz saw. She said that was what the veterinarian had said she had to do to get rid of the fleas Biscuit had brought in and to keep them from reinfesting the clean and groomed dog.

Becca smiled. Theresa probably wouldn't admit it if you put a gun to her head, but she had come to care so much for the dog that she'd have done just about anything for it. Biscuit was slowly dragging the old woman out of the fog of her grief with his wagging tail and big brown eyes.

The only room in the house not shiny by suppertime was the laundry room. Biscuit was afraid of the sounds the washer and dryer made and wouldn't set foot in the room. Since it was likely the only flea-free zone in the house, they hadn't scrubbed it in their clean-athon that afternoon. But fleas or not, the room needed attention. As soon as Theresa was settled in bed, Becca went after the surfaces with Pine-Sol, then got on her hands and knees and attacked the musty-smelling floor drain with bleach.

Becca had put on a load of laundry, so the clunking washer right beside her head blotted out sound. But when she sat back on her heels to inspect her work, the spin cycle glided to a stop and suddenly Becca could hear the ruckus in the garage. Biscuit was going postal! He was barking furiously, growling and scratching at the door outside the laundry room like he intended to claw his way through it. As Becca got up to check on the dog, she thought she heard a sound from upstairs. But Theresa'd taken a pill, so she had to be sleeping soundly.

Becca opened the door to the garage.

"What's the mat—?"

Biscuit streaked past her like his tail was on fire and raced toward the stairs. Becca followed. By the time she was halfway across the kitchen, she could hear Theresa's terrified screams and she began to run, too.

Becca grabbed the key off the hook beside the door. When she turned it in the lock, flung open the bedroom door and switched on the light, what she saw was a horror too awful to countenance. Theresa was lying on her face on the floor beside the dresser and rats were swarming all over her.

Biscuit didn't hesitate for a second. He tore into the creatures in a murderous fury, his growl the rumble of some monstrous enraged beast. He cut like a scythe through their ranks, flinging them aside right and left, attacking the filthy creatures with a savage violence Becca never would have believed possible from the mutt who'd lived a placid life in the home of two old people before Theresa rescued him out of the rain.

The rats swarmed the dog with supernatural strength, biting and clawing, but Biscuit fought them off, his lips curled in a ferocious snarl, vicious fire in his brown eyes. He bit off rats' heads with one snap, disemboweled them with his sharp canines, ripped and tore at them in a brutal assault, driving them back—away from where Theresa lay facedown on the floor.

Becca could see the legions of small demons that possessed the rats. Grotesque bodies, each uniquely hideous. Some were riding the rats like cowboys in a rodeo, others had become so much a part of the rat that they were hardly distinguishable.

One with a beetle-like shell sat atop a huge rat on Theresa's back that had its teeth sunk deep into her shoulder. Its limbs—like tentacles, half a dozen of them—were broken on one side as if they'd been injured and flopped uselessly. It was attached to the rat with something that looked like a beak stuck into the creature's head.

Some were slimy, dripping a yellow or green goo that looked like pus from open sores on their bodies. Everything was out of proportion—heads too large with snouts rather than noses, bloated bodies with leathery skin stretched as tight as the fragile featherless skin on a baby bird's belly. Their mouths were full of broken, blackened, rotting teeth —or with rows of razor knives shiny with drool. Most had tails that swished restlessly back and forth. All of them bore injuries, missing an eye or an ear, scarred from battles unnumbered down through the centuries.

Their cries and maniacal laughter was a symphony of

otherworldly sound that assaulted Becca's ears. The possessed rats were wired into a frenzy—so crazed they were ripping into each other, locked together in writhing clumps of combat on the floor and the bed. Their movements were too frenetic for them to do great damage to Theresa. In a coordinated assault they could literally have torn her apart, but they were incapable of cooperating in anything, merely racing around and over her, nipping, ripping out small hunks of flesh from a dozen bleeding wounds and crying out in glee.

Then a big rat that had leapt off Theresa's back to escape Biscuit's wrath spotted Becca. The demon controlling it cried out and the others turned to look.

"You see us, don't you? You want some of this?"

The rat launched itself at Becca, leapt an impossible distance, and Becca recalled Jack's story of the super-human man in the warehouse, jacked up like a meth-head on his own adrenaline. The rat struck her in the chest, knocked her backward a step and clung to her blouse.

She did not act on conscious thought, didn't even realize what she was doing until the smell of bleach filled her nostrils. She still had the squirt bottle in her hand and she raised it and fired a spray of liquid into the rat's face from inches away. It dropped to the floor, blinded and choking, stumbling, whipping its head frantically from side to side and clawing at its snout with its front paws. Becca tore into the ranks of the rats with the bleach, spraying it into their faces. They fell away from her in a wave, blind and reeling.

Squirt! Squirt!

Even with the heightened strength that tapping into the rats' brains commanded, they were no match for the relentless attack of the savage dog and the burning liquid, and they fled the assault in full retreat—the demons as terrified of Becca's fury as the rats were of Biscuit's fangs.

Becca chased them, squirting them and kicking at them as they tried to squeeze behind the huge armoire against the wall that must have covered the hole they had used to get into the house. But there was a logjam. Only one rat at a time could fit in the tight space and the others were a squirming mass, savaged by the acid bleach in their eyes and noses and the chomping bite of Biscuit's relentless fury.

Becca stomped down into the pack of them jammed together at the armoire, leapt on top of the pile, jumped up and down, hammering them with the heels of her shoes that were slimy with sticky rat blood. Somewhere, Becca had picked up a long, slender vase—on the bedside table? —and was pummeling the rat pack with it. Yelling inarticulate rage as she battered, trampled and poisoned the filthy beasts trying to escape.

The battle could have lasted a few minutes or a few hours. Becca had no idea. She merely found herself beside the armoire, panting, watching the last tail slither back into the crack. Dead and dying rats were everywhere, dozens of them. And the snarling dog with blood and gore on his maw went from one to the next, biting their heads and slinging them out of his mouth one after another to be sure none of them survived.

Becca's throat was raw—had she been screaming? Her face was wet with tears. She dropped the bleach bottle and the bloody vase and raced to Theresa lying in a puddle of blood where she had fainted.

Chapter Seven

Jeff Kendrick's Mercedes screeched into a space in the parking lot in front of Jefferson Memorial Hospital in Harrelton, Ohio, and he leapt out and raced into the building.

"Theresa Washington," he told the woman at the information desk, got the room number and stood anxiously on one foot and then the other, waiting for the elevator to take him to the third floor. He paused in front of the room to calm himself, then eased inside. Theresa lay on the bed—asleep or unconscious. She had bandages on her right hand and the side of her neck and smaller reddened wounds on her arms and face. The sight of them sent Jeff into an inarticulate rage.

Rats! Rats!

He didn't notice Becca sitting in the chair at the foot of the bed until she rose and put her finger to her lips. She led him outside into the hallway.

"Tell me what happened!" he demanded, his voice too loud, but he couldn't seem to get it under control. "How could rats have—?"

Becca looked around at the heads that had turned their way, grabbed his arm and shoved him toward a door a few feet away marked "Waiting Room." As soon as they were alone, Jeff let go.

He wasn't even aware that he was yelling until he saw Becca flinch backward from him, and instantly all the steam whooshed out of him. Fragile little Becca and he was shouting at her.

Get a grip, man.

Jeff clamped hold of his emotions and forced himself to speak calmly—well, in a quieter voice, at least—to find out what had happened. He grew more and more horrified at every grizzly detail—the image of Theresa on the floor with a swarm of rats attacking her was almost more than his mind could take in.

"How could they have gotten in—so many—and why—?"

"You know very well why," Becca told him.

Her words stopped his breath. He stood frozen, gawking at her.

"She warned us something like this could happen, would happen. Don't go looking for some logical explanation because there isn't one."

"That house," Jeff sputtered. "I'll hire a crew of exterminators to stop up every opening, make the place secure—"

"You still don't get it, do you, Jeff? No place is secure. We're at war. You're not safe either, you know. You get tangled up with us and there'll be a target on your chest, too."

Jeff was there when Theresa woke up about an hour later. She came awake in a sudden jolt and cried out, batting at remembered rats, trying to get up and run away.

He grabbed her hands. "Theresa, look at me. You're in the hospital. You're safe. The rats are gone."

The wild-eyed terror receded from her eyes and he felt her arms relax. He let go of them but continued to hold her hand.

"They's gone?" Her voice was raw.

"They won't be back!" Jeff declared. "I've hired exterminators. When they're finished—"

"Exterminators ain't gone help with rats like these," she said, echoing what Becca had already told him. She pulled her hand free of his to feel around on her body, to find the bites and the bandages. Then she rolled over on her side, facing the wall, refused to respond to Jeff or Becca, and wouldn't eat when food was brought to her. Finally, the doctor arrived, said she'd been too traumatized for company and that they were going to give her a powerful sedative. She wouldn't be lucid until morning.

~

"RATS?"

Jack bleated the word so loud several customers turned to look at him. Sudden unease darkened the faces of the others at his table.

Jack, Daniel, Crock and Andi were eating a late dinner at the best eatery Bradford's Ridge had to offer. It was called Boca on Bond Street, which sounded considerably better than "Mouth" on Bond Street, which was how the word translated.

When Jack and Daniel were children, it had been just a storefront, a mom-and-pop operation called simply "Restaurant" that served down-home cooking—country style. It still was that. The three men and Andi sat at a table with bowls piled high with mashed potatoes, Southern-style green beans cooked with ham hock, fried okra, fried squash and, of course, fried chicken or fried fish.

"Sit still in this place for long and somebody's likely to pour batter over your head and plop you into a pan of hot grease," Crock observed. "My cholesterol's spiking from the smell alone."

The men made it through double helpings of almost everything on the table. Andi merely pushed her food around on her plate. Every now and then, she would reach up and touch the Band-Aids on the scratches Ossy's claws had inflicted.

Daniel managed to coax her into sampling a slice of lemon pie made with real lemons and Eagle Brand milk, topped with meringue that towered a full five inches off the filling—just as it had when they were kids. But she'd only taken a bite or two when Jack's cell phone rang and the look on his face took everybody's appetite away.

"Say it again, Becca, slowly. Let me make sure—" He listened and his jaw clenched. "I'll be there as soon as I can." He waited, listening. "I'm glad you called him, but I'm still coming home, won't get there until—" He paused and listened. "Even if the doctor won't let me see her until morning, I'm coming home now. Tonight." He paused. "Are you all right?"

When he hung up, everyone looked at him with dread stapled on their faces.

"Theresa was...attacked by rats."

"Rats!" Daniel exclaimed. Andi gasped and put both hands up over her mouth.

Jack told them what Becca had said to him on the phone. Even repeating it, he still had trouble believing it.

"We're going back to Cincinnati," Daniel said, and began to scoot his chair away from the table as if he intended to leap up and run out the door.

"That's what I said, but Becca said the doctors ordered them out—said Theresa was too upset for company, that she won't be allowed visitors until tomorrow."

"Them?" Daniel asked.

"Becca and Jeff Kendrick." Jack watched Daniel's face tighten, not that he could blame him.

"What's he doing there?"

"Becca called him. We weren't around and she knew he'd want to know." Jack paused, knew Daniel wouldn't want to hear it but said it anyway. "She said he was very helpful."

Jack considered. "I want to go on back to Cincinnati tonight so I can be at the hospital first thing in the morning."

"She doesn't need a whole herd of us descending on her," Crock said. "I think I'll stick here, nose around a little."

"Andi and I will come with you, Jack," Daniel said.

"I think one of us needs to stay here"—Jack nodded at Crock—"to explain the lay of the land to the greenhorn here." Then he gave Daniel a knowing look. "And given who's likely to be hanging around Theresa—and how popular I am here in my hometown—I think I should go and you should stay."

He could see that Daniel understood—didn't like it one bit, but understood. He reluctantly agreed.

"I'm going to see Miss Theresa," Andi said, her voice soft. It wasn't an ask-permission statement. Jack had tried to edit what he told them about what'd happened so as not to upset Andi. But it was what it was, no getting around it.

Before her father had a chance to respond to her un-request, she spoke again, even softer this time.

"Miss Theresa needs me."

Jack and Daniel exchanged a glance over her head. The child was probably right.

"I'll look after Andi," Jack said. "We'll stay at your house so she can sleep in her own bed." Jack leaned over and said to her in a stage whisper, "I'll take you to McDonald's if you want, but we won't tell Daddy."

A ghost of a smile skittered across her solemn features. Her face was way too mature. She'd seen too much for it to be anything else, but Jack mourned the childhood the little girl had left behind.

"When will you be back?" Crock asked.

"Maybe tomorrow afternoon, but probably Sunday morning. That's if Theresa's all right. If not—"

"If not, you'll stay in Cincinnati with her until she is all right," Daniel said. He turned to Crock. "We won't be sitting on our hands here."

Jack noted how pale and drawn Crock was and felt yet again a pang of regret for dragging him into all this.

I warned you.

JEFF WALKED Becca down the hall, through the lobby and out to his car in the parking lot. She had ridden in the ambulance to the hospital with Theresa and he'd offered her a ride home.

How had she managed to fight off an army of crazed rats? She must be made of sterner stuff than what he could see—a delicate woman, so frail she looked like the weight of sunlight alone might topple her over. Her face bore the shadow of great beauty worn away, and there was a haunted look in her eyes he didn't dare engage.

When she smiled, though, which she seldom did, she lit up like a candle in a dark room. Her lips were full and red, her smile heart-shaped and her eyes were the dark blue of still, deep water.

He suddenly felt an overwhelming need to protect her.

"I said I'd give you a ride, but I didn't mean back to that house."

"I live there," she said.

"You're coming home with me." He realized how that sounded—had it actually been a Freudian slip?—and amended quickly. "Sorry, I didn't mean—I'll get you a hotel room. You can't go back to Theresa's."

"Biscuit's there and he's hurt. The rats bit him, too, but I didn't have time to help him before the ambulance came. He needs—"

"Whatever he needs, he'll get. We'll pick him up and you can take him with you." When she started to protest, he said quietly, "Do you really want to go back in there with dead rats on the floor?" She looked horror stricken. "There are crews that clean up crime scenes. I'll have one at Theresa's first thing in the morning."

Nodding, she got into the Mercedes beside him.

She didn't even notice the car—a subdued "Mars red" because a Mercedes was far too dignified for anything as garish as candy-apple red. Or perhaps she noticed and wasn't impressed by it. Jeff couldn't decide whether he was glad or upset that she wasn't. It occurred to him with a jolt that he'd spent most of his life relating to women by impressing them—with his charm, his good looks, his charisma, his money. Emily hadn't cared about superficial things, of course. The stab of pain in his chest at the thought of her took his breath away. Clearly, Becca didn't care about any of that, either.

So how did he relate to her?

He felt pretense loosen, then slide off, a Jell-O mold letting go, freeing the trembling contents. Real felt odd, vulnerable. But good, too, in a way he was too befuddled by then to understand.

"You love that old woman, don't you?" he said as he pulled out onto the parkway and headed east.

"Like she was my own mother. She was, actually. The only one I ever knew. My mother died when I was little."

Jeff had met her father and couldn't help the flashing thought that the man's wife was better off dead than with him. But she had left a fragile little girl behind.

"Tell me about her, what you remember from when you were a kid."

Becca talked then and Jeff listened. Her voice was deeper than he remembered it, maybe hoarse from screaming, and she selected her words carefully and articulately. He said very little, prompting with a question here and there, until they were at Theresa's house. She started to open her door.

"I'll get the dog," he said.

Biscuit was waiting at the front door and bounded out as soon as Jeff unlocked it. Obviously, the dog had no more desire to be in that house than he or Becca did. There was dried blood all over the dog's coat and his snout was crusted with it. There was no way to tell what was rat blood and what was Biscuit's because the dog had open wounds on his ears, paws and sides.

Jeff opened the door to the backseat and the bloody dog bounded up onto the plush leather. When Jeff slid in beside Becca, he told her, "Biscuit's hurt worse than I thought he'd be. He needs more than a little antiseptic—he needs a veterinarian."

The dog was admitted to the veterinary hospital for an overnight stay. It was almost sunup when Jeff handed Becca her room key in the lobby of the Sheraton.

"Basic toiletries are in the room—toothbrush, toothpaste, all that kind of stuff." He pointed down a hallway. "The manager said the hotel shop is still open. Get anything else you might need, whatever you want, and charge it to your room."

Becca was grateful, but not gushingly so. She appreciated his generosity but, again, she wasn't impressed by it. Was that what he was doing—trying to impress her with what a fine dude he was? No, he wasn't. This time, he really wasn't.

"Get some rest and I'll be back later to take you to the hospital. I'm sure they won't have the house cleaned up until after lunch."

She put her hand on his arm and looked up into his face.

"Thank you, Jeff." Simple and sincere.

Then she turned and headed down the hallway toward the hotel shop. He watched her go until she was out of sight. He looked at his Rolex and saw that he had time to go home and change before his weekly Saturday-morning racquetball match with Geoffrey Taylor, one of the senior partners in his firm. Maybe he should cancel. He was exhausted.

Jeff hadn't gone directly home from Theresa's house after the Wednesday night gathering there, where otherwise sane, rational people talked about demons and possessions as matter-of-factly as they'd discuss Notre Dame football or the recipe for clam chowder. He'd driven around for hours afterward trying to—what was it Jack Carpenter'd said?—"Make reality fit into the shape of his personal belief system." He'd gotten only a couple of hours of sleep that night and precious little more the next, tossing and turning, jarred awake by strange nightmares of flames and a pillar of smoke. And he hadn't gone to bed at all last night. He sighed. Well, he let Geoffrey win about half the time anyway and today Jeff was so tired the man might actually beat him.

❧

THE DOCTOR COME in and talked to Theresa about infection and antibiotics and pain medicine. Might as well have saved his breath. She wasn't listenin', didn't hear nothin' he said but the part about how all the bites was shallow. That many rats could have…

Maximum pain, minimum damage. She knew why.

He talked about post-traumatic stress disorder, too, how what'd happened to her had been so awful she'd likely have flashbacks and such for a time—'til she was all healed up and maybe even after that. He told her he wanted her to rest, said a nurse would give her a shot to make her sleep. Then he patted her arm and told her everything was gone be all right. She'd be fine.

Fool.

She was grateful when he quit chatterin' and went away and left her alone in the quiet, with no sound but the drip, drip, drip of that stuff on the pole into the plastic thing that led to a needle in her arm, and the swish-swish-swish of nurses' footsteps outside the door. They was a heart monitor—she supposed that was what it was—with a wavy green line going across it like some video game screen, but they'd turned the beep off after they give her the shot so's it'd be quiet and she could go to sleep.

Sleep. Right. She'd get right on that sleepin' thing soon's she could. It was up there near the top of her to-do list, sleeping was way above gettin' her teeth cleaned and takin' her best Sunday dress to the cleaners to get out that spaghetti sauce you couldn't hardly see 'cause the dress was black.

Theresa wanted to cry, but she couldn't. She wanted to pray, too, but she couldn't do that, either. She lay in the dark on sheets so clean they was stiff and felt all the places on her where she hurt. She hadn't even counted how many, the boils of pain on her legs, her back, her arms and neck where them...

She shut the door in the face of those memories and shuddered. She felt a hot tear slide down her cheek. Then another. She wasn't cryin', but that tear come slipping down her cheek same as if she was bawlin' her eyes out. Could a body be crying and not even know it? The tear ran down the side of her face and down her neck and began to soak into a bandage covering...

Where that rat had bit her!

The door she'd closed on them memories didn't just open. The images knocked it off its hinges, splintered the wood and roared into her mind on custom Harleys.

That big, black stinking rat, with the little feet and the eyes—them eyes. They glowed in the dark, little black marbles. And the stink of it—of what was in it, controllin' it—filled her nostrils again as if that creature was right here in the room, standin' on its hind legs on the foot of the bed, leerin' at her.

Why'd you let that happen, God? Where was you at when I's crying out for help, beggin' you to save me?

Had she cried out to God? Maybe she hadn't, didn't turn toward God because so many of her prayers had bumped they heads on the ceiling ever since Bishop died.

Maybe I didn't ask for help. Is that it? You didn't help me 'cause I didn't ask? Like maybe you didn't notice, was busy causin' a tornado somewhere or an earthquake or something like that, had too much to do to notice that poor old Theresa Washington was locked in her room—

The door'd been locked. She'd tried to run, tried to get

away, but the door was locked and she'd tried to get to the key, but she was covered in rats! Demon-possessed rats!

What's the matter with you, God? They was rats all over me, eatin' me alive and you didn't do nothing 'bout it.

They'd come running up her body like she was a tree they was climbin' and her screaming, fallin' out of bed right into the middle of the whole pack of them, crawlin' toward that key in her underwear drawer. And them rats a'wriggling on her, fightin' and squeakin', bitin' each other. And bitin' her.

Rage suddenly welled up inside her and exploded, like the top of that mountain in Washington had blown up into the sky with a mighty roar and sent clouds of smoke and ash so thick it come night right there in the middle of the day. And then the molten lava had flowed out— red and black and so hot it burned up everything it touched.

Where was you, God? Huh? On vacation? Catchin' some rays on a beach in the Bahamas? I was bein' eat up by rats and you just sat there and let it happen.

Maybe you was leaned back all comfortable in some easy chair in heaven with a bowl of popcorn in your lap, watchin' the show. Whoa—look at that, the big brown one tore a hunk of skin right outa her back. Hey, that one bit her hand and is still hangin' there, just a danglin'—can you beat that!

You invite the angels, didja? Gabriel and Michael, maybe? Had a big ole party watchin' the fat woman get eat alive, you all laughing and carryin' on. Bet you ain't had such a rockin' party since you watched Jesus a'hangin'—

The thought stopped her so totally in her tracks all the other thoughts behind it rammed into the back, slamming one into the other like the cars of a train crashing into a stalled engine. Then them thoughts all bunched up together, fell over on they sides beside the track, derailed, with nowhere to go and nothin' to pull them along.

She did cry, then. Not hysterical crying, but sobbing into her pillow, a little kid whose world had collapsed around her. All beat up and bunged up and hurtin' all over, cryin' from physical pain and psychological pain and spiritual pain. The hurtin' of it all run out of her in hot tears that slathered her cheeks and dripped down her neck and chest under the bandages. The salt in them made the rat bites sting.

Theresa cried for a long time. Soft, not making any noise except snifflin' as her nose ran. She cried until it hurt. The sobbin' became a stabbing agony in her chest and sides, worse than the molten fire in bandaged spots all over her body. The tears continued to flow, though, even when she stopped cryin' outright. Just ran down her cheeks in a river, though she squeezed her eyes up tight to try to stop it.

"I'm done, God," she said aloud, her voice rasping, ragged from screaming. "I can't do this—it's too much. I ain't strong enough. With Bishop here, I coulda...but you took him from me and he was my strength. I'm worn out, ain't got no fight left. It's over—you gone have to find somebody else to do this." She drew in a breath, then said the rest in a soft voice made out of steel. "I quit."

She closed her eyes, let the tears flow, didn't fight the darkness anymore, and allowed the drugs to take her away somewhere that was soft and dark and didn't nothin' hurt nowhere.

Chapter Eight

Andi let go of the big hospital door as soon as she squeezed through the opening and it closed all by itself behind her. She hated doors like that with the big arm on the top that pushed against you, trying to keep you from opening the door in the first place and then closing it quick so nobody else could come in.

Uncle Jack was right outside and the door closed in his face. But he wouldn't push it open again. He'd stay there with Becca until Andi and Theresa were finished talking. He'd agreed to let her come in by herself because...why had he let her? It was like he understood it was something she had to do without her even saying so. She loved that about Uncle Jack. He listened when you said how things were with you and heard a whole lot more than you said out loud.

She crossed the room to where Theresa lay under white sheets that made her black skin shine like that black onyx stone she'd seen all polished up on display when she and Mommy and Daddy had gone to the Smokey Mountains that time. She tried not to think about things like that because the memories made her sad.

Theresa had her eyes closed, but Andi wasn't sure she was asleep. Maybe she was playing possum so she wouldn't have to talk to anybody. There was a straight-backed chair next to the bed, but Andi didn't sit down in it. She used it as a step stool, climbed up on it and sat down on the edge of Theresa's bed. She took Theresa's hand in hers, the one that didn't have a bandage on it. She could see only a couple of other bandages, but she was sure there were lots of others she couldn't see.

Uncle Jack had said rats had bitten her, tried to make it sound like there were only two or three of them, but Andi knew from the expressions on the grownups' faces that it was way worse than that.

"It hurts," she said. It wasn't a question.

Theresa opened her eyes and looked at her then and Andi could tell she'd been awake the whole time. She tried to smile and did manage to get the corners of her mouth to turn up like a smile, but there was nothing smiling about her face.

"It does some," Theresa said. Her voice was deep and hoarse. "But they's little bitty bites, so it ain't bad."

"I don't mean the bites." Andi tapped her chest. "It hurts in here."

Theresa just looked at her.

"That's what she said, the Lady made out of Light." Princess Buttercup had come to her last night, but Andi hadn't told anyone about the visit. "She said that your heart hurts worse than the bites."

Princess Buttercup had been standing by the window in her bedroom after Uncle Jack tucked her in. Uncle Jack didn't know how to do it, though. He didn't sit down on the edge of her bed and pull the covers up around her neck and tell her a story. He didn't even say she ought to say her prayers. If she hadn't mentioned it, he would have walked right out of the room without doing it. But he was trying really hard and she loved him for that.

Andi had sat up in bed, propped herself on pillows, and Princess Buttercup came over to the bed and sat down on it next to her.

"Why'd God let Ossy attack me and scratch my face?" Andi asked. "And why'd he let rats bite Miss Theresa?"

"I don't know," said Princess Buttercup. Oh, Andi knew that wasn't really who she was. In fact, she ought to tell her that it was okay now, that she was a big girl and the angel could be an angel—whatever that looked like—because Andi didn't need her to look like somebody out of a movie anymore.

"You don't know why? Then who does?"

"God."

"Can't you ask him?"

"If God wanted me to know, I wouldn't have to ask. He'd tell me."

"Can you ask him for me, then? I want to know. Why does he let such bad things happen?"

"Like letting your mother die?"

Andi sighed. "It's that same thing again, isn't it? Like with Mommy. God has a reason and He's not required to tell me what it is."

"Something like that."

"Yesterday, we went to this little town called Bradford's Ridge, where Daddy and Uncle Jack and Miss Becca and Miss Theresa used to live. And it was all dark there, like a black fog. And above the town were ugly clouds that weren't fluffy at all and swirled around and around. The darkness was coming out of holes in the ground."

"That's a dark place, sweetheart. The veil between this

world and the demons' world is very thin there. The evil is strong and powerful. It's a scary place, but I'll be close by."

"Really? You'll be there?"

She nodded.

"You need to be kind to Theresa," Princess Buttercup said. "Especially kind. She hurts really bad in her heart. The goodness in you will help her get better."

Theresa was looking at her now and Andi hoped she saw goodness there.

"Your angel talked to you last night?"

"Uh-huh. She told me she'd be with me, help me later when I need it."

"I'm glad she's gone be there, sugar, 'cause I'm not. The rest of you folks is gone have to carry on 'thout me. You'll do just fine." Theresa patted Andi's hand.

"God will let you do that?" Andi asked. "Just...not do this, fight this demon?"

Theresa looked uncomfortable. "It ain't about God lettin' me step aside. I got to, and that's the plain truth of it and...God understands."

"But you said he gave you, gave all of us this thing to do, that we didn't have to be qualified, just willing—"

"How do you know I said that? You was watchin' Prin—"

"I was listening," she said, then plunged ahead. If she was going to get in trouble for eavesdropping, it would have to wait until later. "You said it was our job. If God gives you a job to do, can you just...not do it?"

"Why sure you can, sugar. God tells lots of folks to do things they don't do. In fact, don't none of us ever do all the things he's told us to do, and we do a lot of things he said not to do."

"He didn't let Jonah out of it."

Theresa stared at her but said nothing.

"He told Jonah to go to…Niven-eth—"

"Nineveh," Theresa whispered, like it was a secret she didn't want anybody to hear.

"Yeah, Niven-eth. But Jonah went the other way instead, so God sent a big—"

"A fish. I know about that. Fact is, I might have been the one told you that story in the first place. But God ain't gone send no fish after me. It's all different now. The way things were in Bible times, it's not like that anymore."

"How? Well, except for the fish part. I guess if he still sent fish after people, you'd hear about it on the news. But it's the same thing, isn't it—you and Jonah? He didn't want to go, but God wanted him to and…Jonah didn't get to decide. Why do you get to decide, Miss Theresa?"

Theresa said nothing, just looked at her like she saw something Andi couldn't see.

~

WHEN DANIEL STEPPED out of the shower in his room at the Maple Tree Motel on Saturday morning, the television he'd switched on was awash with news accounts of a restaurant bombing in Phoenix the night before. Nineteen people were dead, forty-six more injured. The news reporter, from a local station, was standing in front of a film clip of a burning building.

"Agents from half a dozen federal agencies have descended on the city, where the mood is fearful and uncertain. Sources tell me that officials are looking into the possibility that this bombing is connected in some way to the explosion two days ago at the Mall of America in Minneapolis. As yet, no one has claimed responsibility for either attack."

The president came on then, urging calm and steadfastness. Daniel shook his head. That man could urge everyone in the country to stand on their heads and whistle Dixie through their left nostrils and fully half the population would be upside down inside thirty seconds.

Daniel brushed his teeth as he listened to the Weekend Today Show's hosts interviewing the top contenders from both parties about the events of the night before. Two of the front-runner presidential wannabes declared their belief that al-Qaida was behind both bombings; the third picked a terrorist group called ISIS that was gaining power as US troops were pulling out of Iraq. Daniel was about to turn off the television when he heard Chapman Whitworth's melodious voice. Clearly, his candidacy had achieved a level of legitimacy that made Daniel's skin crawl.

Whitworth's striking face, with its hard lines and the burn scar he wore as a permanent badge of courage, filled the screen. He talked about making America safe "from enemies without and within"—which had become his mantra, and then he spoke into the camera as if he were speaking directly to those responsible for the bombings.

"Your cowardly acts of terror will engender courage, not fear, will leave us stronger, not weaker. We will defeat you by the power of our national character as well as by the force of our laws. We will crush you beneath our heels, and when all of you and your kind have been brought to justice, we will stand strong on our own soil once more, safe from within as well as without."

Alone among the candidates, Whitworth asserted that the terrorism was homegrown. Though he stopped short of blaming any particular organization, the most likely culprits were the extremists in the Freedom Nation. But Orson Blount, spokesperson for the organization, had adamantly denied they'd had anything to do with it.

"Why would we want to kill children?" he'd said when a reporter had questioned him after the Mall of America bombing. Daniel had believed him. But then, he believed Chapman Whitworth, too, until he stopped talking. As soon as his voice left Daniel's ears, the spell of it fell away, and he—along with most other Americans, he assumed—grasped the absurdity of Whitworth's claim that American antigovernment fanatics were responsible.

Daniel and Crock walked to the restaurant where they were to meet Sheriff Lincoln for breakfast, afoot until Jack returned with the car. But they'd never have found a place to park a car even if they'd had one. Bradford's Ridge's main street was blocked at both ends in preparation for the community's annual Spook Festival, held every year on the last weekend before Halloween. The Spook Festival would kick off on Main Street tonight with a giant costume party/dance called the Monster Mash. All day tomorrow, adults and children dressed in their Halloween costumes would roam the booths selling Frankenstein frankfurters, horror-burgers, ghost cluster cookies complete with green slime, spiderweb cotton candy and ice scream. Children under age eight could bring their Halloween bags and trick-or-treat at all the businesses that lined the street. The weekend festival was birthed by parents who didn't want their children out after dark trick-or-treating on a school night.

He and Crock picked their way around trucks unloading the makings of festival booths and swarms of volunteers putting up decorations to Boca on Bond Street, where they'd had dinner the night before. It was the only non-fast-food restaurant in walking distance from their motel. When Daniel explained to the sheriff that Jack and Andi were in Cincinnati—and why—the big man had listened in horror and revulsion.

"Still, it's not altogether a bad thing that Jack's not here," the sheriff said, looking uncomfortable. "If you're looking for information, folks'll be a whole lot more willing to talk to the two of you than—"

"To a man accused of burning down the Twin Oaks Nursing Home when he was twelve years old," Crock finished for him.

"He didn't do it!" Daniel said.

"He didn't deny it and I gave him the chance," the sheriff countered, sounding defensive.

"He can't deny what he doesn't remember. That whole summer was wiped out of our minds. We only remember little pieces here and there, snippets."

"I didn't grow up in Caverna County," the sheriff said, "but my uncle was a teacher here, junior high school. You're about the right age—you could have been in my uncle's class. He taught shop and all the boys took it—required, I think. His name was—"

"I could have been his star pupil and I wouldn't know it," Daniel said. "The memories are gone. That's why Jack doesn't know—"

"It's been my experience," Crock said, looking full into the sheriff's face, "that sometimes when you don't have all the information, you have to go with your gut." He paused. "What's your gut tell you about the kind of man Jack Carpenter is?"

The sheriff was silent.

"Not the kind who'd burn down a nursing home full of old people," he finally admitted.

"Mine says the same thing. That settles it, then. The internal organs of two law enforcement officers can't be wrong."

He and Crock spent the morning pouring over the map of Caverna County in the courthouse basement, figuring out the nearest cave entrances to the dozen or so places the three children frequented. The sheriff was making arrangements for them to question the children tomorrow morning.

Daniel stood up from the table where the map was spread out and stretched. He longed to take a walk, spend some time alone to clear his head. There was a park only a few blocks away, straight down Bond Street, and Daniel decided he was willing to chance the dicey weather for some fresh air.

With Crock's gimp leg, he wasn't interested in a walk, so he headed toward the newspaper office, instead, to poke around. Never knew what you'd find in the archives of a small-town newspaper.

The park entrance proclaimed Hardwick Memorial Park on an archway. It was the only opening in a solid wall of bushes that looked as impenetrable as the ones that lined the roads in rural England, where Daniel had hitch-hiked for a summer after he graduated from college.

A walking track followed the inside edge of the hedge and there was a large playground area in the center. Between the playground and the hedge were clumps of bushes, stands of trees and neat flower gardens. Daniel was surprised to note that the old-fashioned playground was exactly as he remembered it. No rubber mats beneath the monkey bars, the jungle gym or the slide. Just dirt, where the grass had been worn away by countless little feet. There was an old-fashioned merry-go-round, too, a creaky wooden one.

Wouldn't want to pay the liability insurance on that puppy!

The park was deserted, not surprising given the threatening clouds. Daniel was glad, grateful for the solitude. He took a deep breath of air scented with fresh-mown grass, autumn mums and coming rain and set off around the path. He hadn't walked a hundred yards before he turned a slight bend in the trail and heard it. At first, he thought it was a kitten or a puppy, but he quickly realized the sound was a crying child. He couldn't quite locate the source of the sound, though. He looked around but could see nobody. The crying seemed to be coming from everywhere and nowhere. He hurried farther down the trail where it snaked among huge azaleas and neatly trimmed burning bushes. The sound was louder but still directionless. The crying had ramped up by then, had gone from pitiful tears to heartbroken sobbing.

Daniel became mildly frantic, unable to find the crying child. He searched behind and beneath bushes as if he were hunting for Easter eggs. Then he saw her—sitting right in the middle of the walking path only about fifty feet farther down. A little girl, seven, maybe eight years old, with long red braids hanging down her back. She sat Indian style on the mulched trail with her head in her hands, sobbing.

But the thing was, he would have sworn he could see that section of the trail from the other side of the bushes and she hadn't been there before.

Well, clearly, she was there now, so he approached her —not too fast, didn't want to spook her. She'd likely been warned not to talk to strangers.

The sky grumbled and rumbled. Distant thunder sounded strangely menacing, sending a chill down Daniel's spine that had nothing to do with the cold wind that tugged at his shirt and pushed dry leaves tumbling across the ground with an unpleasant scuttling sound.

When he was about twenty feet away from the little girl, he spoke to her.

"Are you all right? If you're lost, I'd be glad to help you

find your mommy." He held out his hands in front of him as he approached her slowly. "I've got a little girl about your age, only she doesn't have pretty red hair like yours. Her name's Andi."

The little girl didn't acknowledge his presence in any way, maybe hadn't even heard him approach. She simply continued to cry, great heaving, wrenching, brokenhearted sobs.

She still hadn't looked up when he reached her, so he got down on one knee, put out his hand to touch her and then thought better of it and drew it back.

"Honey," he said, calm but loud. She had to hear him, he was less than three feet away. "I don't know what's wrong, but I'd like to help if I can."

She stopped sobbing. Didn't crank down into crying, whimpering, then sniveling. Just stopped, like turning off a faucet. But she kept her face buried in her hands.

"Are you lost?"

She slowly lifted her head and looked at him. Blue eyes in a face so covered in red freckles if she'd had even one more, she'd have had to hold it in her hand. She blinked and big tears ran down the freckled cheeks. She got to her knees as if to stand.

And then she lunged at him.

The little girl hit him square in the chest with such force that even if he hadn't been off balance on one knee, he'd never have been able to stand up to the blow. The impact bowled him over onto his back with her on top of him, hammering his face with her fists, emitting a rumbling sound deep in her throat that sounded like the growl of a wolf or a mad dog.

Daniel put his left arm up in front of his face to shield it and grabbed her with his right hand. But he couldn't hold on. Victor Alexander had broken his wrist, snapped it like a twig the day he shot Emily. Untold hours of physical therapy in the months since had restored much of the use of the hand, but his wrist was still weak. The little girl buried her teeth in the forearm he was using as a shield, bit down through the fabric of his long-sleeved shirt into his flesh, and a lightning bolt of pure pain rocked him.

He tried again to grab her, maybe get hold of her braids. He understood now what he was dealing with. It wasn't the first time he'd seen this kind of superhuman strength. But still…he couldn't hit her! She was a kid. Too quick for him to grab, she dodged his hand and caught the side of it in her mouth and bit him again.

He tried to roll over, to roll her off him, batting at her, but she was relentless. She hammered a fist into his right eye and he couldn't see. He grabbed her arm, held onto it this time and fought to catch the other one when something smashed into the side of his head so solidly he lost his grip on her arm and she wiggled free. Something hit him again, in the forehead this time. A rock, she had grabbed a rock and was hammering him in the face with it.

He got a snapshot of her then, an image. Her freckled face was smeared with his blood where she'd bitten him, and she had the bloody rock raised above her head to slam it down on him again. Her eyes, pretty blue eyes, were the eyes of some wild, deranged animal.

Rain began to fall, coming down in a sudden torrent, and splashed in his face as he lay on his back with the little red-haired girl astride his chest, pounding a rock into his forehead. He felt himself losing consciousness, fought it, but he couldn't escape the shroud of darkness that enveloped him.

Chapter Nine

"It's called a Dr. Pepper," Andi said as she stuffed the three one-dollar bills from Jack's wallet into the hip pocket of her jeans. "Wouldn't you think there'd be a Doctor Pepper in a hospital?"

Andi, Jack and Becca had spent the day with Theresa, at least as much of it as the hospital staff would allow. Jeff Kendrick had arrived later that afternoon to join them. Now, they sat together in the hospital cafeteria, where they'd been banished so Theresa could "eat her dinner in peace" by a nurse who bore more than a passing resemblance to Jabba the Hutt.

Jack smiled at Andi's reasoning, turned back to the others and saw Jeff watching Andi leave the room, studying her with a look on his face Jack couldn't read. Jeff caught his stare and covered smoothly.

"Tell Theresa I'll be back in to see her tomorrow," he said and got to his feet. "I'm closing in on a hot date tonight." He paused. "I scared up a rabbit."

"You managed to find a rodent pretty fast," Jack said. "Can you prove—?"

"Don't be tossing around the p-word. I can't prove anything—yet."

"But you found out something."

Jeff nodded.

"After I graduated from law school, I spent five years earning my chops as a public defender. Among the legion of smarmy characters I represented was a con artist charged with extorting protection money from the owner of Barduchi's Liquor Store. He swore he didn't do it."

"I've never arrested a guilty man."

"Yeah, but this guy might actually have been telling the truth—good for a dozen other crimes but not that particular one. The first time I met with him, he told me, 'Why would I waste my time shaking down a two-bit liquor store? If I was gonna blackmail somebody, I'd start higher up the food chain—like with a federal prosecutor.' He said he had stuff on Chapman Whitworth the man would pay big bucks to keep quiet."

"So you went looking for this guy."

"I have people who can find anybody. A few phone calls, some cash to grease the skids and badda boom, badda bing... Mitchell 'Doughboy' Douglas and I spent some quality time together right after lunch, turned out to be an aeronautical conversation."

Jack was lost.

"Actually, we only talked about one specific airplane— US Air Flight 734 from Cincinnati to Los Angeles on March 4, 2003."

Jack's heart leapt into a gallop. "That wouldn't be the flight where—?"

"A doting grandmother just happened to be lugging a video camera around with her and just happened to have the camera trained on one Chapman Wainwright Whitworth—"

"When Whitworth stopped a knife-wielding lunatic outside the cockpit with the words, 'You'll have to go through me?'"

"Yup. One and the same."

"It was a setup?"

Jeff nodded.

"I knew it! Nobody says crap like that when they're facing a nut job with a knife."

The line had become Whitworth's slogan after he killed the terrorist. But had the man really been a terrorist at all? Maybe. Maybe not. He'd been a mental patient and, given the climate in the country at the time, carrying a weapon onto an airplane was all the proof anybody needed. Just like with the Twin Oaks fire, Chapman Whitworth was an instant hero—add water and stir.

"Why didn't you tell us about this guy when we were fighting to keep Whitworth off the supreme court?" Jack asked. "Maybe he could have given us something to use against him!"

"For starters, I didn't know what he had on Whitworth —if he had anything at all. And besides, everything he'd told me was sealed by attorney-client privilege."

"And now it's unsealed? The tape come loose?"

"No. But after what's happened"—he glanced toward the hallway that led to Theresa's hospital room—"I flat out don't give a rip anymore. My guys have tracked down a certain doting grandmother, too, and I'm on my way to have a little chat with her."

Jeff started for the door as Jack's cell phone rang, and when he heard the urgent tone in Jack's response, he stopped.

"What do you mean 'he's gone'?"

At first, Crock's words didn't register.

"How many things can 'he's gone' mean?" Crock said.

Jack could hear him crunching down on a toothpick. "Daniel's missing. I went to talk to the good folks at the Bradford's Ridge Banner and he said he was going to take a walk in the park. But when I got back to the motel, he wasn't there. I went to the park. He wasn't there either… but I found his shoe."

"You found his shoe?"

"You sound like a parrot, Jack," Crock said. "I'm pretty sure it's his shoe. I remember he was wearing idiot loafers —the ones with tassels on them."

"Where did you find the shoe?"

"On the ground beside the walking trail in the park. I don't know if it's raining in Cincinnati, but it's been pouring for the last couple of hours here—so if there was any other evidence besides Daniel's shoe at the scene, it's gone now."

"Are you sure he didn't just—?"

"Just what? Chuck one shoe and then wander off through a monsoon to have a beer with all the grade school friends he doesn't remember? The sheriff and city police have been looking all afternoon. Nothing."

"He's really gone, then," Jack said. It wasn't a question.

"And wherever he went, he didn't go willingly." He heard Crock's voice soft in his ear. "Jack…you're going to have to tell Andi."

Jack held the phone to his ear, listening to the nothing for a long moment before he told Becca and Jeff the news. The expression on Becca's face so broke his heart he had to look away. That was when he caught the images on the muted television screen on the far wall. A bomb had exploded in a crowded restaurant in Phoenix. The body count stood at forty-six injured and nineteen dead. It never stopped; it went on and on and—

Chapman Whitworth's face filled the screen, straight-out-of-the-tap evil on track to become the president of the United States.

Jack went to the television, picked up a remote on a tray table and flicked on the volume. Then he stood before it, watching, mesmerized in spite of himself by the words Whitworth spoke in a voice like honey poured over shards of glass.

"Men in black hoods on the other side of the planet are not as great a threat to our homeland, our wives and children, as the domestic terrorists who seek to make us afraid to go to a mall...or out to dinner. Those in positions of authority must ensure that our families are protected—we must make America secure without and within."

Whoa, Bessie!

Jack stopped breathing. The face blinked away, but Jack didn't hear the news anchor continue the report.

Two horrific acts of terrorism in four days. Whitworth was hanging his hat on opposition to domestic terrorism—right? Sooooo...if you wanted people to vote for you to keep them safe, wouldn't you first have to make them feel threatened? You don't suppose...?

Jack was so deep in thought he didn't even realize Andi had come to stand beside him until she spoke.

"Found it," she said and held up a red soft drink can in triumph. "Boo-ya!" She was grinning, the dimples in her cheeks deep enough to eat pudding out of. She stretched out her fist to bump with Jack's, but he took her hand in his instead.

"Andi, honey," he said, and felt a lump in his throat the size of a bowling ball, "I have something to tell you."

JEFF KENDRICK ARRIVED at the diner half an hour before closing time. He turned off the purring engine of his Mercedes and tried to order his thoughts. He'd been operating on a couple of hours' sleep for days, was up all night helping Becca with Theresa and had been too busy today to grab a nap. The lack of sleep was catching up with him. But you only needed a couple of synapses firing to figure out that Daniel Burke had been kidnapped—right about the time he'd been talking with Doughboy.

They'd met at Waterfront Park at the railing on the little stone bridge spanning the nameless creek that meandered through the park to make its small contribution to the mighty Ohio River. Doughboy had juked and jived, hadn't wanted to tell him anything, but Jeff had been too tired to play games.

"You still dealing? A little coke, crack maybe?"

Doughboy had looked uncomfortable.

"Still got a meth lab in the basement of that warehouse by the river?" Jeff had leaned close and continued. "One phone call, and I can shut you down and get you an all-expenses-paid trip to the iron house."

"Hey, you can't say nothing about that!" Doughboy had protested. "You're my lawyer. You can't rat me out."

"Try me!"

Mitchell had told Jeff then, all in a rush, about his cellmate in the Kentucky State Penitentiary in Danforth whose girlfriend, a woman named Corrine Talbot, had posed as a doting grandmother videoing her two-year-old grandson's first airplane ride on the US Air flight from Cincinnati to Los Angeles. And who, oh by the way, just happened to capture Chapman Whitworth's singular act of heroism for all the world to see.

"My buddy said Whitworth paid her twenty-five thousand dollars," Doughboy had said. "That money's long gone now. I seen her the other day waiting tables at Shaky's Diner. Better get there quick, though. Waitresses never last more'n a week at Shaky's."

Jeff leaned back in the plush leather seat as the diner's neon sign alternately filled the interior of the car with pink, then blue light. He couldn't threaten Corrine Talbot as he had Mitchell Douglas. If he wanted her to tell him about Whitworth, he'd have to use some method of persuasion other than blackmail or intimidation. He glanced at his Pierce Brosnan doppelganger reflection in the rearview mirror and straightened his tie.

Two hours, three bars and untold numbers of strawberry daiquiris later, Jeff fit his apartment key into the lock. It took him two tries. He'd left his car in the parking garage of their last stop and they'd taken a cab to his place because he hadn't been fit to drive. Hammered as he was by exhaustion, he never should have taken a single drink. He hadn't planned to, but his mission had proved to be harder than he'd thought. Oh, not the getting-Corrine-Talbot-to-talk part. He was certain she'd sing him any song he wanted to hear before the evening was done. But acting believably smitten with an overweight, late-fifties waitress with chipped fingernail polish, bad breath and a maddening nasal giggle—dressed in a too-tight pink uniform with the picture of a hamburger on the back had required frequent fortification of an alcoholic variety.

He stepped into the entry hall but didn't turn on the light. Why get a harsh-reality view of the woman if he could help it? The dark bars had been bad enough.

Jeff lived on the fifth floor of one of the most expensive luxury condo complexes in the city. It was ten stories high, built around a central atrium with pools—outdoor and indoor—restaurants and an amphitheater stage at one end of the marble-columned ground floor. The condos on the inside opened with large balconies looking down into the atrium; the ones on the outside afforded views of downtown Cincinnati. Jeff intended to have an outside condo someday, on the top floor—though he did enjoy the block-party atmosphere of crowded balconies watching concerts or light shows in the amphitheater. There was a show going on tonight, in fact, a Battle of the Bands. Jeff sincerely hoped his neighbors had turned out en masse to watch the local talent so maybe he wouldn't run into anybody he knew before he could spirit his "date" out of sight.

Corrine heard the music when she stepped into his apartment. She saw the strobe lights and hurried to the balcony doors. When she threw them open, the music that had been only a muted beat boomed into the room.

"'Hotel California'—it's the Eagles!" she squealed. He decided not to point out how unlikely it was that Don Henley had shown up in Cincinnati tonight just to serenade her.

Snagging a bottle of wine off a rack in the kitchen, Jeff called out to the woman on the balcony.

"I promised you a Jacuzzi...and wine—remember?" He gestured down the dim hallway and held up the bottle. She came unsteadily back into the living room, giggling.

"It's not red wine, is it?" she asked, kicking off first one shoe and then the other. "Red wine makes my face swell up and I break out in a rash."

He assured her it was white wine and propelled her down the hallway in front of him.

"Oops, forgot the glasses."

As she went into the bedroom, he turned and headed back to the kitchen. He was almost there when he heard her scream.

What in the world...?

Jeff raced down the hallway to the bedroom. He heard the sound before he reached in to turn on the light. In the background behind Corrine's screams was an odd, raspy, scuttling sound. Like corn husks rubbing together. What could possibly make a sound like that? When he stepped into the room, something crunched under his feet like he'd stepped on a bag of potato chips.

He flipped on the light, gasped and staggered backward. Dropping the wine bottle, he cried out in horror, too.

The room was alive with cockroaches!

A lake of them, a sea of them, covering every surface like a swarm of locusts—on the bed, the nightstands, the dresser, crawling up the walls and the curtains—and the woman, whose screams ratcheted into wailing shrieks when the light revealed what she had felt in the darkness.

They were all over her, crawling up her arms onto her face. Batting at them, hopping around, she tried to knock them off, then shoved Jeff out of the way and fled screaming from the room. Jeff's reflexes were slower. He felt the creatures on his legs, looked down and saw them crawling over his shoes and up under the fabric of his suit pants. He kicked at them, leaping from foot to foot in horror. They dropped into his hair from the ceiling and began to crawl around on his head.

With an otherworldly howl of horror, Jeff backed out of the room, slammed the door behind him and staggered backward down the hallway, batting at the bugs that had crawled up his torso onto his chest. The strip of light beneath the bedroom door was instantly blotted out by the tide of bugs that slid under it and scuttled toward him. Corrine's screaming stopped abruptly, like someone had flipped off a switch, but Jeff was too involved in his own battle to be of any help to her.

He turned and ran, but the roaches were so fast they

got to the front door before he did. He flung it open, yelling an inarticulate cry and tearing at his clothes, and staggered out into the hallway, where the light revealed the unbroken sea of roaches that had flowed out the door with him. He slapped at the bugs and felt them crunch beneath his feet as he stumbled toward the stairs door, threw it open and started down the steps. Then a huge cockroach that had been in his hair crawled out and down his forehead. He slapped at it furiously, lost his balance, grabbed for the stairs railing and missed. He fell then and tumbled head over heels down the concrete steps to the fourth-floor landing below, where he lay still, blood oozing out his nose and down his face.

The roaches flowed in a wave across the hallway from Jeff's apartment to the exit door and cascaded in a tide down the stairs to his limp body. They surged over him, covering him until Jeff Kendrick was no longer visible beneath a writhing blanket of bugs.

DANIEL OPENED HIS EYES, grateful to finally shake off the terrible nightmare of finding a pretty little girl in the rain who'd attacked him like some kind of wild animal. He'd awakened with a headache and a searing pain in his right hand. His headache hammered in heartbeat bursts centered in the middle of his forehead, hurt so bad it made him nauseous. The motel room tilted and swam drunkenly, didn't look right, so he closed his eyes again. He wasn't in the motel room. Then where...? On the floor somewhere. A metal floor. And he couldn't move his hands or feet. It was like they were tied...

"You done with your beauty sleep, are you?" said a

voice from above and behind him. "You been out for a good long time."

Daniel opened his eyes again and could see nothing but a wall. The place smelled damp.

He tried to move and discovered that he'd been right. His hands and feet were tied with something.

Then a shadow fell over him and a boot shoved him off his side over onto his back. Hanging above him was a face. It was Billy Ray Hawkins!

"I's beginning to think you might not come around at all," Billy Ray said. "That young'un beat up on you somethin' fierce."

How in the world did Billy Ray Hawkins—?

"You're trying to puzzle out where you're at, but where you're at don't exist," Billy Ray said. "Least nobody believes it exists, which amounts to the same thing. All them tales you heard 'bout a boxcar buried in the woods. Well, you're in it."

Daniel looked out past Billy Ray into the shadowy interior of what must really have been a boxcar. He couldn't tell much about what he saw because his eyes wouldn't focus and the light was dim. There appeared to be shelves all around loaded with bricks. The room swam again for a moment, so he closed his eyes. When he opened them, the world had steadied itself. There were, indeed, shelves all around, a few containing a single brick in the center.

A gold-colored...?

Gold!

His eyes opened wide and Billy Ray began to laugh.

"Figured out what it is, didja? When I got out of the iron house and come in here for the first time in more'n twenty years, it was just like I'd left it. You b'lieve that! Nothing touched. Two hundred and fifty bars, five hundred pounds, of solid gold! Them bars was worth about twelve thousand dollars each when they sent me away. The lot of them was worth twelve million dollars the day I got out."

Daniel closed his eyes again and struggled to calm the sudden machine-gun hammering of his heart. He was in a boxcar buried in the ground with Billy Ray Hawkins's treasure. And since Billy Ray had allowed him to see it, the man had no intention of letting Daniel leave the boxcar alive.

His head began to spin, thoughts flitting across the surface of his mind like water spiders. He opened his eyes and tried to focus on something—anything—to anchor his mind to reality. The dirty metal floor…on to the shelves made of boards on concrete blocks. There was enough space for two hundred fifty bars of gold on those shelves, alright—for more than that even. But there was only a handful of bricks—two dozen or so. Most of the shelf space was empty. He gestured toward the shelves with his chin.

"Two hundred fifty bars—what happened to the rest of it?"

The smile on Billy Ray's face drained away. "Ain't none of your business what I done with it."

The process of trying to understand what he saw ordered Daniel's thoughts.

"That's what—maybe ten million dollars?" The absurdity firmly fastened his mind to the real world again. "You've been out of prison a month—how could you possibly spend ten million—?"

"I didn't spend it."

"If you didn't, who—"

Billy Ray went off like a bottle rocket. "I ain't gonna talk about him, you hear me." He shrieked the words, his voice almost hysterical. "It ain't none of your business! Ain't gonna say a word about him, not a word."

Daniel was stunned by the sudden ferocity, the out-of-proportion response. What could Billy Ray have done with ten million dollars, and who was he so afraid—?

His hammering heart seemed to freeze solid in his chest.

It couldn't possibly be…

But as soon as Daniel thought it, he knew that it was true. It was the only thing that made any sense at all.

"You didn't spend it—" he spoke in wonder as dawning understanding came to him "—Chapman Whitworth did! You're working for him, aren't you, Billy Ray? That's why I'm here and that's where the rest of your gold went. He's got it."

"No!" The little man squealed. "I don't deal with… him. Just his flunkies. I ain't gonna have no truck with The Man."

The mystery of how Billy Ray Hawkins could possibly have gotten connected to Chapman Whitworth was shoved aside by the realization that Billy Ray knew. He knew that Chapman Whitworth was possessed—well, maybe not that, but he knew there was some force and power in the man that was not from this world—and not from any good neighborhoods in any other world.

"Appears you've seen the real Chapman Whitworth," Daniel said, watching Billy Ray's face. Shock registered there first, then something like relief.

"You seen it too, then?"

"Oh, he's real, alright, worse than anything you could possibly dream up. Didn't your old granny ever tell you stories about people who sold their souls to the Devil?"

Billy Ray's eyes opened so wide there was nothing but white all around. He began to breathe hard, to pant.

"That ain't the way of it! You don't know everything. Fact is, you don't know nothin'." Billy Ray grabbed a roll of duct tape that he'd obviously used to bind Daniel's hands and feet and tore off a large piece of it.

"I know that you're screwed," Daniel said. "A deal's a deal and Billy Ray Hawkins always keeps his word."

Billy Ray leaned over and smashed the tape down across Daniel's mouth. "You shut up about devils and such, you hear me! I ain't gonna hear none of that nonsense. You think you're so smart, Mr. Reverend Daniel Burke. Well, you don't know nothin'. Not nothin'!"

His eyes darted from one corner of the boxcar to the other. Wary. Watchful.

Chapter Ten

Jeff couldn't seem to wake up. He tried, then floated back away into darkness. He bobbed up to the edge of consciousness again and struggled harder to wake up. He had to get out of bed or he'd be late for work. He reached up to swat a fly off his nose and opened one eye. A fat brown cockroach was crawling across his nose, its antennae twitching.

All of it slammed back at once with the force of a piano dropped off the Eiffel Tower. He was sitting up, slapping at the bugs that covered him before he had time to will his body to do so. Someone was screaming. It took a second or two to realize it was his own voice echoing off the concrete walls of the stairwell.

He wiggled and writhed on the floor, slapping bugs away that were instantly replaced by the teeming horde that covered the landing floor and walls.

"No...get off!" he sputtered. "Noooooo!" He had to wipe a handful off his face that tried to get into his mouth when he opened it to scream! "Get off me!" In the background behind his screams, he could hear the raspy, scuttling sounds they made as their bodies rubbed against each other. And the crunching sound when he rolled over onto them, smashing them.

All at once, the bugs stopped moving, or so it seemed to Jeff, though he certainly was not rational enough to accurately record reality. The raspy sounds they made silenced instantly.

Then, as suddenly as they had climbed onto his body, they began to scuttle down to the floor and hurry away. He knocked them off his arms and chest to the floor and they ran up the walls—flowed up the walls in a solid wave—and vanished into the crack beside the ceiling tiles. Some ran up the steps and slid between the carpet and the baseboards. Others ran across the landing and down the steps on the other side.

Jeff staggered to his feet, slapping away the stragglers. One crawled out of his shirt pocket; another ran out of his hair and down his face. He slapped them off and stomped them before they could run. Smashing them made a satisfying crushing sound and suddenly he was chasing the last of them across the floor, jumping on them, pulverizing them beneath his feet, grunting, yelling wordless fury. And crying.

Then they were gone, all of them. He whirled around, looking for more to stomp, wanting to find more to stomp. The floor was a gooey mess of bug guts and bug pieces, but all the live ones had vanished, scurrying away and disappearing so quickly it was almost difficult to believe they'd ever been there at all.

He stood panting, patting his clothing to be sure, sobbing. There was wet on his face, and when he swiped at it, his hand came away red. Blood was smeared on his lip and chin and he wiped his mouth with his shirt sleeve. His head hurt, the back of it, and when he touched the spot, he felt a tender lump.

His heart still thundered in his ears so loud its roar muffled sound, but as it calmed, he gradually became aware of the silence broken by nothing but his ragged breathing.

It was only then that he remembered Corrine. His legs felt rubbery, his knees like sacks of water, and he had to hold tight to the railing as he climbed the steps. His vision blurred, his head spun, and he didn't know if the sensation of the world swirling around him was the booze or the blow to the head. The door to his condo stood open, but no sound came from it.

No sound. Nothing from outside in the atrium, either. The band had stopped playing.

He searched the floor for any sign of bugs—they'd left, but they could come back—as he stepped inside and called out, "Corrine?"

He tried to piece together the jumble of images. Corrine had been in the bedroom, covered in cockroaches. Then she'd rushed past him. The bugs came for him. He ran out the front door. So where was Corrine? Where'd she go?

Then he saw the open balcony doors.

He suddenly became very aware of the silence in the atrium. The Don Henley wannabe was no longer wailing "Hotel California." The night breeze ruffled the curtains and brought only a muffled crowd sound from below.

He didn't move, shook his head slowly back and forth and refused to move. Then he was walking, a robot, up onto the landing, through the balcony doors and out into the night air. His neighbors had, indeed, turned out in force to hear the dueling bands that were silent now. They stood in groups on balconies, looking down. Then a woman on a nearby balcony spotted him and pointed, and the four people with her turned and stared at him.

He didn't want to keep going. He wanted to turn around and go back into his condo and close the balcony door behind him.

In there, closed up, with the roaches?

But he did keep walking, of course. He walked to the balcony railing and looked down. Musicians milled around on the stage. Most of the people in the crowd stood in small clumps, talking. Directly below him was a cluster of people gathered around something. He couldn't tell what, didn't want to know. But he couldn't look away, couldn't seem to draw in another breath, either, and then the group of people parted briefly and he caught sight of a figure sprawled on the marble floor. Not recognizable from this height, of course. But it was a woman. And she was dressed in pink.

SEBASTIAN NEMO DECIDED he'd missed his calling. He should have been a financial guru like the know-it-all on the radio he'd been listening to on the long drive from Arizona to Ohio. The radio man was giving advice on buying a car, told his listeners to pay in cash.

Show them greenbacks and all the haggling would silence, the man said. It was human nature. Nothing in the world spoke louder than a wad of bills.

Sebastian barked out a laugh. Really? How about a bar of solid gold!

Of course, Sebastian conducted his business enterprises in a world of cash-and-carry, where finance plans were not an option. No ten easy payments of nine ninety-nine ninety-nine and you could walk off the lot with a mortar, a missile and ten pounds of plastic explosive. But even in that world, the arms dealer's eyes had grown wide when he saw the gold bars. Human nature.

Sebastian had been arranging the purchase of equipment since he'd been notified in the usual fashion that a client was in need of his customized services for a project called Operation Maelstrom. It was the single most ambitious endeavor Sebastian had ever signed on for and it might be his swan song. His fee would set him up for life anywhere in the world, and perhaps it was time to sit on a beach somewhere and sip margaritas. But that was something to consider after. Now, his attention was laser focused on getting the job done—in and out without a trace.

For that, he would need plastic explosives—that was standard. What wasn't standard was the order he placed for two Javelin missile launchers and missiles—man-portable heat-seeking antitank FGM-148 missiles, according to the spec sheet he'd meticulously prepared. Or "Porsches," according to the British—a label they'd applied because at almost ninety thousand dollars each, every round fired from a Javelin cost as much as a Porsche 911.

The total price tag for the equipment alone for this job was snug up against two million dollars. But even when you could afford the sticker price—could plunk down forty bars of pure gold!—such weapons were hard to come by. Even more rare was the personnel trained to fire them. Besides himself, Sebastian needed an additional man for the Javelins, one to plant the on-site explosives and two others.

He would personally topple the first domino in Cincinnati that would start the chain reaction in New York, Chicago, Los Angeles and New Orleans. This would be no 9/11. But it would be close in fear factor and that was how you graded terrorism—in the level of fear generated and the amount of disruption caused. On that scale, Operation Maelstrom would definitely be the valedictorian of the Terrorism Class of 2011.

He pulled into a rustic restaurant outside Louisville, Kentucky, at the Shepherdsville exit off Interstate 65 and parked his nondescript blue van in the back with the employees' cars. It was three o'clock on a Saturday after-noon, so the lunch press was gone and the dinner rush hadn't started. He courteously requested a table in the corner so he'd have his back to the wall, never made eye contact with the waitress and left a reasonable but certainly not generous tip. A forgettable tip from an unremarkable man. Good habits kept you alive.

The roast beef was a bit chewy, but the blackberry cobbler was superb. His were simple tastes and he made it a point to eat well when he was in the United States. A country boy at heart—a lifetime ago—he'd never devel-oped a taste for international cuisine. In most of the coun-tries where he traveled, food was fuel, nothing more.

He thought about the gold bars as he ate. They had oiled all the equipment purchases so they were effortless and smooth, not a single squeak. Paying the hired help had been another matter, however. Recruiting people like Ricky Harrison was fine for a single job where it was vital to throw the authorities off the scent, but there were too many moving parts to pull something like that off multiple times. To pay for services, he needed cash, so he'd had to convert the gold into spendable currency, a service he provided at no additional cost to the client.

In almost every circumstance, Sebastian would prefer to employ a man of simple motivations. Pay him and he'd kill somebody. Pay him enough and he'd kill a lot of some-bodies. Pay him exceptionally and he'd do it flashy if that was what you wanted or stealth if you didn't, and either way he'd get in and get out without leaving so much as an eyelash to mark his passing. Men like that, men of Sebastian's caliber, were worth their weight in gold, but even gold couldn't buy what didn't exist and there were only a handful of such men in all the world. Fortunately, Sebastian was on a first-alias basis with all of them.

He had also started beating the bushes months ago for idiot whack jobs to fill in where the professionals left off. These days, it wasn't hard to procure wide-eyed zealots and wild-eyed fanatics and every stripe in between. The trick was picking those who were honestly willing to die for the cause—not histrionics but genuinely willing to take one for the Gipper. His two professional operatives would vanish like puffs of smoke, as they had done countless times before. And the other two—well, that was why he needed nutcases willing to die. People like that never figured out that even if they somehow managed to survive the mission itself undetected, this would be their last job. You didn't prosper as Sebastian and those like him had all these years by leaving a trail of accomplice/witnesses behind just one offer of immunity away from throwing you under a bus.

As he got back into his van, he wondered momentarily where the gold bars had come from. Sebastian didn't know the name of the man who'd hired him. The man didn't know his name either—well, maybe he did, but he had sense enough to realize the name was bogus. Sebastian didn't know why he'd been hired to blow up the Mall of America, a Phoenix restaurant and five additional targets all across America on Monday. He didn't need to know. Nor did he need to know why his employer was handing out gold bars instead of thousand-dollar bills or numbers to an account in the Cayman Islands. The less you knew, the safer it was for all concerned. When it was over, Sebastian would insert his own gold-bar payment into one end of a complicated money laundering machine and numbered accounts would pop out the other. He'd keep one of the gold bars, though. No, two of them. Souvenir bookends.

BECCA KNEW that whatever lay beyond the next turn in the cave was not merely waiting there for them. It was coming to get them. She could sense its advance, step by step, could feel the earth tremble beneath its feet with every footfall, could hear the otherworldly roar that wasn't a sound you could hear with your ears. Terror consumed her. She had to run, had to get away. She turned…and faced What Comes Behind. How could she—?

Bark! Bark-bark!

The sound brought Becca Hawkins bolt upright in the bed, lying in tangled, sweat-soaked sheets, breathing hard.

Biscuit was at her bedroom door, clawing at it, trying to get out, barking in a yapping frenzy. But it wasn't the growling bark that had rumbled out of his throat when he tore into the rats. The dog wasn't alarmed. His hackles weren't raised.

What time was it? She looked at the glowing numbers on the bedside alarm. Three thirty. Her apprehension grew. What was it Theresa always said—folks never came calling before the sun had shone on the day to give you good news.

She pulled on a robe. As soon as she opened the bedroom door, Biscuit scooted out past her and down the stairs in a doggie gallop. He skidded to a halt at the front door and stood there yapping. She could tell by his bark that whoever was standing on the porch was somebody Biscuit knew. Becca didn't turn on the lights, just went down the stairs in the dark and peeked out the window beside the front door, where the porch was lit by a motion-activated porch light.

Jeff Kendrick.

He balled his hand into a fist and prepared to bang again, but she opened the door before he had a chance.

"Jeff? What are you—?"

He brushed past her into the house, closed the door behind him and leaned against it, trying to catch his breath. Biscuit was still barking his greeting bark.

"She's dead," Jeff said, his voice trembling. "She ran out onto the balcony and fell off. The bugs killed her before she had a chance to tell me anything." He put his head into his hands and his body began to shake. Maybe he was sobbing. Maybe only trembling violently.

Becca flipped on the hallway light, took Jeff's arm and led him wordlessly into the kitchen, where she parked him against the counter by the refrigerator.

"I'll make coffee."

She turned to the cabinet and busied herself with coffee-making activities to allow Jeff time to compose himself. When she turned back to him, there was an odd look in his eyes she couldn't quite define, like something had shifted. Something was profoundly different about the man who stood trembling in her kitchen. He was not the same man who'd raged with her about the rats attacking Theresa the night before.

She didn't want to know—absolutely, one hundred percent did not want to know the answer to the question she was about to ask.

"What happened?"

"Roaches." He strangled on the word. "Everywhere. Roaches."

He told her the story and she listened with growing revulsion. When he described the sensation of the bugs crawling on him, his voice grew strident, high-pitched, as if he were holding on with his fingernails to keep from screaming.

"And the police?"

"More than a dozen witnesses, people on neighboring balconies out watching the battle of the bands, saw that I had nothing to do with what happened to her. They heard her screaming and watched her run out all by herself... with bugs crawling all over her. She was trying to beat them off, unsteady on her feet." He paused. "We were both a little...drunk. She got to the railing and just tripped, they said, stumbled and fell over the edge."

Becca heard the click from the machine on the countertop, telling her the coffee was ready, and she was grateful for the excuse to turn away from him and fiddle with getting cups out of the cupboard, sugar, creamer. When she turned back to him with his cup in her hand, her voice was steady and did not betray the turmoil within.

"Sit down before you fall down," she told him, nodding at the table. When he sank into a chair, she set his coffee in front of him. He picked it up with shaking hands and took two huge gulps—appearing not to notice that the steaming liquid must surely have burned his mouth and throat.

"The police wanted to know about the roaches, where so many had come from, but what could I say? 'Oh, those? —they were sent by a demon to kill Corrine Talbot before she could talk, and to tell me to stay out of this." He looked full into her eyes. "That's what it was, wasn't it? A warning."

Becca nodded. "Butt out or I'll send worse."

"Well, if he wanted to scare me, it worked." He reached out and gripped her hand. "I hope you don't mind me coming over here tonight. I couldn't stay there, wondering when Attila the Roach and his conquering hordes would come back."

There was a glassy look in his eyes. But his words were certainly lucid enough, with the appropriate Jeff-levity to indicate he was firing on all cylinders.

"If he sends any other varmints, we'll freeze 'em like the rats he sent last time!" she said, trying to match his light tone.

"Freeze?" The total incredulity on his face actually made her smile.

"There are fifty or sixty dead rats, maybe more, I didn't count, stuffed in a garbage bag in that old chest freezer in the garage."

"You're serious, aren't you."

"I had to freeze them. The crew you sent cleaned all the blood and mess off everything. But they left the rats in a trash bag beside the can outside the garage door for the garbage truck to remove."

"I'm still not tracking."

"We're on semiweekly service and the garbage truck came day before yesterday. Can you imagine how bad a garbage bag full of dead rats is going to smell after ten days in the sun? I couldn't figure what to do and then I spotted that old freezer in the garage. It works; there's just nothing in it. So I plugged it in and put the garbage bag inside. I'll set it out on trash day."

The total absurdity of frozen rats somehow eased Jeff's tension a little, but he was still jumpy, wary.

"I'll tell you the same thing you told me," Becca continued. "You don't have to go back there. Stay here and get your cleaning crew to go over your place tomorrow and make sure there's not so much as a roach antennae left behind. You're welcome to sleep on the couch." Becca gestured toward the living room. "Or in Bishop's chair. It's definitely the softest piece of furniture in the whole house."

Jeff was visibly relieved. "I couldn't be...alone." He gestured toward the window, where the pink haze of dawn was chasing away the shadows in the yard. "But it doesn't make much sense to go to bed now."

"You should try to sleep, though. You missed a night of sleep tonight and another one last night. Not sleeping will mess with your head."

"If I closed my eyes, I'd see...besides, I don't need sleep as much as I need conversation. I need to know what happened to you and Daniel and Jack when you were children that started all this."

"We didn't start it!" She realized she'd raised her voice and continued in a softer tone. "Somebody started it by drawing a pentagram on the floor and chanting some ancient incantation in a language nobody's spoken in thousands of years. At least that's what I'm beginning to figure out from the books in Bishop's library."

"Chapman Whitworth drew the pentagram?"

"Who else? But it was more than just a pentagram. To summon a king of demons requires all manner of other things, implements, statues—stuff like that. It's all there in Bishop's books, but you have to dig it out—one bit here, another part there. But Bishop told us about the final ingredient when we were kids: a human sacrifice, the blood of a murder victim."

"So Chapman Whitworth killed somebody?"

"Must have. And not just anybody—somebody with the 'mark of evil.'"

"What's the 'mark of evil'?"

"Theresa said Bishop tried for years to find out what

that meant, but as far as she knew, he never did. She said he had a theory, though." Images flooded her mind, shifting and changing like the colors in a kaleidoscope. "And if his theory was right, I've got more marks of evil on me than zits on a freshman."

Chapter Eleven

Jack made a swing by the hospital with Andi to see Theresa before they left Cincinnati to go back to Bradford's Ridge—to talk to three possessed children and to look for Daniel! Becca was in Theresa's room and so was Jeff Kendrick. Becca looked pale and haunted, not all that different from the way she'd looked the day he, Theresa, and Andi had bailed her out of an Indiana jail.

But Jeff Kendrick looked way worse than she did! The self-possessed, immaculately dressed, coiffed and manicured junior partner in the law firm of Taylor, Murray and Kendrick was as unkempt as a wino under a bridge. Dark circles beneath his eyes, hair askew, tie undone, suit wrinkled. And more important—profound fearfulness pulsed off him like heat from the basement boiler.

Theresa picked up on it, too, shot a knowing look at Jack and cocked her head toward Jeff. Jack shrugged. But the moment Andi had been dispatched to the cafeteria to get jelly doughnuts, Jack asked him quietly, "Did you find that woman last night, the one from the airplane?"

"Yeah, I found her." His voice had no expression.

"What happened to you, man?"

"Bugs," Jeff said, and a shudder ran through him that Jack could see even sitting three feet away. "Cockroaches."

Jack listened spellbound and horrified as Jeff related the story of what'd happened to him the night before.

"So I stayed at your house, Theresa, for what was left of the night," Jeff said. "I'm not in legal trouble. I didn't break the law. The police have eye-witness testimony that Corrine Talbot's death wasn't my faul—" He stopped. "But it was my fault, wasn't it? It's my fault she's dead."

"No, Jeff," Theresa said. "That bird's roosting in Chapman Whitworth's henhouse!"

SOMEWHERE BETWEEN THE hospital cafeteria and the Mercedes Jeff had retrieved from the parking garage of Sweet Meets Bar, Jeff Kendrick's exhaustion/shock/terror morphed into anger. It grew on him slowly and he was so sleep-deprived that he didn't even recognize its presence until a little red sports car cut him off in traffic and he started screaming at the driver. When the car stopped in front of him at a traffic light, he slammed his car into park, leapt out and advanced on the car ahead with such murderous rage boiling in his chest he could hardly contain himself.

He'd drag the driver out of the car, slam him up against the door and beat his face in, put his hands around his throat and—

A blonde teenage girl looked up at him in surprise when he reached the door. Then her surprise changed to fear and he realized what a sight he must be—rumpled, disheveled, unshaven.

He backed away, saying nothing, got back into his car,

and when the traffic light changed, he drove away—slowly, because his hands were shaking so badly on the steering wheel he feared he might lose control of the car altogether.

And at that moment Jeff Kendrick snapped back into himself like he'd reached the end of a bungee cord. The Jeff Kendrick who knew how to get it done, who was strong, forceful, confident and, yes, cocky. That Jeff was back. And that Jeff was pissed.

He realized then that he'd been in some sort of shock ever since he came to in the stairwell of his condo complex with…go on, say it—with roaches crawling all over him. Roaches! He yelled the word as loud as he could, along with a colorful stream of obscenities. His hands calmed then and stopped shaking.

He'd been horrified, terrified, revolted and trauma-tized, but now all that was replaced by a single clarifying emotion, one that superseded them all, that burned them away like the sun drying up creek mist. Jeff Kendrick was furious! He'd never in his life been so angry.

Jeff believed it now, oh yes, indeed—every word of it! He was one hundred percent in. All the crazy talk about demons and possessions—it was just as Jack Carpenter had said: whether you liked it or not, it was true.

Chapman Whitworth and whatever monster from hell drove him had stolen from Jeff the only woman he'd ever loved. Had murdered Emily. The power of the thing that possessed the man had sent rats to attack a sweet old woman. Had unleashed cockroaches to frighten him and silence the only witness to the chicanery that'd made him a hero. And had kidnapped, maybe murdered Daniel Burke.

If Jeff could have seized Chapman Whitworth by the throat at that moment, he'd have squeezed the life out of the man and cheerfully suffered whatever the consequences might be. He sat very still for a moment, until the car behind beeped and he realized the traffic light had turned green.

The heat of his rage was slowly replaced by a cold ball of determination that sank down through his chest into his belly like cold water sinks because it's heavier. He knew then what had to be done.

~

MAJOR CHARLES CROCKER put his index fingers to his temples, closed his eyes and leaned his head back.

"Don't tell me," he said to Sheriff Hezekiah Lincoln. "Let me impress you with my psychic powers." He paused. "Yes, it's coming to me now…when Daniel Burke was snatched from the park yesterday, nobody saw anything or heard anything—right?"

Crock sat in the sheriff's cramped office with puddles forming all around him where his raincoat was shedding the water from the morning's downpour. The sky had since turned sunny, but frequent rumbles of thunder in the distance made it clear the rain could start up again anytime it liked, thank you very much, so don't make any plans.

Which was playing havoc with preparations for the Spook Festival.

Crock had spent the morning getting needlessly soaked, tramping around the muddy "crime scene," looking for anything that would shed any light at all on the disappearance of Daniel Burke. All he'd managed to do was get Sonny and Cher wet.

"Never would have pegged you for a cynical man," Sheriff Lincoln said. "You've spent too much time in the big city and it's soured you on the ways of common folk."

"If Harrelton, Ohio, is the big city, I'm a three-eyed crow."

Crock reached up and pulled Cher out of his right ear, opened the battery compartment of the hearing aid and blew into it, trying to dislodge any droplets of water that might have seeped in. Then he gently thumped it against his palm. Sonny seemed to be functioning fine. It was always Cher that gave him trouble—just like a woman!— and he didn't want to spend the rest of the time he was in Bradford's Ridge deaf in one ear. Well, not deaf. His hearing loss was strange. Some speech sounds were clear. Other frequencies were missing altogether. Without both hearing aids working, words lacked key sounds, granting conversations a stuttering quality that was maddening. He fit the small earpiece back into his ear canal and the hearing aid itself, connected to it by a translucent wire, behind his ear. Then he punched the small button on the bottom and was rewarded with the five-note chime indicating the hearing aid was working properly.

"Actually, you're mostly right, though. Nobody saw or heard anything. All we know is that Ariel Murphy was seen near the park and nobody's seen her since."

"And that's significant because...?"

"Because she's an eight-year-old child that nobody reported missing! And because Ariel is one of the three children who're...the children you came down here to see. I sent deputies around to talk to the parents of all three of them this morning and managed to get out of Ariel's mother—who came to the door already falling-down drunk—that she didn't know where the child was. Rita'd just got her five-year sobriety chip in AA, but I bet the woman hasn't drawn a sober breath since all the strange things started happening. Got her husband's number and called him. He drives a whiskey barrel truck, just dropped off a load at a winery in California. He's worried sick about both of them, said he'd deadhead home as fast as he could. But even straight through, it's going to take him a couple of days."

"You saying this kid might have had something to do with——?"

"I'm saying this kid—who looks like a life-sized Raggedy Ann doll—is the child who ripped up my daughter's entire rose garden by the roots. If she really is…"

The sheriff was having as much trouble saying "possessed" as Crock was. That was comforting somehow, in a way Crock didn't bother to pick at.

"If she is, she'd have been physically capable of taking on Daniel, three NFL linebackers and Batman," Crock said.

The sheriff was clearly struggling with all this. Who wouldn't be?

"How about the other two?" Crock asked. "What are their names?"

"Cassidy Davenport and Russell Willis."

"Their folks know where they are?"

"I can testify to where one of them is—in my administrator's office. I had a deputy bring in Rusty Willis so we could have a little chat. Cassidy Davenport's family went to church this morning and I assume she went with them." The sheriff paused. "That wouldn't seem likely though, would it? I mean, if the child's…?"

"No idea. I've already told you seventy-five percent more than I actually know about"—he forced the word out with only a slight hesitation and was right proud of himself —"demons."

Crock had intended to wait until Jack got back to Bradford's Ridge before attempting to interrogate any of the possessed children—so the two of them could haul out their well-oiled good cop/bad cop routine. But Jack had stopped at the hospital to see Theresa this morning and he wasn't back yet. Crock would have to start without him.

The boy was small—Crock would have guessed he was about six instead of eight except he wasn't missing any front teeth. He had curly brown hair, a button nose and was sitting in a chair so big for him his feet didn't even touch the floor. He swung them absentmindedly back and forth as he flipped through a Spiderman comic book. His mother sat in the chair next to him, clearly far more concerned about the goings-on than he was.

As soon as the sheriff stepped into the room, the mother was on him.

"What do you want from my Rusty? You've already asked him about those spiders and that burned-up cat and he couldn't tell you anything about any of it. He's a good boy! You have no right to keep hauling him in here every time there's some petty crime or vandalism and you don't have anybody else to pin it on."

She went on in that vein and Crock watched her closely, listened to what she said and balanced that against the silent monologue of her body language. He quickly picked up on two things. For one, she didn't believe a word she was saying. She absolutely did not think little Rusty was a good boy. In a quarter of a century as a police officer, he'd listened to enough other parents haul out that line to recognize sincerity when he heard it. No, she wasn't defending the kid because she thought he was innocent. She was defending him because she was scared to death of him.

The other thing Crock noticed was that the police station, the presence of all manner of firepower and the implied "you're in a heap of trouble, son" atmosphere had not cowed the boy in the slightest.

When the woman finally paused for breath, Sheriff Lincoln spoke in the slow, measured tone you used with a hysteric, which this woman would likely become with the slightest provocation.

"Now, Mary Ellen, we're not saying little Rusty's committed any crime. We only need to talk to him, ask him a few questions. Shoot, he may know something that'd help us out without even realizing it's important."

Before the woman could launch back into her diatribe, the sheriff gestured toward Crock. "This is Major Charles Crocker from the Harrelton, Ohio, Police Department."

The boy was instantly alert. He didn't look up from the comic book he was feigning reading, but he tensed, stopped swinging his legs and grew very still.

"Major Crocker wants to ask Rusty some questions that might shed some light on a case he's working on."

"How could Rusty know anything about something that happened in Cinci—"

"There's a connection to Caverna County or we wouldn't be troubling you and the boy." The sheriff's tone was kind and conciliatory but firm. Just the right mix. The man was a good cop, Crock decided, and with a little prep time could have played Jack's part in Crock's traveling good cop/bad cop show. It was too late for that now, though.

"But…"

"This will only take a few minutes and then you and Rusty can be on your way. Why don't you come with me and let's get some hot chocolate. The Lions Club booth is open, I think, and they're serving funnel cakes, too."

"I'm not leaving Rusty with—"

"Go on, Mom, do what he says." The boy's words ran a chill up Crock's spine. His was not the tone of a little boy talking to his mother. And the voice was somehow deeper than a child's voice and was…Crock couldn't put his finger on—it was cold, that was it. The voice was as devoid of personality as an automated attendant.

Rusty then turned his gaze on Crock. "I'm glad to answer any questions the major here has for me." The tone was insolent and mocking, and a small smirk crawled out onto the boy's face.

MAIN STREET WAS BLOCKED off for the Spook Festival, so Uncle Jack couldn't park in front of the courthouse. He parked a couple of blocks away and they walked to the center of town. Then Uncle Jack headed off to talk to the sheriff and Major Crocker, and Andi stayed behind to wander around the festival setup. She knew he'd been concerned she might be upset by all the Halloween decorations. Most of the workers and volunteers were dressed in some kind of costume. Witches and vampires and lots of zombies because it didn't take much effort—some ratty-looking torn clothes and fake blood—to look like a zombie. Signs said the festival would open at noon and the morning's storm had delayed preparations, so all the volunteers rushed around in a panic and didn't even notice Andi. She'd stand out later as the lone costume-less kid after families rushed home from church and returned with Ninja Turtles, Luke Skywalkers and Little Mermaids in tow.

As she passed by, workers splashed water on her shoes when they dumped a puddle off the top of a blow-up spider that was bigger than a car. Farther down the street was a gigantic blow-up Frankenstein and a trio of ghosts attached by ropes to light posts. The biggest blow-up figure was a red demon fifty feet tall that towered higher than the buildings. It had horns, a forked tail and wide, crazy eyes.

She stood before the pudgy demon and shook her head. It didn't upset her. It made her sad. This was what people thought he was like—and they laughed and joked about him. If only they could see…

Mostly, she wasn't looking at the decorations at all. She was searching the faces, looking for Daddy. Maybe he wasn't really lost at all, like Uncle Jack had said he was. Maybe it wasn't anything bad like that. Maybe he'd just gone somewhere without telling Major Crocker and now he was back.

There were pillars on either side of the huge oak door at the top of the courthouse steps, each set on a marble base about four feet square. Andi climbed up onto the base beside one of the pillars so she could see the whole crowd. She scanned up and down, looking for hair the same color as hers and a red jacket. He might have been wearing his black and orange Cincinnati Bengals jacket, though, so she looked for that, too. But she saw neither.

Andi slumped back against the pillar. Trying not to cry, she touched the silver cross necklace that had been her mother's. Uncle Jack had fastened it around her neck at Mommy's funeral and Andi had silently sworn she'd never take it off, that she would wear it every day for the rest of her life. Sometimes touching it made her feel closer to Mommy, but not this time.

Where is Daddy?

How could he just be…gone like that? Uncle Jack hadn't told her all of it. Grownups never told you all of it. They tried to protect you from the truth, which was stupid because sometimes you knew the truth better than they did. This was one of those times. Whether Uncle Jack said it outright or not, she knew what had happened to Daddy. He'd been kidnapped, like when she'd been on her way to her piano lesson and Dreadlock Man and Speedy

Gonzales had snatched her off the sidewalk. But Daddy was in more danger than she'd been. Daddy'd been kidnapped because of that...thing...that efreet the grownups wouldn't talk about in front of her. Though she wasn't sure what it was, she was sure that an efreet was way worse than Tattoo Man with a knife.

Somehow the efreet thing and Daddy and her vision were all tangled up together, but she didn't know how. She'd seen it again this morning on the way to Bradford's Ridge from Cincinnati. She'd been riding shotgun and Uncle Jack had reached over and taken her hand and squeezed it, then held on. Sitting there holding Uncle Jack's hand, she'd felt better, like maybe Daddy would be okay because Uncle Jack would find him just like he'd found her.

Then the red-and-gold-leafed trees outside the window had dissolved and she saw the Big Bad Thing.

The vision was different every time she saw it, not because it changed but because she was seeing it from different angles. Like looking at a tree from the ground below, then from the sky above and then out through its limbs. This time there was the smell of fried chicken and something cinnamon—apple pie, maybe. Then a big booming sound rumbled as loud as being right up next to thunder. People were screaming and wailing like before, and smoke and things flew past her so quickly she didn't have time to get a good look at any of them. Glass was breaking, a lot of glass, and shards of it flew through the air like jagged icicles, stabbing and cutting people. Dead bodies with bloody bandages, pieces of people, a leg from the knee down, ripped off, and the shoe on the foot had a funny-looking curled-up toe.

Something big and round appeared. She'd seen it in the vision before, and when she'd described it to Daddy, she'd said it looked like a big dinner plate. But this time it looked more like a Frisbee. It was spinning through the air as if someone had tossed it at her. It flashed across her vision in an instant, but she concentrated hard to see what was written on it. She'd seen that part before, too, numbers and letters. The first one was a zero, but the right side was smashed flat. Then OSW7. Then there were flames everywhere, followed by darkness.

As quickly as the vision had appeared, it disappeared, leaving Andi staring at nothing for a moment before the real world returned. She must have looked funny because Uncle Jack asked what was wrong and she described how the Big Bad Thing had looked this time.

As she spoke, they'd rounded the last bend before the Welcome to Caverna County sign and she could see the gathering darkness. It was blacker now, much darker than it'd been before. Almost so dark it blotted out the sunlight altogether, sucking all the color from the world and casting it in shades of gray with deep black shadows—odd shadows. It took a moment to figure out what was strange about the shadows. She remembered playing in the backyard on summer evenings in the glow of big security lights on posts around the deck. She'd play with the long black shadow she cast with the lights behind her and she'd chase it to the back fence, trying to catch it. These shadows didn't extend out from trees and signs and fences like there was a light behind them. These shadows settled in black pools around everything, puddles of darkness on all sides. Andi thought maybe if she walked into one, it would be too dark there to see anything at all.

Chapter Twelve

Though Rusty's mother appeared hesitant to leave the boy alone with a stranger, she wasn't really reluctant at all. Her body language screamed that she was desperate to put as much distance as she could between her and the freckle-faced little boy in the big chair.

As soon as the door closed behind her and the sheriff, Crock sat down on the edge of the desk facing the boy and tossed the cinnamon toothpick he'd been chewing into a trash basket. This was an office, not a typical interrogation room. The nameplate on the desk read Juanita Torres, administrative assistant. It was a small, stuffy, windowless room cluttered with the paraphernalia common to all secretaries—Crock still called them that. There was a tape dispenser, Post-it notes, scissors, stapler and a pad of the little pink "While you were out" notes for phone messages. Did people still use those? You'd think that even in a backwater hamlet like Bradford's Ridge, Kentucky, voicemail would have rendered them obsolete. Apparently not.

A huge aquarium, four feet by six feet, rested on a stand across from the desk. Illuminated with its own light,

the murky water was teeming with aquatic life, the obligatory goldfish and guppies plus four or five other varieties
of colorful fish Crock couldn't identify. A small turtle
climbed on a rock on the bottom. The air breather on the
tank offered comforting plunk-swish white noise, and the
watery blue glow from it mitigated, at least a little bit, the
sallow yellow illumination from the lone overhead fluores-
cent bulb.

"Can I get you anything?" Crock asked. "Would you
like a soft drink? I think the root beer slot in the machine
down the hall still has cans."

The boy didn't answer, just looked at Crock.

It was unnerving, but Crock didn't let his discomfort
show.

"I'm an A&W fan myself," Crock said. "House brand
root beer tastes like swamp water. You sure you don't want
anything?"

"Go get yourself a root beer if you want one," the boy
said. "Judging from that fat belly, you've sucked down more
than a few already."

With great effort, Crock kept his reaction off his face.

"Yeah, but I've already had my quota for the morning
—two for breakfast along with a dozen doughnuts and a
piece of cherry pie. Cherries are a fruit, you know, so technically I tapped a couple of food groups."

"Why are you here?" the boy asked. "What do you
want from me?"

"Just want to chat, that's all."

"You didn't drive all the way down here from Cincinnati to chat with a snot-nosed eight-year-old kid." The
casual reference to himself in third person added another
layer of otherworldliness to the scene.

Then he saw it, only for a second. Or thought he did.
Might have imagined it. Yeah, probably imagined it. But

for a moment there seemed to be a shadow behind the boy, like the "ghosts" cast behind people in a flashed picture. Only the shadow wasn't in the shape of a boy. It wasn't in the shape of anything recognizable.

"You ever go exploring in the caves?"

Crock's bluntness was rewarded with the shock and surprise he was hoping for. And alarm. Definitely alarm.

"No, I never go in the caves. Nobody does. They're dangerous. You could get lost in there and never be found."

"Yeah, that's what I hear, but they're caves, for crying out loud. Nothing cooler to explore than a cave. A remote cave, maybe, one nobody's been in before."

"I told you I don't ever go in the caves."

"Not even once? You and Ariel and Cassidy out playing in the woods and you come upon—"

The look that distorted the child's features was one Crock was certain he would carry to his grave. Rage, loathing, hatred all wrapped up and poured undiluted onto the features of an innocent freckled face, twisting and molding it into a sneer of such revulsion Crock couldn't help pulling back from it.

"Those caves are dangerous, all right, fat man." The voice that spoke the words was a growl, an animal sound, from the throat of a wolf with dripping fangs, ready to pounce. "More dangerous than you could possibly imagine."

The air in the room instantly became too thick to breathe and Crock was suddenly sucking in a substance his lungs couldn't process. Dark shapes fluttered around the edges of his vision in the darkness of the room. Darkness. In the gloom, the boy's eyes shone. They were brown. Not a pretty chocolate brown or caramel color. They were muddy, the color of stagnant water, a pond with green

slime along the edge, water that more than one stray creature had wandered into and drowned.

Water closes over his head and he flails with his arms
and legs, trying to get his head back up into the air. The
breath strains at his lungs and the terror in his chest is so
huge there's hardly room for any air at all. He kicks frantically, trying to propel his body upward, but he only sinks
farther. The pressure to breathe has become unbearable.
Sunlight streams down through the water above, refracted
into a shower of silver spangles, a shaft of brilliance that he
knows will be the last thing he ever sees.

Then there is bright all around him. Hands grab his
arm, yanking him upward, and he somehow manages to
hold onto that breath until his head breaks the surface into
the air. He gasps air in great heaving lungfuls, then catches
a bit of water and strangles, coughs, feels himself hauled to
shore as if he weighed no more than a loaf of bread.
There is water in Crock's eyes; he can't see. But as the man
who saved him lays him gently on his back on the riverbank, he catches a glimpse of one thing in crisp focus. The
man is wearing black cowboy boots.

The memory was there and then gone between one
heartbeat and another. But that was enough. The darkness
receded from around Crock's vision, the oppression in the
room lifted, and he drew in a breath—not the gasp of a
drowning boy but the relieved sigh of one to whom evil has
come way too close.

The look that had curdled the boy's features was gone
as quickly as it had appeared, leaving them innocent and
totally blank.

"You ever explored a cave, Mister?" The too-sweet
childishness was cloying. "What's it like in a cave?" Rusty
slid down off the seat of the chair and began to wander

aimlessly around the room. He fingered the paperweight on the desk and lifted the little glass ball next to it that was filled with a Currier and Ives scene. He turned it upside down and shook it and snow began to fall from the sky. "I'd be too scared to go in a cave. I bet it's real dark in there. Mommy always turns on my nightlight at night because I'm afraid of the dark."

Crock turned and watched as the boy made a circuit around the room. He stopped at the desk beside Crock, picked up the Post-it notes and began tearing off one after another as he spoke.

"What was the cave you went exploring in? Was it dangerous?"

"The only cave I was ever in was Carlsbad Caverns, and—"

Crock caught the movement out of the corner of his eye. Or maybe just sensed it. Cop's instinct. The boy was lightning fast. He snatched up the scissors off the desktop, turned and stabbed them at Crock in a single motion so fluid it was hard to follow.

All Crock could do was deflect. He reached out and knocked the scissors aside, so the motion that would have plunged the six inches of sharp blade into his heart plunged downward instead, and he felt a white-hot dagger of pain in his thigh.

The boy made a horrible, guttural sound, yanked the scissors out of Crock's leg and stabbed again at his chest. Crock staggered down off the desk and shoved the child away before the blade found its target. The force of the shove sent the boy flying across the room, where he collided with the aquarium, knocking it off its stand to crash to the floor in a flood of rank, fish-food-smelling water.

The boy was drenched, lying on his back amid dying,

flopping fish. He had lost his grip on the scissors when he fell, but as fast as a rattlesnake, he leapt to pick them up off the floor and started for Crock with them upraised, his eyes gleaming, his teeth bared.

The door flew open then, officers and staff responding to the sound of the crash, and the adults were frozen in place by the sight of the child advancing on Crock with the bloody scissors.

"You'll die, you fat pig," the voice that came from the child's mouth said. "I'll kill you, cut your heart out and—"

Finally, one of the deputies moved and his response unfroze the other officers. Three of them tried to grab the boy, but he turned and plunged the scissors into the chest of the first man who reached him. The deputy looked down in surprise at the scissors sticking out of his shirt below the badge on his right side, then sank to the floor and fell over into the puddle of aquarium water.

The other officers advanced on the boy, but the kid fought like a wild animal. He bit the second officer, tore out a hunk of flesh from his hand and spat it out on the floor as the man howled in pain. Wet and as slippery as an eel, the boy dodged around them, slipped out of their grasping hands and made for the door, jumping over the body of the officer lying in a growing puddle of blood.

Crock reached out, grabbed him by the back of his skinny neck and yanked him off his feet. The boy kicked and flailed frantically, but Crock had lifted him off the floor and was holding the child out from his body the way you'd hold a dead mouse by the tail.

The room was suddenly filled with people.

Someone was screaming—a woman, shrieking, "Rusty! Rusty! What have you done to my boy?"

Other hands took the boy out of Crock's grasp. The child continued to writhe and twist. He kicked, spat and tried to bite them. It took five big men to subdue him—one on each side gripping an arm or leg and another behind with his fingers encircling the boy's neck so when he tried to wriggle free, the movement choked him.

Crock heard the wail of a siren—an ambulance. Someone had had the good judgment to summon one. He looked down and saw that his whole pants leg was drenched in blood. But it was the officer on the floor he was concerned about. The sheriff—when did he get here? —turned the man over on his back where he lay in a puddle of water and blood, gasping, every breath producing a bubbly red spittle on his lips that dripped down his chin.

"You hang in there, Ed," the sheriff told him. "Ambulance is on its way. You're gonna be just fine."

Crock knew the officer wouldn't make it to the hospital alive.

"Crock!"

Jack was standing wide-eyed in the doorway. Then Crock discovered that his legs didn't want to hold him upright anymore and he sank down into the water on the floor beside the dying deputy.

JEFF KENDRICK CHECKED into the downtown Sheraton after he left the hospital. He couldn't face going home, not yet, but he was exhausted, dead on his feet. He hadn't slept in...he didn't know how long. Forty-eight hours? More? The lack of sleep had set his head spinning, and he had to think, to make a plan. He collapsed on the bed in his hotel room, didn't pull the bedspread back or take his shoes off, merely lay where he had fallen, closed his eyes, and blessed darkness took him.

They came for him then, thousands of them—roaches and spiders and beetles. A blanket of them a foot deep swarmed over his body and his face so thick he couldn't see light through them. They crawled up his nostrils and into his ears. He tried to scream, but when he opened his mouth, they crawled in, jamming themselves in so tight he couldn't close it. And they kept coming, crawling through his mouth and down his throat. He beat at them, trying to knock them off, but there were too many. The skin on his neck began to stretch out, swelling with wriggling lumps as they packed his throat. He couldn't breathe. They were crawling into his stomach now, filling his lungs and—

Jeff sat bolt upright on the bed, gasping for breath, batting at the horrors all over him, spitting out...

There was nothing in his mouth. Nothing on him. It had been a nightmare. He sat panting, his face wet—was he crying? Then he leapt up and paced. Back and forth. Back and forth.

Bugs. And rats! Biting Theresa, eating Theresa. And then there was Daniel. Andi's daddy gone!

The buzzing in his head grew louder and louder, flies on a rotting corpse. His breathing began to hitch in and out in an irregular rhythm that he could not control. Bugs and rats and death.

The gift that keeps on giving from Chapman Wainwright Whitworth. He had to be stopped. But Jeff's head was spinning and he couldn't plan—

Suddenly, the plan and the will to implement it was just there. He didn't have to figure it out. It appeared in his mind as seamless as a file downloaded off the Internet. He already knew what had to be done, had already decided that part. Now, he knew how. He accepted the fact of it without question. No second-guessing, no doubt.

The High Court of Common Sense and the Commissioner of Reasonable Behavior made halfhearted attempts to sway him as he drove across Cincinnati to the sleazy part of town. But Jeff could barely hear their pleas. It was as if they were on a pier, shouting to him as he sat on a raft being carried out to sea by the tide. Even if he'd heard and listened to them, it wouldn't have mattered. He was being carried along by a current so powerful that he could not have returned to the dock—to sanity, maybe?—even if he tried. And he didn't have a paddle.

His life and the purpose of it had been distilled into a single pure, shining thing. Jeff Kendrick was about that shining thing, that deed, that act of retribution that would pay for all that had come before.

He found himself at a bar on Conrad Street, where the debris of trash and empty bottles from the Saturday night crowd still littered the parking lot. He had no memory of driving there. He was in the hotel room and then he was there. Nothing in between. The bar wouldn't open until Sunday evening, of course, but the proprietor lived in an apartment on the back side with an entrance off the alley, and Jeff banged on the door until the man answered—in his skivvies, bleary-eyed, with bedhead tangling his thick black hair and a sheet crease across his beard-stubbled right cheek. Jeff had defended him on a drug charge a year ago and he'd never paid the outstanding balance on his bill. Jeff told him he could forget the bill, that he'd trade that for what he needed and the man willingly agreed.

Back in his car, he hit Google on his cell phone, got the number and called the Cincinnati campaign headquarters of the Chapman Whitworth for President Campaign— Making America Safe from Without and Within. Mild threats and an indignant do-you-know-who-I-am? got his call kicked upstairs from the barely pubescent volunteer manning the phone bank to one of Whitworth's aides.

Jeff was brief and clear. He needed an appointment with Mr. Whitworth today.

The man almost laughed in Jeff's face.

"I'm sorry Mr....what did you say your name was... Kendrick? I'm sorry, Mr. Kendrick, but Mr. Whitworth can't possibly squeeze you in. He doesn't land in Cincinnati until four o'clock and he's booked solid until he's introduced with the other candidates at the Better Day Society ball tomorrow night.

"He'll see me today," Jeff told the man. "Tell him I want to talk to him about a video shot by a mutual friend —Corrine Talbot. I only need five minutes of his time."

Jeff waited on hold and was not at all surprised a few minutes later to hear that Chapman Whitworth would be able to shoehorn him into his schedule today after all. Would Jeff join him for an early dinner at Andolini's Restaurant?

Jeff would. Perfect.

And then...?

Beyond was only blankness, the color of a computer screen that wouldn't make the universal computer-starting boing because the hard drive was fried. His future was a gray blankness. But that was okay. It had really been that way since the day he'd dropped scalding coffee into his lap when the breaking news report on WCIN described a shooting at Voice of Hope Community Church. He'd stared at the family picture of Emily, Daniel and Andi on the screen—the photo that'd been on the front of last year's Christmas card—and listened as the news anchor told him that Emily Burke was dead.

In truth, Jeff had died that day, too. Like a gyroscope, the momentum of his spinning life kept him upright for a time afterward, but now he was running out of steam, beginning to wobble, about to topple over. When he did, there was no life force to start him spinning again, so maybe he should use another bullet out of the chamber of the gun he'd gotten from the drug dealer to turn his own screen permanently dark.

Maybe he would do just that.

But first Chapman Whitworth had to die.

Chapter Thirteen

Andi had been standing on the marble base of the pillar on the left side of the huge oak door of the courthouse when the commotion started. Shouting. Screams. People running in and out. A crowd had quickly gathered—from where?—on the courthouse steps.

There was a babble of talk all around Andi, people curious or upset.

"…said it was a prisoner got loose and shot…"

"Two of the officers is down. I heard it on the scanner when they called the ambulance."

"…standing right here on the steps and I didn't hear no gunshots."

"It's some kid. Must be Mary Ellen Willis's boy because she's the one in there doing all the screaming."

Andi could hear her, a woman's voice wailing, "Rusty! Rusty!"

Then the crowd parted to allow EMTs through with a stretcher. And in no time they were wheeling the stretcher back out with a man on it. His face was deathly pale. The crowd recognized him, a hum of sympathy buzzed around.

"Charley Parker's oldest…"

"Somebody'd ought to tell his wife—she's playing the organ right now at First Baptist."

The crowd was watching the EMTs load the man into the ambulance and nobody noticed the four deputies come out the front door, each holding the limb of a little boy with wet brown hair hanging in his eyes, thrashing about, writhing, struggling to get free.

A bat-like creature clung to the boy's shoulders, its scaled wings draped over his back. The creature had the head of some kind of bug—a beetle—with gigantic eyes and a drooling mouth with pinchers on either side that snapped together in front of its face and antennae that twitched restlessly. The creature's head snapped from side to side, watchful and alert. It spotted Andi immediately and put up a huge, clawed hand to shield its lidless eyes, like it was looking into the sun.

The boy who was its host suddenly froze, stopped trying to wrench away.

"Who are you?" the creature demanded, its voice the sound of metal scraping against metal, a grating sound that set Andi's teeth on edge.

Andi shrank back in revulsion, all the air knocked out of her, and squeezed her eyes tight shut. But she opened them again whether she wanted to or not. She had to look; she always had to look. The rage and loathing that pulsed off the creature in a wave struck her a blow in the chest and she staggered, almost stepping off the edge of the marble base of the column.

"You will die," the creature threatened, but the menace in its voice seemed somehow almost…shaky…"We will come for you in the night and—"

"No, you won't. You won't come anywhere near her."

The voice was soft, such a contrast to the rasping rumble of the creature, it seemed musical.

Andi turned to find Princess Buttercup standing next to her on the marble base of the column. Not Princess Buttercup exactly. It was a young woman with long blond hair that hung down her back in a single braid. She was dressed in a pair of jeans with a hole above the right knee and a chambray shirt sprinkled with tiny yellow flowers. She'd rolled the long sleeves up to her elbows, had well-worn New Balance running shoes on her feet and carried a rain jacket. No flowing white gown, but the face was Princess Buttercup's. Andi would recognize that face anywhere.

The creature cowered backward, shielding its eyes as if they were scorched by a thousand suns.

"You can't hurt me here," the creature cried. Maybe it was trying to sound cocky and confident, but Andi could see it didn't feel confident at all. It felt scared. At the sight of that horrible creature cowering back, a thrill of elation ran through Andi's whole body and she stood up tall and didn't shrink away from the sight of it like before.

When the boy had gone limp, the woman behind him had cried out, "Rusty! Rusty, are you all right?" Then she rushed around in front of the officers, looking up pleadingly into their faces.

"Please…he's…when he's asleep, he's not…"

The two officers holding his ankles set them down. She reached out and tenderly gathered into her arms the child the other two officers held between them. He hung as limp as a rag doll. The officers looked at each other; then one picked the limp boy up into his arms out of the other officers' grips and they continued down the steps with him. It was a brief tableau. The crowd missed it altogether, but

Andi watched from the top of the column base, following the progress of the officers, the boy and his mother, and the creature as they got into a squad car parked out front.

The creature never stopped squinting in Andi's direction, trying to look, but unable to tolerate the brightness that sparkled in the dark, ashy air.

As the officers were loading the child into the backseat beside his mother, the creature cried out in defiance at Andi.

"We'll kill you all, you know," it shouted with its ragged, rusty voice. "Starting with your daddy."

Andi gasped and couldn't drag her eyes away as the boy was loaded into the car and the officers drove with him slowly away. Then she turned to Princess Buttercup. But Princess Buttercup was gone. The ambulance edged through the spot where the barricades on the street had been moved to let it pass; then it tore out fast with lights flashing and the siren screaming. Another ambulance pulled into the space left by the first and EMTs from it rushed into the courthouse.

A few minutes later, Uncle Jack emerged through the crowd around the courthouse doors, moving people out of the way of the stretcher pushed by the two EMTs right behind him.

The man on the stretcher was Major Crocker.

Andi jumped down and shoved her way through the crowd to his side.

"Major Crocker!"

He tried to smile but couldn't quite pull it off. "Wanna play rock, paper, scissors?" he asked, but his voice was breathy, the way you talked when you were trying not to cry because you just stubbed your toe or got a brain freeze.

When the EMTs began to load the stretcher into the

ambulance, Uncle Jack told her, "We'll follow the ambulance to the hospital."

Andi looked around one last time. But she didn't see Princess Buttercup. She didn't see Daddy either.

THERESA TRIED to act like didn't nothing hurt, that she was fine, but she wasn't foolin' nobody. Truth was everything hurt, and whatever part didn't hurt was sympathizin' with the parts that did hurt by hurtin' right along with 'em.

Dr. Paul Richardson had said she had been bitten more than two dozen times—miraculous given how many rats they was. Most was only little punctures where they teeth sunk in, but five of the bites required a stitch or two to close wounds where the sharp teeth tore her flesh. Only two of the stitched and bandaged bites—the one on the side of her neck and the one on her right hand—were in places you could see. But all the rest had been thoroughly disinfected. They'd pumped her full of all kind of IV antibiotics, give her bottles of the pills to take home with her and said she was to go to Dr. Richardson's office in Lancaster if she had any problems.

"I want to see you immediately if any of your wounds start to ooze or get red and puffy or if you start to run a fever," Dr. Richardson had said. "It is almost impossible to totally disinfect the bite of the filthiest animal on the planet."

While Becca went to fetch the car, Theresa waited in a wheelchair at the main entrance to the hospital. She'd told them nurses she didn't need no wheelchair and they'd told her she wasn't leaving 'less she got in one! As she watched other folks pass by who 'peared to be in a lot worse shape than she was, Theresa struggled to have a good attitude about what'd happened. Truth was she hadn't been shot or nothing like that. Didn't break her arm or get hit by a bus. Everybody was making a fuss about somethin' wasn't all that bad. She had a bunch of little bitty holes in her—only a few even needed Band-Aids—that was all.

And she could believe that as long as she thought of the pains as little holes and not as where rats had sunk their sharp teeth into her.

She always stopped herself any time she started talkin' to Bishop, in her head or out loud even, because he'd gone on home and she needed to be talkin' to the one who had been waitin' for him when he got there. It still didn't feel like her prayers made it as far as the attic, but she'd read once not to judge the effectiveness of a prayer by how you felt while you was prayin' it, so she went on ahead even if it didn't feel like God was listenin'.

Okay, Lord, I ain't Jonah and I ain't gonna run away— and by the way, do you think it was fair to sic that little girl on me with all her sweetness and wide-eyed innocence?

But I'm stickin' and I'm sorry for unloadin' on you like I done. I was just being honest and you could see it all in my heart anyway so I might as well a'said it out my mouth.

Lord, it's getting darker and darker. That monster's got Daniel now and the rest of us is floatin' around, not knowing what to do.

Bottom line is, you got to do something. You, not us. We're doing all we know to do, but it ain't enough. You gone have to step in or we ain't never even gonna find that efreet, let alone send it back where it come from.

And you done give Andi that vision about explosions rippin' people apart. But how we supposed to stop it from happenin' if we don't even know what it is? In fact, how could we stop it even if we did know what it is—only the handful of us, nobody special, garden-variety folks like we is. How we supposed to stand up to the Prince of Darkness hisself?

You got to give us what we need. You got to make a way, 'cause we stuck here. Ain't nothing else we can do on our own.

Later that afternoon, she had dozed off in Bishop's big old chair as the afternoon shadows lengthened across the lawn when there come a knock at the door. It was Jeff Kendrick, but a very different Jeff Kendrick from the hotshot lawyer who'd sat in that conference room in the police station that time, telling her all confident like that he was gone win her case and get her off and she wasn't gonna have to go to prison.

What'd happened to him with them roaches—it'd changed him. Course wasn't none of them the folks they was before, and wouldn't none of them ever be again.

Still, it looked like the man had aged ten years, had bags under his eyes big enough to pack for two weeks in Hawaii. Jeff's face was dark, too, with…what? She wasn't sure. But she was sure that he was all strung out. Like them wires in the back of that grand piano she seen once in Macy's at Christmastime. The little short ones was pulled the tightest and they was the ones made the high notes. The Jeff Kendrick she'd known before could have played you a song on that piano, but the one standing before her right now wasn't capable of nothin' but high notes.

"I stopped by to check on you…and to tell you I'm having dinner with Chapman Whitworth this evening," Jeff said. No preamble, said it flat out without even taking time to sit down.

"You'll want to back up a little, sugar, 'cause I'm still loopy from all them drugs they gave me. I thought you said you's going to see Chapman Whitworth."

"His 'you'll have to go through me' video was a fraud."

"Can you prove that?"

"No, but I can convince him I can. All I had to do was mention it and suddenly he had time to see me today."

"Been my experience trying to bluff the devil don't usually end well. Daniel and Jack and Senator LaHayne had in mind to do the same thing—bluff him—and the senator got hisself dead over it."

"I'm not going to demand he withdraw from the presidential race or anything like that," Jeff said. "I'm going to tell him that we know what he did and he knows where Daniel Burke is—'let's trade.'"

Theresa was so incredulous she could hardly find her voice. "Jeff, listen to yourself, son. Do you really think he's gone say, 'why, sure, Jeff, I'd be glad to trade what I got for what you got'? You know better than that."

This was all wrong. Wasn't a thing about any of it that felt genuine. Theresa's instincts about people had alarm bells, and right now, every one of them bells was clanging ding, ding, ding.

Why on earth would Jeff Kendrick…?

"You ain't doin' this to rescue Daniel Burke!" She hadn't thought the words before she said them, but she knew they was true soon's they come out of her mouth. "You just made that part up so you'd look noble." His surprised face told her she'd guessed right. "You want revenge!"

That was what she'd seen darkening his face—unspent rage.

"And you think you can waltz in there—"

"You said demons don't know what we're thinking —right?"

"They can't get inside your head, if that's what you're askin'. But most times they don't need to 'cause one of 'em was probably right there when—"

Jeff went right on like he hadn't heard a word she said. Most likely he hadn't. "Then Chapman Whitworth is in for a big surprise." He paused. "Goodbye, Theresa."

There was an awful finality to his words; then he turned and walked out the door.

Chapter Fourteen

Ariel Murphy was totally alone. She was cold, sitting in the dark, shivering.

She wanted to cry, to scream, to yell, but she had done all that before and it brought the thing, got the attention of the thing, and that was worse than sitting in the cold dark alone, so she remained silent.

What her eyes could see was large in front of her, like she was sitting in a movie theater in front of a big IMAX screen. But she was a spectator, had no control, couldn't even blink the eyes she looked through, could not stop the legs that took small creeping steps along the side of a rock wall on a chilly October evening that smelled of mums and burning leaves.

Ariel watched, trembling, wondering what awful act the thing had planned for her body to do.

She saw on the screen a car pull into a parking space at the Maple Tree Inn Motel. Two men got out of it, one of them leaning on a crutch. He must be the man Rusty Willis had stabbed in the courthouse, an attack that had sent the police out looking for her.

Oh, how Ariel wanted the police to catch her, to stop the creature that controlled her from using her body to do terrible things. The monster was watchful now, though, on guard. He had brought her here to spy on the outsiders and he would make her run away before anyone could catch her.

The police were looking for Cassidy Davenport, too, and Ariel knew the monster in her would do anything to keep her from being caught.

A third person got out of the backseat of the car at the motel then, a little girl who glowed with a white light that hurt Ariel's eyes. The thing that controlled Ariel's body recoiled in horror from the light! Ariel staggered back, tripped and fell into the side of a rosebush, its thorns ripping her arm and back. The thing couldn't feel the pain, but Ariel could.

The light upset the thing—confused it. Frightened it. Yes, the thing was afraid of the light that lit the world around the little girl! It had never been afraid of anything before. Not once since that nightmare afternoon when she, Rusty and Cassidy had gone looking for their soccer ball, the day a beast came into her head and body and shoved her aside and took control—not once since that day had Ariel ever felt the beast fear.

It hated. She felt the hate that pulsed out from it at every living thing, every good and beautiful thing. It loathed all creation, from the smallest flower to butterflies and birds. And people! They sent it into such a rage of revulsion it sometimes pounded her fists on the ground until they bled.

The beast constantly raged in a barely controllable anger that sent it into bouts of destruction where it used her hands and body to break dishes, hurl chairs through windows, uproot flowers or unleash spiders in a Sunday school class.

And kill. The thing lived to kill. Killing gave it a thrill that Ariel felt run up and down her spine. When it used her hands to choke the life out of puppies, it was full of an emotion, an elation, Ariel did not know existed. When it used her fingers to slip the switch on a lighter to set a gasoline-soaked cat afire, it laughed a maniacal laugh that tore at her ears and wounded her deeper than the agonized wailing of the murdered animal.

The thing watched people, waiting for an opportunity, and Ariel knew sooner or later it would come. Eventually someone would make a mistake, would leave a baby or small child unattended near her and…

Ariel told herself she would stop it. She would not let it use her body to…But she knew she wasn't strong enough to stop it. She had tried a time or two—had taken back power over her own limbs for a time—a moment, had spoken or cried out. It was stronger than she was, though and it always wrenched control back out of her hands and screeched at her inside her head until she felt her ears and nose bleed.

But now it was afraid. Of the little girl filled with light. That lone thought warmed Ariel Murphy. A spark of hope glowed in her deepest heart. If it was afraid of the girl, the girl must be able to harm it. Maybe the girl was stronger than it was.

Ariel watched from the rosebush, her thorn-scratched arms and back bleeding, as the three stood together in front of their rooms, talking. Then the little girl who glowed had gone into the room on the right with the big black man, and the bald man with the crutch had gone alone into the room on the left. After that, it was quiet.

Ariel would go now, she knew, but she didn't want to!

She wanted to stay here, near the shining girl who had some kind of power so strong it frightened the beast. Then the door to the motel room on the right opened and the little girl appeared. She held something in her hand, punched a button and the car beeped. She went to it, opened the back passenger-side door, climbed in and then back out again, holding an iPad. She swung the door closed and—

Ariel cried out. She didn't mean to, didn't intend or plan to. That was probably why she got away with it. The cry just burst out of her lips. She had caught the thing when it was distracted and somehow got the words out past it.

"Help me! Please! Get it out of me! Make it go away."

The thing turned on her in a rage. Shrieked at her in a rumbling howl that was so overwhelming she could hear or see nothing else. The cry of rage echoed as if off stone walls until it multiplied all around her, fracturing and shattering, and her aloneness increased, her otherness grew larger, and she felt herself shoved farther back down into the dark depths of herself so deep she might never climb out again.

From a great distance she saw out her eyes that the little girl had stopped and turned her way; then Ariel's body was running, the thing in a seething rage that burned white hot but did not warm the cold where she hid, down deep in the depths. He was screeching inarticulately at her, the cries opening up great fissures in her head, cracking her open, and she closed her own eyes, buried her head in her lap and tried not to respond to anything at all.

Ariel didn't really feel it when her leg broke. She knew that it hurt, but somehow knowing it hurt and feeling the pain were two different things, and she'd been shoved so far down in the bottom of herself that she could only know and not feel.

She had been running through the woods, away from the little girl she'd seen at the motel, running like a deer, leaping over bushes or rocks or anything in her path, and she could hear the frantic pounding of her heart, knew she shouldn't be able to do the things her body was doing, but she'd been watching her body do things she couldn't really do for…how long? She had no idea. It was growing harder and harder to remember a time when she wasn't hiding here in the dark, terrified, cold and alone. Harder to remember the people she could see out the eyes she didn't control anymore. Harder to remember what feelings there were except terror and pain.

She knew as she ran that the creature that controlled her was feeling something she'd never sensed in it before. It was terrified. It was maybe as scared of that little girl as Ariel was of it. That was a wondrous thing—incredible—but the fact of it wouldn't change her existence. She couldn't make her body go back to the place where she'd seen the little girl and she was certain the creature would take her as far away from here as possible.

A vine slapped her in the face as she ran and she swatted it out of the way, but it covered her vision for a moment, long enough that in the shadowy evening light she didn't see the drop-off a few feet ahead in time to stop. She fell probably twenty feet—not straight down. She bounced off the cragged face of a rock, hit it twice before she landed at the base of it in what was probably a creek bed when it rained. She came to rest with her right leg twisted beneath her and the cracking sound it made when it shattered was so distant and otherworldly Ariel didn't respond in any way.

Then she tried to stand, but the leg would not hold her

weight and she collapsed on her butt with her back against the rock. She looked out through her own eyes that she could not control and could see the leg now stretched out in front of her. But it looked more like a sack of marbles than a leg, which she supposed meant it was broken in more than one place, too badly damaged to use even if the creature demanded it.

She felt the creature's rage like a blast of hot air in her face and then felt her body begin to crawl, dragging her right leg behind her like a snail. The jagged rocks quickly tore the skin on the palms of her hands and on her belly where it dragged across the rocks. She was making no progress at all. She'd fallen into a crevice between two ledges. It was blocked at one end by a tree and the other by a rockslide. The only way out was to climb back up the way she'd fallen. Ariel couldn't do that, but the creature was determined that she try. So she felt her body haul itself up across jagged rocks, tumbling back down again and again until she lay on her back, looking up at the sky, and all the anger and determination of the beast that controlled her could not make her move. She was totally spent.

Ariel looked up through the tree limbs as darkness stole the bright red and gold fall colors from the leaves. The sky grew black and the first sprinkle of stars began to twinkle and she wondered what it would feel like to die. She wasn't afraid of dying—she welcomed death! Though she didn't know anything much about heaven and hell, she did know that when you died, your soul left your body—which meant she could escape the creature that held her hostage. And no matter where she went after that, it would be better than here.

ANDI WAITED until she had heard Uncle Jack gently snoring before she slipped out of the bed and changed out of the candy-striped pajamas Daddy had packed for her and into her jeans and T-shirt. She pulled a hoodie over her head and carried her shoes with her to the door. Achingly slowly, she opened it, just far enough—the key!

She stopped and hurried to the desk where Uncle Jack had put the credit card thing you inserted in the door to open it. If she didn't take it with her, she'd have to knock on the door to wake him up to let her back in. That would be a problem. She didn't want him to know she'd been gone at all, wanted to slip out and away and then back while he was still asleep.

If she woke him, he wouldn't let her leave and she had to go! Uncle Jack wouldn't understand, but she had to. That little girl by the fence…there was a slimy thing, like the green larvae of some insect, on her shoulders—and she'd cried out. Only it was the little girl. Andi didn't know how she knew that, but she did. It was the little girl who had called for help, not the thing on her shoulder.

She had sounded so scared, so alone and desperate. Andi had to go, had to find her somehow. Had to help. She thought she could do that—help. That was another thing she didn't know why or how she knew, but she did. She thought she could help the little girl and she had to try— even if Uncle Jack got mad about it. Even if Daddy grounded her for a week.

Daddy.

Where is Daddy?

She snatched up Uncle Jack's car keys, too. She'd need them to get into the car for the flashlight in the glove box. There'd be no way to find that little girl in the woods without a flashlight.

Then she stepped out into night air that smelled of

bacon frying from the Waffle House next door to the motel. And roses. Mommy had planted rosebushes around the front and back doors of their house in Harrelton, and every time Andi stepped outside, she inhaled the sweet aroma and her mother's face swam before her.

It did that now, an image of her mother smiling. A lump came up in her throat so big it hurt to swallow back the tears. Mommy. And now Daddy. Gone.

She didn't sniffle, though, didn't make a sound, just eased the door closed behind her and rested her forehead against it, feeling hot tears run down her face. It only lasted a moment, though. Then she straightened up, squared her shoulders and turned around.

Princess Buttercup was standing a few feet away, watching her.

Andi couldn't help it, she rushed to the blonde woman in the pale blue shirt with little yellow flowers, threw her arms around her waist and began to sob. The more she cried, the more she wanted to cry, until she was sobbing so hard her chest hurt. On and on she cried as Princess Buttercup held her, patted her back, brushed her hair off her face and rocked gently back and forth.

It seemed like a long time before the crying jag ended, and when it was over, she couldn't seem to breathe right. The air hitched in and out almost like the hiccups. Andi had nothing to wipe her face, so she used the bottom of her hoodie to clear the tears off her cheeks.

"Aren't you going to ask me what I'm doing out here?" she asked.

"I know what you're doing out here," Princess Buttercup said.

"You don't have to be Princess Buttercup, you know," Andi said. "You can be…well, whoever you are. I'm not a little kid anymore."

Princess Buttercup smiled. "One day, you'll see who I am." Her smile turned into a grin. "But I do like these jeans better than that peasant dress. Don't know how those people ever got anything done dragging those long skirts along in the dirt behind them."

It occurred to Andi then that the angel had come to stop her like Daddy or Uncle Jack would. Andi couldn't let that happen.

"There was a little girl over there by the fence and she called out for help and it was her calling not the green thing on her shoulders. I'm going to get a flashlight out of the car and look for her in the woods. I have to find her."

She said it all in a rush, hiccupping air in and out as she spoke.

"Of course you do," Princess Buttercup said. "But you won't need a flashlight. I'm going with you."

Chapter Fifteen

Becca couldn't concentrate. Even though it was a big room, Bishop's study was stuffy. She usually kept the door closed when she was at work because she suspected it was painful for Theresa to pass by and see her in Bishop's chair behind the desk. But it was stuffy tonight, and she had left the door ajar, hoping for a breeze that didn't come.

She was worried about Theresa. Worried that the bites would get infected, sure, but more worried about the gray pallor to her skin and the bone weariness she saw in the old woman's eyes even after she'd had a good night's sleep…if any of them ever got a good night's sleep anymore.

Leaning back in the oversized chair, she rubbed her neck, trying to massage out the stiffness. The action caused her index finger to throb. She didn't know what she'd done to it to blacken the nail. It looked like she'd smashed it in a car door and maybe she had. She didn't remember much about the day she'd gone to her father's house to trade herself for Andi.

Careful of the finger, she continued to massage her stiff neck. She had pored over documents, ancient texts, papers and files almost nonstop for days and had hardly put a dent in the masses of information Bishop had collected and stored in the room over the years.

"That day he figured out how to get rid of an efreet, he said he'd noted it and wrote it out clear," Theresa had said. It was somewhere here, a needle in a haystack.

The books and documents were journeys into a darkness the human heart and mind could not conceive. Becca read about the horror of pure evil, the deeds demonic presences had performed over the centuries, and every day she felt her grasp on the real world grow less secure. She willed herself to hold on because to lose her grip would be to slide down into that black abyss of evil and psychosis and never return.

She cried out silently in frustration.

I can't find it. I've looked and looked and…I can't keep reading his horror. Help me! Show me where—

And then she knew she was no longer alone in the room. She sensed the presence even before she lifted her head and saw it there by the door.

Just a shadow, like a wisp of dark smoke in the shape of a hooded form. Cold eyes blazed red inside the hood, but she turned her gaze away. To look into those eyes was to be lost forever.

It wasn't real, of course. She was alone in a room, riffling through papers written by a dear old man who had given his life to save a room full of children.

That was reality. She understood that.

And it made absolutely no difference at all.

"You are condemned to remain forever in this mortal world." The voice reminded her of the sound of tires on gravel. "Because you refuse to come home where you belong, you will be trapped in your dead body when we kill you."

It took every speck of will Becca possessed to move her left hand over to her right, inch it, drag it against the force that held her motionless. As the figure of smoke continued to speak, she inched her left index finger under the thick rubber band around her right wrist and began to pull it tight. Slowly, she dragged it away from her skin, feeling the band dig into the flesh of her right wrist.

"You will live to feel worms eat your flesh, beetles chew your skin, rot bloat your belly and your bones turn to—"

She let go. The rubber band snapped back against her wrist with a painful sting and the creature of smoke was instantly gone. Poof.

An old wino in a shelter had taught her that trick, a woman who saw monsters, too, but not the ones Becca saw. The woman had said that sometimes a little sting was enough to bring back the real world.

Becca let out her breath in a whoosh and put her head in her hands. She burst into tears of terror and relief, and the crying covered the sound for a little while. But as soon as she calmed down, she heard it. She didn't want to lift her head, did not want to see.

Then she heard it again, clearly. The rattle.

She slowly raised her head and stared into the dead eyes of a rattlesnake coiled right inside the door. Attached to its head was a spiderlike creature covered in bristling black hair. It had one eye and it fixed that eye on her. Then the snake uncoiled and began to slither across the floor toward her.

This was no illusion. This was real.

THERESA FELT Biscuit suddenly go rigid. She was propped up in bed, trying to read her Bible but not having

much success at it. She was gone have to go down to the
Dollar Store and get her another pair of cheater reading
glasses, maybe 2.75 this time. She'd started out with 1.50.
Bishop had bought her that first pair, said he was tired of
watching her wrinkle her face all squinty like every time
she read the word of God.

That'd been—

The dog didn't bark. Just lay there on the bed beside
her with his ears turning around like them satellite dishes,
trying to pick up a signal.

Theresa's heart took up the beat of a kettle drum in
her chest.

No more rats, Lord. Please.

Then the dog leapt off her bed and went tearing out
her bedroom door and down the stairs, silently, like a
mountain lion on the attack.

She hefted her bulk up out of the bed fast as she could,
but she knew that whatever evil thing had invaded her
house would likely do whatever it was gone do long before
she could get there to stop it.

BECCA JUMPED out of the chair and climbed on top of
the desk. The snake was at the base of the desk in seconds,
coiling again. She knew rattlesnakes could strike farther
from a coil and this was a big one—with the superhuman
strength granted it by the one-eyed spider creature
attached to its head. There was nowhere in the room,
nowhere in the whole house, she could climb tall enough to
be out of the snake's striking range.

She didn't hear Biscuit coming. The dog hadn't
barked, hadn't made a sound, was just suddenly in the
room, leaping at the snake. A vicious, ugly growl

rumbled from his throat as he sank his teeth deep into the creature's body and whipped it sideways. The snake twisted in his grasp and struck at him, but Biscuit shook his head and the snake missed. He whipped it back and forth again and again, and the snake kept striking and missing.

Then Biscuit yelped, a pained, pitiful cry. The snake had buried its fangs deep in his shoulder. Biscuit jerked, tried to shake the snake off, but his legs didn't seem to work anymore and he collapsed. The dog rolled over on his side, twitching as the snake slithered away from him and back toward Becca.

THERESA RUSHED FAST as she could to the door of Bishop's study that Biscuit had pushed open. She could smell the demon stink on the other side. Becca was standing on the desk and Biscuit had a snake in his teeth! A rattlesnake.

Then it bit Biscuit! And the dog tried to keep fighting, but it couldn't. It collapsed and the snake started slithering toward Becca on the desk.

Theresa didn't think what to do. Didn't have to, wouldn't have been able to, probably, even if she'd tried. It was like somebody—Bishop?—moved her arms and legs for her.

The old woman took two steps into the room, reached up above the bulletin board on the wall by the door and lifted the scimitar down off the rack. The motion knocked the board loose and it crashed to the floor, sending out a spray of papers and Post-it notes and pushpins around it.

Theresa raised the blade high above her head and brought it down in a great chopping motion that severed the snake into two pieces neat as slicing a knife through a ripe tomato.

What was left of it turned toward her, tried to bunch up to come after her but didn't have enough body left to coil. She lifted the blade again and this time when she brought it down it severed the head off the snake—clean, left the rest of the body twitching.

Then Theresa dropped the blade and got down on the floor beside Biscuit. She had trouble with her knees, they didn't bend good, but she knelt beside the animal anyway and they bent fine.

The dog was breathing in short, gasping breaths. His eyes were rolled back in his head and he was twitching a little, like the dead snake. She'd seen folks after a rattlesnake had bitten them—that day years ago when a coffin full of poisonous snakes had attacked a crowd. She knew wasn't no way that dog could survive—then Biscuit breathed a great shuddering sigh and was still.

BECCA HOPPED down off the desk and knelt beside Theresa and the dead dog.

"Oh, Biscuit," she cried, and reached out a hand to stroke the fur on his belly. The dog liked to have his belly stroked, would roll over on his back, and look up at Becca with big pleading eyes that said, don't stop, don't stop.

Theresa gathered the animal up in her arms and rocked him like he was a baby, back and forth, tears streaming down her cheeks and dripping into his fur.

Becca rose slowly to her feet and surveyed the room, shuddering at the pieces of dead snake that had left bloody trails on the floor.

The severed head of the snake had come to rest beside

the pile of papers that had cascaded out from the bulletin board when it crashed to the floor. In fact, the fangs had stuck in something. Like twin pushpins, they affixed a lone yellowed Post-it note to the floor.

Becca stepped slowly closer. Then she began to tremble. She could make out Bishop's handwriting on the note. She leaned over and read his words, only a handful, and she knew this was what she'd been looking for.

JACK WAS JARRED SO ABRUPTLY from sleep by the banging sound he was momentarily disoriented, couldn't remember where he was or what he was doing there. Even so, he looked down and saw his pistol in his hand. He'd reached up instinctively and snatched it out of the holster he'd left hanging on the bedpost. Well, wherever he was, he was armed!

Then it all flooded back. The motel room. Andi. He glanced over to the bed where she was asleep.

Andi wasn't there!

He heard her voice then, from outside the door. She was the one banging on it.

"Uncle Jack, open the door. Hurry!"

He leapt out of the bed, stepped to the door and pulled it open.

"Andi, what are you doing out—?"

"You have to come now." She grabbed his hand and yanked him toward the parking lot. "There's a little girl— her name's Ariel—she's hurt really bad. You have to help."

"What are you talking about? And what are you doing out—?"

"Please," she pleaded. "I'll tell you everything, all about it, but right now you have to come with me—hurry."

Jack didn't have to dress. With Andi in the room with him—and he certainly wasn't going to allow the child to stay in her father's empty room all by herself!—he slept in sweatpants and a Fraternal Order of Police T-shirt. He stepped back into the room, shoved the gun down the back of his pants, his feet into his shoes—no socks, snatched up his cell phone and followed Andi.

She had his hand and was dragging him toward the fence on the other side of the parking lot like a big dog pulling at a leash.

"Hurry!" she said, then stopped and raced back across the lot. She dug in her pocket and pulled out—his car keys! —punched the unlock button, opened the passenger side door and grabbed the flashlight out of the glove box.

She turned it on as she ran back toward him, then plunged ahead of him into the dark woods.

"I found her at the bottom of a cliff," she said. "This way!" And she raced off into the darkness.

The flashlight was locked in the car...so how had she found somebody in the dark woods without it?

Following Andi in the darkness was like trying to keep up with a firefly. She darted ahead, a bobbing light here and there. He stumbled along behind, tripping over roots and stubbing his toe on rocks.

Andi pulled up so sharply in front of him he almost ran into her.

"There!" She pointed with the flashlight down into a rocky creek bed where a little girl lay crumpled on the ground.

Jack climbed down the rocky embankment and knelt beside the child. She was lying so still he couldn't even tell if she was breathing. He was reaching out to feel for the carotid artery in her neck when her huge blue eyes popped open.

"Where did she go?" she whispered, her voice so soft and weak he could barely hear her.

"Her name's Ariel Murphy," Andi said. "She fell from up there." Andi pointed the flashlight to the ridge above them. "Her leg's broken, and maybe other stuff, too." She shone the light on the child's body, where her right leg was twisted at an impossible angle.

Since Jack didn't know if there was such a thing as "dial 911" in a town as small as Bradford's Ridge, he pulled out his phone and punched "call back" on the last number. He'd spoken to the sheriff only a couple of hours ago when he'd called to let Jack know that Ed Blackwell, the deputy attacked by Rusty Willis, had died.

Sheriff Lincoln answered on the first ring, totally alert.

"Andi found a little girl in the woods—badly hurt. I'll send Andi back to the motel parking lot to lead you here—you'd never find us on your own. I'll stay here with Ariel."

"Ariel?" the sheriff asked. "That's the little girl? Ariel Murphy?"

Then it hit Jack, too. Ariel Murphy was the child who'd pulled up the rosebushes in the sheriff's yard. She was one of the three children who were possessed.

Andi and the light bobbed off into the darkness and Jack settled himself on the ground beside the little girl, sitting with his legs crossed Indian style, holding her small cold hand. He didn't dare touch her anywhere else since he had no idea what other injuries she might have. As soon as his eyes adjusted to the darkness with no flashlight glare, Jack could make out the features of the child lying still beside him, her eyes closed.

She seemed so badly hurt she couldn't possibly move, but Jack remained alert. He'd fought a man juiced up by a demon once and the fact that this was a little girl didn't matter in the least. If she could tear rosebushes out of the ground, she was fully capable of ripping his head off his shoulders.

How in the world had Andi—?

The child spoke, or he thought she did, but he couldn't hear her. He leaned over until his face was only inches from hers.

"What?"

"It's gone now," the child said. Her breathing was shallow and rapid. Clearly, she was in shock. "It's still cold, though. So cold."

He knew then. There was only a little girl lying dirty and broken on the ground. He could not have said how he knew, but he was certain there was no other presence here.

The night air was cold, but Jack knew that kind of chill was not what the little girl was talking about. Still, he pulled his T-shirt off over his head and snuggled it around the child the best he could. It was only cotton, but his body heat was in it.

"That better?"

Her eyes were closed and she didn't speak again.

Chapter Sixteen

Jack looked out the glass doors of the emergency room waiting area at the fury of the storm that had come up as the EMTs were loading Ariel into the ambulance.

He felt Andi beside him and reached out to put his arm around her shoulders and pull her to him. The way the child melted into his side brought a tightness to his chest and he hugged her tenderly.

"It's really dark out there," she said.

Jack wasn't sure if she was referring to the storm or the pall that hung over the whole county, a darkness of evil so profound that even Jack imagined he could see it now.

Thunder crashed so loud the glass in the windows rattled. Sheriff Lincoln stepped up beside him and stared with him and Andi sightlessly out into the maelstrom.

"STAT Flight helicopter lifted off from University Hospital in Louisville half an hour ago—the same crew that took Ed." Deputy Blackwell, killed by a little boy—no, by a demon. But what would happen to the little boy who'd been its host? "The chopper had to turn back, though, because of the storm. And driving an ambulance through a downpour like this." He shook his head. "It could get washed off the road into a ditch. That little girl's stuck here until this storm passes." His voice grew soft, but Jack could still hear the awe and fear in it. "Caverna County is the only place in the whole state of Kentucky where it's raining."

He and Jack exchanged a long look. Then Jack spoke to the little girl he held tight against his side. "I say we get some hot chocolate."

"You don't want hot chocolate, you want coffee," Andi said. "Major Crocker says you're an addict."

"And you believed him?" He took her hand and led her toward the cafeteria. "The man's a pathological liar. Can't trust a word he says."

Jack had sat with the injured child in the woods for what seemed like forever, and it'd been chilly with no shirt on. He'd talked to her, even sang to her! Told her the only story he knew—the three bears, but he'd mixed it all together with the three little pigs and it ended with a big bad wolf eating Goldilocks. It didn't matter. He knew she wasn't listening. He only wanted to fill the silence around the child with the sound of a human voice.

When the sheriff, Andi and the EMTs showed up, he stood back with his hands on Andi's shoulders as they worked feverishly to stabilize the child so they could move her. They said she was too badly injured to be treated at the local hospital. Bradford's Ridge Regional Hospital would be a pit stop on her way to University Hospital in Louisville.

But then the storm hit.

Jack settled himself in a plastic hospital cafeteria chair, nursing a cup of coffee from a machine. Andi went to the window there and continued to stare sightlessly out into the rain.

"Ariel's mother was passed out, dead drunk, when we went to tell her about the child. Her daddy's somewhere in New Mexico on his way home. I've got deputies out trying to find her grandparents—her father's folks still live here—or maybe one of her aunts. She needs family around her when she wakes up."

"When does the doctor think that will be?"

The sheriff shrugged. "They filled her full of pain meds, packed her leg in ice and put it in a sling to keep down the swelling, but she needs an orthopedic surgeon to put the pieces back together." He paused. "The little girl who pulled up my daughter's rosebushes isn't strong enough anymore to pick a single flower. That...demon thing...it's gone, isn't it?"

"Appears so."

"How'd that happen?"

"Beats me." Jack glanced at the chestnut-haired little girl. "But Andi knows. I think Andi had something to do with getting rid of it."

The sheriff spoke the thoughts that had been chasing themselves around in circles in Jack's head ever since he'd knelt beside the blue-eyed child in the woods.

"With that thing gone, the little girl's just a kid again—"

"And that kid knows where to find the efreet," Jack finished for him. "She knows, and there's no reason anymore for her not to tell us."

Rusty Willis and now Ariel Murphy. Rusty was under restraint and heavily sedated.

"Any news on Cassidy Davenport?"

"Nope. Last anybody saw her was this morning at Sunday school. She left the room to go to the bathroom and never came back."

"What do her parents think of all this?"

"They're good people, in denial. They're convinced she wouldn't have run away—not their sweet little girl—so somebody must have taken her. It's not going to do any good, but I put out an Amber Alert."

"Wouldn't want to be the person who spotted her."

The sheriff nodded, then looked over Jack's shoulder at Crock limping into the cafeteria. He wasn't using the crutch. Andi turned from the window and raced to meet him, but stopped before she got there, didn't bowl him over, just spread her arms in the air to encircle something imaginary.

"Virtual hug," she said.

Crock smiled, but it was a pained smile. It had only taken a couple of stitches to close the stab wound Rusty Willis had inflicted with the scissors. But the wound was deep. Another inch to the left and the blade would have severed the femoral artery and he would have bled to death in minutes.

Crock fished in his pocket and pulled out his wallet, extracted two bills and held them out to Andi, then intoned: "Your mission, should you choose to accept it." He stopped. "You don't have any idea what I'm talking about, do you?"

She shook her head.

"Just roll with it," he said. "Your mission is to find two Dr. Peppers. Cold ones. This tape will self-destruct in three seconds."

Andi looked at him quizzically, then snatched the bills out of his hand and raced out of the cafeteria. Crock hobbled up to Jack and the sheriff.

"Got your phone turned off?" he asked Jack.

Jack pulled it out of his pocket and groaned. "Not turned off. Dead. Had it plugged in by the bed, but it didn't get a full charge before I went dashing out into the night."

"Figured it was that or the storm," Crock said. "Becca tried to reach you, and when she couldn't, she called me. She and Theresa had company tonight."

Jack felt the bottom drop out of the pit of his stomach. "Anybody I know?"

"Probably not on your Christmas card list. It was company of the slithering variety. Rattlesnake."

The storm outside seemed to intensify as Crock described what had happened to Becca and Theresa. It battered the walls of the building, a lighthouse on a rocky promontory with waves crashing over it. Lightning torched the sky. Thunder rumbled on its heels.

"And the dog?" Jack asked.

Crock shook his head as Andi came through the double doors. She carried no soft drinks and was still clinging to the one-dollar bills Crock'd given her.

"I saw it again," she said, with no preamble. "The vision."

"The same one as before?"

"No...well, yes, the same. But it's bigger." She paused, struggling to come up with the right words. "Like at the airport. You can see the planes that are about to land from a long way off. They look like toys, but the closer they get, the bigger they look. This vision is like that. It's big now because it's very close."

Jack reached into his pocket for his cell phone, then remembered it was out of juice. "Borrow your phone?" he asked Crock.

Jack dialed Theresa's number. Becca answered and he told her to get Theresa. Bishop had put the new FaceTime app on the iPhone he'd gotten Theresa for her birthday, but she had absolutely no idea how to use it—how to do anything at all on the phone except make a phone call. Becca knew how, though.

They all gathered around Crock's iPhone in the hospital cafeteria—Andi, Crock, Jack and the sheriff. On the other end, Becca and Theresa sat in her kitchen.

"You guys need to hear this," Jack said. Then he turned to Andi. "Tell them what you saw, sweetheart."

When Andi was finished, Jack asked, "Any of you know what this could possibly mean?"

No one spoke.

"I think I…might have an idea," he said. "It's only a thought, but…the terrorist acts in the past few days, the Mall of America bombing and the restaurant in Phoenix. Front-page news, which means all the politicians are talking about it. But have you noticed—Chapman Whitworth is the only candidate crying 'domestic terrorism.' He's hanging his campaign on it—so what if it is home-grown terrorism and our scar-faced friend is the farmer planting the seeds."

"Which means Andi's vision is of some act of terrorism Whitworth's planning," Crock continued Jack's train of thought. "If we could understand the vision, maybe we could stop it."

"It seems clear the vision's about an explosion—but where?" Jack said. "There's no clue where."

They were quiet for a moment and then Becca changed the subject.

"You know what happened here earlier tonight…" she said and Jack knew she was being vague to keep from upsetting Andi further. "Our 'visitor' showed me what we have to do when we find the efreet."

"Yes!" he said and let out a big sigh as relief loosened some knot he hadn't even realized had been tied in his guts. He'd been prepared to go after the efreet as soon as

Ariel told them where to find it even though he had no idea how to fight it once he got there. Now, they could go armed. "Okay, we'll come back to Cincinnati in the morning so we can sit down together and study—"

"There's nothing to study," Becca said. "It's not complicated. It's actually very simple."

"God usually makes things simple so simple folks can understand," Theresa said. "It's people who make everything all complex, adding this thing and that thing the Lord never did intend to be in there. We've spent two thousand years complicatin' a simple message, tangling it up 'til you got to have a seminary degree to figure it out."

"How can it possibly be easy?" Jack protested.

"I didn't say it was easy," Becca said. "I said it was simple."

It occurred to Jack then, in a forehead-slapping duh, that the doing of it, whatever it was, couldn't have involved all manner of erudite information, secret incantations and the like because somehow he, Daniel and Becca had pulled it off all by themselves when they were twelve years old.

"What do we have to do?" he asked.

The voice that answered the question didn't come from the speaker of the phone on the table. It came from the little girl standing beside him, her face so solemn no dimples dinted her freckled cheeks.

"You have to tell it to go," Andi said.

The silence that followed her words was palpable.

"How do you know that, sugar?" Theresa asked.

"That's what I did...what Princess Buttercup told me to do and the demon left Ariel and went away."

"We'd have figured this out a whole lot sooner if I'd listened to my own self complain 'bout folks complicating simple things," Theresa said. "I s'posed Bishop was in that study diggin' words in some dead language out of some book that he had the only copy of...somethin' like that. He told me, but I didn't have ears to hear, didn't realize when he said he'd 'Post-it' clear, he meant he'd written the whole thing down on a Post-it note."

"Let me get this straight," Crock said, fumbling. "You're saying all we have to do to send a demon back to hell is to tell it to go away?"

"'Parently it's that simple, but that don't mean it's easy. Bishop said doin' that would be the hardest thing he'd ever have to do."

"Hard how?" Crock asked.

"I been thinking about how you'd do it ever since Becca found that Post-it note, putting it together with other things Bishop told me over the years. You gone have to set your will against the will of the demon. And the bigger the demon, the harder that'll be. You got to demand that it do what you say—in the name of God. You can't flinch. You can't back down. You can't even blink. You can't let it confuse you or trick you with all the things it knows to do to trip you up, all the things it knows about you that it'll throw in your face. You got to stand rock solid and make the demon back down." She paused, then added in a soft voice, "And if you try and fail...the demon will destroy you."

"It doesn't want to go," Andi said. "It says things, terrible things. Princess Buttercup warned me, though. She said 'Satan is the father of lies,' so I wasn't to believe anything this demon said to me, even if it made sense."

She dropped her chin on her chest and her next words were only a whisper. "It talked about Daddy. About what it was going to do to Daddy. And I was so scared, but it was a lie! It had to be a lie!"

Jack reached out and drew Andi into a hug again, holding her close. "What did it say, sweetheart?"

"It said"—the rest was so soft, nobody heard her but Jack—"it was going to chop off his head."

"And you stood your ground against the…thing inside Ariel?" the sheriff asked. The sheriff's voice had a trembly quality Jack hadn't heard before. His face was ashen. Welcome to the real world.

"Uh-huh. Princess Buttercup was there and she must have been shining like a spotlight because the demon couldn't even look at us. And Ariel helped, too. She was fighting as hard as we were."

"It's one thing to kick out a demon only powerful enough to possess a little girl—with the child helping you do it," Theresa said. "It's something else altogether to impose your will on a mighty prince of demons, an immortal Lord from the dark realm that has totally melded with the heart, mind and soul of a human being. We talking the difference 'tween fightin' a kitten ain't got its eyes open yet and a rabid Bengal tiger with a sinus infection."

"But you did it once," Crock said, looking at Jack. "You and Daniel and Becca—you defeated it. How—?"

"I don't know!" Jack said, louder than he meant to. Then he added in a softer, resigned voice, "I don't remember."

"I do," Becca said.

"You remember?" Jack was incredulous.

"A little. The things in Bishop's office—reading about…must have knocked something loose, and all sorts of things, pieces of things have come back. I remember what it said to me." But she didn't elaborate and Jack didn't press the point.

"So now we know what it is you're going to have to do," Crock said. "We have to find that thing so you can go there and do it."

"And Ariel Murphy knows where it is," Jack said.

"Which ones of you...?" The sheriff stopped and looked around the table. "Who's going to go in after that thing once you find it."

"Jack and I have unfinished business with that monster," Becca said without hesitation.

Daniel did, too, of course, but nobody mentioned that. Nobody had to.

"And me," Theresa said. "Bishop was gone go and he never got the chance. I'll be taking his place."

There didn't seem to be anything left to say. Jack would have to locate the efreet and contact Becca and Theresa. Then they would take up where the Three Musketeers had left off in 1985.

When the phone call was over, Andi looked at the sheriff. "You think maybe I could go sit with Ariel?"

"She's all drugged up. She won't know you're there."

"I'll know I'm there. I don't want her to be alone." Andi's voice got soft. "She's been...alone...and scared for a very long time."

"She's not supposed to have any visitors," the sheriff said. "And even if she could, it's not visiting hours and they don't allow children—"

"Please," Andi begged. "She needs me."

The sheriff nodded. "She probably does. I'll see if I can throw my weight around."

Crock cleared his throat. "Jack, I need to talk to you for a minute."

Jack nodded and turned to the sheriff. "Would you mind taking Andi to Ariel's room? I'll be right up."

As soon as the elevator doors closed behind the sheriff and Andi, Jack turned to Crock. "What is it?"

"I suspect we got ourselves a problem with Jeff

Kendrick," Crock said. "Becca and Theresa think he's lost it."

～

JEFF SAT in the car for a few minutes, composing himself. If he could just get rid of the infernal buzzing in his head, an ugly sound from the low-rent district in a beehive.

He pulled down the visor and checked his appearance. All shined up and ready for the party. New everything, from his skivvies to his tie pin. He'd bought a whole new outfit. Had to. All his clothes were in his condo, and if he went back there, the bugs might…

He slammed the door on the thoughts with a resounding bang!

Time had gotten squirrelly. It expanded sometimes like one of those concertinas clowns used in a circus—so everything took too long, minutes dragged by wearing the shackles of hours. Other times, it squeezed together so tight he couldn't find it. He was at Theresa's and then he was in his hotel room, changing clothes, and then he was here. No time in between.

He started to breathe too fast again at the thought of losing hours he couldn't account for. Hyperventilating. Couldn't do that, not now, so he clamped down on his diaphragm and willed himself to inhale and exhale regularly.

In. Slowly. Out. Slowly.

He adjusted his tie. A two-hundred-fifty-dollar Charvet silk. Things like that mattered to him once—wearing an Armani suit, Gucci shoes. Now nothing mattered to him except the cold metal in his coat pocket and the cold resolve in his heart.

And then he was in the main dining room of Andolini's

Restaurant. No memory of the walk from the car to the restaurant. Just here, following the maître d'. He'd never been to Andolini's and he had to stifle a giggle at the image that filled his head—Michael Corleone walking slowly to the table where the crooked cop and the mafia boss had only seconds to live, clutching the gun he'd retrieved from behind the water tank in the bathroom.

Mr. Whitworth was awaiting him in a private dining room on the fourth floor, the maître d' told him.

Perfect.

A man wearing a suit as expensive as Jeff's stood outside the elevator door.

"Mr. Kendrick?" he inquired.

Jeff nodded.

The man said something into his shirt cuff—oh, please! —and obviously heard something in the earbud with a cord leading up the left side of his neck because he smiled pleasantly and punched the number four on the elevator light panel.

Jeff stepped inside.

The elevator opened into a small, candlelit dining room with only a handful of white- tableclothed tables. But the room wasn't alive with diners and servers, music and the subdued clatter of knives and forks on plates. It was empty and silent.

A man stood on the far side of it in front of a huge floor-to-ceiling picture window with a view of the distant Ohio River, where a paddleboat ablaze with bright strings of colored lights carried its dinner guests downstream.

The man turned slowly around and looked at him, and a hatchet of ragged panic hacked into Jeff's chest. He knew instantly that coming here had been the biggest mistake he'd ever made.

Chapter Seventeen

Andi and Sheriff Lincoln exited the elevator. Though Ariel's room was right across from the elevator and stairs, the sheriff led Andi past it to the center of the long hallway where the nurses' station sat in a pool of light in the otherwise dim stretch of linoleum. Andi waited impatiently as he explained to the only nurse there, whose nose was as sharp as an ax blade, that they'd not yet been able to locate the family of the little girl in room number 201, and did his best to convince her that it would do no harm to allow Andi to sit quietly with her.

"The little Murphy girl ought to be in intensive care and no visitors are allowed in the ICU," said Hatchet Face. "But the ICU is full, so she has a nurse in her room for around-the-clock care, which makes us shorthanded out here until we can send her to Louisville—" she looked almost apprehensively out the window at the far end of the hallway, where lightning torched the sky—"when the storm clears." She shook her head in wonder. "It came up so fast —did you see it? One minute the sky was cloudless and the next..."

Concerned at first that the ugly nurse would turn her away, Andi listened in growing respect as the sheriff "gently" threw his weight around, and before she knew it, Hatchet Face was agreeing.

"She won't even know you're there," the nurse told Andi. "But the morphine she received when she got here should be wearing off by now, so she could be hovering on the edge of consciousness—don't disturb her. If she does begin to come around, Nurse Jankowski will ask you to leave."

"Don't listen to what that nurse said," the sheriff told her as they walked back toward the elevator and Ariel's room. "Nobody knows what somebody who's unconscious can or can't hear or see. You go in there and talk quiet to her like you would if she was awake. Let her know she's not alone."

They stopped in front of Ariel's room. "I need to go out to my cruiser to use the radio, see if my deputies have had any luck locating her grandparents. But your Uncle Jack and Major Crocker will be outside here in the hallway or down in the cafeteria when you're done."

Andi pushed open the door—one of those awful hospital doors that tried to keep you out if you weren't big enough to push it hard—stepped inside and felt the door swish soundlessly shut behind her.

Thunder rumbled outside the window and rain attacked the glass like it was trying to break in to the room. Andi shivered, grateful it hadn't been raining when Ariel was lying out there in the woods. Hurt as badly as she'd been and then cold and wet—she might have died right there where she had fallen.

The sight of Ariel there in the dirt had broken Andi's heart, and for the first time ever she was not afraid of the ugly green slimy thing on Ariel's shoulders. She was mad at it.

It wasn't angry at her, though. It was scared of her. Well, maybe not of her, but definitely of the shining white light of Princess Buttercup beside her.

Ariel's was a double room, but nobody was in the bed beside the door. Ariel barely made a lump in the bed against the far wall. The only light in the room came from the glow of the muted television mounted near the ceiling on the wall opposite the bed. Its flickering brightness danced across the sheets. Ariel was attached by tubes to machines and bottles hanging from IV stands at the head of her bed. Her right leg was all wrapped up—must have been ice packs of some kind—and suspended in a sling above the bed.

The nurse was sitting in the shadows near the foot of the bed beyond the spill of light. Andi was afraid she would try to keep her away, but she said nothing as Andi walked quietly from the door to the chair beside the bed. As with Theresa, Andi didn't sit in the chair, just used it as a stepping stool so she could climb up and sit on the edge of the bed.

She reached out and took Ariel's hand. It was icy cold. She had to look closely to be certain the crisp white sheet was moving at all. Her eyes were adjusting to the dim light and now she could make out shapes and forms in the darkness.

The sheriff had said to talk.

"You were real scared, weren't you? I know how that feels, being so scared you're afraid you're going to throw up. I felt like that once."

When the bad man had come into the church and said he was going to shoot her or shoot her mother, and her mother had stepped up and told him he better shoot her because he would have to kill her anyway if he tried to hurt Andi. Then her mother had taken her to the choir robe closet and shoved her inside, leaning near to tell her, "When I close this door, you run! And hide somewhere he'll never find you."

She had run, bounded up the ladder into the pageant storage room the stupid man didn't know was there and hid in a basket. She'd heard a gunshot from the sanctuary but wouldn't believe, couldn't believe...She'd been so scared.

"But you're okay now," Andi said. "You won't ever be alone...locked inside with...You're safe now. I promise."

She heard a sound from the nurse at the foot of the bed, who had probably dozed off and only now realized Andi was there. She might try to make Andi leave after all.

But it was a grunt, like a small bark of laughter. Andi turned and could see her now. Her head was plopped back onto the chair back. The front of her uniform was stained red where blood had gushed down the front of it from the gory red gash on her neck that looked like a smile.

Then she heard a little girl's giggle.

THE MAN who turned to face Jeff Kendrick was ordinary in every respect. He was dressed in a proper pin-striped suit, coat buttoned, French blue shirt and the obligatory red power tie.

He was a reasonably good-looking man, well groomed, with a distinguishing scar. Jeff couldn't see from the door, but he was certain Whitworth's nails had been manicured and his shoes were polished to a shine you could see your face in.

He looked like he looked on television. Except when he was on television you couldn't see the winged shadow that rose up to the ceiling behind him, the gigantic bat-like shape that was made out of darkness. It wasn't a form you could see. It was a black hole in the universe you couldn't see through.

Then it opened eyes made of flames and looked at Jeff, and Jeff tried to scream, but the sight gut-punched him so hard it knocked the wind out of him.

The creature rumbled, words came from its fanged mouth that were more a roaring sound than syllables, a hoary, rasping noise that tore at Jeff's ears, banged into him and knocked him backward. Except he didn't move.

"You pathetic fool!" the creature said.

Suddenly, Jeff's nose was bleeding. He could feel the blood running down his upper lip, a great flood of it, across his mouth and down his chin, where it plopped in red teardrops on the brand-new shirt he had bought just for this occasion at Macys.

The same time he'd bought the suit. The suit that had a gun in the pocket.

He tried to wrench his will back out of the grasp of the thing on the other side of the room that hung in the air above the ordinary-looking man who was smiling in amusement, as if he knew the punchline of a joke and you didn't. Knew that the joke was on you.

Then he felt his hand moving slowly toward his coat pocket. But he wasn't moving it. The hand slipped inside and drew out the Beretta M9 and raised it slowly until it was pointed at Chapman Whitworth's chest.

Whitworth's smile broadened and Jeff felt his hand begin to turn. He tried to resist this time, grunting with the effort to keep his arm pointed forward with the gun aimed at Whitworth. He held his muscles as tight as he could, felt a thin sheen of sweat break out on his forehead. But it was like being in an arm-wrestling match with a forklift. He didn't have a chance, and finally, he gave up, panting, and watched in fascination as his hand pointed the gun at his own face.

The hand moved slowly forward and he felt his mouth begin to open, pried open the way his mother used to do when he refused to take the foul-tasting medicine that was administered every time the color, texture or nature of his bowel movements didn't satisfy her. Pressure applied right at the jaw joint, so no matter how hard you tried, you couldn't keep your jaws clamped shut. He didn't even try to resist this time. He felt the hand that was no longer his own place the barrel of the gun in his open mouth. The gun barrel was as cold as death.

"Pathetic fool." The same words, but not from the creature this time. In fact, the darkness of the creature had dissolved into an amorphous shadow behind the man in the pin-striped suit who had spoken in the melodious tones that mystified and mesmerized everyone who heard them.

Jeff wasn't mesmerized. In fact, he wasn't even frightened anymore. And when the hand that wasn't his own thumbed back the hammer on the pistol, he relaxed altogether.

Game over.

JACK FELT a headache curl up behind his right eye. He needed more coffee. Caffeine would help. An Aspirin would help, too, and he was in a hospital. But there were so many thoughts ahead of "take an Aspirin" in the queue of his mind, he couldn't possibly get to it until after Christmas.

Jeff Kendrick. In the grand scheme of things, he was small potatoes. If the dude who'd been shacking up with Daniel's wife went off the deep end, well…nobody'd invited him to the party in the first place.

Jack felt instantly contrite. Jeff had saved Becca's and Theresa's lives, kept Billy Ray from killing them. And he was, after all, on their side.

He sighed, pushed his chair back and rose, looked at the rain pouring down outside and shivered—not from cold.

"Can he do that?" Crock cocked his chin toward the windows. "That…thing. Can he control the weather, make it—?"

"I guess he can. He is."

"I don't know about you, Jack, but I am feeling major outgunned here." Crock flinched and looked down at the spot where a big bandage bloated the leg of his pants. "When he can use little kids…"

Yeah, little kids. Ariel. Perhaps she had regained consciousness. It was time to find out.

He avoided the elevator, of course. Something had happened to him when he was a kid that had left him with raging claustrophobia, but Jack couldn't remember what it was. And that was one of a hoard of memories he wasn't looking forward to recovering. He shoved open the stairway door beside the elevator and stepped into the bilious glow of the yellow light high overhead. His footfalls echoed with a particularly lonely sound against the concrete walls. He stepped in a small puddle of water, turned the corner and started up the stairs to the second floor. Then he stopped and looked carefully at the steps.

A small pool of water, black in the yellow light, decorated every step. All the way up. Not large puddles, the marks of someone with big feet. He followed the little puddles up the steps to the landing, where the steps switched back to continue upward. From there he could see that the little puddles didn't turn the corner with the stairs for the third floor. They stretched out uniformly across the landing to the second-floor door.

And then Jack was running, bounding up the final stairs. He yanked open the door into the hallway, where the glow from an empty nurses' station spilled down toward him from the center of the building. The puddles of water didn't turn down the hallway toward the station, though. He knew they wouldn't. They stretched out across the hall to the doorway of room 201.

Jack leapt across the hall and shoved open the door. The room was dark. The spill of light from the dim hallway only stretched as far as the first bed in the double room. It was empty. But there were shapes in the darkness beyond it.

"Close the door, Jack," said a voice out of the black. A child's voice, only it wasn't a child speaking.

"SHOULD YOU PULL THE TRIGGER, do you think? Kill yourself?"

Chapman Whitworth spoke the words as he crossed the room to stand in front of where a statue of Jeff Kendrick held the barrel of a pistol in his mouth. The dark shadow had melted away. Almost melted away. Maybe he was imagining it, but Jeff seemed to see a thin darkness around the man, as if his form had been outlined in Magic Marker. He wasn't as tall as Jeff. He seemed bigger on television.

Whitworth cocked his head to one side. "You're not afraid, are you."

It wasn't a question, but even if it had been, Jeff couldn't have answered it with a gun barrel stuck halfway down his throat.

"You don't appear to care one way or the other whether you live or die. Interesting. Now, why would that be?"

He studied Jeff, like a mountain lion regarding his prey before he pounces.

"That woman, Daniel Burke's wife, who committed adultery with you—what was her name? Oh, yes. Emily. Surely you didn't actually care when my Victor Alexander blew out her skull and splattered her brain all over the floor—did you?"

Jeff screamed silently at him.

"Or were you so terribly upset by the visit my friends paid you last night?"

Out of the corner of his eye Jeff spotted a lone cockroach—huge, five or six inches long and three inches across —crawl up onto the back side of the white tablecloth of the nearest table and stop in the middle of a shiny white plate, its antenna twitching. The shudder of revulsion started in Jeff's chest even before the bug scuttled off the plate and began to crawl down the front side of the tablecloth. He was frozen in place, couldn't move, but the shudders racked his body like seizures as the bug crossed the floor toward him. He could watch it with his eyes without turning his head, but lost sight of it a few feet from his shoe because his body blocked his view.

He felt it, though. Felt the movement of it as it climbed up his pants leg and across his shirt, felt its stickery feet on his neck as it crawled from his shoulder to the top of his head. Then it crawled down his forehead to his face. Jeff was shrieking inside his head, in unreserved hysteria, making no sound at all. He tried to shut his eyes so he couldn't see it. But he could no longer control his eyelids.

So he watched its progress as it crawled down his left cheek and back up the other side. It stopped beneath his right eye and shoved its head between his eyelid and eyeball, looking for a way to crawl in, got part of its body up to its front legs into the space, its stickery feet scratching his eyeball. His eyes flooded with tears as it pulled back out and crawled onto the barrel of the gun stuck in his mouth, went over his hand and followed the barrel to his lips. He could feel its head nudging his lips aside so it could crawl inside. Tears of horror—and pain from his scratched eyeball—slid down his face and slathered his cheeks. The bug got most of its body into his mouth, all but the very end. He could feel it exploring in there, stickery legs on the insides of his cheek and on his tongue. It had no…taste. If it had had a taste, Jeff's heart would have burst out of his chest and he would have fallen dead to the floor.

After a few moments, it stopped trying to shove itself into his mouth, either couldn't fit the rest inside or changed its mind. It backed out, climbed his lip and stuck its head up into his left nostril. It shoved in farther, but then withdrew after a few moments and Jeff felt the blood from his nosebleed on its feet as it crawled up onto the top of his nose and sat there, its antenna twitching, looking at him.

Looking at it cross-eyed, there were two roaches instead of only one.

Tears flowed in buckets down Jeff's cheeks. Inside his head, he was screaming, mindlessly hysterical, but he remained rigid, standing in the middle of a private dining room in a five-star restaurant with a gun in his mouth and a cockroach on his nose.

Whitworth reached over and put out his index finger, the way you'd extend a finger to a parakeet, and the bug crawled off Jeff's nose and onto the finger. Whitworth held the bug up to his own face, puckered his lips and made kissing noises. The bug moved forward and pecked its head at his lips. Then the roach turned on his finger, ran down his hand, arm and body and out onto the floor and began to skitter back toward the table it'd crawled up on. Just as it got to the tablecloth, Chapman Whitworth lifted his foot and slammed it down, crushing the bug into the carpet. He rubbed his shoe back and forth, like he was grinding out a cigarette butt, and when he lifted it, there was nothing left but a brown-yellow smear of goo.

"Hate roaches," he said casually. "Filthy creatures."

He focused his attention on Jeff.

"So what am I going to do with you, my stupid friend?" He sighed. "Certainly can't have you blowing your brains out all over the carpet—there'll probably be an extra charge for the bug stain already and I am on a tight budget, as I'm sure you've heard. Don't have money in my 'underdog, grassroots' campaign to throw around on unnecessary expenses."

He held out his hand. "Give me that." The gun popped out of Jeff's mouth so fast the sight on the top of the barrel chipped off a small piece of his front tooth, and flew across the space between them into Whitworth's hand. Jeff discovered he'd been set free, was once again in control of his own body. He reached up and scrubbed his face with his hands to get the feel of stickery feet off his skin, smearing the blood and the tears. He dug at his itching eye, unable to keep himself from scratching it further.

"I suppose I could throw you out the window."

Jeff's body lifted a few inches off the floor and then dropped back down.

"But the noise...and the broken glass, and it might be

possible to survive a fall from a fourth-floor window—every bone in your body broken, but alive. If the fall killed you, it certainly would seem a plausible end to your miserable life. You throw yourself to your death like the fat waitress you wined and dined did from your balcony."

Jeff picked up his two-hundred-dollar tie and used it to wipe the blood, snot and tears off his face. He'd already figured out that all the speculation was for his benefit. Chapman Whitworth knew exactly what he planned to do with him and was only toying with him by ticking off the list of possible outcomes.

"Just do it," Jeff said, surprised that his voice was level. "Quit playing games and just do it."

The black cloud sprang up behind Chapman Whitworth in a nanosecond. It towered all the way to the arched ceiling, and there were flames licking off it. The creature smelled, too, this close up. A stink of rot and decay and burning flesh. And sulphur.

Jeff had never before felt the kind of elemental, raw terror that gripped him then. A special-effects movie monster that was real. Real! He could feel the hatred and anger pulsing off the creature in waves of loathing. Jeff's knees buckled out from under him and he collapsed to the floor, where he curled up in a fetal position, his knees under him, his arms across his head, his eyes squeezed tight shut.

"Please…" He felt the sniveling whine whisper out his lips but would have sworn it was so soft no one could hear.

"Please?" the roaring voice mocked. "Please!" it shouted and the sound tore holes in Jeff's head and he knew he would die from the blows.

Then Jeff's prostrate form began to rise off the floor, higher and higher until he felt his head bump the ceiling.

He had watched his own ascent in stunned horror, but now he shut his eyes, cringing away from what he knew was coming. His body didn't just fall. It was hurled down like a child throwing a rag doll on the sidewalk.

And everything went black.

Chapter Eighteen

Andi saw in the shadows behind the nurse a hunched form.

"Who's there?"

Her voice was trembling, breathless.

All in a rush, the form leapt, sprang like a cat hopping up onto a windowsill. It went from behind the nurse to the foot of Ariel's bed in a single leap and crouched there, glaring at her.

Andi had seen demons and demon-possessed people before. It was always horrible, but it didn't shock her anymore. But she had not seen anything like what crouched before her on the foot of the bed. The figure was small, a black child—whether girl or boy she couldn't tell. No, she could see the shorts were pink, with lace trim, had to be a girl. Maybe the little girl had been in some kind of accident. But Andi didn't believe that was what had happened even though the figure in front of her could well have walked out of a five-car pileup on an expressway.

It was hard to tell the figure was human at all. And a thought suddenly struck Andi, the way they sometimes did, and she knew she was right even though it was only a guess. The little girl before her was possessed and she had fought back. She had tried to get free and the demon had punished her for it, had turned her on herself.

The face was a ruin. Great claw marks sliced across it, her nose was almost ripped off and the mouth below was full of blood—whether the child's or...Andi didn't know. But her teeth were broken and jagged. The child's hair had been fixed in layers of beaded braids—her mother had gone to a lot of trouble to do that, Andi knew. She'd tried it once with a doll and quickly ran out of rubber bands, beads and patience. But hunks of the little girl's hair were missing, leaving bloody bald spots where the braids should have been. Her arms and legs were bleeding from wounds both large and small and she was breathing funny, with a gurgling sound.

The creature that controlled the body of the little girl was not on her shoulders, riding her as the others Andi had seen had done. It grew out of the center of her chest, like a deformed dog's head with a snout that twisted at the end, and had canine teeth—fangs on either side. Its tongue was lolling out one side and its lidless eyes had no whites at all —were black holes with red centers that glowed.

Then the creature pulled the little girl's lips back in a horror of a broken-toothed smile. Even on the blood-drenched face, Andi could pick out dimples like her own.

"I'm not afraid of you," the thing told her. It spoke to her. The little girl whose body it possessed said nothing. "You're not strong enough by yourself, and if you've placed your chips on the Light coming to save you, you lose—crapped out, snake eyes. Let's just say she's...busy right now."

The creature laughed, then turned and looked up into the face of the little girl it owned. When it did, the child reached up and took hold of one of the beaded braids above her forehead. In a swift motion that made a little sucking sound, she yanked the braid out and tossed it on the floor. Blood poured down over her face.

Andi felt vomit rear up in the back of her throat so suddenly she couldn't control it. She barely had time to turn her head before the hot chocolate she'd had in the hospital cafeteria spewed out her mouth and nose.

"Sensitive stomach?" the creature asked in mock sympathy.

BILLY RAY'D BEEN SUMMONED. Like somebody calling a dog. Was told he was to show up at an address in Cincinnati—an old warehouse down by the river—and collect two boxes that'd be lying next to a loading dock there. Didn't say what to do with 'em, just to pick 'em up and put 'em in the back of his pickup truck and take them back to the boxcar with him. So he'd done as he was told. Hated the feeling of helplessness—that he couldn't, didn't dare refuse.

But it was his money! His. Didn't matter. He still done whatever that voice said he was supposed to do.

The boxes were corrugated cardboard, sealed with wax to be waterproof.

One was almost as flat as a pizza box, but much bigger, maybe four feet square, lying with another box in the weeds beside the dock. It wasn't particularly heavy, but awkward to lift, and he could feel something in there that was solid, one piece, like whatever it was didn't come "assembly required." The other box was bigger, not flat. It wasn't heavy either, but whatever was inside wasn't all one piece. He could hear and feel loose things inside. He'd been told to handle the big box with care, like maybe the contents was breakable, and he didn't like to think what might happen to him if he broke something. Both boxes was taped shut and he didn't make no effort to see what was in 'em, had an awful feeling he didn't want to know what it was.

Then he'd got the call on his cell phone, saying not to go back to Caverna County yet—there was something else he needed to pick up and take back there with him.

And there had, indeed, been something else. Now, he couldn't stop the quaking in his belly that sent trembles out his arms and legs so violent he feared he couldn't keep his pickup truck from plunging into a ditch.

You got to get a grip, man!

Billy Ray's mind was hopping around frantic as spit on a griddle and he couldn't seem to grab hold of it long enough to think.

He had to think.

He had got in way over his head here. Waaaay over his head. And he might be able to think his way out if he could think at all, but every time he tried, images popped into his mind that sent him off in some other direction.

He'd been waiting where the voice on his cell phone had told him to wait, with his truck parked up close to the back side of a building in the alley between a dumpster and a long black car, a limousine. That limousine'd had tinted windows, so's whoever was in there could see you, but you couldn't see them. And the longer he sat there, the more certain Billy Ray was that there was somebody behind the tinted windows of that limousine. Watching every move he made. With eyes made of fire.

That was when he'd heard some sound above him, hopped out of his truck and looked up. He'd seen a man leaning out a window high above, the fourth or fifth floor maybe, and then the man had fallen, his body hurling down right at Billy Ray. Billy Ray'd leapt back—something big as a man falls on you from that high—it'd squash you flat as a fried egg.

But the body had stopped. Right there in midair, the body had pulled up short like it had got to the end of one of them bungee cords, only it hadn't flown right back up where it come from. It had hung there, about four feet off the ground, right behind the pickup. Staring at it hanging there—a man in a suit, with his face bloody—Billy Ray's mind had started to get squirrelly, thinking a hundred things and nothing at all.

His cell phone had rung, then. He'd let it ring and ring, knew who it was and didn't want to answer it, but finally he'd reached into his pocket with a trembling hand. The voice on the other end of the line had been oily and slick, so smooth draining into his ear it'd soaked into his brain, a drop of food coloring in a glass of water.

No hello. Just said to put the man who was dangling there into the back of the truck with the boxes and take 'em all to where Billy Ray'd stashed Daniel Burke. Said he'd get a call later about the contents of the boxes he'd picked up. Nothing more than that. The phone had gone dead, and the man who'd been hanging suspended in the air had dropped like a sack of potatoes the final four feet to the ground and cracked his head a nasty blow on the asphalt.

When Billy Ray'd got down to lift the body into the bed of his truck, he'd recognized the man. It was Jeff Kendrick, the smart-ass lawyer who'd kicked Billy Ray in the face, broke his nose and—more important—deprived him of the privilege of killing Becca and that fat pig Theresa Washington. In a flash of rage at the memory, Billy Ray had slammed his fist into Kendrick's face—let him see what a broken nose felt like! He'd punched him in the face another time or two, but wasn't no fun hitting a man who couldn't feel no pain.

Kendrick had been heavy, limp as he was. Dead weight.

Yep, dead weight all right, just like Daniel Burke.

Billy Ray Hawkins didn't have no qualms 'bout killing a man. He'd killed many—he hadn't kept track of how many, but a whole lot. He was looking forward to puttin' a bullet in Daniel's brain and now he'd have the satisfaction of offing that big-city lawyer, too. No, wasn't killing that was makin' him squirrelly. It was the voice, the man, the thing that was calling the shots and givin' Billy Ray orders. His mind went skittering off again soon's it went anywhere near the black shadow that had risen up behind Chapman Whitworth.

Had to think. Had to think. Had to get out of this somehow.

But he didn't think. He merely covered the boxes and the body up with a big tarp and drove south down Interstate 71 away from Cincinnati. Once he was out of the city's lights, an endless black sky opened above him. The stars were as big as ice chips and looked twice as cold. The vast emptiness of the night had never seemed scary before, but now he found himself hunkerin' down behind the wheel, flinchin' away. He knew now that the black was just a curtain. On the other side of darkness they was things that maybe you didn't want to get a good look at. Things that was waitin' to eat you alive.

He turned off the interstate and wound through narrow, twisting country roads toward the north end of Caverna County. As soon as he crossed the county line, the empty sky above him vanished and rain poured down. It was like steppin' under a waterfall, so sudden he almost wrecked as he scrambled to turn on his windshield wipers. That tarp would keep everythin' in the back of the truck dry for now, but if it was still rainin' when he got home, it'd all get soaked when he carried it to the boxcar.

Billy Ray was a whole lot stronger'n he looked, but it was still no easy thing to get that smart-mouth lawyer into his hidden boxcar. He hadn't been gentle. With Daniel, he'd hauled him in a fireman-carry to the Butt Cheek Rocks and left his limp body sprawled unconscious across the rocks while he climbed down behind 'em. Then he'd reached up and dragged Daniel off into his arms. But it hadn't been raining then.

In the downpour, he'd just chucked Mr. Suit and Tie Man's body down into the crevice behind the rocks. Coulda broke his fool neck. But he was moanin', so he wasn't hurt too bad.

Didn't want him to wake up before Billy Ray got him all trussed up, though, so Billy Ray hurried to roll the rock away that hid the cave and the gate. The slab of rock was taller than a refrigerator, but only about six inches wide, rounded on one side. He rolled it on that edge away from the crack that opened into the cave and then jammed a chock in place to hold it there. After he dragged Kendrick's limp body out of the downpour, through the crack in the rock into the cave, he dug around in his pocket for the key to unlock the padlock on the metal gate across the cave entrance. He'd built it decades ago when he'd buried the boxcar—fixed the gate hinges to the cave wall with iron spikes and hollowed out a trench on the cave floor so he could set the bottom bar of the gate frame into a base of five-inch-thick concrete.

Once inside the boxcar, Billy Ray quickly secured Kendrick's hands and feet with duct tape.

Daniel Burke was watching his every move, not sayin' nothin'.

"I thought you might like some company," Billy Ray said. "Brought you a chum. Be nice, now, don't want you to get no 'unsatisfactory' in that space on your report card where it says 'plays well with others.'"

Daniel just looked at the wet, crumpled body.

"This fella's a friend of yours, ain't he?" Billy Ray said.

"He's no friend of mine."

"Now, why is it that I don't hardly believe that? Seein' as how he was the big-city lawyer kept you out of jail after you attacked that woman."

"I didn't say I didn't know him. I said he wasn't a friend of mine."

"Oh, so that's how it is, huh? You boys don't get along, do ya?"

He stepped back and looked at them from a spot next to the bars of gold on the shelves.

"Well, whatever it is you got against each other, you best kiss and make up." He grinned and watched with glee to see the effect his next words would have on Daniel. "'Cause it would be a shame for a fact to die alongside somebody you don't like. Ain't neither one of you ever gonna see another sunset."

Then Billy Ray left the boxcar, banging its metal door shut behind him.

❧

WON'T LIVE to see another sunset.

Now there was a conversation stopper, pulled everything up short and into perspective. Daniel was stiff and hurt all over—especially his forearm and hand where the little girl had bitten him. His head throbbed in heartbeat bursts. He was so thirsty the roof of his mouth and his tongue came apart as reluctantly as two strips of Velcro and his legs ached from being cramped together by the duct-tape restraints.

None of that mattered now. One thought drove everything else off the stage and stood alone in the glaring spotlight.

Billy Ray Hawkins was going to kill him.

Jeff Kendrick began to moan. He was coming to. It was such a cosmic joke that it was laughable if you had that kind of sick sense of humor. Daniel was going to die alongside Jeff Kendrick, his wife's lover.

"What is this?" Jeff muttered and tried to sit up, but couldn't with his hands taped together in front of him and his arms taped down to his body from shoulder to elbow. "Where am…what…?" He continued to wiggle until Daniel spoke to him for the first time.

"Give up, Jeff. You're tied up with duct tape. Can you see?"

Jeff's nose was clearly broken, smashed over onto his left cheek in a puffy mass that was painful to look at. One eye was blacked and swollen almost shut; the other was crusted with blood that had drained into it from some wound on his head.

He quit struggling and lay still, then opened his eyes—eye, the one with blood on it. The lids stuck together at first, but he finally got the upper lid free. His gaze darted around and landed on Daniel. He stared, looking puzzled.

"Daniel?" His voice sounded like he had a cold.

Daniel realized then that he probably didn't look a whole lot better than Jeff. He must have the mother of all lumps on his forehead where that little girl—beautiful until he saw the look in her eyes—had slammed a rock into it. Maybe the blow blacked his eyes, too.

"Where...?" Jeff looked around. "What is this place?"

"It's a boxcar full of gold bricks—several million dollars' worth—buried in a cave somewhere in Caverna County."

Jeff's face was as blank as the first page in a brand-new school notebook.

"Billy Ray Hawkins buried his money here. It's his 'secret fortress.' You and I are probably the only people in the world who've ever seen it. And he doesn't intend for us to live to tell about it."

As if on cue, Billy Ray opened the door to the boxcar, pitched a flat cardboard box onto the floor, then reached down and picked up a square box, carried it into the boxcar, set it down and closed the door behind him. He didn't turn around, just stood there facing the door, shaking his head.

Then he turned around slowly. His eyes clearly were not seeing the inside of a buried boxcar, and whatever they were seeing was not a good thing. Billy Ray's face was a mask of such abject terror and revulsion Daniel instinctively shrank back from the sight. Jeff actually gasped, or maybe he was just trying to suck in a breath through the swollen ruin that was his nose.

Billy Ray did not acknowledge their presence, just cowered before whatever he imagined he saw on the wall above their heads.

Perhaps the image vanished then because he began to pace from one end of the boxcar to the other, talking to himself in nonsense, his wet boots tracing a trail of puddles behind him. "Not going to...see if he makes me...that's crazy, sick crazy—" He stopped in the middle of the floor and shook his head violently from side to side. "No! Won't do it. No! Can't make...yes, he can. He can make anybody do…I gotta run, get away—find me, find me and…he'll eat me alive."

Back and forth he went, growing more and more agitated with every passing moment, walking faster and faster, mumbling and shaking his head.

Daniel had never actually seen a person have a psychotic episode, but it was obvious that was what this was. If there were any way at all to get free from the tape, he could escape and Billy Ray would never even notice. But the tape was secure.

Billy Ray stopped, panting, then went to the far corner away from Jeff and Daniel. He slid to the floor there and lay whimpering, curled up in something resembling a fetal position.

"Have a flat tire, did you?" Jeff called out and Daniel wanted to choke him. He whispered harshly, "Shut up, you idiot. Can't you see he—"

But Jeff ignored him.

"Girlfriend dump you? No, wait, I know—your favorite M&M was the red one they discontinued."

Billy Ray looked at them then, actually seemed to register the reality of them. He got slowly to his feet.

"He wants lots of blood, wants it everywhere—so folks can see it."

Daniel didn't have to ask who "he" was.

"Let's come back to the spectators later," Jeff said, in his stopped-up-nose voice. "I want to back up to the 'your blood' part."

Billy Ray crossed the width of the boxcar to Jeff in a rush, drew back his foot and drove a savage blow with it into Jeff's belly, buried the pointed toe of his boot there. Jeff curled up in a ball, unable to breathe at all.

Then Billy Ray started shouting, his voice high pitched and hysterical.

"Your blood!" he said to Daniel, then turned to Jeff. "Yours, too. Both of you." He seemed to be speaking to himself again. "He don't care how big a mess it makes 'cause he ain't the one has to clean it up. But maybe it ain't even gonna be here at all."

"You're going to take us somewhere else to shoot us?"

"Shoot? I didn't say nothin' about shootin' you. Ain't going to be no shootin'."

Then the energy drained out of Billy Ray like water out the hole in the bottom of a bucket. He seemed to physically shrink. Pulling his cell phone out of his pocket, he looked at it as if it were a scorpion or poisonous snake. He held it out in front of him and began to talk to it as if someone were on speakerphone.

"Opened up them boxes, just like you said, and it was all there, the robe, the sword—everything…"

Sword? The word kicked Daniel in the gut as solidly as Billy Ray had kicked Jeff, and he could not draw in another breath.

"…be sure to shoot the video up close so you can see their faces, so you can tell who they are. I got that part, uh-huh." He paused as if he were in a real conversation, listening to someone else speak. "Save Burke for last, he's the main attraction—right."

He listened, then set the phone down on a shelf and used both hands to pantomime as he repeated the instructions only he could hear from the cell phone.

"Grab a handful of his hair—get a good hold on it—then bring the sword down hard, slice across his throat, just one clean blow so you're left holding his head in your hand."

Chapter Nineteen

Sebastian Nemo stared down at the maps he'd stretched out across the bed and tables in his hotel room. Coordinating six attacks to go off almost simultaneously was challenging enough without the added wrinkle of ensuring a proper target for them in four different time zones. Fortunately, it was not Sebastian's responsibility to get the video posted online at the same time. That was somebody else's headache.

Sebastian had spent several weeks in each of the five target cities—Cincinnati, New York, New Orleans, Chicago and Los Angeles. He'd studied the area between SoHo and Greenwich Village in New York, beginning on Sixth Avenue at Spring Street and following it to Twenty-Third Street in Chelsea. The streets between Bleecker and Fourteenth Street would likely be the most crowded, so he'd concentrated on finding a spot there.

He'd walked streets bordering Halsted and Belmont in Chicago and along Lower Decatur Street in New Orleans, from Molly's at the Market to Bourbon Street.

He'd already been familiar with Santa Monica Boulevard in Los Angeles—where he might possibly get the highest body count. It would still be daylight there. The Halloween parade in Los Angeles didn't start until six o'clock, which was nine o'clock on the East Coast—long after he expected to topple the first domino. Still, more than half a million people would attend "the world's largest Halloween street party," and with all the major streets in West Hollywood shut down, they'd have to show up early.

His study of the locations had informed his decisions about what kinds of weapons he'd use at each, what he could conceal and which ones would do the most damage.

Oh, he could have chosen bigger weapons with more firepower. He had access to the brand-new M224A light-weight mortar system sent into battle this year. That'd been tempting because it could be fired from four thousand yards away and the survivors would later recount in hushed horror how they'd heard the whistle of the round's approach. And mortars would produce a high body count, too.

But in the end, it really didn't matter how many people were killed or wounded. The fact of the attacks was the point, not how effective they were in producing casualties. A week later, nobody'd remember how many people died, but ten years from now they'd remember there'd been an attack. A coordinated assault on five American cities—even if all you did was toss a hand grenade into a crowd—would be paralyzing. Psychological damage was how you kept score.

In that regard, driving the ambulance loaded with explosives into the crowd of freaks prancing around in Los Angeles would likely be the most effective. Mowing people down in broad daylight in full view of who knew how many security cameras—with a bomb-loaded vehicle police had allowed inside the blocked-off streets—made for great footage on the eleven o'clock news. Of course, the explosion at the end was to take out the driver and the evidence, not to increase the body count.

The backpack bomb in Chicago, similar to the one he'd used so effectively with Ricky Harrison in Minneapolis, was its own special horror because it would come out of nowhere, no warning. And expedient because it, too, took out the operative along with the victims.

The on-site explosives in New Orleans, the ones in false-bottomed trash barrels, blue metal mailboxes and other semipermanent structures, would demonstrate that terrorists didn't even have to be present to kill. And the Javelins…ahhh, they were the coup de grâce. Killing civilians with sophisticated military weapons designed to take out Taliban bunkers, fortified heavy machine guns, T-55 tanks and armored personnel carriers rated a plus ten on the horror scale.

Sebastian leaned back and stretched. He'd been hunched over the maps for more than two hours. He massaged his neck as he walked to the window, moved the curtain back an inch, enough to see out a crack. The city skyline was superimposed on the backdrop of a bright red-golden sky, a silhouette backlit by the setting sun. A coal barge was making its way across the glass top of the Ohio River, slowly and silently. Sebastian smiled.

DANIEL WAS HAVING TROUBLE BREATHING. His chest didn't want to rise and fall properly. It merely hitched up an inch or two—not far enough to admit enough air—then collapsed and expelled a puff in a gasp. In and out like that, again and again. Daniel's head began to swim and the scene took on an eerie unreality.

Hyperventilating. Was that what he was doing?

His lips felt numb and he watched through a fog as Billy Ray stopped talking, picked up the phone and moved back and forth around the boxcar, obviously figuring something out. Planning it. He stood back and eyed the two captives near the wall, walked to the other side of the boxcar and back again.

He lifted the cell phone in his hand and held it up toward Daniel and Jeff to take a picture. But he didn't snap the photo, only looked at the angle, then placed the cell phone—propped up on a bar of pure gold worth probably fifty thousand dollars—and got behind it to see that it was the angle he wanted.

He noticed Daniel watching him and grinned, his eyes far too bright.

"I'm about to take you boys' pictures," he said. "You be sure and smile real wide for the camera."

Then he turned to the cardboard boxes on the floor. He pulled out his knife, slit the sealing tape on the flat one and took something out of it that was wrapped in black fabric. He unwound the fabric—it was a garment, a robe or tunic—and dropped it on the floor and stood gaping at what it had concealed, turning it over and over in his hand in wonder. Daniel heard a gasp beside him. He'd been so fixated on Billy Ray he'd completely forgotten that Jeff Kendrick was lying on the floor next to him.

Billy Ray lifted the huge scimitar above his head, examining it in the bilious light. Its curved blade was about three feet long, much bigger than the one that hung above the bulletin board beside the door in Bishop's office. The carvings and designs on that one had been on the handle. On this larger one, the whole blade was adorned with runes—words in some ancient language, one nobody on the planet spoke anymore. When Billy Ray moved the sword, the symbols…no, it couldn't be! But it was. Movement brought the tiny markings to life and they crawled over the blade like so many tiny spiders. The metal was satin gray, not silver like Bishop's, and there seemed to be a shadow around it like smoke, as if it reflected darkness rather than light.

It looked like—was it?—points of red fire were licking up from the handle where the shiny black wood had been carved into the shape of a serpent with rubies the size of grapes for eyes. Even from where he lay, Daniel could see that the scimitar blade had been honed to a razor edge.

Billy Ray hefted the sword from hand to hand and swished it downward in the air in a hacking motion. Then he held it with both hands like a baseball bat and sliced it through the air horizontally.

Daniel was suddenly nauseous. He struggled mightily, determined not to retch, held on with all his might, tears rolling down his cheeks from the effort, as waves of convulsive retching crashed again and again into his rigid diaphragm. Billy Ray leaned the blade against the wall and Daniel's heaving subsided. But he still couldn't breathe.

He and Jeff watched as Billy Ray picked the fabric up off the floor and shook it out, then pulled the black hooded robe over his head. Its long sleeves covered the tattoos on his arms and the cowl hid his face in shadow. He looked like a skinny monk. Or the Grim Reaper. When he had the garment adjusted to suit him, Billy Ray addressed Jeff and Daniel.

"I want you boys on your knees," he said.

With their hands and feet bound, it was hard to assume that position on their own. Billy Ray went first to Jeff and yanked on his elbow, lifting him off the floor and setting him unsteadily on his knees. Jeff promptly flopped back over on his side on the floor.

"This can go easy, or this can go hard," Billy Ray told him, the hysterical edge that had been in his voice replaced by a black threatening tone. He nodded toward the heavy metal door on the boxcar. "Want me to slam that door shut on your hand? Becca was so out of it she didn't feel her finger in the car door that time, but you'll feel every one of the bones in your hand break."

Becca's finger—the one with the blackened nail.

Billy Ray reached down and pulled Jeff up a second time. He wobbled but remained in place. Then he lifted Daniel up beside him so the two of them were kneeling in front of a blank wall—not one with shelves of gold on it.

After he went to the cell phone and fiddled with it, he grabbed the sword and moved with it behind them—but the timer on the camera fired the picture before he was in place. He took half a dozen pictures before he was satisfied. When he finally had the picture he wanted, he lifted his foot and kicked Jeff in the back, propelling him forward. With his hands bound behind him, he could not break his own fall and his already damaged face smashed into the floor.

Daniel winced reflexively and braced himself, but Billy Ray only kicked him out of the way and he landed on his shoulder. Stepping over Daniel, Billy Ray removed his robe and hung it over the post of one of the shelf units that held his gold bars. He slipped his cell phone into his pocket and turned for the door.

Daniel had to say something. "You got any plans for a potty break before you leave?"

Billy Ray had probably used a whole roll of duct tape on the two of them. He'd bound their wrists together in front of them, then wrapped tape around and around them to secure their arms to their bodies from the elbows up. They still had limited use of their hands and fingers—enough—and Billy Ray had set out a pail beside Daniel. He'd also brought in a McDonald's burger, fries and a soft drink with a straw and set them on the floor. Daniel had managed to get to his knees and kneel over the straw in the soft drink. He'd tried taking bites of the burger on the floor, too, though it was like bobbing for apples. But he gave up after a bite or two—didn't have much appetite.

Gesturing toward the bucket in the far corner of the boxcar, Billy Ray said, "You need to go bad enough, you'll figure out a way to scoot over there and use it by yourself. You got nothing but time." Then he picked up the scimitar. "'Til I use this to stop your clocks—permanently."

JACK STEPPED into Ariel Murphy's hospital room and let the door swing closed by itself behind him. He stifled the reflex that came next. He'd seen it a hundred times. A perp reaches over unconsciously and pats his pocket to reassure himself his gun is still there. He needed no reassurance. The gun he'd shoved into his sweatpants in the motel room had rubbed his back raw.

"Come on over and join the party," the voice said, and he walked toward the bed on the back wall, where he could see Ariel under the white sheet and Andi perched on the foot of the bed with her feet dangling off the side. The only light in the room was the flickering of the muted television mounted on the wall across from Ariel's bed. He didn't look at it and willed himself to move slowly to give his eyes time to adjust to the semidarkness.

The hall downstairs outside the elevator where he'd been talking to Crock and the stairwell had been dimly lit, but still it'd be three—maybe five—minutes before he could make out clearly all the shapes around the bed. No way he'd get five minutes.

He'd have to flush the thing out into the light.

"Uncle Jack, I—"

"Quiet, you—!" Then the voice spilled obscenities into the room as foul as the stench of a stagnant pool, words Jack would wager Andi had never heard in her life. The voice came from the shadows directly behind where Andi sat.

"If this is a party, what are we celebrating?" Jack asked.

There was a giggle, a little girl's giggle, only it wasn't. "We're celebrating death, of course. I only came for one kill. All the rest of you are a bonus. Sometimes, you just get lucky."

Jack stepped on something and glanced down but couldn't make out what it was—a piece of black yarn maybe with beads in it. There was blood on one end.

"Shame I won't get to keep the trophies. You bag one, you're supposed to get to stuff it and hang it on your wall. Right? Isn't that the way big-game hunting works?"

The monster was babbling, clearly enjoying itself. Good. Keep it talking. Every second granted Jack a little more edge. If he was going to take a shot, he had to be able to see his target better than he could right now. From here, it was nothing more than an indistinct lump behind Andi. And Jack would rather die than shoot Andi…again.

"I wouldn't know," Jack said, edging a few inches to the side as he did to try to get a sight line behind Andi. "I'm a fisherman, not a hunter."

"Fool," the child's voice that wasn't a child rumbled, a sound so ragged surely it must have shredded the vocal cords of the one making it. "They'll be dead before you can untangle it from your underwear. Scalpels were designed to slice through flesh, you know."

Jack froze, remembering the rattlesnake speed of the hyped-up-on-adrenaline monster that had almost killed him last summer.

Suddenly, the voice turned almost cheery.

"Why look at that, Andi," it said. "Your daddy's on television, only this time he's not preaching."

Andi looked up at the television screen. When Jack saw the shock on her face, he looked, too. Pictured there was a hooded man holding a scimitar, standing behind two bound men on their knees, facing the camera.

"Daddy!" Andi cried.

It took Jack a beat longer. A wound on his forehead crusted in dried blood had spread bruising downward to black both his eyes, but it was Daniel.

Words ran across the bottom of the screen.

"...and other national media outlets received an email containing this photograph from a group identifying itself as 'Maelstrom' that claimed responsibility for bombing the Mall of America in Minneapolis on Wednesday and the Desert Dolphin Restaurant in Phoenix on Friday.

"Though we don't yet have independent confirmation, the two men pictured here on their knees were identified in the email as the Reverend Daniel Burke, senior minister of the twenty-thousand-member Voice of Hope Community Church in Cincinnati, Ohio, and Jeff Kendrick, an attorney with the Cincinnati law firm Taylor, Murray and Kendrick."

Until the words identified Jeff, Jack didn't recognize him. His face was in much worse shape than Daniel's.

"The email threatened that a video of the beheadings of these two men would be posted online tomorrow evening—I'm quoting here—'as we unleash coordinated catastrophic attacks with thousands of casualties in five American cities.'

"The email said the beheadings would mark the birth of a revolutionary movement that would plunge America into chaos. I'm quoting again, 'We kill one who corrupted the sacred and one who prevented the sword of retribution from falling—to symbolize chopping off the heads of religion and law to expose the rot within.'

"It's possible that's a reference to a recent investigation of Reverend Burke on a rape charge that was eventually dropped. Kendrick represented Reverend Burke in that case."

Andi had leapt to her knees at the sight of her father and was clutching the footboard of the bed, gawking at the images on the screen and sobbing. Now Jack could see the thing on the bed behind her, a horror unrecognizable as the child Cassidy Davenport.

"Noooo," Andi shrieked. "Daddy! Daaaddy!"

The voice that spoke from the thing was barely a whisper, but its viciousness sliced through all other sound.

"We warned you, sweet meat. We told you we'd chop off your daddy's head."

Jack's heart began to hammer so hard in his chest that little bursts of light exploded in his eyes with every beat.

BILLY RAY STARTED out the door of the boxcar with the scimitar, then looked back at Daniel and Jeff with a grin before he reached over and flipped off the light. He'd left the light on while he'd been gone before.

"Finding that bucket's gonna be a challenge now," he said, standing in the doorway in the spill of light cast by the bulb that hung suspended from the cave roof outside the boxcar. "It'll give you something to do to pass the time."

He stepped out into the cave and closed the door behind him, plunging the room into darkness. Not a single ray of light. Blind-man black. Inside-a-lump-of-coal black. And quiet.

Daniel heard him fasten the padlock in place on the outside of the door, then a muffled clanging as he closed another door or gate of some kind. Then it was silent. Daniel could hear the sound of Jeff's breathing a few feet away, but he couldn't see him, couldn't have seen his own hand in front of his face if he'd been able to lift it up that high.

Beheaded.

Somehow the word wouldn't fit into his brain. He'd shove it in there and it would tumble right back out. How could you get your mind around a thing like that? Somebody was going to chop off your head. What did you do with that?

"Got any idea what's up with the beheading?" The words in a stopped-up-nose voice came from the nearby darkness. "You want to kill a man, there are easier, less… messy…ways to do it."

Daniel hadn't yet adjusted to the prospect of getting his head lopped off with a scimitar. It was way beyond his bandwidth right now to puzzle out why Chapman Whitworth was going to the trouble. Instead of answering, he began to scoot toward the back corner of the boxcar.

The silence returned, broken only by the sounds Daniel made propelling himself along the floor of the boxcar.

"You won't feel anything," the stuffed-nose voice continued. "It's actually a pretty humane way to kill someone, if you think about it. There's no pain. You just—"

Daniel felt emotion rise in his chest like vomit.

"Shut up!" He fired the words into the darkness like arrows. "Even now, knowing you're about to die, you still have to be the big shot, don't you, the know-it-all. Always playing 'can you top this?' Just. Shut. Up. You owe me that much—the privilege of not having to hear your voice."

There was silence then, and Daniel could hear only his own thudding heartbeat and his heavy breathing as anger coursed through him.

The word dropped into his mind—he could almost see it—a pure drop of water surrounding it as it fell slowly down into the still pool below. Rage. When it hit the surface, the liquid rose around it like in those slow-motion videos where you watched the action of the milk in a bowl of cereal when the first raisin from the raisin brand box plopped in.

That was what he was about. Daniel Burke was about rage. Anger. Fury! He was about bitterness and jealousy. He was about hatred. He hated the man lying only a few feet away in the dark. Loathed him. He had stolen Emily. Images of the two of them together downloaded then with such power he almost groaned out loud. He was too tired, too hungry and thirsty and hurt to mount defenses against them. And so they came and overwhelmed him, visions of Jeff and Emily walking hand in hand, laughing together, staring into each other's eyes. In bed.

For a long time, Daniel Burke was swallowed up in depths of rage and loathing far darker than the lightless boxcar buried deep in the earth.

Chapter Twenty

You were real scared, weren't you?

Ariel heard the voice from a long way off.

I know how that feels, being so scared you're afraid you're going to throw up. I felt like that once.

It was the voice of the little girl from the woods.

But you're okay now. You won't ever be alone, locked inside with...you won't ever have to do that again. I promise.

Part of Ariel wanted to sink back into darkness, but another part struggled to return to the world. She had a huge fishbowl full of goldfish in her room at home. She'd watch the fish swimming and the turtles crawling around on the rocks on the bottom. Then a bubble would come out from under a rock, a tiny circle of air, and she would watch it float upward, up and up until it burst out into the air of the surface.

Ariel was a bubble. She felt herself begin to rise from the bottom toward the light.

She had hidden far down inside herself when the monster had screamed at her and they ran away into the woods. She hadn't come back up when she fell, just watched it from the dark depths, accepted that she was going to die with her eyes turned up to the sky while the creature roared in filthy hatred and rage.

And then the light had come.

It was there above her, a light so bright it shone in through her eyes and all the way down into the depths of her where she had hidden. It lit everything with a warm, shadowless radiance.

Ariel crept out of hiding. She could hear and feel the creature in her, terrified, trying to get her body to move and carry it away, but Ariel's body could not obey. It was spent.

The monster roared, screamed obscenities, thundered in terror and rage, banging around. She crept through the hallways of darkness inside herself. It had been achingly cold before, the touch of every surface the feel of a rock in the snow. The stench of the creature, the fetid reek of excrement, from some animal too horrible to imagine filled every breath.

It wasn't cold now, though. There was a warm breeze sweeping through the hallways, carrying with it the sweet scent of roses and honeysuckle and Ariel found herself running toward the glow she could see far off. She had hidden so deep, it was a long way. But the closer she got, the warmer and brighter it got.

Suddenly, the creature was there, all around, everywhere. The cold of it bit into her bones, the stink so vile and thick you could almost touch it. Ariel dropped to her knees and covered her head. She could feel the creature's terror, feel it struggling.

She realized it was paying no attention to her, so Ariel tried again to do what she had done before. She focused all her will on taking her body back—only for a moment, an instant long enough to cry out. But instead of turning on her in fury when she did, the creature faltered. Some great force from outside her was applying pressure on the monster, and Ariel felt the creature's grip begin to loosen. That gave her such a surge of wild hope and joy that she shoved at it with all the will she had, every ounce of her strength. It squalled out a great, awful, guttural cry with her voice, so loud it made her throat hurt.

Then it was gone.

Quiet.

Nothing.

She lifted her head slowly, and when she did, everything snapped back. She was no longer looking out big screens that showed the world she couldn't get to or touch. She was just...looking. She blinked. Again, slowly closing her eyes and opening them just as slowly. Her eyelids did as she told them.

She realized then that even the stink of him was gone.

A little girl with curly brown hair and deep dimples was leaning over her, her lips moving, and as if stoppers had been pulled from her ears, Ariel heard the voice.

"Ariel, come back," the little girl said. "It's gone now."

Behind the little girl stood a beautiful woman with long blond hair, clothed in a gown of sparkling diamonds. They shimmered, each giving off its own light, hundreds of thousands of points of brilliance made of stones that refracted all the lights of the spectrum she'd seen on display in science class at school. Only hundreds of times brighter and more beautiful.

She heard the woman tell the little girl to go for help, that she'd stay here with Ariel.

"But how can I find the way in the dark without a light?"

"The way is lit for you," the woman said.

Ariel saw sparkles of light, like a trail of multicolored glitter, appear all around the woman. Then it moved toward the woods, like a tail following a kite, and wound its way through the trees. The little girl followed it and was gone.

"Ariel." The woman called her name. "It's safe now. I'm here and I won't let anything harm you."

Ariel stared at the beauty of the brilliant light. She was so tired, but so peaceful. She could go to sleep now. The nightmare couldn't get her anymore.

There was a man, then, a big black man who held her hand, spoke softly to her and wrapped her in his warm T-shirt. She'd looked at him, then closed her eyes—not yet ready to return to the world. It was dark after that, but not cold dark. Just no-light dark. That was when she became the bubble and started toward the surface. She could feel the bubble of her consciousness continue to rise now. Higher and higher until she burst out into the air. She opened her eyes. Then closed them again, and the terror she knew so well grabbed hold of her heart and squeezed. She'd only caught a glimpse of the thing that sat at the foot of her bed, but a glimpse was all she needed. Cassidy Davenport—but not now.

With her heart pounding, she carefully peeked out a forest of eyelashes. Nothing she saw made sense; then reason settled around her and she understood she was in a hospital. Her leg! She remembered then, the sickening snapping sound she'd heard when she landed at the bottom of the cliff. She could see her leg now, wrapped round and round like a big club, suspended by a sling in the air behind the head of the thing that had taken over the body of Cassidy Davenport crouched on the foot of the bed.

Ariel lay perfectly still. Watched. Listened.

The thing had come to kill her with the scalpel clutched in its bloody hand. It meant to kill the little girl, too, the one who had found Ariel in the woods. The kind man who'd wrapped his warm shirt around her wanted to stop the thing, but it would move too quickly. Ariel knew about such things. He wouldn't get to it before it plunged the blade into the little girl's back and then into Ariel's chest.

Ariel couldn't run away and hide from it. She couldn't move at all with her leg hanging up there…like a club.

JEFF SHOOK his head and opened his eyes wider as if that would somehow admit some light from the lightless room. He hadn't slept in—how long? He couldn't even remember anymore. Didn't matter. He wouldn't nod off now, didn't intend to spend the last hours of his life asleep! Besides, he didn't feel sleepy. A little loopy, maybe…no, actually a lot loopy—spinning.

He was turning slowly, suspended by a single crystal strand above a darkness that was somehow darker than where he lay now. It was a darkness that collected and pooled in its depths, a darkness that was more than merely the absence of light. The darkness itself was a thing, an entity. A malevolent being with shiny teeth you couldn't see and great crushing jaws invisible now, but Jeff would feel them both when the strand broke and he fell into the nothingness.

His mind kept hopping from one random thought to another. They slid across the expanse of his consciousness like sailboats on a glassy pond and they moved so fast he couldn't catch any one of them long enough to think it.

"Got any idea what's up with the beheading?" he

thought the words as he spoke them. No, he spoke them several seconds before he thought them. He said something else, too, that had the word messy in it. Daniel didn't reply, but Jeff could hear him scooting slowly across the floor toward the bucket in the corner.

Jeff was afraid, but he couldn't even catch that to feel the emotion. It scampered away out of reach.

Would it hurt?

No. He'd read that somewhere—about Anne Boleyn, he thought, how she'd begged not to have her head lopped off with an ax on a chopping block, that she'd feared that ever since she was a little girl. So they'd arranged to bring in someone—from France, he remembered. Why did he remember that?—who would use a sword instead of an ax. She was saying her final prayers and he came up behind her, sliced her head off so instantly that as it rolled across the floor, her lips were still moving in prayer.

"You won't feel anything," he said. It was hard to talk with his nose smashed. "It's actually a pretty humane way to kill someone, if you think about it. There's no pain. You just—"

"Shut up!" The words exploded out of the nearby darkness. "Just. Shut. Up. You owe me that much—the privilege of not having to hear your voice."

Daniel said other things, too, about Jeff playing the big shot. The ferocity of the words was stunning. The level of loathing and hatred contained in them staggering.

And for the first time since the moment he'd set his sights on Emily Burke, Jeff Kendrick paused to consider Daniel. What did he feel? What would it feel like for the woman you loved, your wife, the mother of your child, to betray you? Because that was what she'd done. You could put all the pretty words on it you wanted to—call it an affair, a fling, a flirtation, a romance—but the bottom line was that the fair Emily Marie Burke had decided to break the promise to remain faithful forever that she'd made to Daniel Burke fourteen years ago. She had made a decision to betray him.

Jeff had never considered Emily in that light before.

He'd never considered the consequences—the fallout—from his decision to take her.

But he'd loved her. He had!

So had Daniel Burke. And Daniel had seen her first.

AT FIRST, Jack thought he was imagining it. But he'd spent too many years training his senses to collect information for that. He really was seeing it. Movement. Slow, gradual. But movement. Ariel Murphy's leg was moving back away from the monster crouched on the foot of the bed. Inching back, farther and farther. Millimetering back.

It took less than a heartbeat for Jack to record that information. Another heartbeat to figure out...to grasp what was happening, what must be happening.

Andi was staring up at the flickering television, the image of her father and the other man still shown as words continued to flow across the bottom of the screen. She was crying, "Daddy, Daddy!"

The monster behind her was giggling in glee, almost dancing.

"Now!" he called out.

The monster immediately turned to him, lifting the blade as it did to plunge it into Andi's back.

Ariel let go and her ice-pack-encased leg hit the creature in the back of the head. It wasn't a hard blow. Ariel was incapable of putting any force behind it. But the blow was enough to knock the creature off balance for a second, and a second was all Jack needed.

Then came rogue time—the suspension of reality as the world saw it, where everything cranked down into slow motion and words were dragged out in loooong syllables. Or it sped up in a dizzying fast-forward that turned voices into the chipmunks from the annual Christmas special.

It was slow now. Jack reached back. He always left his shirt untucked to cover the weapon. But he must have stuffed it down inside his pants behind the gun as he crossed the hallway to Ariel's room. He didn't remember doing it. Instinct.

In a loping slow-motion movement, he pulled the gun free and raised it. The monster on the bed was knocked sideways in equal slow motion, lost its balance and began to tumble toward the edge of the bed. It twisted as it fell, lifting the blade to stab it down into the lump under the sheet that was Ariel Murphy.

Jack was a crack shot, the firearms instructor for his department, and the target was less than ten feet away. Still, it was a gamble—but a risk he had to take. He wasn't shooting a killer. She was only a little girl.

Ignoring the deadly-fire protocol that required him to "aim for the largest target," he took less than a second to draw a bead and then squeezed the trigger. The report of the gunshot sounded like a cannon in the confined space. The sound released time and it snapped back, a rubber band pulled taut and released. Blood squirted out of the skinny thigh of the monster and the scalpel flew from its grasp. It jerked backward, hit the bed, then crumpled to the floor with a sickening thud.

Someone was shrieking.

It was Andi. She had turned halfway at the sound of the gunshot, saw her uncle Jack with a pistol in both hands, the monster on the floor in a puddle of blood and her father's image on the screen, kneeling in front of the hooded man who was going to chop off his head—and she snapped, went completely hysterical, screaming and banging her fists on the footboard of the bed.

After that, everything happened at once. Jack stood with his gun pointed at the floor as the room suddenly filled with people. First nurses, doctors and orderlies, then Crock and the sheriff. The wounded little girl on the floor wasn't behaving like a severely injured child. She was a wild animal—kicking and screaming. It took three nurses and a burly orderly to subdue Cassidy, and it would have taken considerably more if loss of blood hadn't weakened her. She writhed until the contents of a syringe buried in her arm turned her into a limp rag doll. Crock took in the whole scene in one glance.

"Ariel's awake," Jack told him. It was hard to get the words out in the wake of the adrenaline rush that had sent his body into pulsing action. Jack stepped to the small child under the sheet and spoke her name softly. Ariel's eyes popped open and she stared at him in terror. The fear dissipated and the suggestion of a smile briefly lit her face.

"You did good, sweetheart," he told her. "Real good."

Then he turned to the sheriff. "You'll want this," he said and offered his weapon, handgrip first.

"Eventually, yeah," the sheriff said. "Not now. Keep it. You might need it."

Jack shoved the gun back into the waistband of his sweatpants and pulled his shirt out over it.

Then he went to the hysterical child at the foot of the bed. He tried to put his arms around Andi. She fought him off, shaking her head, beating on his chest with little fists, crying and wailing. He took hold of her in a bear hug from behind, letting her scream and kick and hit, expending her terror and sorrow. Eventually, she began to relax.

Activity went on around them, but they were an island. Andi and Jack. As soon as she stopped struggling, he lifted the crying child into his arms and carried her out of the room, past the pandemonium in the hallway to the stairway door. He shoved it open, stepped inside and sat down with Andi cradled in his lap on the steps leading up to the next floor. He rocked her back and forth as she sobbed, wiped her hair out of her face, hummed some nameless tune and felt the warmth of her body against his chest. Eventually, she stopped trembling. When she had wound down to hiccuping breaths, she drew back out of his arms and looked up at him.

Her eyes were red-rimmed, her face slathered with tears, her nose running. She was absolutely beautiful.

"They're g-g-going to cho—"

"No, sweetheart, nobody's going to hurt your daddy."

"How can you stop them? You don't even know where he is."

The last word went up in volume and tears threatened to return.

"Cut off the head of a snake, the rest of it dies." He gestured with his chin toward Ariel's room. "She knows where to find the snake."

IN ABSOLUTE DARKNESS, it was impossible for Daniel to judge the passage of time. Had Billy Ray been gone an hour? Five? Ten minutes? Daniel had tried counting slowly, but gave up the effort because he couldn't focus on it. He'd get to twenty-nine and go blank, didn't know if the next number was thirty or forty or fifty. Besides, what was the point? He couldn't count off every second of every minute until the end. And knowing how many were left, how many breaths, how many heartbeats—why would he want to know?

"Would you mind not doing that?"

The voice out of the nearby darkness startled Daniel. It wasn't that he'd forgotten about Jeff's presence, but he was no longer acutely aware of it, either. The rage had drained away after—how long? No way to tell. When the emotion had begun to fade, Daniel had clung to it, seized it with both hands and clenched his fists. But he couldn't hold onto that level of rage, couldn't maintain the intensity. The energy of the bright hot emotion was replaced by dull anger and loathing that ached like a rotten tooth.

"Doing what?"

"Tapping your foot."

"I'm not tapping my foot."

"Yes, you are. I've been listening to it for the past fifteen minutes."

"How do you know it's been fifteen minutes?"

"I've been counting the seconds."

The shared humanity of that—of counting—hit Daniel hard. Jeff was going to die, too, after all. They both had a finite number of seconds left.

"I guess I was tapping my foot to…stay in the world. The sensory deprivation…I needed something…"

"I think my right index finger is broken. I've been concentrating on the throbbing in it, willing myself to feel it, holding onto the pain. I even…squeezed it to make it hurt worse. Same reason, I guess."

Daniel said nothing else and the silence flowed in a wave back into the small space. But Daniel was aware of Jeff now, could almost feel him only a few feet away—the warmth of his body, maybe. Or smell him. The sweat. Fear sweat.

"How did you get here?" Daniel didn't decide to speak, merely heard himself say the words, maybe from the same reflex that had set his foot tapping. The silence was as oppressive as the dark.

"I rode here on a bug's back," Jeff said, with the lazy, sardonic ease that always yanked a knot of instant animosity in Daniel's belly. It did this time, too, but the blinding rage didn't return with it. "A cockroach. Several, actually."

Jeff told Daniel about the bugs without embellishment, and the story of how he'd lost it and had gone after Chapman Whitworth in a rueful tone without rationalization or self-justification. Daniel listened in growing horror. The thought of being covered in crawling bugs—

In the cave, when they were kids, Daniel had only looked back once, and from that moment on his skin had crawled in revulsion and horror. What Comes Behind. The sea of spiders and slithering snakes out there in the dark beyond the light. And the big one he never saw until it was too late.

"Daniel?" Jeff's voice pierced the profound dark.

"What?"

"You made a sound, a cry."

"I've...met some of his 'bugs.'" Daniel didn't elaborate and Jeff asked for no explanation.

The silence returned.

Then Daniel heard his own voice again, speaking his thoughts out into the darkness. "The efreet put a black widow spider into the cuff of my pants in the cave and I carried it home with me. It crawled out when my parents were away and I was babysitting my little sister."

The memory of her precious face, jade green eyes

sparkling, filled his mind so bright it drove the darkness into the corners.

"She held it out to me, said it tickled her palm." He paused and his voice was as thin and fragile as tissue paper. "'Look it, Dan-Dan.' That's what she called me. 'Look I find.'"

"How old was she?"

"Three."

"How old were you?"

"Twelve." Daniel didn't will his voice to continue speaking, but it went on without him. "The spider turned toward me, looked at me before it bit her." He'd never told that part to anybody. Not Jack. Not Theresa. Not Becca. No one. It had been his private agony.

"I tried to get help. I picked her up and carried her, ran as fast as...Marianne died in my arms."

Daniel heard a groan from the darkness. Jeff's voice was husky. "I'm sorry, Daniel," he said. And maybe he was.

Chapter Twenty-One

Becca and Theresa sat across from each other at the kitchen table, each nursing a cup of cold coffee. They said nothing. Theresa didn't look good. Though her skin was so dark it was hard to tell, Becca could see the old woman's face had a gray pallor. The doctor'd said she was to come to his office in Lancaster at the slightest sign of an infection and maybe...

But first, they had to bury Biscuit.

Becca had gotten a spade from the garage and begun to dig a hole in the shade of the pink dogwood tree by the fence as soon as there was enough light in the morning sky to see. Though there was frost on the grass, the ground was not frozen. But it was so full of roots she abandoned that spot and tried one nearer the house, next to the rose trellis beside the gate. She found digging easier there, but still the ground was hard and she was neither big nor strong. By the time she had a hole dug two feet deep and three feet across, she was exhausted. If it wasn't deep enough...

Well, it would have to do anyway.

Theresa scooted her chair back slowly and got to her feet.

"We best get to it, child," she said. "I'll go get Biscuit."

"He's too big for you to be lifting." Theresa's back had been giving her trouble off and on ever since the day she'd come to Bradford's Ridge with Jeff to find Becca. She wasn't wearing her cookie-sheet corset now and she might really hurt herself. "I'll get him."

Theresa put her hand on Becca's arm. "Let me carry him this one last time."

Theresa moved slowly toward the garage, where they had laid the animal on the floor, wrapped in a blanket. When she returned carrying him, Becca could see that he'd already gotten stiff. Theresa held the blanket-covered dog tenderly against her breast—stiff as he was—and the two women went together out into the backyard.

It was chilly. Neither she nor Theresa had stopped to put on a jacket, but they didn't care about the cold.

Becca dropped to her knees beside the grave and Theresa handed her the dog to lower into the shallow hole. That was when Becca saw it. The bandage on one of the rat bites on Theresa's calf had come loose, and Becca could see that the area around it was puffy and thick yellow liquid oozed out.

"Lord, I don't know about dogs and going to heaven and such," Theresa said as Becca got to her feet, dusted the dirt off her knees and stood beside her. "The Bible don't say one way or the other, so I guess we's free to speculate. I never give it much thought before Biscuit. Now, I think…I choose to believe that at this very moment Biscuit is running around chasing butterflies in heaven." She sucked in a shuddering breath but didn't break down. "He was a good dog. You look after him for me 'til I get there."

Theresa said nothing as Becca shoveled back into the

hole the dirt she had dug out of it, then tamped it down in a mound on top. There was no cross. Maybe someday when they had time to…maybe someday.

"You need to get dressed now," Becca said and Theresa looked at her quizzically. "I'm calling the doctor and taking you in to see him. One of the bites on your leg is infected."

Theresa didn't argue, merely turned away from the grave and walked ponderously toward the house.

THERESA FELT her age as she stood on the sidewalk—had to stand, wasn't nowhere to sit—while Becca circled the block, looking for a parking space near Lancaster North, one of four big buildings that formed Lancaster Plaza, where Dr. Paul Richardson's office was located. Becca had took to driving again like a pig to mud. Actually seemed to enjoy it. She didn't have her license yet, but Theresa wasn't up to driving today, so she give her the wheel anyway.

Theresa felt more than old—old and sick, too. She felt beat down. The ever-present evil was sucking the life out of her. But she was too tired even to protest. God knew how old she was. He was sending her down into a dark hole in the ground to fight a monster, so must be he knew she could handle it—or planned to take her on home during the fight, which was fine with her, too.

The weight of what she, Daniel, Jack and Becca was gone have to do when they found the efreet was painted on the backdrop of Andi's vision. God give visions for a reason. As a warning, so people could get ready for somethin'. Or so they could stop some bad thing from happenin'. Theresa suddenly smiled as Isaac's face burst full blown into her mind.

They'd been standing in the back of the church right

after services and he'd tugged on her sleeve and drawn himself up serious like—and him not even nine years old. "Why didn't God tell Joseph what he wanted him to know? Why'd God make him figure it out on his own?"

"I don't rightly know," she'd said, and he'd crossed his arms over his little chest and said all self-righteous, "If I was God, I'd say things flat out and clear. Or I'd write them on the sky with a red Magic Marker." Then he'd pantomimed the act of writing. "'Dear Joseph. There is going to be a famine, so you need to save up food. Sincerely, your friend, God.'"

She chuckled at the memory, but the mirth drained away as Andi's latest description of the Big Bad Thing filled her head. Andi had said last night that it was getting bigger, closer. A roaring boom, smoke, fire, people screaming, pieces of bodies flying through the air. A bomb, of course, but that didn't narrow it down much. An explosion like them ones at that mall in Minnesota and the restaurant in Arizona—innocent people ripped apart. Theresa shuddered, a full body shake that made her so weak she was afraid she was gonna have to sit down right there on the sidewalk if Becca didn't get here pretty soon.

"There's a…leg, only a leg, not the whole person, like it'd been torn off at the knee, and blood's coming out of it," Andi'd said. "On the foot—the shoe it's wearing is funny-looking. The toe's all curled up."

She'd said there were bodies of "dead people, white and pasty and all bandaged up." Which didn't make no sense at all 'cause how could they have been bandaged already if they'd just got injured? "And this big gold Frisbee flies through the air and hits a man wearing a cowboy hat and a vest like Woody's and almost cuts him in half."

Theresa didn't know who Woody might be. But did the hat mean the Big Bad Thing was going to happen in

Texas, maybe? Big place to search for a bomb, Texas was. "And he falls down on top of the Frisbee, bleeding on the letters."

OSW7.

Theresa and all the others had racked their brains, trying to figure out what that could mean but had come up with nothing. Jack had Googled it. It was the abbreviation of the scientific name for some protein. It was the number on a race car. It was a kind of fishhook with little brass beads on it. It was the username for some guy on Instagram in Ecuador, the brand of a lady's watch, and of accessories to put on trucks, and other random, meaningless things. They'd checked them all out, every one, but none of them had anything to do with golden Frisbees or with folks getting blown up and dying.

Theresa and Becca spent more than two hours at the doctor's office—most of that time waiting to see him, of course. On account of it being Halloween, one of the receptionists was dressed up like Princess Leia—looked like she had cinnamon rolls stuck to both ears—and the other was all green, likely supposed to be Yoda. Or Kermit the Frog. Or the Incredible Hulk. Maybe a head of lettuce.

While Becca read a five-month-old magazine full of stuff about the royal wedding that'd done come and gone, Theresa thumbed through the morning newspaper. Course, there was Chapman Whitworth's picture smack on the front page—not by his lonesome, though, but alongside the other candidates for the nomination. They'd be guests at the Better Day Society ball tonight at the Rivergate's Balloon Ballroom on the waterfront.

Theresa'd worked as a hotel maid in lots of places, but the Rivergate had been one of her all-time favorites. She liked to stand in that top-floor ballroom at night, look up at the stars and watch the balloon shows. The roof was retractable like the roof of Lucas Stadium in Indianapolis, where she and Bishop had gone that time to see the Drum Corps International Championships.

The Balloon Ballroom often filled the night sky over Cincinnati with balloons. Red and green ones at Christmastime, orange and black at Halloween, green ones on Saint Patrick's Day, red-white-and-blue ones on the Fourth of July—and random multicolored ones for other occasions, both public and private, throughout the year.

The pillars in the huge ballroom were shaped like tree trunks, and hundreds of helium-filled balloons tied with strings to tiny hooks on the limbs formed the leaves. They could all be released at once by retracting the hooks, or guests could remove the balloons from the trees and hold them by the strings until some signal to set them free.

Sometimes, the balloons fell down instead of floating up. The newspaper story said that was what was planned for the ball tonight. Mesh netting filled with thousands of tiny balloons no bigger than a fist—somebody told her once they was more'n ten thousand of 'em—would be stretched across the opening in the roof and ceiling. She'd been there when they released balloons like that, watched the air fill solid with 'em as they fell to the floor.

When the doctor finally took a look at Theresa's leg, he ordered the nurse to clean it all out and put a fresh bandage on it, and to give her a shot that hurt worse than them bites ever did—right in her backside! She got another prescription, too, and instructions to put hydrogen peroxide on all them bites twice a day. That was gone feel swell.

Becca left Theresa on the sidewalk where she'd waited before and went down the street for the car. By the time Becca pulled up in front of the building, Theresa had stood so long her legs was all trembly-like. When she stepped out into the street to get in the car, she come real close to face-planting on the asphalt, stubbing her toe on a manhole cover that was sticking up just enough to—

Theresa stopped and stood totally still, looking down at the street. Then she walked slowly around in a circle. Becca leaned across the front seat, rolled down the passenger side window and called out to her, "Get in. This is a no parking zone."

"You need to git out and come over here and look at this."

Becca got out of the car, put it in park right there in the street, and came to stand beside Theresa.

"What is it you want me to see?"

Theresa pointed at the storm drain cover she'd stumbled over. "What's that mean?"

"It's initials, stands for Lancaster Metropolitan Sewer District," Becca said.

Theresa walked slowly around to the other side of the manhole cover. "Now, come look at it from over here."

Becca followed her, looked down, and when she saw it, she gasped.

LMSD read upside down became O—with one side smashed flat just like Andi'd said—SW7.

"That Frisbee flying through the air was turning over and over, so Andi seen it upside down!"

"OSW7 is a manhole cover?" Becca was incredulous.

Theresa felt her throat tighten so she could barely talk. "That newspaper story about the Better Day Society said they give a community service award every year to some business for being a 'good corporate neighbor.' The award is a gold-plated manhole cover."

Becca looked up, her eyes huge. "It's here, then," she said, her voice a whisper of awe and dread. "Right here in Lancaster. Somebody's going to blow up that ball tonight."

Then all the pieces fell into place and everything Andi'd seen made sense. The Better Day Society's ball was a costume ball! People would be dressed up like witches with curled-toe shoes, white-faced zombies in bandages or cowboys.

"But isn't Chapman Whitworth supposed to be there?" Becca asked.

"Uh-huh. And so is every one of the other candidates that's runnin' against him! All of them together in one spot. I'd say Mr. Whitworth's likely to be a no-show. Or he'll get an urgent call of nature so he just happens to be out of the room when the fun starts."

"We have to stop this!" Becca said.

"Course we do."

"How?"

"We got to tell somebody…warn…"

But even as she said the words, Theresa knew how futile that would be:

Somebody's going to blow up the Better Day Society's ball tonight!!

And you know that because…?

Because a little girl saw it in a vision.

Riiiight.

It was like when Andi'd been kidnapped and Daniel couldn't call the FBI. He knew details about where she was being held that he couldn't tell the police because they'd never have believed Andi's vision meant anything.

So Jack'd had to go find her his own self.

Jack!

"We got to call Jack," Theresa said, snatching her cell phone out of her purse. "He's gone have to…do something." The call went directly to voicemail. Jack's phone was turned off. She tried Crock's. His rang, but he didn't answer.

Theresa didn't even realize she was trembling until Becca took her by the elbow and directed her to the car.

"Come on," Becca said. "I'm taking you home. We'll keep trying Jack on the way."

~

TIME RACED AHEAD, stopped, looked over its shoulder and waited for Jeff to catch up. Then off it went again. Had he always breathed this slow? Or was it fast? Was he panting?

He jumped at every imagined sound—and they had to be imagined, didn't they? What was there in a cave to make noise? Blind cave fish weren't a particularly rambunctious lot as fish go, at least not as far as he knew. Now, blind cave crickets were another thing altogether. Crickets would—

What was that?

Was it footsteps? Was Billy Ray coming to chop off their heads?

Coming to chop off their heads—you die!

Lions and tigers and bears—oh my!

He waited, breathless, heart pounding.

Nothing.

But the mad hammering of his heart took a long time to subside. Or did it? Who knew? The absolute darkness erased the borders, the fences both real and psychological that fit the essential you snug on one side and everything else on the other. He didn't know anymore where he stopped and forever-dark started. He felt himself leaking away into it little by little, a small steady stream, and when there was light again, if there ever was light again, part of him would be missing. Some essential element of his Jeff-ness was being gobbled up by the Black Nothing.

He concentrated on his throbbing nose and on the pain that stabbed all the way up his arm whenever he moved his finger. That helped to keep him tethered in reality. Not that reality was exactly a tour bus destination right now. In the place called "reality," Jefferson Monroe Kendrick was about to die—a singularly grizzly death.

The Jeff Kendrick who'd cheated to pass the bar examination, using an elaborate scheme that surely required more time and energy than studying for the exam would have taken. And certainly much more ingenuity, initiative and resourcefulness.

The Jeff Kendrick who had shirts to pick up at the laundry, who'd just paid a five-hundred-dollar annual fee on a gym membership, and who now would never climb Mount Everest, go skinny-dipping in the Mediterranean with some dark-eyed Italian beauty or hang glide over a volcano in Hawaii—or any of the other things on his bucket list. Shoot, he'd never even get to see the final Batman movie! He was going to die! Today. In how many minutes—who knew?—he was going to cease to exist on this planet.

Was that it? You just ceased to exist?

He genuinely did not know, but he suspected Daniel did. No, he was certain Daniel did. Daniel Burke was…

Was what?

Everything Jeff Kendrick should have been, could have been, but wasn't.

Chapter Twenty-Two

Neither Jack nor Crock ever picked up. Becca reached the sheriff, though, and he promised to have Jack call. Theresa was sitting at her kitchen table when her phone finally rang in her hand, startling her so she almost dropped it.

"Jack, somethin' terrible's 'bout to happen," she told him, all the pent-up scared flooding out with the words.

"I know," he said. The sound of his voice—she'd never heard that tone before—stopped her.

"How do you know? Me and Becca just did figure it out our own selves."

"Figure what out? You didn't see it on television?"

"See what on television?"

"Turn the television on. It's still all over the news."

Becca crossed the room and turned on the set. She changed the channel a time or two, looking for—an image burst on the screen that took a second to process. Two men were—Daniel!—on their knees.

The sight swallowed up every bit of oxygen in the air. Theresa heard Becca cry out from a great distance and then she could hear the voice of the news anchor reading from an email he said had been sent to all the national media outlets last night.

"No one is safe. Nowhere is safe. The blood of these two will herald the shedding of blood this day in cities all across the country. The revolution has begun, and from the ashes of destruction will rise the phoenix of a new order. A new America. Be afraid. Be very afraid."

Theresa was afraid, alright. So scared for Daniel she had to swallow hard to keep from chucking up her breakfast.

Daniel. They was a man standin' behind him a-fixin' to chop off his head!

"Only one voice in American politics called this one," the talking head droned on as Theresa's eyes gobbled up Daniel's face. He'd been beat up somethin' fierce.

"Democratic party candidate Chapman Whitworth has been saying ever since he entered the race that domestic terrorism posed the greatest threat to America."

The screen then showed a clip of one of Whitworth's speeches.

"Chasing hooded figures in the desert is a dangerous misdirection of resources. We must look within our own borders for those who seek to destroy us."

Jack had been right! All that death, all those innocent people—Chapman Whitworth had planned and executed it all. And he meant to orchestrate more death—would attack other cities just like he was planning to do in Cincinnati. Was she and Becca supposed to stop them other attacks, too? How did God intend to pull that off?

"…know where the efreet is," Jack was saying and she tried to concentrate, focus on that. "Ariel told us. We have to get to it to…stop it. That's Daniel's only hope. The only hope of all the people Whitworth is planning to massacre today. That doesn't give us much time and it'll take you and Becca an hour and a half to get here."

Theresa couldn't breathe. There was a sudden tightness in her chest, an overwhelming sense that something was terribly wrong with all this. Like she'd felt the whole time Chapman Whitworth was tricking them into getting him publicity. She'd ignored the feeling then, but it was bigger and stronger now and she wasn't gone ignore it again!

"You got to give me some time." Theresa choked out the words, then shoved the phone at Becca. "You tell him what we know about them letters and that manhole cover. And tell him we'll call him back."

She got up from the table and walked in an unsteady gait out of the kitchen and down the hallway to Bishop's office. She pushed the door open. She could see brown bloodstains on the floor where they'd killed the snake last night. She stood for a moment on the threshold, then stepped inside and closed the door behind her.

Theresa had only been in this room three or four times in all the long years she and Bishop had lived in this house. Two walls were covered with floor-to-ceiling bookcases so jammed with books they spilled out onto the floor. And even more volumes had been shoved into the space between the tops of the books and the bottoms of the shelves above. Becca'd put the bulletin board back up on the wall and hung on the rack above it the scimitar Theresa'd used to kill the snake.

She stood looking at the scimitar for a moment, hadn't never paid much heed to it before. It was old, with swirls and hand-carved designs and symbols on the handle that might have been words in some language she didn't know. The blade was silver, maybe even real silver from the tarnished look of it, and it coulda sliced through a solid hickory mop handle easy as it did that snake.

She never come in Bishop's study or into the one in their house in Bradford's Ridge because Bishop didn't want her to. And she didn't want to, neither. She knew what was in all them books—some so old the bindings had rotted away so's Bishop'd had to lift 'em careful or they'd fall apart in his hands. On the pages of them books was descriptions of pure evil. What it looked like. What it acted like. What it done in the world. On and on.

How that man of hers—and frail little Becca!—had come in here day after day and let consummate evil out of them books into the air with 'em was more than Theresa could comprehend.

She went to the desk and sat down in Bishop's chair, all broke down from him sittin' in it, and let the reality sink in. Jack knew where the efreet was hidin' and needed her and Becca to hurry on down there so's they could go into that dark evil hidey-hole and do what it was they had to do. Or maybe die tryin'.

But Theresa's mind kept swerving away from that and back to them people who was gone be at the Better Day Society ball.

What was gone happen to them? They was expecting more than a thousand people, all decked out in costumes and looking forward to havin' theirselves a good time. And somebody—maybe a whole bunch of somebodies for all she knew—was working right this minute on a plan to butcher the lot of them. Every last one.

Fire. Smoke. Broken glass. Body parts flying through the air.

A Frisbee with OSW7—no, with LMSD—printed on it cutting a man in half.

Jack wasn't gone come back here and save them people

like he saved Andi. He couldn't. Not with what he had to do, what he'd been assigned to do. So was all them people just gone have to get murdered?

She closed her eyes and prayed.

What are you doin' here, Lord? You just want me to get in the car and drive away and let all them people get blown into little bitty pieces?

I know you done said I got to go fight this—

She stopped then, thinking.

When was that, exactly? When was it God had picked her out to do battle with the efreet?

Why, it was…was…

Dawning awareness lit her mind like turning up the dimmer switch on the chandelier in Miss Minnie and Mr. Gerald's foyer.

Point of fact was it'd been Theresa who'd decided that was her job, not God. She'd made up her mind she was s'posed to take Bishop's place and she hadn't never bothered to run that decision by God to see what he might have to say about it one way or the other.

Maybe that wasn't what she was s'posed to do a'tall.

It'd been orchestrated so's she and Becca wasn't down there in Bradford's Ridge right now, when it was time.

Things happened for a reason.

When she returned to the kitchen, where Becca sat with big tears streaming down her cheeks, Theresa felt even more exhausted than she had before, if that was possible. She knew her face showed it. Had to. She was running pretty near empty now and wasn't no way to hide a thing like that. It occurred to her, not for the first time, that she might not survive what lay ahead. Might be that none of them would. That wasn't for her to say, though. Her job was to suit up and show up—as Bishop used to say—and let those a whole lot higher on the food chain than a fat old woman figure out the rest of it.

"Do what you done before, sugar," Theresa said, gesturing to the phone in Becca's hand. "That FaceTime thing. We all need to talk."

When Jack's face appeared in the phone's view window, Theresa sat down next to her, snuggled close so they could both see.

"Everybody there on that end?" she asked Jack. "We all need to have a say in this."

"All aboard," Jack said, panning the phone so Theresa could see the others. They had gotten into Jack's car—for privacy, Theresa supposed. Crock was in the front passenger seat and Andi leaned over from the backseat.

Theresa got right to the point. "Me and Becca...we ain't gone be comin' down there today, Jack."

Becca stared at Theresa, dumbstruck. "What do you mean we're not going?"

Theresa rolled her eyes. "How many things can 'we not going' mean, child? We stayin' here. The thing down in Bradford's Ridge—it's not for us to do."

Jack's face registered shock, distress and fear. He tried real hard to keep emotion out of his voice when he spoke. He didn't manage it, but he did try.

"You mean...I'm going to...go after the efreet alone?"

"That ain't what I said. I said that task there is not what's been laid out for me and Becca to do. But you ain't gone be by yourself. You'll have Crock and Andi with you."

IT BUILT up and built up until it just finally blew out of Jeff's mouth and into the world.

"This is an awfully small place to have such a big

elephant in the middle of the room," he said. "What we're not talking about...who we're not talking about is—"

"Don't!" Daniel's voice came out of a silence as thick as mud. "Just...don't."

"Look, I don't know about this kind of thing—you do, you're the minister. All I know is that we're both going to stop breathing, permanently, in—"

"Do you think I want to spend my last breaths talking about...my wife and you?" Suddenly, Daniel barked out a sardonic laugh. "This ought to be one of Dante's Nine Levels of Hell—spending your last hours on earth locked in a dark room with the man who was sleeping with the woman you love."

"Or with the man who got her first. Who gave her his name. Who fathered her child."

The silence breathed. In and out. Jeff could hear the sound of it pounding like surf in his ears.

"You loved Emily." It wasn't even a question. Daniel's voice was devoid of emotion, sounding like an automated attendant.

"Not...as well as you did. Or as purely as you did. Or as faithfully as you did. I'm not the man you are, Daniel. But with whatever there is in me to love, I gave it all to Emily."

The silence lasted one heartbeat. Two. When the question came out of the darkness, Jeff was sure Daniel Burke would rather have cut his own tongue out than ask it.

"And did she—?"

"Love me?" Jeff let the silent surf pound, listening to it crash on the rocks again and again. "If you'd asked me a week ago, I'd have puffed out my chest and said absolutely! That's what I told myself, convinced myself. But the truth...all the truth I know is that I think...not."

He was surprised that the last word came out in a

strangled sob. He hadn't known he was going to say that. If he planned it, he wouldn't have said any of it. Because now that he'd said it, he had to face the reality that it was —to the best of his understanding—true. She'd been smitten with him, enjoyed him, wanted him. But she hadn't loved him, not really. She'd said as much.

"Her cell phone…after she died, what did you do with it?" Jeff asked. "Did you read her texts?"

"I didn't spy on Emily!" Daniel's voice was as full of emotion then as it had been devoid of emotion before. "I think he…Victor Alexander stomped it. It was lying broken on the floor beside…"

Beside her body.

Jeff heard himself speaking again, words he'd never even thought before, truth he hadn't accepted at the time and had never even peeked at in the months since.

"I sent her a text that day, that afternoon right before…" He dragged his mind away from the image of her his pain had sketched in his mind when he'd learned she'd been murdered, an image that'd haunted the dark hallways of his worst nightmares ever since. For all its horrific detail, though, it was imaginary. Daniel had seen reality. "I just asked her, 'Are you okay?'"

"Why are you telling me this—do you really think I want to hear about your conversations, what you said to each other!"

"She texted me back. The time stamp…it was a few minutes before she died." She hadn't meant it, he'd told himself. She was just upset. He'd change her mind. As soon as he saw her, held her, kissed her…

He felt a sudden lump in his throat and had trouble pushing the words out into the darkness, heard his voice thick and tear-clotted. "She said, 'It's over, Jeff. I'm sorry. Goodbye.'"

The silence flowed like oil back into his ears.

"Why are you telling me this?" It was the same question, but it was only that this time—a question.

"Oh, don't think I would have let that be the end of it," Jeff said. "Just: 'Bye-bye, see ya, have a nice life.' No way! I'd have gone after her, I'd…"

He would have done anything to win her back. No matter what it took. He'd never have let her go. But before he had a chance, a demon had stolen her from him. From both of them. "I'm telling you because you have a right to know…Emily picked you."

As Jeff Kendrick accepted the truth of those words for the first time, he decided dying wasn't such a bad thing after all.

A STAB WOUND in the thigh was not the most serious injury Major Charles Crocker had sustained in more than a quarter of a century in law enforcement. Not even close. He'd been a beat patrolman in Chicago in 1980, off duty, on his way to the hospital for the birth of his second child, when an "officer needs assistance" call came over the radio. He'd been the closest unit, so he'd responded to the call and found an officer pinned down by a teenager hyped-up on meth, waving a pistol around, trying to shoot out all the streetlights. In a hurry to cap the kid so he could be on his way, Crock tried to take him down before any more backup arrived. That departure from procedure earned him a bullet in the kneecap at point-blank range—and a lifetime devotion to following safety protocols. If the kid'd been using anything but a .22-caliber popgun, Crock probably would never have walked again. Back then, there was no such thing as knee-replacement surgery. As it was, the subsequent limp contributed to the peculiar bow-legged gait that had been mimicked unmercifully by every officer who'd served with him in the thirty-three years since.

The knee wasn't his only world-class wound. A few years after that, working crowd control during a riot over some perceived injustice or another, Crock had been stabbed in the side with an icepick that slid in between the front and back panels of his Kevlar vest. Punctured a lung.

He'd once fought off the attack of a pit bull, too, and had the scars on his hands and arms to prove it. He'd been whacked on the head more times than he could count and kicked in the privates easily as many.

But no injury he'd ever sustained in all those years had caused him as much pain as the one he'd suffered when a little boy with curly brown hair stabbed a pair of scissors into his leg.

It hurt all out of proportion to the severity of the injury, spearing jagged shards of pain in heartbeat bursts through his body from his groin to his knee. The agonizing throb, throb, throb hadn't even blinked at the massive doses of pain relievers he'd popped like some crackhead after he left the hospital. The drugs had made him dopey —that was all—so he'd stopped taking them, just gutted it out. He'd gnawed down to splinters every cinnamon tooth-pick he'd brought with him as the pain robbed him of even a dozing rest last night. He'd been sitting up in a chair fully dressed—why go to bed if he wasn't going to sleep?— when the troops had arrived that Jack had summoned to care for Ariel Murphy.

And the thing was, he knew why the wound hurt so bad. There was pure evil in it. It was not random violence by a meth-head teenager, it had not been inflicted by a fanatic in the throes of mob mentality or some drunk in a bar, angling for a fight. It was focused, intentional evil from the pit of hell itself. He'd seen it in the little boy's eyes as he drove the scissors as far as he could into Crock's leg—a maniacal, unrestrained, raging hatred that was breathtaking in its ferocity. Crock had barely caught the briefest glimpse of the demon's shadow and that had been bad enough. He could not imagine the horror it must have been for three twelve-year-old children years ago to behold a demon prince up close and personal.

Now, it looked like Theresa intended for him to find out.

He was the first to react to her glib pronouncement that he was to accompany Jack and Andi—Andi!—into the belly of the beast, into the cave in the bowels of the earth where hell had opened up a door into the world and evil had slithered unencumbered through it.

"Whoa there," he said. "Let's back up, take the bologna off the bread and start over with this sandwich. What could possibly make you think I'm qualified to fight an efreet?"

"Course you ain't qualified," Theresa said. Her big earnest face filled the whole screen of Jack's phone. Crock wished Becca would tell her to hold it farther out in front of her because she had a mildly cyclops-ian look. "Ain't none of us qualified, come to that. God don't need qualified, he just—"

"Needs willing. I know, you said that before. But there's unqualified and then there's un-qualified. I haven't darkened the door of a church since sometime during the Bush administration—Bush one. His first term. And come to think of it, that was a synagogue, not a church—for a bar mitzvah."

He knew he was babbling, dodging and weaving while he tried to get his mind to face head-on what she was suggesting. "Maybe a synagogue'd get you a few points, but not nearly enough—"

"It ain't about points, Major Crocker," she said. "It's about having a pure soul." She rushed on before he could interrupt. "I don't mean one ain't got no splotches on it. We all got them and some of us's got more'n others. I mean a soul that's protected by God as one of his own."

Okay, he was a believer. Check that box. But so were millions of other people, any one of them better suited to this task than he was.

"You think it's an accident that it's come to this?" Theresa wasn't just talking to Crock anymore but to all of them. "Like maybe God was busy makin' babies or designin' butterflies or paintin' rainbows in the sky and all that's happening here just kinda slipped his notice? Don't you see? God orchestrated it this way—with you there and us here. So that means it's the way God had in mind to do it all along."

There was silence. Nobody spoke. But Crock couldn't let go yet.

"You...the rest of you, you've been thinking about this, or things like this, your whole lives." In his own ears, his voice sounded echoey and hollow, like he was speaking out of the bottom of a rain barrel. "How am I supposed to get ready to fight a demon, to cast it out or whatever it is we're supposed to do with it, in half an hour?"

"Ain't no way to get 'ready' to cast out a demon. You just got to stand, refuse to be cowed by pure evil. There ain't nothin' to prepare you for a thing like that. Ain't like you can practice—get a little better at it and a little better at it 'til you finally master the skill. Either you can do it or you can't."

Crock felt a stab of pain in his leg. The pain of evil. And the thought of seeing face-to-face an evil far more powerful than what glowed in the eyes of the little boy who'd stabbed him froze his breath in his throat and he couldn't speak.

Theresa spoke to him again. Her voice was gentle and kind. "Major Crocker...Crock...I'll admit you is an unlikely choice, but Moses wouldn't have been no first-round draft pick, neither."

He finally managed to get words out. "Just my luck." His voice was airless, though, with no volume at all. "The one-millionth customer, winner of a year's supply of microwave popcorn."

"It ain't luck. It ain't chance. He picked you to do this —for a reason, though it ain't likely you'll ever find out what that reason is. You told me God give you back your life twice and you been askin' why for years. I s'pect this is why."

Chapter Twenty-Three

Daniel was trying to concentrate, but the dark and silence made it hard. It was as if the pressure of the world and light and people and sound was the force that kept all the thoughts and intentions inside his head. And when that force was taken away, the contents of his mind leaked out into the nothingness and evaporated—disappeared like the smoke from a dying campfire.

He needed to make an accounting of himself. That was what you did, right? You were minutes—how many?—away from coming face-to-face with God, so you took some kind of moral inventory. Saw where you stood.

Oh, Daniel had proclaimed from the pulpit for years that there existed no celestial scorecard where more yes votes than no votes would get you in. Heaven was a gift—one you didn't and couldn't earn.

And all that sounded profound and pious—if you said it with an appropriately weighty level of humility and gratitude. It was particularly engaging if you added a little hitch in your voice to indicate that perhaps—just perhaps —you were fighting back tears.

When the image-magnification screen blew your face up twenty feet tall and cameras fed the image live into the homes of hundreds of thousands of people, believability was measured in millimeters, in knowing exactly how far to duck your chin when you prayed so the overhead lights wouldn't drape the shadow of your nose down your lip in a black smudge that looked like a cleft pallet scar.

But all those years of sermons didn't mean squat now! It didn't matter what he'd said. What he had to figure out now, at the end, was what he really believed. Good, evil, heaven, hell, God, Satan. Those were not metaphysical terms—not anymore. They were walking-around-in-an-ordinary-world reality. He knew. He'd seen.

What about the rest of it, though? Not the belief system he kept tucked in his wallet like a Triple A card to rescue him when he got in trouble—fire insurance, some people called it. What was real? What was true?

True.

The word seemed to float like a brightly lit movie title on a marquis in the darkness in front of him. Then it began to blink, a Joe's Beer Joint sign, on and off, on and off, faster and faster. He shook his head violently to clear his vision and the motion flung apart the thoughts he'd been so carefully cobbling together.

What scuttled in behind them to fill the darkness of his mind was absolute chaos. Unmitigated confusion. The roaring turmoil of an earthquake, the grinding rumble of rocks, dirt and boulders dropping away, crumbling and falling into a bottomless pit of utter darkness.

Then Theresa spoke in his head—the words she'd said that day she'd come to Andi's hospital room and called Daniel a phony. She sounded like a voice-over in a catastrophe movie now, with the tumult rumbling so loud behind her he had to strain to hear.

"You done traded in real faith for 'religion' from the Dollar General Store—the kind that don't cost nothing and ain't worth nothin'. You's just skatin' around on the shiny outside of believing, gliding along barely even touching the surface."

He'd been offended, of course.

And she'd been right, of course.

The maelstrom roared on, its rumble an avalanche in his head. The whole world was coming apart, imploding. Mountains fell in on themselves, their jagged peaks hurling toward the earth like serrated swords, impaling the world on their spikes. Gigantic cracks formed in the ground and raced out across it, the split in a melon rushing out ahead of the knife, tearing the world asunder with great ripping, straining sounds.

Andi's face burst into his mind, shining like a thousand suns. It lit the great darkness of the empty pit eating the world. The rumbling and roaring ceased; land masses stopped moving. Chaos shrank away from her brilliance, cowering small and terrified before the splendor of it. At that moment, Daniel's confusion didn't matter, his questions didn't matter, his belief system didn't matter. Having his head chopped off didn't matter.

All that mattered was Andi!

Where was she?

Who was taking care of her?

Was she alone?

Was she safe?

Was she hurt?

Was she frightened?

Was she calling for her daddy?

He loved that child. Loving that little girl was the purest, best, most holy thing Daniel Burke had ever done!

He paused, stopped breathing.

That was it, then, wasn't it.

Love.

As you sucked in your final breath at the end of all things, love was what mattered. It was all that mattered.

Love was true.

Love was good, too, the force that stood against the evil Daniel had not wanted to know existed. The evil he'd caught glimpses of—in the eyes of the madman who'd butchered Emily, and distorting the innocent features of a little girl who looked like a life-sized Raggedy Ann doll.

If good really existed, were true, all the rest of it was true, too—all the things he'd said Sunday after Sunday about good versus evil and light against darkness. And about love that was pure and good. He hadn't really believed a single word of it when he'd said it—in feigned faith and counterfeit humility. But his glib insincerity didn't change reality. It was still true.

What was it Jack had told Jeff—that he'd been struggling to wedge truth into the shape of his personal belief system? That was backwards, of course. What was required of all of them, Jack and Daniel and the others, was to re-form their personal belief systems into the shape of truth.

Silence settled back around Daniel then, gentle, a warm blanket on a cold night. There was just one more thing now, here at the end—the matter of Jeff Kendrick to attend to before it was all over.

IT TOOK Jack a few moments to absorb the enormity of Theresa's words. She and Becca weren't coming. So it wasn't going to go down the way Jack had designed it in his head. As soon as pieces of memory about the beast began to form in their minds, they'd all understood they were going to have to complete the job they'd started years ago. It had been a given who the cast of characters would be. The three musketeers would take up where they'd left off in 1985—wherever that was. He, Daniel and Becca would finish the task they'd begun when they were twelve years old.

And this time, they wouldn't be all on their own. This time, Theresa Washington, a spiritual leviathan, would lead the charge.

Then his plan began to fall apart. Daniel'd been kidnapped. And now Theresa was saying she and Becca wouldn't be on the expedition, either. The enormity of it rammed a boot into his belly. He—Jack Carpenter—would be in charge.

He and Crock would have to do it on their own—because Andi was not setting foot in that cave. That point was absolutely nonnegotiable.

"Andi's not going," he said firmly.

Theresa didn't argue with him, just asked, "How you figure to do it without her?"

"We'll have to come up with something because Andi's not going anywhere near that cave."

"Don't you think maybe you'd ought to ask her how she feels 'bout that?"

"It doesn't matter how she feels about it. For crying out loud, Theresa, she's ten years old. She's not old enough to make a decision like that."

"That child's a whole lot older than ten and you know it, Jack."

"I'm scared, Uncle Jack," Andi said. He turned from the image of Theresa on the screen to the little girl leaned over the front seat from the back. The child's face was white. All the blood had drained out of it and she was so pale her lips almost looked blue. He reached over and patted her arm.

"Of course you're scared, sweetheart. But you'll be safe here—I'll see if you can stay with the sheriff for a little while. You liked him and he has a little girl about your age."

"No, it's not safe here," she said.

"Why, sure it is. The sheriff has a gun almost as big as mine and—"

"It's not safe anywhere," she said. Theresa was right. She wasn't ten years old.

"When Mr. Bishop came into Miss Lunde's classroom that day, I was in the storage closet, sharpening my pencil. So I just closed the door and the man with the demon made out of flies didn't know I was there."

The non sequitur was jarring.

"That man, the one who killed Mommy, do you know what he said?"

"No, what did he say?"

"He told her he didn't want two hostages. Either she had to die or I did, and she told him that he didn't have a decision to make, that he'd have to kill her to get to me. She told me to run and hide and I hid where he'd never find me." She paused for a beat, then whispered, "I heard the gunshot, though."

Andi was quiet then, a thousand-mile stare in her eyes, looking at nothing, or maybe at something they couldn't see, out the front window.

"Why did you tell me that story, honey?" As he said it, Jack felt a hole begin to open up in front of him. He was standing on the edge, the ground crumbling beneath his feet.

She didn't respond, like she hadn't heard him.

"Andi...why—?"

She turned to look at him; then she shook her head and turned back to stare out the window. "I don't know"—her voice began to tremble—"except…I just…I can't hide anymore, Uncle Jack, while people I love die." The ground let go and Jack was tumbling down into nothing. It was dark there and the hole had no bottom.

Andi's voice broke altogether and she began to cry, had to choke out the rest. "I don't want my daddy to die while I hide." Then she put her head in her hands and sobbed.

Jack looked past her at Crock. His face was absolutely blank, devoid of any expression at all. Then he turned back to the face on the phone. Theresa looked like she was about to burst into tears, too, and Jack felt utter helplessness wash over him. He recognized the feeling.

He instantly spotted the red dress, watched it billow around Lyla as she fell.

"This is the way it's supposed to be," Theresa whispered. "Ain't no use trying to be Jonah. Andi pointed that out to me just the other day. Said it was best to go on to Nevanah and get it over with." There was a heartbeat pause; then Theresa added softly, "Andi was dead, Jack. The heart monitor flatlined. Then you called her name and she come back—she was sent back. You remember what she said?"

Jack remembered, all right.

A little girl with brown curls, cinnamon-sprinkled freckles and dimples had poked her head up out of a sea of stuffed animals on a hospital bed.

"I heard you, Mr. Jack. When you called me, I knew who you were and that you needed me. So I came back."

~

DIDN'T SURPRISE THERESA that wasn't nobody happy about the way things had turned out—might even be mad at her about it. But she didn't have no choice but to deliver the message she'd been give. Oh, God didn't talk to her out loud. She never had known whether she'd ought to envy or pity the folks he did talk to that way. Granted, it'd be nice to be absolutely, one hundred percent sure you's doing what you's supposed to be doin'. There was a lot to be said for that. But there was something so…intimate and personal about hearin' God's voice in your head. And wonderin' if you's making it all up, listenin' to your own self and then sayin' it was God talkin'. That was where the faith part come in, where you had to draw up real close to the Almighty, and she always wondered if the people God talked to out loud ever had to do that part.

Of course, the chief thing Theresa Washington had to do to find out what God was telling her was to shut up her own mouth and listen. Soon's she did this time, she knew how he intended things to be. Jack and Crock and Andi was supposed to face down that demon. She and Becca'd been give another task.

Come to think of it, it would be better to hear God talking out loud—so when he told you to do something, you could ask him how.

Becca spoke to Theresa and she turned the screen so everybody down in Bradford's Ridge could see what she was sayin', too.

"You don't understand," Becca said. "I have to go. It's my fault he's back."

"Your fault—why would you think that?" Jack asked.

Becca's voice got so quiet Theresa hoped the folks on the phone could hear it.

"I remembered," she said.

"The efreet? When we…defeated it, made it go away

—whatever? You remember that part?" Jack was incredulous.

"Uh-huh. And big pieces of the rest of the summer, too. The memories started coming back as soon as I found that note where Bishop wrote down what had to be done. It's what we did, what the Cat in the Hat told me to do. But I...failed."

"The Cat in the Hat?" Crock was confused.

"Like Princess Buttercup," Andi said, and it struck Theresa how ridiculous they sounded.

"How did you fail?" Jack asked.

"I—"

"It don't matter 'cause what happened to her ain't gone be what happens to you," Theresa said. "That ole demon can appear any way he wants to. He won't come at you the way he come at Becca."

"I still want to know," Jack said.

Becca wouldn't look at Jack's face on the screen. Or at Theresa. She studied her hands in her lap. "When I was a little girl, my father...did things. Made me do things, awful things. The efreet knew all about it, every sick, disgusting detail. He said I wanted it, I asked for it, I liked it." She took a deep, shuddery breath.

"Becca, you never said." Jack's voice was pained and tender.

"I didn't tell anybody. Back then, nobody would have believed me, and if I'd ever breathed a word, Daddy would have killed me. It was an ugly, festering secret. And when that monster knew, and described it. One incident after another—every tiny detail, the way the dust motes floated in a beam of sunlight that time in the barn when..."

She looked up then, her face a mask of revulsion. "I didn't just remember those times, I relived them. It's like I...fell down in a crack of time and every horrible thing he ever did to me—starting when I was four years old—was happening to me all over again. I lived those times again, one after the other, right there in that cave."

Theresa reached out and put her arm around Becca. The girl's whole body was vibrating.

"And something inside me...shattered. I could almost hear the sound of it—a wineglass on a stone floor. Pieces of it, tiny sharp shards of me, flew in all directions. I fell to my knees and I think Jack crawled over to me." She looked at Jack. "You didn't come in with Daniel and me. You were already there. The Bad Kids brought you. Do you remember?"

Jack shook his head. "I still can't...I don't remember any of it."

"Daniel was standing beside me. I bowed my head, couldn't look up because the demon had won. He had beaten me and he had to know it."

"Not necessarily," Theresa said, but Becca continued as if she hadn't heard her.

"I only remember bits and pieces of what happened after that—not because the memories are gone, but because I was gone. I had...some kind of mental breakdown. They use other words now. The clinical diagnosis is paranoid schizophrenia. That's when the psychosis started —that day, what I experienced in the cave. Hallucinations and voices...I don't guess I have to tell you that I'm still not 'right.' Probably never will be."

Theresa patted her shoulder reassuringly and Becca gave her an odd look, then turned back to Jack.

"So you don't remember what the efreet said to you?"

Jack shook his head.

"I think he must have—" she darted a glance at Theresa "—become Isaac to you."

Theresa's whole body went cold at the mention of her son's name.

"I only saw a monster, but I think you saw Isaac, and Isaac accused you, said what had happened to him was your fault, that he got killed because of you."

Theresa's heart hammered in her chest, thoughts and emotions crashing into her like the waves on rocks. Isaac was dead. Dead. Oh, she knew. A boy don't just vanish into thin air and not make a peep for twenty-six years unless he was…But still, in her mother's heart, there had always been a little flame of hope burning, telling her that one day there'd be a big strapping young man standin' in her doorway and he'd smile and hold out his arms to her and…

Pfffft. The little flame of hope flickered like a candle in the wind and guttered out.

Words tripped over themselves as they tumbled out of her mouth.

"Isaac? How could…what did Jack have to do with…?" She turned to Jack then. His face was a frozen mask of shock. "Jack, what did you do, son?"

Jack's voice sounded vacant, uninhabited. "I've always known it was my fault, but I couldn't remember what happened until that night at your house—the night the hospital called Daniel about Mikey Rutherford. Daniel and I were asking what you remembered about that summer and you said you'd been a wreck after Isaac disappeared. And suddenly the memory was there, one of those 'expelled memories,' and I could see it all like it was a movie playing in my head."

He stopped and took a deep breath.

"The night Isaac disappeared, Daniel and I went out drinking in the barn at Becca's, got so drunk we couldn't ride my bike back home. So I sneaked into her house and called Isaac, asked him to come get us and made him promise he wouldn't tell anybody. But he never showed up. That's why it was my fault—if I hadn't called him, Isaac would have been safe at home in his own bed."

So that was why Isaac never said where he was going. Well, it was good to know that much at least. Theresa let out the breath she'd been holding, a sad form of relief flooding over her.

"Wasn't no way you coulda known," she said. "Somebody had in mind to"—she couldn't say the word—"take my Isaac, and if it hadn't a'been then, it'd a been some other time."

Jack didn't look into that phone Crock was holding out there in front of him. She barely caught his whisper.

"The night at your house when I remembered, I should have told you then. I started to tell you, but…" Then he did look at her. "I'm so sorry, Theresa."

"Nothing to be sorry about. Wasn't your fault."

It was quiet for a moment. Then Crock turned the conversation back to where it'd been before Becca'd mentioned Isaac.

"What else do you remember, Becca—any detail that you might not even think is important?" Theresa could hear the police officer in the question.

"Only flashes, images." She paused. "When I fell down on the floor, I saw—there was something drawn on the floor of the cave, in chalk, I think. And I remember Jack had been kneeling where the Bad Kids had dropped him, but then he was there beside me. Daniel was standing on the other side—his face was so scared—holding onto that cross he always wore. I think Jack took my hand, and I reached to take Daniel's. That's all, really. Just darkness. And then being outside and hearing birds in the trees."

Crock spoke to Theresa. "That still doesn't explain

what made the demon…go away. Did Jack and Daniel do something? And why did it come back?"

"No, wasn't Jack and Daniel done it. Only somebody with the knowing can do that. Any person whose soul belongs to God can exorcize a demon that's possessed another person—ain't sayin' it's easy, but the Catholic Church has been doing it for centuries. But a demon that's been summoned, one whose whole being ain't in the spirit world no more but here in this world—only someone who can see the demon as it really is can send it back where it come from. That's why Bishop was going to go after it."

"So if we couldn't banish it, and Becca didn't banish it —what did happen?" Jack asked.

"I don't rightly know, but if I's to guess what happened, I'd say…maybe that demon wasn't never banished at all. Hearing how it happened…I 'spect that efreet decided its own self to leave."

"Why would it do that?" Becca asked.

"Demon can't read your mind, sugar. Only God can do that. You may have been a mess in your own heart and mind, but that demon didn't know that. You just sunk down on your knees—right? Didn't say nothing? That efreet musta thought you was about to come right back at him. He'd thrown the worst he had at you, and far as he could tell, it hadn't stopped you. And…seeing all three of you side by side in front of him…"

She turned to Becca. "You said you was about to take Jack's and Daniel's hands, right? There's something about that, I think, some power in that kind of connection." She thought for a moment. "Yep, I think that's it. I think that efreet decided he'd ought to pick up his marbles and go home, live to fight again another day."

"Why did he wait so long to come back, all these years?" Jack asked.

"Shoot, Jack, it wasn't no long time to that demon! They's eternal creatures—a few years, why, probably seemed to him like he just went out to Starbucks for a latte."

"And first thing he did when he came back was send his troops out looking for Becca so he could keep her from finishing what she started," Jack said. He paused, thoughtful. "He screwed up the first time, didn't see three little kids as a threat, and he didn't intend to be surprised again."

Theresa remembered how Bishop'd sounded the day he'd told her gettin' rid of the efreet would take everything there was in him.

"That demon will do anything to distract you from what you's there to do," Theresa said. "That beast will bewilder and confound you, keep you tied in knots—upset, scared, confused—so you won't have no strength to use against him."

Bishop had said the monster would prey on ugly emotions—rage, jealousy, guilt—that he could sniff 'em out like a hound dog.

"He'll use the worst things in your lives—all the ugly— to take you out, break you, make you back down and run away," Theresa said. "You can't be no dirty ole sewer pipe with scared and guilt and hate jammed in there so tight can't nothing good get through."

When she turned her attention to Crock, her face and voice were tender. "I don't know what you done in your life, Major Crocker, but I 'spect you ain't pure as the driven snow—none of us is. You best make your peace with God 'bout whatever's blackening your soul 'fore you go in there."

Andi spoke then, for the first time. "Miss Theresa, you said that God didn't intend for you to fight the efreet—that he had another job for you. What job?"

"Me and Becca—we got to stop them people of Chapman Whitworth's, the ones that's plannin' the Big Bad Thing. God don't give you a warning 'bout somethin' as a kind of heads-up so you don't miss the story on the eleven o'clock news. If he tells you in advance, he means for you to do something about it."

"What are you going to do?" Andi asked.

"Why, I don't have no idea."

Chapter Twenty-Four

"How did we get here?"

Jeff's voice cut through the darkness again after—how long? Fifteen minutes? Five? Two hours? Daniel had given up trying to keep track of the passage of time.

"I thought you said you rode here on a cockroach's back."

"No, how did we get here? All of us. To this? You and me and Crock and Theresa. Jack ought to be out pulling over a drunk driver somewhere, and Andi ought to be home in a room with a lacy pink bedspread, playing with dolls. How did we get caught up in all this? We're normal people."

"Theresa told me once that normal is just a setting on a dryer."

"I caught myself a minute ago getting angry because I paid five hundred dollars for a gym membership last week and now I won't be able to use it. It was…humbling to realize that everything I ever did or wanted or said in my whole life didn't matter at all. Dying changes the way you look at everything."

That struck Daniel as funny and he laughed. "Yeah, I suppose death would have a profound effect on the way you lived your life—if you weren't dead."

"I see a self-help book in there somewhere," Jeff said. "Lessons From The Grave—Ten Ways to Improve the Quality of Your Life by Dying."

"I forgive you," Daniel said. The words popped out unbidden. Like "Emily's having an affair" had popped out of his mouth that day in the car with Jack after they'd spoken with Mikey Rutherford. He was tempted to ask Jeff the same thing he'd asked Jack that day—did I actually say that out loud? But he knew he'd said it.

"No," Jeff said.

"No what?"

"Save your forgiveness for somebody who cares." Jeff's voice was thick, but without seeing his face, Daniel didn't recognize the emotion. "You can't forgive me because I'm not sorry. And if you're holding your breath waiting for me to say that I am, you can resume your regularly scheduled respirations because I—"

"You don't have to be sorry for me to forgive you. It doesn't work that way." Daniel felt emotion rise in his own chest and he didn't have to wonder what it was. "Understand what I'm saying here, okay! I didn't say I like you. I didn't say I trust you. I didn't say I want to be your new best friend. I said I forgive you."

"Why would you—?"

"I didn't do it for you!" Daniel stopped and took a calming breath. "I did it for me. Forgiveness isn't optional; it's not a suggestion. And it's not an emotion, either. It's a decision—plain and simple. You have to make it over and over and...I'd have to decide again tomorrow to forgive you—except we'll both be dead tomorrow."

"Your choice, pal. Whatever gets you through the

night." Jeff was silent. Then he spoke again and the thickness had left his voice. What had replaced it was…what? Resignation, maybe. Despair.

"Emily was the best thing that ever happened to me and I won't walk out there into the great nothingness saying I'm sorry I loved her. I'm not."

"That's what you think? It's a great nothingness? Poof, you're gone. Not with a bang but a whimper?"

Jeff barked out a sardonic laugh. "I wouldn't have made you for a T. S. Elliot fan."

"The Hollow Men was required reading in English 101."

"The poof-you're-gone part…I don't think it's like that. I think…I believe that your energy, your essence, your life force remains and—"

"That's word salad, Jeff!" How many times had Daniel heard that nonsense! "Energy. Essence. Life force. What does that mean? It's gobbledygook to make people feel better when they refuse to believe the truth."

"And the truth is…?"

"Oh, come on, Jeff. You asked how we got here. We got here courtesy of a demon—not a life force or a magnetic ball of protoplasm or energy—a real being. You saw what it could do, for Pete's sake. Or have you convinced yourself you were hallucinating, that all those cockroaches were looking for crumbs in your pockets?"

"I saw a thing…a beast rose up out of Chapman Whitworth!"

"Aw, that was a hologram, a computer-generated image. Jack, Theresa, Becca, Andi, Chapman Whitworth and I have conspired to perpetrate a monumental practical joke on Jeff Kendrick. Or maybe we're all in the grip of a shared delusion." He took a breath and spoke softly.

"Maybe Emily's murder was nothing more than 'a random act of violence.'"

"What I saw was real. It's all...real."

"And it's pure evil—unadulterated, no-additives-or-artificial-colors-or-flavors evil. If pure evil exists then—knock-knock, Jeff—doesn't it follow that pure good exists, too? Andi can see angels. They're as real as the demon you saw. Where do you think they come from? They're the newest animations from Pixar?"

"I don't know what I think about all that."

"That wouldn't be a bad place to start if you had the luxury of ruminating on it, of spending years 'seeking the wisdom of the ancients' or some other idiot thing, of wasting your life trying all the rest of it—which doesn't work—so you end up right back where you started. But you don't have that kind of time. Truth exists. God exists. You either believe that or you don't. If you do, you'd better figure out real quick what that means."

"That preacher thing. You're doing it, aren't you. You get paid to convert—"

"I'm not trying to convert anybody! If I were, I'd be a whole lot nicer about it. You're going to die. I'm going to die. I know the truth and I have an obligation to tell you what it is. What you do with the truth..." Daniel paused and he could hear a smile in his own voice. "You never met Bishop Washington, but he would have said 'that chicken'll come home to roost in your henhouse.'"

The silence rolled back in, waves of it crashing on the shore. Again and again the surf dashed against the rocks. Jeff was in that black water somewhere, struggling with the forces of the universe. When he finally spoke, Daniel could hear the exhaustion in his voice. Wherever he was, he'd fought to get there. His words rang with absolute finality.

"Message received and duly noted," he said. "You fulfilled your obligation. You told me. Now move on."

Daniel's sigh seemed overloud in the dark silence. That was it, then. On the brink of death or not, this was as far as Jeff Kendrick was willing to go. Game over.

"Billy Ray's about to lose it," Jeff said.

Daniel's mind stumbled trying to catch the train of Jeff's thought, which had pulled out of the station and headed off in an entirely different direction.

"He's seen the real Chapman Whitworth," Daniel said. "That'd be enough to freak anybody out and Billy Ray Hawkins wasn't exactly the poster boy for National Mental Health Week going in. Are you making a point here?"

"I'm wondering if we could use that somehow. I don't think it would take much to push our Neanderthal friend over the edge."

"And you think we should start shoving."

"Why not? It's not like we have anything to lose."

BECCA SAT VERY STILL after the conversation ended with Jack, Andi and Crock. Trying to process it all. Everything was happening too fast. There was no time to adjust to a given reality before it changed and the world was different. She wasn't going to face the efreet again. That truth sank slowly down through her whole body. She felt it the way she used to feel hot chocolate spread heat down her throat into her belly on cold winter mornings when she was a kid.

Instead, she had to stop a terrorist.

Riiiight. Becca Hawkins wouldn't have weighed a hundred pounds with three running jumps at the scales. How was she supposed to fight who knew how many burly madmen?

Apparently, Theresa's thoughts were running in a similar vein because she murmured to herself, "Ain't no way a fat black woman and a skinny white girl is gonna beat up on a bunch of Chapman Whitworth's hired nut jobs right here in Cincinnati—so how we supposed to take on a whole herd of 'em all over the country? That's crazy."

She let out a sigh and turned to Becca. "It is what it is, sugar. We can only do what we can do. We here in Cincinnati, so must be we s'posed to make our stand right here."

She seemed to shift some kind of gear.

"All righty then—it's plain we can't fight 'em, so we gone have to outsmart 'em."

"And you plan to do that…how?"

"I been thinking…what if we didn't even worry about them terrorists. Can't do nothing 'bout 'em anyway. What if we concentrated on the crowd of people they's plannin' to blow up? If we could figure a way to get all them people out of that room, wouldn't matter if a bomb went off in there—right?"

Becca nodded. "How do we get them out—call the police and tell them there's a bomb?"

"We could do that. But if we's to make an anonymous call, they'd blow it off. If we tell 'em who we are, then we got to tell them how we know they's a bomb gone go off in that ballroom. And when we do that, they's gone haul the both of us off to Saint Somebody's Home for the Bewildered."

"Or to jail."

"'Sides, if I'm rememberin' right, they said they thought the bomb that blew up the Mall of America was strapped to somebody who walked out into that crowd of children. If that's the way these folks operate—put the bomb somewhere at the last minute—then the police could search that building top to bottom—if they b'lieved us, which they wouldn't—and still wouldn't find nothin'."

"Which leads us back to my original question. How are we going to get all the people at that ball out of the room?"

There was a sudden twinkle in Theresa's eyes. "I ain't got it all worked out in my head yet, sugar, but I think we might be able to manage that with the resources the good Lord done already blessed us with."

"And those resources are?"

The twinkle in Theresa's eyes grew brighter.

"Six dozen frozen rats."

BILLY RAY WAS HALFWAY across the meadow next to his house when he seen the car sitting in his driveway beside his truck.

He sucked in a gasp, but it didn't do no good because there wasn't no oxygen in the air he pulled into his lungs. The car was black with tinted windows so you couldn't see inside. But he didn't need to see to know who was inside, what was inside. It was the car that'd been parked in the alley behind that building where Jeff Kendrick fell out the window but didn't hit the ground.

The Man was here!

Run!

No, hide!

Which?

He looked around, trying to see everywhere at once, which meant he couldn't register the sight of anything at all. Then he heard a sound, the pitiful, whining, mewling sound of a dog you find all torn up on the side of the road, waiting to die. He jerked around, looking behind him for what was making that awful sound.

Wasn't nothing behind him. Then he realized the whining cry was coming from his own mouth!

He turned slowly back toward the house. The car was gone.

He shook his head, closed his eyes, then opened them again. His truck was the only vehicle in the driveway.

His heart was banging away in his chest so hard he could see each individual beat through his shirt. He even halfway expected to see tire tracks where that car had been before it'd vanished, but he knew it'd never really been there at all. Just his mind playin' tricks on him.

When he pulled his cell phone out of his pocket, his hands were shaking so violently he could barely keep hold of it. Didn't have no cell coverage in the boxcar, so he'd had to leave and get near his house, where he had reception. He tried to calm down, took deep breaths, walked around in circles. Still, it was a long time before he could hit them little buttons and make the call he'd been told to make to get "further instructions."

He wanted nothing more in life than to drop that phone in the dirt and take off runnin' and never look back. He didn't do that, of course, just listened, growing more mystified and horrified with every word.

His knees felt all wobbly-like. There was so much he had to do and he'd by golly better not mess any of it up! Whitworth didn't say nothing about what'd happen to Billy Ray if he did screw it up. He didn't have to. Billy Ray understood that failure was not an option.

Whitworth had given very specific instructions on how he was to kill Daniel Burke and Jeff Kendrick—all kinda crazy stuff—for effect, Billy Ray supposed, to make the whole thing look even more sinister.

What he was supposed to do was troubling, but where he was supposed to do it upset him even more. Whitworth had told him he wanted the murders committed in that strange cavern the boxcar's cave emptied into, the one Billy Ray didn't think anybody'd ever laid eyes on but him!

When Billy Ray'd first put the boxcar in the ground, he'd taken a kerosene lantern one day and went to explore the cave that extended beyond the cavern where he'd lowered the boxcar from the field above. Folks weren't disposed to go nosing around the caves much—afraid of getting lost or falling in a hole or something. But he still had to make sure the cave that went on beyond the boxcar didn't have no other entrance somewhere that some fool might wander in and then stumble upon his treasure.

The cave turned east from the boxcar and went on more or less straight for what must have been near to a mile. Weren't no tunnels branching off from the main cave to confuse him or he'd have turned back. If his sense of direction was right, he had likely gone under the mountain halfway to Milkstone, and he knew there was a cave entrance there.

Little black bats of memory beat their skin-covered wings in his mind, but he'd chased them away.

Finally, the cave had opened up into a huge chamber, way bigger than the one where the boxcar was buried— so big the kerosene lantern light didn't reach all the way to the ceiling or the walls. This wasn't no ordinary cave! It was like something out of a movie, so vast his feet echoed on the stone floor like he was in one of them cathedrals with high ceilings. Billy Ray had gone on a field trip with his fifth-grade class to Cave City, about a hundred miles south of Bradford's Ridge, to visit Mammoth Cave, which claimed to be the longest cave in the world. At the very end of the tour there'd been a chamber that had stalagmites and stalactites—he always got them confused—coming up from the floor and hanging down from the ceiling and rocks that looked like a frozen waterfall.

Them stalag-things was pitiful, though, compared to the ones in this cave! They hung down from beyond the lantern light in the ceiling above and rose up from the floor taller than he was. A forest of 'em. He'd turned up the lantern as bright as it would go and shadows leapt back against the walls, creating an army of black beings that stretched up into the gloom above.

The forest of stalag-things thinned out to just a few sprinkled round on an area where the stone floor was polished so shiny it looked like the marble floor of the capital building in Columbus. He didn't have to worry about no cave entrances on the other side of that bare spot, though! On the far side of it, the floor'd been ripped open in a huge crack with jagged edges that stretched all the way across the chamber from one side to the other—probably thirty feet across at the narrowest spot.

He'd approached it carefully, and when he'd got right to the edge, his lantern light had stretched out across it and lit the opposite wall where there was, indeed, a tunnel opening. Directly opposite the tunnel he'd come in, the cave continued past that big chamber. But he didn't have to worry about somebody stumbling on his boxcar by coming through that cave. Wasn't nobody gonna jump across that crack in the floor and wasn't no way around it.

He'd peeked down into it, shone the lantern down, and it'd been dark as a well, no telling how deep. But maybe it just looked deep because the walls of the crack was black—which was odd because the cavern floor was the cream color of polished marble. So he'd picked up a piece broken off one of them stalag-things and chucked it into the crack and listened for the plunk but never heard a sound, nothing. Which meant the bottom must have been so deep the sound of the rock hitting it didn't carry back up to him.

How did Whitworth know about that giant cavern? And when had Whitworth come and made "all the necessary arrangements" in it—the ones he'd said had been "waiting there for years"? The Man hadn't come in past the boxcar, that was for sure! You could tell hadn't nobody got past the rusty lock that sealed the entrance to the gate while he was in prison. Only explanation was that he'd come from the other direction, through the cave on the other side of the fissure in the floor.

Billy Ray shivered. That crack in the floor of the cavern wouldn't even have slowed Whitworth down. He could picture the man with the scarred face rising in the air himself, like he'd picked up Billy Ray that time and threw him up against…

His mind started sliding sideways again and he giggled.

Giggled!

He'd been doing that a lot lately when his mind wouldn't stop hopping around. It was like a kid's giggle, a little girl's. He didn't like the eerie sound of it, but he couldn't stop it no more'n he'd a'been able to stop a sneeze. It just burst out.

He giggled again.

Well, doing the killing in the big cavern would mean he wouldn't have to clean up the mess of chopping two men's heads off right there in his boxcar—splattering blood all over twelve million dollars' worth of gold bars. No, two million. That was all that was left after he'd give more'n two hundred bars to Whitworth. Hauled them up out of that boxcar ten at a time 'cause they weighed two pounds each and wasn't no way to get up out of the space in front of the butt cheek rocks carrying any more than that. It'd taken him a whole day, and that evening he loaded them bars in the back of a van driven by some flunky—which was better than dealing with Whitworth. Anything was better than that.

Billy Ray shuddered. He didn't want to go back into that cavern again, hadn't set foot in any cave but the one that held his boxcar since his twenty-ninth birthday when —no! Not going there. Uh-uh.

But flashes of memory leapt into his mind whether he liked it or not, and it was getting harder and harder to keep them locked up in that place where nightmares and ghost stories was supposed to be.

It's because they ain't kiddie stories, buddy-roe, they're real, said the voice inside his head, the scornful Billy Ray who had taken up residence outside him and commented on what was going on like he wasn't even Billy Ray at all but some observer watching Billy Ray.

"Hush up, you," he said aloud. He'd taken to doing that, too, talking to himself out loud. Talking to the other self, that is.

Giggling and talking to himself. Sounded like he was losing his marbles. Might be he was.

Chapter Twenty-Five

It'd come to her when she set the phone down on the table after talking to Jack. When she did, she bumped that rat bite on her hand—the worst one, where it bit all the way through and hung there while she was tryin' to shake it off. The pain had set her to rememberin' that night, them rats all over her, how rats was about the awfullest thing a body could possibly imagine.

The thought dropped into her mind, then. Plop. If she'd a'heard a ding, she'd a'thought it was an email.

Anybody'd run from rats.

And there it was. Could they come up with a way to use them rats to freak out them people at the ball so bad they'd get up and run out of the room? And right on the heels of that question come the answer!

"That newspaper story said the staff of the Rivergate would be all dressed up in costumes like the guests. We ain't got no tickets for that ball, but we can get ourselves in as servers. All's we need is Halloween costumes."

"So we get into the ball...then what? Start throwing frozen rats at people?"

"They'll be thawed out by then, sugar."

"Okay, throw thawed-out rats at people?"

"Didn't you say them cleaning men hosed the rats down, got 'em presentable?"

"Presentable?"

"Not all bloody like they just did get hit by a truck. They'll just be dead."

"They weren't in real good shape when they died, you know."

"Oh, that part don't matter. Folks ain't gone get a very good look at 'em anyway. Long's they look like they could be alive, we're good."

"So how are we going to get six dozen thawed-out dead rats into that ballroom and what are we going to do with them once we get them there?"

"We ain't gone take them into the ballroom." She stopped. "You ain't 'fraid of heights, are you?"

Becca barked a mirthless laugh. "Theresa, I'm afraid of everything!"

"That newspaper story said they was gone be a balloon drop at the ball tonight."

"And somehow we're going to put the rats in with the balloons?"

Theresa nodded. Then she waved off the questions she could see Becca forming.

"The answer is I don't know," she said.

She patted Becca's arm. "I once heard a preacher compare God to them motion-activated lights folks use to line they sidewalks. They only come on when you're close enough that you need 'em and they only light up what you got to see right in front of you. I got some of this figured out and I'm trustin' I'll figure out the rest of it when the time comes."

She started toward the garage door.

"Grab another garbage bag, sugar. Soon's them rats thaw out enough we can separate 'em, we gone need to divide 'em up." She shuddered at the thought of touching the rats. But they was dead. She comforted herself with that thought.

They was dead, right?

Becca took the garbage bag full of rats out of the freezer in the garage and set it with a clunk into the trunk of the car. Theresa wondered how long it would be before them rats was…usable. She didn't have no experience with how long it took a dead rat to thaw out.

She and Becca swung by Hedringer's Novelties and Party Supplies and done the best they could to outfit themselves. It being Halloween, them costumes was mighty picked over, and she and Becca wasn't 'xactly average size eights. They was only two costumes in the whole store big enough to fit Theresa. One was an outfit with alternating rows of red, green, gold, purple and orange fringe sewn around and around it.

"If I go dressed as a piñata, I'm gone spend the whole night dodging people trying to whack me with a stick," she said.

Resigned, she picked up the other costume and made a humph sound in her throat. "Fat as I am, the Big Bad Wolf's gonna have to take home a doggie bag."

Theresa's face was completely hidden when she put the hood of the red cape up over her head. Wasn't nothing showing from behind Becca's mask but her chin. Theresa stopped before they checked out and selected a pair of fancy white gloves with lace around the top for herself—fit snug over the rat-bite bandage on her right hand—and red gloves for Becca.

"I don't know if what we's plannin' is technically illegal, but I 'spect there's a little bitty law or two we's gone break along the way. Might be a plan not to leave no fingerprints behind."

The ball didn't start until six o'clock, but they had to get there soon's they could so they'd have time to figure out a way to pull this off. Theresa figured she'd ought to make sure the both of them was singin' from the same sheet of music.

"Have you thought 'bout what's gone happen—to us—if this don't work?" she asked.

"We'll be in the room when the bomb goes off," Becca said. Then she turned to Theresa and her eyes looked haunted. "I'd rather be in a room with a bomb than in a room with...where Jack and Andi and Crock are going."

SEBASTIAN NEMO LEFT his hotel room fifteen minutes before checkout time on Monday morning. Sometimes hotel maids remembered people who made them wait to clean the room. He stopped at a fast-food restaurant for lunch and drove to a crowded Walmart parking lot, where he sat in his van until mid-afternoon. Then he set out for the half-hour drive northeast along the Ohio River upstream from Cincinnati. Five miles below the speed limit even though it was a rural two-lane road. It wouldn't do to get pulled over packing a Javelin missile in the back of the van.

He'd selected the spot along the riverbank carefully. As he approached it, he slowed to allow the pickup truck behind him to pass. He pulled to the side of the road and waited until the truck vanished over the next hill and no other vehicles were in sight in either direction. Then he drove the van off the road through the undergrowth and around trees to the bank of a small inlet a quarter mile away. He parked among a stand of bushes and hurried back to the road to remove the tire tracks he'd left behind.

When he returned to the van, he checked his perimeter. The area was so densely overgrown with brush that the inlet was invisible from the road and from the riverbank both upstream and downstream. He parked the van longways, facing downriver, to block the view from passing boats and barges, then pulled the inflatable dinghy out of the back of the van and went to work.

Inside an hour, he was set. The black dinghy with its twenty-horse-power outboard motor was ready to shove into the water in the inlet. The missile lay on the floor of the dinghy. A Javelin had two components—the reusable command launch unit and the missile, which was sealed in a disposable launch tube. Fully assembled—locked and loaded—it was less than five feet long and weighed less than fifty pounds.

As he donned his black jumpsuit, pulled the black cap low on his head and applied eyeblack to his face and hands, he went over the plan again. It was simple. All good plans were.

No plan ever survived the first contact with the enemy, a former Navy SEAL instructor had told him years ago, so reducing the number of moving parts that could… would…go wrong minimized the damage control you had to do when things inevitably began to unravel.

The Javelin was the perfect weapon for the job at the Rivergate Hotel because you could fire it two ways. You could fire it directly at the target. Or you could set it to come down on top of the target, in this case right through the hotel's rolled-back roof to detonate in the Balloon Ballroom on the top floor. Like shooting ducks in a washtub—

sight in on the gigantic neon-flashing balloons on the four corners of the hotel roof and fire.

For all its accuracy and ease of use, however, the Javelin had a drawback that had presented a significant challenge. Mortars used coordinates to hurl incendiary devices off into the blue. With a Javelin, the man firing it had to be able to see the target.

That was the manufacturer's slogan: "If you can see it, you can destroy it."

That proved problematic in the case of this mission. Though the missile's range was more than a mile and a half, there was no land-side approach to the Rivergate Hotel that offered a sightline view of it. The hotel was part of a four-building riverfront complex called The Cedars, and the Stabler Building sat directly behind it. The Bank of Ohio Building sat beside the Rivergate on the east and the Regency Plaza was snuggled up beside it on the west. All three buildings surrounding it were two to four stories taller than the hotel. The only open approach was on the river side—but not from the opposite shore. On the Kentucky side of the Ohio River across from the Rivergate was a collection of buildings that held the government offices of Boone County as well as the Northern Kentucky State Police post!

There was only one option left—he would have to hit the building from a position on the river itself, and because the Rivergate was set back from the water farther than the buildings on either side of it, even the river approach had limitations.

When he'd first set up the hit on the Balloon Ballroom, there'd been talk that the First Lady might attend the Better Day Society Ball—which would have meant security out the wazoo. Most people didn't know that after 9/11, the US Coast Guard stopped routinely policing inland waterways. Their resources instead were trained on security for locks, dams and bridges. But with the First Lady nearby, you'd probably be able to walk across the river on Coast Guard vessels. They'd be all over every pleasure craft on the water, every yacht, pontoon boat, speedboat, raft and kayak—if they didn't just ban pleasure boat traffic on the river altogether until she left.

Even though, to Sebastian's vast relief, the First Lady's plans changed, he wasn't sure what kind of security—if any—there might be for the four main contenders for the Democratic presidential nomination. So he'd decided to stick with the original First-Lady-in-Attendance plan. It was simple and safe—though its small window of opportunity made it a little more challenging than other alternatives. But Nemo enjoyed the adrenaline rush of danger every now and then. He usually let the hired help take all the risks. Not tonight. He would be the man firing the Javelin…from a position on a coal barge chugging down the Ohio River.

A standard barge was thirty-five feet wide and one hundred ninety-five feet long, twelve feet deep and sank nine feet below the surface of the water when it was loaded. A standard tow for one tugboat had fifteen such barges—three wide and five long—winched together with cables. That amounted to roughly a thousand feet of surface area piled high with thirty thousand tons of coal— a floating island. It would take an army to find one man dressed in black in the dark, carrying a pipe a little bigger than a fence post in an area the size of four football fields placed end to end.

A barge's only drawback was the fact that it was moving. Slowly, though, less than six miles per hour—not a whole lot faster than a brisk walk. Still, Sebastian would have a limited window of opportunity to fire, from the time the Rivergate came into view from behind the Bank of Ohio Building upstream until it was blocked from view by the Regency Plaza Building downstream. By Nemo's calculations, that would be somewhere between nine and fifteen minutes—plenty of time for the Boss, who apparently intended to be on the site of the explosion, to get clear.

Nemo hadn't intended to launch the dinghy out into the river until it was full dark, and sundown would be at 6:29 p.m. But shortly after five o'clock, it began to get foggy. It was a strange fog that had appeared out of nowhere, not settling first in low-lying areas and around streams. It was suddenly there, all around, reducing visibility to fifteen or twenty feet.

Well, no plan ever survived the first contact...

The presence of fog would require adjustments, but it did mean the launch would not be visible from the Kentucky State Police Post on the Kentucky side of the river—if anybody chanced to be looking in his direction when he fired. And it also closed the loophole of his only vulnerability. It would be possible to spot him from the air with a helicopter and searchlight. Fog this thick would ground all choppers, and it would hide the small tail of fire and smoke produced when the round fired. The fog would cause no sighting problem for Sebastian, though. The neon balloons on the four corners of the Rivergate's roof were brightly lit spheres three times the size of Volkswagens.

HE'D THOUGHT LONG and hard about it, figuring out how he was gonna get them boys out of the boxcar and all the way to that cavern to kill them the way Chapman Whitworth had told him he had to kill them. And how he was gonna carry all the stuff he had to take with him to do it like Chapman Whitworth said he had to. Finally, he decided he'd use Daniel and Kendrick as pack mules.

It took a couple of trips back and forth to the house to get the supplies to the boxcar. Until he was ready to go in and retrieve his captives, he left the things sitting in the open area in the front of the cave next to the shelves where he kept his own supplies. He had containers of water, a few tools and a great big stack of extra car batteries—and he had to have spares. Couldn't be down here with no 'lectricity. In the dark.

They'd been in there stewing a long time, staring death in the face. That was why he'd left the light off. It was a lot scarier to think about dying when it was dark.

He stepped into the boxcar, flipped on the light and watched the two of them squint.

"It's showtime," he announced cheerily. He walked to where they lay. "Let me tell you how this is gonna go down. We're gonna go out into this here cave and down it to the spot where I'm going to send you fellas on to meet your maker. I figure you've spent a good bit of the time you been in here coming up with all kinda plans on how you're gonna escape. You need to know what's gonna happen if you decide to try one of them plans."

He pulled a Glock 17 semiautomatic pistol from a holster on his belt.

"Either one of you so much as sneezes or looks at me funny and I'm gonna shoot you. I ain't gonna kill you— that'd spoil all the fun, but I am gonna shoot you. I'll take out your kneecaps, point-blank range. You can still kneel to get executed with busted kneecaps."

Kendrick and Daniel just looked at him and said nothing.

"That's for the first offense even if you didn't mean nothin' by it, so you better be real careful. But if you pull something where I know you really are coming after me…" He pulled a small but vicious-looking knife from a scabbard on the other side of his belt and turned it so it flashed silver in the overhead light. "I'll take out your knees and then I'm gonna use this on you, fix it so you won't want to escape anymore because ain't no point in living after I castrate you."

He liked it that they both flinched visibly. He'd got their attention alright.

"Anybody unsure of what's at stake if you screw up?"

They didn't respond.

"I said are we clear on this?"

"Whatever you say, boss," Kendrick said. He was probably smirking, but you couldn't really tell with his face all messed up like it was.

"I heard you," Daniel said.

"Since I ain't plannin' on carryin' you, you're gonna have to walk, so I'm gonna cut your feet lose." He sniffed. "Don't think that gives you no advantage. You're gonna be blindfolded. Good luck trying to run away when you can't see! And good luck getting out of this cave with the gate padlocked and I got the only key." He held a key ring with a lone key up for them to see, then stuffed it down in his pants pocket.

He used the knife to cut the tape binding Kendrick's ankles together, then tied a piece of the rope around both ankles, leaving about three feet in between.

"A hobbled horse don't do no kicking."

After he'd freed Daniel's ankles, he took hold of his upper arm and lifted him to his feet. He swayed, almost fell, so Billy Ray kept hold of his arm until he was steady, then did the same with Kendrick and shoved both of them out the door of the boxcar into the cave.

He picked up the roll of duct tape and went to Daniel

first. Using his teeth to rip off a piece of tape about two feet long, Billy Ray wrapped the tape around Daniel's head and over his eyes, then tore off several more pieces and covered his face with them so wasn't no way he could even see light.

He turned to Kendrick and noticed how he was looking around, taking everything in.

"I done a good job on this place," he said. "Course, ain't nobody ever gonna know that since everybody who sees it ends up dead."

He ripped off a piece of tape and began to wrap Kendrick's head, making a special effort to poke his swollen, broken nose, and enjoyed hearing him moan in pain.

"Broke nose hurts, don't it," he said. "You broke mine when you kicked me in the face and I ain't forgot it! Time for payback!" He made a fist and slammed it like a hammer into the tape covering Kendrick's face. The man screamed, staggered backwards and fell to the cave floor.

As Kendrick lay moaning on the floor, Billy Ray studied the both of them. Puzzled on it hard as he could, but he couldn't figure a way two blind men with their hands taped together and their arms taped to their bodies could put up any kind of fight. Still, he'd be ready if they tried anything.

He reached down and picked up a long length of the rope he'd bought special at that fancy hunting/fishing/hiking store that'd opened up in town after he was sent off. It was rock climbing rope—light and strong and easy to work with. He tied a slipknot in both ends, placed one end around Kendrick's neck—blood was seeping out the edges of the tape covering his face—and the other around Daniel's. The slightest pull from one of them would yank the rope tight around both their necks.

He had tied the handles of two halogen lanterns together and he draped the lanterns around Daniel's neck like a scarf hanging down on his chest. He did the same thing with another set of lanterns. Then he took two additional lanterns he'd tied together and draped them around Daniel's neck to hang down in back. Six lanterns in all. The weight of them combined with the choke rope made it hard for Daniel to breathe—and that was a good thing.

He dragged Kendrick to his feet and draped him with lanterns, too—made it a dozen lanterns in all—then slid a second slipknot-tied rope around Daniel's neck as a lead rope. It was a long piece so he'd be way out in front. He gathered up a duffle bag with the rest of what he needed in one hand and a lantern in the other, stepped out in front of Daniel and gave the rope a tug.

"We're starting out now, boys. One of you falls, gonna choke the other. If I figure you didn't fall on purpose, I'll only take out one kneecap, and then the other one's gonna have to drag you. Make it easy on yourselves, walk careful and don't try nothing. We'll take it slow."

And so they started. It was hard for the men to keep their footing with their hands tied, trying to stay balanced with the weight of the lanterns and the ropes. He'd planned it that way. They had to concentrate just to stay upright, so their minds were occupied, no time to stew about what was about to happen and start to panic.

The two of them finally got a rhythm going, timed and measured their steps so it wasn't so herky-jerky on the ropes around their necks. He walked backwards for probably a hundred yards of slow going, keepin' his eyes on 'em, but finally relaxed. There was no way for them to try anything.

Eventually, they made the final turn in the tunnel before the cavern—if Billy Ray was remembering it right, and he'd only been here the one time right after he buried the boxcar.

When the cavern opened up in front of him, Billy Ray was as awed by it as he'd been that first time. He'd never been in any place as strange, as otherworldly as this. He led the men through the forest of stalag-things out into the middle of the almost-marble floor and then stood very still, looking around. He set down the duffle bag and his lantern, took one set of lanterns from around Kendrick's neck, untied them and flipped the switches.

The light revealed two things that hadn't been here the only other time he'd been here. One was a table-like thing in the center of the cavern. It was made from rocks and broken pieces of stalag-things, piled up about four feet high with a huge flat rock four feet by six feet lying across the top. Billy Ray'd bet ten strong men wouldn't have been able to lift that thing into place…but ten strong men hadn't been who put it there.

The second thing that was different was the drawings. Something had been drawn with black chalk on the floor that'd looked like frozen water before.

This must be what Whitworth had meant when he said things was all ready—had been waiting for today for more than twenty years.

Images suddenly splashed on the walls of his memory and he shook his head to get rid of them. That nightmare, dream, whatever it was—there'd been something drawn on the floor that time, too. He'd seen the lines when he fell. And there'd been a table—he remembered now, a table, and he'd looked up past it—

He clamped back down on the images, shoving them out of his mind with a great force of will. But they were right behind the door and he couldn't keep the door locked anymore. He couldn't even keep it closed all the way anymore and they were right there, ready to come rushing in all the time.

He went to Daniel and lifted off the lanterns. He had a raw rope burn on the front of his neck.

Billy Ray giggled, reached out and touched the mark.

"You're making this easy. All I gotta do is cut on the dotted line." He roared at his own joke, his ragged, damaged voice bouncing around the walls of the huge cavern, echoing in such an eerie fashion that the humor drained out of him at the sound. The place was creepy in a way he didn't remember from before. He had to hurry up and do this, get it over with so he could get out of here.

He worked as quickly as he could then. He turned on the other of the set of lanterns he'd taken from Kendrick and set it on the edge of the fissure in the floor—wanted to light that up real well. Wouldn't want to accidentally step off into it. If he did, he'd still be falling by the middle of next week.

He took all the lanterns Kendrick and Daniel had hauled from the boxcar and left the two men standing where they were with the rope around their necks still tethering them to each other.

"Case you were considerin' running off blind, you need to know there's a crevice in the floor in this cavern—probably thirty feet wide and so deep you can't see the bottom. You best stand real still right where you are."

He set the lanterns in a circle around the edges of the cavern, trying to light it as evenly and effectively as he could. He'd use that table thing to set the video camera on so it'd catch every detail. He'd saved two lanterns to set right up next to them two men when he was ready to do the deed so's their faces would be lit up and recognizable. Wouldn't do no good to video him whacking off their heads if it was too dark to see who they were. Chapman

Whitworth had been very specific about that—make sure we see their faces!

Billy Ray remembered his voice and shivered. He'd been specific about everything—not only the light. So much crazy stuff to do...

Chapter Twenty-Six

The ride from Bradford's Ridge to the cave entrance Ariel had told them about was quiet. As Jack drove through town, he and the others saw early trick-or-treaters, mostly very small children out with their parents before sunset. Toddlers in pumpkin suits, two-year-old Spidermen and three-year-old Little Mermaids. They carried grocery sacks to collect their loot and would be picking through it on the kitchen table before the big kids came out after dark. Andi should have been one of those kids, should have been knocking on doors with a gang of friends, crying "trick or treat" instead of on her way to confront a real demon from hell.

Jack took Bethel Park Road, which followed the river-bank for a couple of miles before it connected to US 31, the road that'd brought them into town. He was thinking about Ariel's description of her attack on Daniel, how she'd waited for him, then left him unconscious on the walking path. That was when one of Chapman Whitworth's minions had kidnapped him and taken him —where?

Jack turned south on US 31, heading toward a land-mark that had been a part of his life for all of it that he could remember. Milkstone. They were almost there when they saw the smoke. A gray pall—dark as a ten-penny nail—hung like a shroud above the treetops on the hills.

"Something's on fire, a big something from the look of that smoke," Crock said.

"It's not smoke," Andi said softly from the backseat.

"Is this the darkness you saw hanging above Bradford's Ridge when we first drove into town?" Jack asked. "Why can I see it now when I couldn't before?"

"It's the same thing," Andi said. "But it's…worse, so bad, so evil anybody can see it. It's coming up out of the caves like the other. It's so dark and thick I can barely see through it."

She shivered. For a moment he regretted not telling her to wear a jacket. But the autumn chill was not what she felt. A jacket wouldn't have warmed her.

"It's colder, too," Andi said. "Can't you feel it?"

Jack could see only a thick gray fog, not a malevolent darkness. And it struck him that what Andi could see was reality. A reality to which he and Crock were totally blind. The bright sunshine and the blue sky—with white puffy clouds tethered like hot-air balloons to treetops dressed in autumn splendor—protected them from the horror. Almost every human being on the planet had been born, lived their four-score-and-ten, and died without ever seeing what reality actually looked like.

He pulled off the road onto the grass, trying with no success to conjure up memories of being here before with the Bad Kids, with Daniel or Becca or Mikey. No memories came.

Milkstone was an outcrop of pure white limestone that extended into the Three Forks River, a popular haunt for generations of teenagers, who hung out on the riverbank and swam in the deep pool formed by the rushing water around the rock. The mouth of an enormous cave gaped in the hillside next to Milkstone, a hundred feet tall and probably twice as wide, completely blocked in the back by a rockfall. The little house where Becca had lived before her mother died and her father built the mansion was on the opposite side of the mountain from Milkstone, only a couple of miles away as the crow flies. Ariel's grandmother lived a quarter of a mile down US 31.

Ariel had described how she, Rusty and Cassidy had been in the open field next to Milkstone, kicking a soccer ball. Rusty had whacked it really hard; it had taken a crazy bounce and had flown into the cave and disappeared in the pile of boulders that stretched from the cave floor to the roof in the back right corner. The three children had clambered up the pile of rocks, looking for the ball.

"You can't see it from below," Ariel had said, "but there's a crack in the rock up there at the top behind a big boulder."

Rusty had spotted the ball first, snatched it up, but Cassidy'd tried to take it away from him. In the scuffle that followed, they'd dropped the ball and it had rolled away from them into the crack. The cave beyond the crack was dark, but the ball was only a few feet away, lying in the spill of light from the entrance, and the children went in to get it. When they turned to leave, their path back out had been blocked.

"It was just there, between us and the crack," she'd said and shivered at the memory. "A huge rattlesnake was coiled up, rattling, ready to strike."

The children had bolted away from the snake into the cave, going deeper and deeper with the sound of the rattling snake always behind them. The light from the

crack faded and soon they were in absolute darkness, terrified, feeling their way through a labyrinth of twisting and
turning tunnels until a red light began to glow, to pulse, in
the black cave ahead of them.

Jack parked next to a falling-down split-rail fence that
might once have been somebody's attempt to keep
teenagers away. He was pretty sure it hadn't been there
when he was a kid and its condition testified to its ineffec-
tiveness, as did the litter of cans, trash and campfire-black-
ened marks in the dirt in front of the cave.

Even before the car had come to a full stop, Andi leapt
out the back door and ran through the swirling fog to a
light the fog didn't make fuzzy, a light so bright Jack should
have had to squint to look at it—but he didn't.

"I knew you'd be here, Princess Buttercup," Andi cried.

Jack got out of the car and watched the light envelop
Andi. The light grew brighter by the second until the
whole world around Milkstone was filled with a golden
luminescence, a sourceless incandescence that lit every
surface, the tops and bottoms, without forming shadows.
The autumn leaves, blazing in bright yellow, gold, red and
russet on the nearby trees burst into even brighter colors,
as if a Christmas light had been turned on inside each
individual leaf. The Three Forks River became flowing
gold glitter, sparkling as it cascaded past them.

What he saw at the center of the light was a young
woman with long blond hair in a single braid, wearing
jeans with a hole above the right knee, and a denim
jacket over a T-shirt with words he couldn't make out
printed on the front. And yes, she did resemble Princess
Buttercup.

"Where else would I be?" she asked.

The voice of the young woman in the light was so rich
and pure Jack thought wildly that if he'd had a wineglass

with him, just the voice's normal tones would have shattered the glass into a million sparkling shards.

Crock got out of the car on the passenger side. Jack couldn't read the look on his face, lit a golden hue by the light that enveloped Andi. Surprise, shock, awe—certainly. But it was almost as if...Crock had spotted an old friend.

When Crock limped around the front of the car, Jack's concern returned. They'd have to climb up that rockfall and then find their way through the labyrinth of caves beyond to the chamber where the efreet lay. It was going to be hard on Crock, all that climbing and walking. Jack hoped he was up to it.

Though when it came right down to it, Jack doubted that any of them was up to what lay ahead. He felt so unprepared. Until half an hour ago, he'd been counting on Theresa and Becca to bring or do or say whatever was needed. They were the experts; they were the generals. Jack was just a foot soldier. He was prepared to take orders; was he now expected to give them?

He watched Andi, her face lit by the light, and he suddenly found himself praying. He couldn't remember the last time he'd prayed.

God, please don't let anything happen to that little girl. Keep her safe.

Right, safe. We're about to do battle with the devil—there's no such thing as safe.

It was Jack's job to find the snake and cut off its head and trust that without the direction and power of the efreet, its plans to kill Daniel would fall apart.

And it was his job to take care of Andi, to give his life for her if he had to.

The words of Todd Beamer, the young man who'd led the passenger revolt on United Flight 93 that went down in the Pennsylvania countryside on 9/11 came to mind and he whispered them to himself.

"Let's roll."

~

ONCE HE'D GOT the whole place lit up right, Billy Ray stepped back to see how it looked. It was only then that he noticed that the black chalk lines on the floor fit together into complicated shapes with points and circles. The table was on a bare spot in the center of all the shapes. Why had Whitworth gone to the trouble to draw all that stuff on the floor when you wouldn't even see it in the video of the beheadings?

And the other stuff—the chanting Billy Ray was supposed to do, the words he was supposed to say and the numbers.

What if he just didn't do it, any of it?

How would Whitworth know?

He peered around the cavern. The shadow shapes on the walls extending from those pointy stalag-things on the floor shifted and moved as if the lantern light were flickering—but they were halogen lanterns. They didn't flicker. Still, the shadows danced like they were alive. Were they watching, maybe? He looked up at the sharp points coming down from the ceiling and then at the ones rising up from the floor and he saw them as jagged teeth in a huge open mouth, ready to bite down and chew him up.

All at once, he couldn't be in here alone anymore. He leapt up and went to where Daniel and Kendrick stood linked together by the rope tied in nooses around their necks.

"Get down on your knees," he commanded, then held their arms for balance so they didn't fall over and choke each other when they did. Once they were both kneeling, he started ripping the duct tape off Kendrick's face. He had to have somebody else in the cavern with him, even if it was the somebody he was going to behead in a few minutes.

Yanking off the duct tape pulled out hunks of Kendrick's hair, stripped off most of his left eyebrow and dragged his broken nose across his face. Kendrick cried out in pain, but Billy Ray didn't slow down until he had all the tape off.

"Open your eyes and look at me," he commanded. Kendrick opened the one eye that would open and stared at him. Another person here, alive, awake. Not alone. Yeah, that was better.

Kendrick turned his head as best he could and took in his surroundings while Billy Ray went to work on Daniel. Daniel lost some hair, too, and the tape left a huge raw spot on his left cheek when Billy Ray yanked it off. But Daniel didn't cry out. Wasn't as painful as a broken nose. All in all, Daniel's face had fared better than Kendrick's—just the bruises on his forehead and the black eyes from the rock— and that was good. Daniel was the one that mattered, The Man had said—which didn't make no sense to Billy Ray a'tall. Seemed to him like beheadin' a big-shot lawyer would be a bigger deal than some minister. But Billy Ray hadn't been consulted.

When both of them were looking around like chicks just hatched out of their shells, Billy Ray made a grand gesture that took in the whole cavern.

"Welcome to your new digs—your last digs."

"Where are we?" Daniel asked. He raised himself up off his heels and looked around, turning his head from side to side, taking it all in.

"The last place you're ever gonna see, that's where."

Billy Ray looked at his watch. He still had plenty of time—even counting how long it would take him to get back to the boxcar and out of the cave into the open where he had coverage so he could send off the video. Even so, he was in a hurry. And if he didn't do all that crap Whitworth had said he had to do, he could be out of here in half the time.

"I ain't gonna do it," he said out loud. That talking-to-himself thing again. "Gonna chop off their heads and get out of here. I ain't gonna do all that crazy stuff. He'll never know."

He saw Daniel shoot Kendrick a brief look; then Kendrick said, "You mean Chapman Whitworth? You know who he is, don't you? What he is? You've seen it, haven't you, Billy Ray?"

"I ain't seen nothing. Shut your mouth. Me and him's partners, and when he's president, he's—"

"Partners?" Kendrick sneered. "With Chapman Whitworth? Demons don't have 'partners,' Billy Ray. Demons have slaves."

Daniel wasn't saying anything, just looking around at the marks on the floor with a strange expression.

"You think I b'lieve in fairy tales. Ain't no such thing as a demon. Ain't—"

"Do you know what these are?" Daniel's voice sounded like he'd got the wind knocked out of him. And the look on his face—he was scared worse'n he'd been when Billy Ray'd told him he was gonna chop his head off!

"Them marks, aw, they don't mean nothing." But Billy Ray wasn't sure of that. Not sure at all.

Daniel turned to Kendrick. "Jeff, these are pentagrams."

Kendrick was startled, then looked, really looked, and all the color drained out of his face, too. "Pentagrams…"

His voice was as thin as a mouse's whisker. "That's what Becca said…"

Daniel started in on Billy Ray then. "Chapman Whitworth told you to do some things here besides cut off our heads—didn't he?"

How'd he know that? Billy Ray's mind started jumping around again—bouncing—couldn't think with it doing that. He put his hands up to his temples, as if pushing in on them would somehow keep his head from exploding. He bit down hard, clamping his jaw to keep that whimpering sound in his throat from leaking out his mouth.

"That's what you said you didn't want to do." Daniel's voice drilled into him. "Because it was crazy."

"I don't know what you're talking about. You're the one's cra—"

"You're supposed to start at that altar." Daniel nodded toward the flat rock on the pile of stones.

Altar? The table was an altar?

"And he's given you words to say there."

Billy Ray found he could only take short, shallow breaths.

"They're not really words, though, at least not English words. They don't sound like any language you ever heard."

Billy Ray was going to shut him up, yes, sir, put that tape back over his mouth so he couldn't say nothing else. But Billy Ray couldn't move.

"Then you're supposed to go to the five points of these stars—"

"They're upside down," Kendrick said. "The point of a pentagram is supposed to be at the top."

"When it's upside down, the points are hooves. They're called the 'sign of the cloven hoof' or the 'footprint of the devil.'"

Daniel turned back to Billy Ray, who found he couldn't seem to make his mouth form words anymore.

"Each point of the star has a name—earth, fire, water, air and spirit. You're supposed to call out its name and then say—"

Billy Ray finally found his voice, a wave of emotion erupted from his throat—panicked confusion—but it came out as rage. "Shut up!" he screamed in the voice that ever since his twenty-ninth birthday had been so hoarse it sounded like he had laryngitis. The words echoed off the cavern walls—up...up...up..."You shut your mouth or I'll cut off your—"

He fumbled to get the knife out of its sheath, but his hands were trembling so badly the knife clattered to the stone floor in front of him. He got to his knees to pick it up.

"The books in Bishop's office..." Kendrick said. His voice was all airy like, the way you talk when you can't catch your breath. "When I went to Theresa's after the bugs, Becca said..." His mouth kept forming words, but there was no sound and finally he quit trying to talk altogether.

"The day before we came to Bradford's Ridge, she told me about that part," Daniel said to Kendrick.

Then he turned back to Billy Ray. "Your daughter knows what all this is really about. The beheading part is window dressing, to scare people into believing Chapman Whitworth is right about domestic terrorism. But that's not why we're here."

He gestured with his chin at the shapes on the floor and spoke very slowly. "First, you draw an upside-down pentagram in a circle on the floor..." Daniel paused, like he was waiting for Billy Ray to look at him. But he wouldn't. He wouldn't!

"And then you say certain words." Daniel paused again and this time Billy Ray did look at him—didn't want to, didn't intend to. He just found himself lifting his head. He was staring dead into Daniel Burke's eyes when Daniel said, "That's how you summon a demon from Hell."

His words plowed into Billy Ray's gut with the force of a sledgehammer.

"But you have to have one more thing besides the right words and a pentagram," Daniel said. "You have to have a human sacrifice. You have to have the blood of a murder victim."

There wasn't no air. It'd all got sucked out of that cavern by Daniel's words, and when Billy Ray tried to breathe, it was like his face was covered in a plastic bag and him trying to suck in air pulled the bag tight across his nose and mouth. His eyes bugged out, his face got red, and the tendons on his neck stood out like ropes.

A black frame formed around the edges of his vision and began to close in on him. The sides of the frame rushed at him, and when they slammed shut in front of him, the world vanished and Billy Ray was trapped in the black hole of his memory, alone and naked. What was there in the darkness came for him then. It'd been lurking in the shadows for years, hungry, fangs dripping. Now, there was nowhere to run from it, nowhere to hide.

The marks on the floor. The table...altar! The shattered amulet—the one he'd filled with Isaac Washington's blood...after he'd murdered him.

The monster in the lake of fire.

It happened then. His mind tore apart. You could almost hear the sound, like the cry of ripping fabric. The terror and horror had finally burst the stitches, the ones he'd sewn in desperation half a century ago to close the rip. When the threads unraveled, he came apart, his senses, his wits, who he was…it all floated away, leaving behind only scraps of sanity that dangled in shreds, twisting and fluttering listlessly in a cold wind. He caught a single breath, the last breath the man who had been Billy Ray Hawkins would ever draw. It was a giant lungful of air, and he used it to scream.

Chapter Twenty-Seven

Andi and Princess Buttercup scampered up the rockfall like squirrels, hopping from one rock to the next. Now, they stood on the flat area beside the big boulder at the top, looking down at Jack and Crock as they labored to the top.

Jack was next up; Crock was having a hard time of it. He was fifty-eight years old, had a bad knee from an old gunshot wound, and Jack could see that blood had started to seep through the bandage over the wound caused by an eight-year-old boy and a pair of scissors.

"You okay?" he called down to Crock, who had managed to make it most of the way up, but was having trouble negotiating the rock outcrop at the top.

"Do I look okay?" Crock asked, gasping. "I'm too old for this."

"Moses was eighty years old when he went to Egypt to free his people, and Abraham was a hundred years old when his son Isaac was born," Andi chirped. From the moment she'd spotted Princess Buttercup, Andi had been as cheery as if she'd been going on a picnic, her eyes as bright as twin pilot lights.

"Children are to be seen and not heard, little girl," Crock said, grunting from exertion. "Didn't you get the memo?"

Jack climbed back down off the outcrop and extended his hand and helped haul Crock up to the top.

"You're bleeding," Andi said.

"Catsup. Spilled it. Can't take me anywhere."

Jack turned toward the glowing presence beside Andi, unsure how to address her. Princess Buttercup?

"Are we ready?" he asked.

The light dimmed, at least the brightness did, but the glow remained. He looked into her face, an ordinary face with large compassionate blue eyes. Now he could read the slogan on her T-shirt: "That love thy neighbor thing—I meant that." God. He somehow found a genuine smile on his lips.

"Are you ready?" she asked.

He looked at Crock and they both nodded wordlessly.

"Then," the angel said, in that voice that would shatter crystal, "let's roll."

How did she…?

The angel stepped into the cave and the glow around her was concentrated by the darkness, focused by the black border into a beam of light like a flashlight. She went first, of course, because she was the only one of them who knew the way—though flashes of memory were returning to Jack. He was the last to step through the crack and he suddenly remembered how it looked from inside—a jagged crack of light that had grown more and more distant as the Bad Kids had dragged him farther and farther into the cave's depths. He also remembered that it was here, in the spill of light from outside, that he saw the first of the creatures that would grow and grow in number until they were crawling and slithering all over each other.

Spiders and snakes. Daniel had called them What Comes Behind.

Now, the puddle of light inside the crack was empty. There were no spiders or snakes to herd them forward and block their retreat.

He let out a little sigh of relief.

Up ahead of him Andi gasped.

Jack turned toward the interior of the cave, and in the glow from the angel, he saw them. The walls and ceiling of the cave ahead were black, but that wasn't the color of the rock. That was the color of the writhing blanket of spiders that coated every surface. Fat, hairy spiders as big as a dinner plate, a kind Jack had never seen before. Wolf spiders and brown recluse spiders and, of course, black widows like the one that had crawled into the cuff of Daniel's pants and killed his little sister.

He heard the first rattle then, but it was quickly joined by others until the sound echoed off the walls and rocks all around. Snakes covered the cave floor, so thick there was no way to move forward without stepping on them. Copperheads. Timber rattlers. Diamondbacks and water moccasins.

This time, they weren't behind to herd them forward. They were ahead to keep them out.

At the sight of the spiders and snakes, Crock stepped back involuntarily and bumped into Jack. He turned to Jack, his face pale and panic-stricken.

"Jack, I can't. I...hate spiders...ever since I was a kid, arachnophobia so bad I ran through a glass door once to get away from a daddy longlegs. I can't go in there."

"Don't look at them. They can't hurt you, the angel won't let them. Look at the angel, nothing else. Just the angel."

Crock was balanced on a knife blade of panic, a heartbeat or two away from bolting. Jack could see the crazed terror in his eyes, the irrational, mindless fear only a phobia could produce. And if he chose to quit now and go back, Jack would step out of his way and let him go. No shame in that. What was being asked of him—of all of them—was way over the top too much. A man could only do what he could do.

Crock's eyes pleaded with Jack; then Jack watched him grab his fear and wrestle it, struggling with all his strength to get a grip on it. His jaw clenched so tight Jack actually heard his teeth grind together. Then he turned slowly back around toward the interior of the cave—clearly the single hardest thing the man had ever done in his life.

The angel and Andi had stopped. Andi was holding the angel's hand, looking up into her face. When Crock made eye contact with the angel and nodded, she smiled with compassion and reassurance. Then the glow around her instantly got brighter until it formed a puddle of light that extended on both sides and beyond Jack. And he understood that she'd created a no-fly zone—that nothing could harm anyone within that glow.

Jack tried the best he could to take the advice he'd given to Crock, tried not to allow his gaze to stray from the bright light of the angel in front of them. That wasn't always possible, though. The cave wasn't a tunnel here. It was fissures in the rock that ran off in every direction, connecting to other fissures and tunnels—a hopeless maze you'd never find your way through without help. As they moved forward, the light was a force that cleared away the tangle of snakes on the floor and spiders on the walls and ceiling like a leaf blower, sending every creature in their path tumbling away. Still, the fissures were so narrow in places that Crock had to turn sideways to pass through, his considerable belly only inches away from where spiders had been crawling only moments before.

When they finally entered a proper cave tunnel, the light dimmed slightly, but became more vibrantly gold at the same time, sparkling, shimmering like glitter, as if it weren't really one light at all but millions of tiny ones. Here, the mass of spiders and snakes fell back from the glow, the Red Sea parting. Jack never looked back, though. Not once. He knew better. He knew they'd closed ranks and become What Comes Behind, a clotted mass of spiders and snakes crawling and slithering over each other only inches beyond the light.

He, Crock and Andi were committed now, had effectively burned their ships. To turn around and plunge into the darkness beyond the light was to be overwhelmed by pure evil. It flashed through Jack's mind that that was as good a metaphor for life as he had ever heard, but the thought skittered away as quickly as it came.

The tunnel seemed to go on forever, to stretch out in front of them, a black hole into infinity. He knew that in reality they probably had not been walking long, but time seemed somehow suspended here, as if what happened was not governed by the rest of the laws of the universe. And maybe it wasn't. Certainly, what they faced stood outside those laws, a creature that had stepped into their world from beyond. Forces for good and evil linked in battle for all eternity would collide here today. He and Crock and Andi were just pawns.

But play the game right and a pawn could take a king.

Then he saw the red glow up ahead, flickering on the cave walls. There was a fire of some kind beyond the next bend and Jack knew what was burning.

～

THE LOOK that transformed Billy Ray's face took Daniel's breath away. The wiry little man had sunk to his hands and knees and was fumbling for the knife he'd dropped until Daniel said "murder victim." Then he froze. Daniel watched his eyes begin to move, to follow the action in a movie in the air in front of him that Daniel didn't want to see.

Billy Ray's face turned red, his neck muscles bulged as if he couldn't breathe and his eyes bugged out of his head —literally. His face squeezed up like the strings on a draw-string bag yanked tight. He began to scream then, his ugly hoarse voice scraping and rasping, a rusty chain dragged across a metal floor. Sound tore out of his throat in one long breath, his prominent Adam's apple working franti-cally up and down, and then he stopped screaming abruptly. In the silence, his face sagged, almost like it… melted. Whatever muscles had kept his features in place went limp—a stroke victim—and the angular bony lines reshaped soft and flaccid. The teardrop tattoo beneath his left eye slid down his sagging cheek as if he were crying.

He turned toward Daniel and Jeff and looked at them with eyes as vacant as an empty tomb.

"Billy Ray Hawkins has left the building," Jeff whispered.

Though the man in front of him was clearly incapable of rational thought, Daniel had to try. "You've seen a demon from hell, haven't you, Billy Ray?"

"I broke my necklace," he said, looking forlorn. "Cut my chest on the glass when I hit the floor. Isaac's blood started to drip out and I—"

"Isaac's blood?"

Billy Ray's face registered that he actually heard Daniel this time. But his eyes never lost their vacant stare.

"I stood right up next to Bishop at the Derby Festival

parade on Main Street, close as you two boys are, 'cept I didn't touch him. Get the stink of nigger flesh on your hands and you can't get it off with nothing but lye soap. I said to him, 'Why, hello, Bishop, you doin' all right today?' Nice as you please. And the whole time I had his boy's blood in a little bottle 'round my neck." Billy Ray let out a peal of tittering, high-pitched laughter that bounced and echoed off the walls of the empty chamber, creating a crowd of ghosts laughing with him.

Daniel felt sick. Bishop and Theresa hoping all these years and Billy Ray had…

Billy Ray rolled over on his back, lost in the laughter, slapped the floor and bellowed with glee. "Collected it—" he gasped between peals of laughter "—in a mason jar—" more laughter "—after I cut him up with a chain saw. Him screamin' and screamin' until I lopped his head off—"

He froze.

"Yes, sir, Mr. Whitworth. I'll do it just the way you say," he said to nobody.

He turned to Daniel and Jeff, his eyes not vacant but deranged.

"It's showtime, boys!" He snatched up the knife and stuck it in its scabbard and scrambled to his feet. He grabbed Daniel and dragged him to the altar encircled by pentagrams. Then he dragged Jeff and set them up side by side on their knees in front of it. He started digging around in a gym bag he must have brought with him, pulled out a notepad and set it on the altar.

"Billy Ray, listen to me," Daniel said, his voice urgent but calm, the tone you'd use with an injured animal, one you didn't want to upset because it could bite your head off. "You saw it—the big red monster—"

Billy Ray put his hands over his ears and shook his head violently. "All a dream—too much whiskey—only wanted to drink that bottle of Maker's in the cave where it was cool, that's all." He took his hands off his ears and continued to unload the gym bag. "Didn't see a thing, not a thing."

"Yes, you did," Daniel said. "You saw the red—"

Billy Ray turned with the speed of a striking cobra, crossed the distance between them in two steps, grabbed a handful of Daniel's hair and tilted his head back. When he put the knife to Daniel's throat, he held it so tight against his skin that a thin line of blood formed there and began to ooze down his neck.

"Don't you tell me what I saw," he shouted into Daniel's face. "I didn't see nothin'. You say I did and I'm gonna"—he moved the knife from Daniel's neck to his face, digging the point into the skin beneath his right eye—"put out your eyes. Cut 'em out and feed 'em to them buzzards a-circling up there." He gestured up toward the empty ceiling of the cavern. "Them birds'll make a fine meal out of 'em." He stopped. "And out of you, too! Was wondering what I was gonna do with your headless bodies and now I know. I ain't gonna do nothin' with 'em. I'll let the buzzards eat you."

He returned the knife to its scabbard on his belt and went back to the altar.

"These marks on the floor, the pentagrams—you draw those?" Jeff asked, in the casual way you'd ask a fly fisherman if he made his own lures.

Billy Ray didn't turn around, but answered just as amicably. "Nah, Whitworth musta done it. Said it was a long time ago. He didn't get in here past my boxcar, though, I had that puppy locked up tight."

"There's another way in? Weren't you afraid some-body'd come in that way and find your gold?"

Billy Ray turned back to face Jeff, his tone exasperated

rather than angry. "You think I'm stupid or somethin'? You don't think I checked? Only other way in here is through that tunnel over there." He cocked his thumb over his shoulder at the other side of the cavern beyond the crevice but didn't look that way. "And the only way to get over that crack in the floor between here and there is to…" He started to giggle then, high pitched like a teenage girl. "Float! The Man musta picked up his own self and— what's it called?—levitated over to this side."

"There are five pentagrams, Billy Ray," Daniel said quietly.

Billy Ray glanced around. "Yeah, I guess. Five."

"Billy Ray, do you realize that when you drip blood in those pentagrams, the same thing is going to happen that happened in the cave the night you broke your necklace," Daniel said.

Billy Ray froze in place with his back to them.

"Only this time, Billy Ray, there won't be one monster, there will be five—"

"I've about decided I'm not even gonna plant pole beans in my garden next spring," Billy Ray said as he consulted the notebook and took objects Daniel couldn't see and placed them on the altar. "Lots of tomato plants, though. Then I'll have some for fried green tomatoes. Mama got mad when we let 'em all get ripe this year, so next year…"

Billy Ray continued to prattle on about gardens and planting and building a henhouse as he arranged the arti-facts on the altar. Then Billy Ray lifted each in a Lion-King-hold-the-baby-to-the-sky pose and began to read what sounded like gibberish off a page of the notebook he'd laid on the altar. The first three artifacts were ancient stone statues. One was small, fit like a baseball in Billy Ray's hand. The other two were larger. Even from where he sat, Daniel could tell that the faces carved into the rock were monstrous.

Then Billy Ray lifted a book very carefully. It was in tatters, the cover all but falling off, many of the pages loose and all of them yellowed with age. He picked up a ring. The gold of the band glinted in the lantern light and the black stone as big as a walnut in the setting cast shards of refracted light in shiny arrows around the room. If that was a real diamond—of course it was a real diamond! A black diamond that size would be worth...it truly was priceless.

Billy Ray placed the ring on the ring finger of his left hand after he offered it up to the darkened ceiling, where imaginary buzzards circled overhead. He picked up a necklace and fit it over his head. It hung almost to his waist. Its chain was fashioned of alternating gold and silver links and a gigantic gold pendant dangled from it. The pendant was covered with runes and pictographs and the black diamond in the center of it was bigger than a golf ball. One by one he blessed them—clay pots, a mortar and pestle, two tablets with hieroglyphics—or some other ancient writing—on them. Daniel counted thirteen different items.

With the pendant necklace around his neck and the ring on his finger, Billy Ray put the other items back into the bag and carried the bag to the bottom point of the five-pointed star to their left. He took the small statue out of the bag, placed it on the point of the star, then stopped to consult his notebook. Then he stepped back and shook his head, put the small statue back into the bag, rummaged around, and came up with the largest statue. It appeared vaguely human, with a potbelly and legs, but three long horns protruded from the forehead of a hideous skull. He placed that one on the star point instead, eyed it and seemed satisfied, then began to read more gibberish from his notebook. He took out the tattered book and appeared to read a passage from it, his Kentucky accent rendering the words ludicrous—the sound of Charlie Brown's teacher. He went to the second point of the star and repeated the process with the small statue he'd mistakenly put in the place reserved for the biggest one.

"Look at the wall over there," Daniel said, and gestured with his chin to the cavern wall on the other side of the floor crack. There was a red glow that hadn't been there before coming from the cave entrance on the wall.

"The light, you mean?"

"I'm betting the efreet's there." He paused for a heart-beat. "That must be where we misplaced it."

Jeff looked appropriately chagrined.

"Chapman Whitworth's father was a 'sticky-fingered' anthropologist, pilfered artifacts from the Middle East for years, and Chapman either stumbled on—or maybe went looking for—how to summon a demon with them. So he decided to try his luck, drew a pentagram on the floor of a cave and did all the rest of it—but nothing happened. Either he didn't know about the blood or couldn't find anybody with the mark of evil to murder."

"Becca wasn't sure what 'the mark of evil' part meant," Jeff said. "She just said if Bishop's theory about it was right, she'd be a prime candidate."

"Bishop thought it might mean someone who'd actu-ally seen a demon—because seeing pure evil leaves a mark on a person's soul."

"Somebody with the knowing, then—like Becca. Did Isaac Washington—?"

Daniel nodded, then felt another piece slip into place.

"Milkstone! That must be where the cave over there comes out—the Bad Kids went there to drink that Sunday night. And somehow the efreet herded them into a cave nobody knew was there—probably used his eight-legged and no-legged friends to do it. Then they came out and went looking for the 'summoner'—that's what Becca said they called the person who'd drawn the pentagram—located Whitworth and he got himself absorbed by the efreet—"

"And the efreet wanted to bring all his rowdy buddies to the party, so—"

"Whitworth needed somewhere big enough to draw more pentagrams and this cavern was it. But the Three Musketeers stopped him before he had a chance. Now, he plans to finish what he started twenty-six years ago."

"That's a plausible scenario except for one thing—he can't use our blood. We don't qualify."

"You don't qualify," Daniel said. "I do."

"You don't have the knowing."

"No, but when I was twelve years old, I saw the efreet. That left the 'mark of evil' on me."

"So I'm just—what? A practice shot?"

"I was prepared to die. I'd made my peace with that. But five more efreets! No! I can't let him do that."

"You planning on stopping him?"

"I'm the only one who can."

Chapter Twenty-Eight

As Becca headed east along the Ohio River, Theresa spotted a smudge of smoke in the sky ahead. Whatever was burning was something big to be producing that much smoke.

But it was funny-looking smoke.

"Do you see that?" Becca asked. "Or is it just me?"

"That smoke, you mean?"

"It's not smoke."

And it wasn't smoke, couldn't be, didn't act like smoke. Smoke spewed up from a fire into the sky, going higher and higher. This gray…cloud, fog spread out on the ground.

"If it ain't smoke, what is it?"

"I don't know what it is, but I know where it's coming from."

"You think he's…"

"It's happening because of him and maybe he's doing it on purpose to hide something. Or maybe when that kind of evil uses all its power—it produces…that, the way boiling water makes steam."

It was clear to Theresa and Becca, though maybe not

to anybody else, that the center of the fog was the River-gate Hotel. The fog got thicker and darker as they approached it, blotting out the late afternoon sun so completely that automatic street lights came on and cars had to turn on their headlights.

Becca parked where Theresa directed her, in the back lot. They got out and donned their masks and Theresa pulled up her hood so she looked like a red Grim Reaper. It was early, so there was no crowd yet. Still, the lobby held all manner of strange beings, Vikings and clowns and Indian maidens—lots of color, too, with a red M&M, a yellow Minion, a blue Dorie the Fish, a purple dinosaur and a green Alf the Elf.

Theresa led them through a labyrinth of hallways, winding toward the back of the building where the employee lounges, huge industrial kitchens and laundry rooms were located.

Nobody noticed when she snatched one of the rolling laundry hampers, dumped most of the dirty sheets and towels from it into the one beside it and pushed the almost empty one down the hall.

"Pull the car up to the back door on the east side," Theresa said, "the one beside the dumpsters. I'll be waiting."

When Becca appeared out of the fog, the image startled Theresa. Not because the horned mask, the red suit with black batwings and a forked tail was scary. It was disturbing because the outfit was the shape of the figure hidden by the pillar of smoke in the painting of the efreet in Bishop's office. Whoever it was who'd drawn the first cartoon devil had obviously seen a real one.

The two women stepped between the big green dumpsters and the building, Becca with the bag full of rats and the other garbage bag Theresa'd told her to get. When

Becca opened up the "rat bag," Theresa recoiled so violently she bumped her head on the dumpster. How could she touch one of them creatures? Pick it up? Might even be the one that took that hunk outta her leg, or the one that bit her on the neck. How could—?

"You hold the bag open and I'll put the rats in," Becca said, and Theresa knew that skinny little thing would dig every last one of them rats outa that bag so Theresa wouldn't have to touch 'em.

Becca reached in and pulled out the first one, its head barely affixed to its body. Musta been one of them Biscuit got a'hold of. Biscuit. Pain swelled in Theresa's heart.

"They're still…well, not frozen solid, but stiff." Theresa could hear the revulsion in Becca's voice. "I don't know how lifelike they're going to look."

"They'll serve," Theresa said. "They got to." Theresa continued to babble, trying to distract Becca from the grisly task.

"When I worked here as a maid, my partner cleanin' rooms was the prettiest little thing you ever seen, sweet and innocent, only sixteen. Nyree had a face like an angel and a body like…well, not like an angel."

As Becca pried the frozen rats apart to distribute the dead bodies in the bags, Theresa described how every bellhop with a pulse had had a thing for Nyree—even the ones old enough to be her grandfather. Especially the ones old enough to be her grandfather.

"Them men was always comin' up with interestin' things to show Nyree, tryin' to get her alone somewhere. They didn't like it much when I'd show up to tag along."

There was hardly a nook or cranny of the Rivergate Theresa hadn't seen on them "scenic tours." Pulleys big as truck tires in the elevator shafts. HVAC ductwork you could drive a Humvee through. She'd "toured" the top floor of the building where the roof retracted for balloon shows. A bellhop had even pointed out the switch in that 'lectronics room behind the ballroom on the ground floor that released the netting for a balloon drop. Theresa'd thought at the time she wasn't doin' nothing but protecting a young girl's virtue, never dreamed she'd ever use any of the stuff she was findin' out. The Lord worked in mysterious ways.

After Becca divided the rats into two garbage bags, they set the bags over into the laundry basket, covered them with towels and sheets and rolled the basket back into the building.

They continued down a labyrinth of hallways to the lobby and the atrium, now crowded with all manner of strange beings on their way to the ball. The service elevator was located in the big hallway behind the Balloon Ballroom.

"Only the service elevator goes all the way to the top floor above the ceiling. It ain't out here with the regular elevators. It's—"

"Hey, you!" snarled a voice from behind them.

They turned to see Darth Vader striding toward them, the glowing light saber in his hand raised high.

"What do you think you're doing with a laundry basket out here among the guests?"

Theresa turned toward him. "It ain't laundry in this here basket," she said. "It's dead rats. Couldn't very well haul dead rats through the lobby right out in front of everybody, now could we?"

OHIO RIVER COAL barges didn't keep to tight schedules, so it was impossible for Sebastian to find out exactly when one would pass the Rivergate tonight—only that sometime between six o'clock and ten o'clock at least one barge, and probably more than one, would glide silently by. He had a spotter upstream who had targeted a barge about half an hour away and another about twenty minutes behind that one. He'd use the first.

Though the fog had grown so thick Sebastian could have launched an aircraft carrier out into the river unseen, he waited until the barge was still a few minutes out, then pushed the dinghy into the inlet and pulled out into the river—not into the shipping channel.

If the barges had been empty, they'd have been floating so high in the water that the tugboat's radar would pass right over something as small as a dinghy out front. But the barges were fully loaded, sunk ten feet deep, so anything at all beyond the lead barge would show up as a blip on the tug's screen.

Watching a barge come around a bend in the river was like watching lead screw slowly out of a pencil. But in this fog, it would be impossible to see the front barge coming. You wouldn't be able to hear it, either. For all their size and girth, Ohio River coal barges traveled almost silently. The rumble of the tug pushing them was more than four football fields behind the front barge.

Sebastian killed the dinghy's outboard motor and put his hand down into the water. He felt it instantly—the vibration of the tug's engines. Sound didn't carry, but the vibration in the water did. The barge was close.

A minute, two maybe, and then it was there in front of him, slicing silently through the water. He waited. Watched the first barge in the tow pass and then the second. He began to ease out into the shipping channel then, turned and matched his speed to the speed of the tug as he pulled up close to the third barge. Though the spotlight on the tug was nothing but a bright blur in the distance now, if the fog should suddenly lift, that searchlight would sweep back and forth over the lead barge and out into the water in front of it. But the light was mounted on the roof of the tug, so it would pass over the tops of the nearest barges.

He pulled alongside a barge that was so heavily loaded that the waterline came within two feet of the narrow walkway that surrounded the cargo area. He slid closer to it until he spotted a cleat, then nudged the dinghy up to the barge there, grabbed the cleat and secured a line around it. He stood and carefully lifted the Javelin up onto the walkway before he hopped out behind it.

Though there was a crew of nine men on the tugboat, on rigid six-hours-on, six-hours-off schedules, their duties mostly involved the tug itself rather than the barges—which were nothing more than floating boxes with no moving parts. Two deckhands, one on each side, would make a circuit of the whole tow sometime during their six-hour watch. Maybe they'd already made their circuit. If they hadn't, there'd certainly be no reason to send anybody out in the fog to inspect barges they couldn't see. Sebastian wanted to get on and off the barge without anybody knowing he'd ever been there. That was ideal. He'd rather not have to silence some wandering deckhand who happened to stumble over him—but he would if he had to.

Sebastian slipped the strap on the launcher over his shoulder and stepped over the three-foot-tall edge of the coal compartment and into the coal in neat stacks about thirty feet tall. Ten feet of the stacked coal was below the waterline, which left twenty-foot piles sticking out above. Sebastian made his way toward the center of the barge and selected a spot between two piles of coal. He'd be impossible to see there in the dark even with good visibility.

He knelt, rested the missile launcher on his right

shoulder and lowered his face to the sight, an integrated day/night sight that provided such good visibility even in bad weather conditions that it was often used by itself for battlefield surveillance and reconnaissance. The shoreline instantly popped into view and he could make out bushes, trees and rocks. Excellent. He didn't need such a powerful sight for his purposes, though. You could see the neon balloons on the roof of the Rivergate through mud!

Then Sebastian Nemo relaxed back against the pile of coal with the missile launcher in his lap and waited.

CROCK NOTICED it when they came out of a narrow fissure into what might actually be a cave—with an ominous red glow at the far end of it. He was so surprised, he almost stopped in his tracks, but Jack would have rear-ended him if he had. They were all huddled as close together as they could, shrinking involuntarily away from the horror that existed beyond the light.

What Crock noticed was that his leg where that boy had stabbed him with scissors had stopped hurting! Well, not entirely, but it hurt like it was supposed to—an amount of pain commensurate with the severity of the wound. Which was plenty. But it was nothing like the hot coal of agony that had kept him awake through the night. He'd never felt a pain like that in his life, a thrumming ache that —okay, this was nuts, but it was what it was—an ache that felt alive. Like it was wiggling and squirming and gnawing away at him deep inside. Sometime in the wee hours of the morning, as he lay awake grinding his teeth to keep from moaning, he thought about that movie he'd gone to because everybody was talking about it and he was tired of having nothing to say. There was a little guy in it with furry feet, Frodo, who got stabbed by a see-through ghost king, and somebody, he couldn't remember who, had said a piece of the blade had broken off inside him and was moving toward his heart. That was how Crock's leg had felt.

Except it didn't feel that way now. He tried to think when it had stopped throbbing, but he couldn't be sure. He'd been concentrating so hard on not looking around, on seeing nothing but the top of Andi's head and the back of that angel's denim jacket that a shark could have bit his leg off at the knee and he wouldn't have noticed. But he believed the pain had eased up as soon as that angel's light touched him. Which made sense. Jack said evil couldn't harm them—at least not physically—when they were protected by the angel's light.

Would it start hurting again like that after this was over and—?

Blank.

Nothing there.

No room anywhere in his head to think about the world of sunshine, baseball games and triple-cheese pizzas and about this world of dark, unfathomable horror. One or the other. There was no way to consider any reality beyond this tunnel and a sound behind them like crinkling tissue paper and the light from the angel that left no shadows.

The red glow ahead was getting nearer with each step. Crock's heart began to bang away in his chest and his terror began to swell, bigger and bigger, a sperm whale in a fish tank. The pressure of it made it hard to breathe.

God! Are you here? In the light maybe, in the sparkles?

That thing up there in front of us...I can't...I've done some pretty sorry things in my life and he's going to rub my nose in all of it. Theresa says we have to stand tall, be courageous and...God, I'm not brave. You know that. I'm the worst sniveling coward in the world. If there was any possible way I could get out of this right now, I would. I would! I'd leave the rest of them behind—sorry 'bout your luck—bolt out of here and never look back. I'm going to fail, God. I know it. He's going to come after me and I won't be able to hold it together. You shouldn't have picked me. You should have tapped somebody else on the shoulder...anybody else. I'm telling you now while I can. You got the wrong guy in Charles Allen Crocker.

YOU GOT the wrong man in Jack Carpenter.

Jack thought it or prayed it. It was hard for him to tell here when he was praying and when he wasn't. There were random, crazy thoughts in his head, firing like popcorn—the oil in the car needs changing...could he really find season tickets to the Reds' games on eBay?—and a sickening terror groaned in his mind. Was he praying all that, too? Yeah, probably.

That last part, though, he knew that was a prayer.

You should have picked somebody else! Daniel could do this. I can't. Why couldn't you let me get my head chopped off and use Daniel to fight this monster? You need a man of faith and that's not me. I'm...okay, here it is. Theresa would call this "truth in long johns with the butt flap down." I don't trust you, God. And most of the time, I don't like you. You let good people, innocent people get hurt and die. You let this thing we're facing come here and didn't do a thing to stop it. Why not? You could have sent him back where he came from—but no, you're making us do it for you. That pisses me off! See, I'm an angry, doubting man. How can you use a man like that?

And you let Andi get dragged into this. What's wrong

with you, God—how could you do a thing like that? She's only a little girl! You have to protect her.

Look, if somebody's got to get hurt here today…die here today…I volunteer. Take me. Keep her safe and take me. My life for Andi's. Deal? Please!

∾

<

I know I'm not supposed to be—I'm holding the hand of an angel—but God, I'm scared. I'm afraid of spiders and snakes. All crawly and slimy—I guess snakes are slimy. I never touched one, but they look slimy. I just…I want to go home!

Tears began to slide down Andi's cheeks and she couldn't do anything to stop them. Her lip was trembling and she bit it to keep from crying out loud.

The angel squeezed her hand then. She looked up into the angel's face—she didn't much look like Princess Buttercup anymore—and she saw an expression there like she used to see on her mommy's face when she'd play possum, pretend to be asleep so she could watch Mommy stand in the doorway, looking down at her.

And that should have made her feel better, but it really made her feel worse because she was about to let the angel down. Let everybody down. She tried to tell the angel that she wanted to go home, she couldn't do this, but if she stopped biting her lip to talk, she'd burst out crying.

I want my daddy! Please, God, don't let those bad people chop off his head.

She sucked in a single sob at the image that burst into her mind of Daddy and Mr. Kendrick on their knees and the bad man with the sword behind them.

No, she couldn't think about that or she'd start crying

and never be able to stop. Uncle Jack had said if you cut off a snake's head, the rest of it would die and that this monster thing was the snake's head. If they...got rid of it or killed it or banished it or whatever they were supposed to do—the people it controlled wouldn't be puppets anymore. That was the only hope Daddy had.

She squeezed the angel's hand—hard. Didn't look up at her this time, though. She had to concentrate on being brave, on being good and saying the right thing so this monster would go away and leave her and Daddy and the others alone.

Besides, it wouldn't do any good to run away, to go home—God would just send a big fish or something after her. Miss Theresa had wanted to pick, to decide if she was going to do what God told her to do or not. So had Jonah. But they didn't get to pick.

Andi Burke didn't get to pick either.

But I'm so scared, God. I'm afraid I'll cry or something —maybe wet my pants. How can I do this if I'm so scared?

There was a red glow at the end of the tunnel and it'd been getting bigger and bigger as they got near it. Now she could see the light was flickering like from a candle. At the far end, the tunnel turned to the left and the red light was coming from there.

He was in there. That thing. He was right around the corner. Andi took a deep, shuddering breath.

Help.

Her mind went suddenly blank and the only thing in it was that one word. Help. Not as a cry, a plea. Just a word. Help. Maybe that meant God was promising to help her! Or maybe it meant God was telling her to help somebody else.

Chapter Twenty-Nine

Halfway down the tunnel that led to where Jack could see a red light glowing, flickering, off to the left, the angel stopped. She turned and spoke to them. It was the first time she had uttered a word since they stepped into the cave.

"There's a pentagram drawn on the floor in that cavern," she said, gesturing with her chin to the flickering red light. "Don't step inside it." Her voice was soft but clear and strong. "And remember who this beast serves…"

She turned from one to the other of them, each one in turn, catching their gaze and holding it, staring deep into their eyes.

"He serves the Father of Lies."

The words hung in the air for a heartbeat. Then the angel turned back around and continued down the tunnel toward the red glow.

That was it? No pep talk? No coaching? Nothing profound that they'd remember the rest of their lives—if they had a rest of their lives?

Nope. They just went on.

Jack was not aware of taking steps, couldn't feel his legs at all, as a matter of fact. But he had to be walking because he was getting closer to the tunnel that turned left at the far end, where red, flickering light pulsed.

Well, this was where the proverbial Michelin Radial made contact with the asphalt. Jack's heart was a frantic woodpecker in his chest and he was breathing hard—was he panting?—but he didn't feel like he was taking in enough oxygen. He felt like he was suffocating.

He'd been here before!

There, on the wall opposite the opening to the cavern where the beast was waiting for them, were Mickey Mouse ears! Or that was what he'd thought the two cup-shaped rocks on top of a round one had looked like when the Bad Kids dragged him past them twenty-six years ago. Why would he remember a stupid thing like that when he couldn't remember the important stuff? He'd been twelve years old then, but he was certain he felt more fear now than that young man had been capable of feeling. Of course, he hadn't known what he was facing that time. Returning to the horror now created some emotion way on the other side of fear in his belly. A nameless emotion made of equal parts disbelief, terror and…and anger.

Yeah, anger! He was flat out done with having his life and the lives of every person in the world he cared about terrorized by this monster.

It's showtime, pal. Come on, give it your best shot. Make my day.

The bravado lasted only as long as it took Jack to round the corner and see what actually did lie in the cavern that opened off the left side of the tunnel.

That one sight melted Jack's resolve, his courage and his will. They gushed out of him—water through a hole in a wading pool—leaving him parched, so dry and brittle a single touch would turn his whole being to dust.

∿

"YOU'RE GOING to stop Billy Ray from summoning more efreets?" Jeff's voice had regained its customary sardonic edge. "How? I must have missed that part."

Daniel had been considering it ever since Billy Ray ripped the duct tape off his face and he got a good look at the cavern. As soon as Billy Ray started performing the ceremony, he knew.

"What he's doing is a ritual," he said. "Billy Ray has to go around to each of the five points of every star in those pentagrams and chant certain words."

Jeff nodded.

"When he gets to the bottom point on the fifth star, the one next to the crack in the floor, he'll have his back to us while he says his mumbo jumbo. I'm going to jump him then and bowl him over into the crevice."

Jeff spoke slowly and deliberately, probably the way he talked to drunk or nutcase clients.

"Daniel, you can't knock him into the hole without—"

"Falling in with him? I know that. What have I got to lose? Either he kills me and uses my blood to summon demons, or I kill him—and myself. I die either way. Even if I screw it up and miss Billy Ray somehow, I've stopped him. He can't do what he came here to do without my blood."

Jeff stared at him, an odd expression on his face. At least it appeared to be odd. His face was a train wreck, though, so it was hard to tell.

If Emily could see him now, would she think he was such hot stuff?

Daniel was instantly ashamed of that thought. Ashamed? That was crazy. But things had shifted somehow. Daniel didn't know and had neither the emotional wherewithal, the energy nor the time to puzzle out why.

"We'll both jump him," Jeff said.

"Why? You don't have to—"

"—do anything I don't want to? I'm well aware of that. But look at it from my perspective. Best-case scenario: you succeed, you kill him. Where does that leave me? In a cavern I can't find my way out of. Oh, maybe I could find the boxcar, but then I'd have to chew my way through that gate. Maybe you didn't notice, but the base is sunk in five inches of concrete. And the key to the padlock on it is in Billy Ray's pocket. Worst-case scenario: he sidesteps and you go diving off into nowhere all by yourself. Where does that leave me? The same place the best-case scenario does —but add in a homicidal lunatic with a scimitar, a pissed-off lunatic. If I'm lucky, he might only use that blade to cut my head off, but I figure it's more likely he'll be in chop-Mr.-Suit-and-Tie-Man-into-little-pieces mode."

Jeff was right, of course.

"I want to take that stupid hillbilly with me when I buy the farm." Jeff growled. "Revenge is a whole lot more satisfying than forgiveness."

"Can you do it hobbled?" Daniel asked.

"I'd rather kick his face in, but yeah, I can move fast enough to pull it off."

In truth, Daniel was glad Jeff was going with him. Surely, the two of them could knock Billy Ray over the edge. And he very much wanted to rid the world of Billy Ray Hawkins.

"Did you play football in high school, by any chance?" Jeff asked.

"Marching band."

"Seriously?"

"Tuba."

Jeff rolled his eyes. "Well, I played football. A real man's sport, by the way. I'll hit him high, body-slam him. You hit him low, knock his legs out from under him."

Daniel nodded.

Billy Ray slowly made his way around the pentagrams, spouting ancient words at the point of each star in a twangy Kentucky accent—words that would unleash monsters from the dawn of time on mankind.

"Sulfuric acid will eat right through concrete," Jeff muttered thoughtfully to himself.

What?

The non sequitur was jarring. Daniel looked at him quizzically, but Jeff offered no explanation. Neither spoke again, just listened as Billy Ray made unintelligible sounds in his gravelly, guttural voice. They watched him progress from one point of the stars to the next, and when he finished the fourth pentagram and started for the fifth, Jeff whispered, "Stand up slow; stay in a crouch. Don't rush him until I give the signal."

Somehow, Jeff had taken over and was running the show. He was a man accustomed to being in charge. Daniel let him have that, here at the end.

"Body slam..." Daniel said. "That chest-bump thing football players do, very macho."

"There are car batteries on a shelf outside the boxcar," Jeff said. Another non sequitur. Then he tensed. "Get ready."

Billy Ray turned to face the crack. Jeff and Daniel rose clumsily from their knees to a crouch, staying low.

Jeff suddenly whispered, "You can get out of here. Take good care of Emily's little girl!"

He banged his shoulder into Daniel, shoving him sideways. Crouched as he was, the blow knocked Daniel off balance and he tumbled over onto his side. As he fell to the floor, he watched Jeff spring up and race toward Billy Ray.

Billy Ray had heard the scuffle, or Jeff's footsteps, and he was turning, pulling the gun from his holster, when Jeff yelled a wordless, primal cry and slammed his body into the smaller man. Billy Ray flew backwards with Jeff on top of him and they both disappeared into the abyss.

Stunned, Daniel lay where he'd fallen, listening—waiting for a cry, a thump, some kind of sound. Nothing. He struggled to get to his knees, rolled to a nearby stalagmite and used it for balance. Then he stood and walked on trembling legs to the edge of the crack and looked down. Impenetrable darkness was all that looked back up at him.

THE DEAD-RATS STATEMENT had the desired effect, stopping Darth Vader in his tracks. He lowered his light saber, pulled his mask up off his face and gaped at her.

Theresa hoped Becca didn't pass out from shock.

When the black-caped Star Wars bad guy, whose name tag said he was the concierge of the hotel, had called out to them, Theresa'd known she had about three seconds to come up with a plausible explanation or this little party was gone be over before it started. It was Bishop who could think fast on his feet—not Theresa. Why'd God give this to her to do when she was gone mess up the whole thing?

What can I say?

And it had happened to her again, like it'd done that day when she'd faced Chapman Whitworth in Miss Minnie and Mr. Gerald's parlor with them lying hacked to death with an ax not ten feet away. Words had come out of her mouth, words she hadn't thought or formed or willed her lips to speak.

"It ain't towels in this here laundry basket," she said. "It's dead rats. Couldn't very well haul dead rats through the lobby right out in front of everybody, now could we?"

Theresa heard herself continue, "You know, rubber rats."

She babbled on as chatty as she'd have been giving somebody her granny's special recipe for corn fritters.

"Didn't nobody tell you about 'em?"

She reached down into the laundry basket to one of the sacks and stuck her hand inside. "They's real lifelike, look just like the genuine article."

She pulled a rat out of the sack by its tail and held it up right in front of Darth Vader's face.

The big man took a step back.

The rat wasn't completely thawed out yet. Its neck was broke and its head was laid back and stuck to its backbone. Revulsion threatened to gag her, but she swallowed hard, reached up and pulled the head into place like it was an action figure doll, praying as hard as she'd ever prayed for anything in her life that the head wouldn't come off in her hand.

"There," she said with pride. "Don't that look real?"

The concierge only glanced at the beast, clearly could not stand to get a good look at it. And that was a fine thing, because if he'd looked closely, he'd have seen the drop of blood slide down off its nose and plop on the floor.

"Very real," he said. "But what—?"

"You didn't get no memo?" Theresa shook her head. "Somebody higher up on the food chain than me was in charge of tellin' the folks as needed to know. Not everybody, of course. Then word woulda got out and spoiled the surprise."

"What are they—?"

Theresa rolled over him like Sherman marching through Atlanta.

"All's I know is I was s'posed to pick these up at the loading dock and deliver 'em to the kitchen staff. They's gonna put 'em on the dessert trays of important people is what I heard."

"Rubber rats—?"

"I didn't think it was funny my own self but didn't nobody ask for my opinion. If you got a problem with it, though, that is fine with me." She shoved the rat at him. "Here. You take care of 'em!"

Theresa watched in horror as the movement dislodged several drips of blood from the dead rat's smashed nose— one of which landed on Darth Vader's shiny black boot.

"No, I…" He shot another glance off the rat, didn't look at it full on. Didn't look at his boot, neither. "It's so real." He actually shuddered then. Hard to fathom a squeamish Darth Vader. "Go on about…whatever you were doing." He turned on his heel and strode purposefully away.

The smile melted off Theresa's face, candle wax from a flame, as soon as his back was turned. While they'd been talking, the lobby around them had emptied as the throng of costumed revelers filed into the Balloon Ballroom. Theresa heard a brief squawk of feedback from the microphone on the dais in the front of the room. The ball had begun; the clock was ticking.

Turning wordlessly, Theresa piloted the laundry basket with shaking hands out of the lobby into the huge hallway behind the ballroom, where the service elevator was located on the back wall. She was breathing now, great heaving gulps of relief. She got two or three good lungfuls before she noticed that the red button on the wall beside the elevator had a keyhole beneath it. The elevator required a key to operate. The bellhop trying to impress Nyree had had one. Theresa didn't.

CROCK HAD PREPARED himself the best he could for what he would see when they stepped into the cavern lit by the red glow. He'd dropped his gaze, pried it off the back of the angel walking in front holding Andi's hand, and deliberately looked down at his shoes, concentrated on his shoes—granting his anguished mind a few more seconds before the blow.

One step.

Two.

Couldn't look at his feet forever.

When he lifted his head, he gasped. From surprise and shock rather than terror.

The cavern was enormous. Bigger than the inside of a cathedral, than a football stadium. Its walls looked like streams of frozen cream. Water-polished flow formations cascaded in swirls and eddies, an unseen current of glossy rock rising seamlessly off the floor and up to the ceiling in the shadows above. Stalactites hung there, stretching down out of the darkness, each with a shiny point, a gigantic chandelier that sparkled but provided no light. The room was lit with the glow of thousands of candles affixed to the shiny, polished walls—how? He couldn't tell. Their tiny flames danced and flickered as if a breeze gently brushed them. They didn't give off normal light, though—soft white light. Each candle glowed the color of blood, a garish luminescence that reminded him of college parties when he and his fraternity brothers screwed red light bulbs into every socket.

But the cavern with its otherworldly glow was not what shocked him. What knocked the breath out of him was the young woman standing alone in the center of the otherwise empty expanse of cream-colored rock.

A strikingly beautiful black woman in her twenties, her face looked hauntingly familiar, but Crock couldn't recall where he'd seen her before. Her hair lay in soft curls, her eyes were wide and sad, her cheeks tearstained. She had the kind of sensually plump lips men went all stupid over, with bright red lipstick. The color matched her dress.

But below her head, the rest of her body was a ruin. If she'd been hit by a train, she couldn't have been more severely injured. Her arms and legs were twisted and bent, a prickly forest of compound fractures with bloody bones sticking out through her ripped flesh. Her torso had been torn open, her internal organs visible in a smashed tangle that hung out through a hole in the skirt of her bright red dress.

She couldn't possibly be standing, of course. But she was. In her right hand she held a man's hand—only the hand. The arm extending from it dangled almost to the floor, ending in bloody flesh and shattered bone, torn off at the shoulder.

She began to shamble toward them on grotesquely broken legs. When she spoke, her voice was tear clotted. She sounded like she'd been crying for a long time.

"I only wanted a baby, Jack," she said, and stifled a sob. "But you said no." She mimicked Jack's voice. "'I don't want children. They take up all your time and energy. I don't even like kids.'"

Then Crock knew where he'd seen her before. In a picture on the wall in Jack's living room. This was his wife, Lyla, who'd been at work in Tower One on 9/11."

Crock turned toward Jack. He'd never seen on

anybody's face a look quite like the one on Jack's. He was surprised and horrified…and glad. Even in such a horrible condition, here was his wife, right in front of him. And she'd been dead for a decade.

But it wasn't Lyla, of course. It was pure evil. Crock reached out and touched Jack's arm, but Jack shook off his hand as if he wanted nothing to distract him. He stared at the vision in fascination, horror and delight.

"Lyla?" he said, wonder in his voice.

"Jack, that's not Lyla," Crock said. He reached out to him again to get his attention. "Lyla's dead."

The not-Lyla turned on Crock in the grip of such loathing rage her face was more horrifying than her shattered body.

"Mind your own business, fat man," she shrieked like a harpy. "You'll get your turn!"

A dark black cloud thicker than smoke suddenly rose behind Lyla and filled the cavern from top to bottom, bubbling and boiling like a thunderstorm. The color of the cloud changed to the sick gray-black of tornado clouds, the edges tinged the greenish purple of a day-old bruise.

…and there was something in the cloud.

Crock couldn't see what it was. Not with his eyes. But somewhere in his most basic self, he could sense it. The form, the dark shape, the thing needed no image to communicate its presence. Even in the not-seeing, there was horror. Orange and red and black. A mouth with too many teeth. A head with horns. A face that defined ugliness.

Lyla went limp, like a marionette when the puppeteer lets go of the strings.

A horrifying roar issued from the depths of the black cloud, a sound that echoed off the chamber walls, fracturing and multiplying.

A rumbling roar like that could not possibly form words. But it did.

"How dare you come here!"

Thunder from the throat of Niagara Falls, the sound itself had substance, took up space in the world like a mountain or an ocean.

"Get out!"

The last words came at Crock with a force like the repercussion of an explosion. An invisible hand slapped him backwards. He stumbled and fell to the chamber floor, banging his head painfully, in the grip of a cold terror that wound through every twist and turn of his bowels.

"—leave now or—" The voice full of boulders broke up. There was static, then sputtering sounds. "—be sorry —" More static.

When Crock's head'd hit the floor, the hearing aid in his right ear had blinked off, then back on. Cher. She'd always been the one that gave him trouble. Now, her sputtering made the monster sound like it had a speech defect.

"—Maggots! Wretched fools—" Static. "—out of—" More static. Then silence, no sound of any kind in his right ear. He couldn't hear—

And there it was. That simple. The why Theresa'd told him he'd likely never find out. Charles Allen Crocker had not been selected by God to do battle with a lord of evil because of some remarkable character trait. Or because of his great faith. He hadn't been twice saved by angels so he could be right here, right now because of his unshakeable courage and resolve. He'd been picked because he was deaf. God had given him a unique hearing loss at birth for just this occasion. No, he wasn't the one-millionth customer, but the reason he was here was as simple and unpretentious. Crock could stand tall against the malicious, hate-filled lies of the enemy if he couldn't hear them.

Crock sat up and put his hands over his ears, shaking his head violently, appearing to be so frightened he could barely hold onto his terror. But it wasn't his terror he was holding onto. It was Sonny and Cher. As he shook his head, he switched both of them off.

Theresa had said a demon couldn't read your mind, that it didn't know Becca was down for the count all those years ago and so feared her. That monster surely knew Crock wore hearing aids, but it didn't know Crock couldn't hear a single word it was saying right now. And Crock had no intention of letting it find out. As far as this efreet thing knew, Harrelton, Ohio, Police Department Major Charles Crocker was resolute and defiant, uncowed by the worst the monster could throw at him. Surely to goodness, that'd unnerve the beast.

Crock got to his feet as the Lyla puppet came back to life.

"It's your fault, Jack! I died because of you," she said. "If you had let me go to that doctor's appointment, I wouldn't have—"

"Lyla...baby..." Anguish broke Jack's voice. "I'm so sorry."

Crock grabbed his arm and yanked Jack around to face him.

"That's not Lyla, Jack. Remember what the angel said —he serves the Father of Lies."

Crock felt the nudge of a percussive force and knew the creature must be speaking. It wasn't yelling this time, though, and it was not addressing him at all. But whatever it was saying was ripping open Jack Carpenter's soul.

The arm attached to the man's hand the Lyla Carpenter monster was holding began to move.

Crock kept his grip on Jack's arm, refusing to allow

him to turn back toward the abomination that was not Lyla Carpenter.

"Look at me, Jack! Make eye contact. "That's not Lyla!"

Then more Lylas appeared. Literally out of nowhere. Each was a unique abomination—horribly injured but in different ways. One had no face at all, only mashed flesh, broken bones and gore below the soft black curls. One had no head at all, but carried it, held it out in front like offering a plate of cookies. Another was a decayed corpse from the grave, covered in maggots. Three of them. Four. A half dozen. They circled around where Jack and Crock stood, jackals closing in for the kill. And the stench, they reeked of rotted decaying flesh.

"Don't look at them," Crock said. "Look at me. Look at my ugly mug."

The percussion again, the cloud speaking. Crock was profoundly glad he could not hear what it must be saying because he could see the effect of it on Jack's face.

"I'm real, Jack. They're not. They're evil in human-being suits. I'm your friend. Look at me!"

Then someone appeared beside Crock and the strength went out of his arms and he let Jack go. Crock didn't have to turn to know who it was. But he turned anyway.

Chapter Thirty

It couldn't be, of course. Except it was.

Lyla.

Jack felt everything inside him come loose and begin to float away. Courage, will, resolve. They'd been tethered to the man who was Jack Carpenter, anchored there his whole life with firm, sturdy ropes. Now, the moorings fell away and a great wave carried them all out to sea. Left on the shore was a parched, brittle soul, fragile and frail, strength drained away by the apparition before him.

Then Jack felt sudden joy well up in his chest. He recognized it for what it was—unhinged and mad. But she was here. His precious…

Not Lyla. Not Lyla. Not Lyla! Can't be.

Her face—animated, not just a photograph—was as beautiful as it had been the last time he saw her. She'd been crying then, too.

When she spoke, her voice was deeper, throatier than the woman he loved. But her words drilled down into his soul. She'd only wanted a baby, she said, but Jack didn't like children.

It wasn't that he hadn't noticed the horror of her body. It was that his mind could attend to one thing or the other —her beautiful face or the carnage below it. Not both. When he allowed himself to take in the extent of her injuries, he was suddenly nauseated, afraid he might actually vomit right there at her feet.

Her body! She had fallen so far.

He felt a grip on his arm, but shook it off and finally found his voice.

"Lyla?" His voice was weak and made a scratchy sound like wind-driven sleet against a windowpane or scarabs on the walls of an ancient tomb. It was how he'd sounded the night he'd wandered through their apartment, calling out to her, crying out in disbelieving agony while dust still hung in the air in the city.

"Jack, that's not Lyla. Lyla's dead."

He could hear Crock, but his words seemed to come not only from a great distance but from another time altogether. From a distant past. Not from now. Now was Lyla.

She turned to Crock and screamed at him to mind his own business, that his turn would come.

Then a black cloud bubbled up behind Lyla, the black-purple turbulence of an approaching hurricane. Its roiling ugliness filled the cavern behind her all the way to the ceiling.

Lyla froze, became a lifeless mannequin.

No, Lyla. Don't go.

A roar rumbled out of the cloud, ricocheting off the walls. The roaring voice addressed Crock and the force of the words knocked him to the floor. The cloud continued to rumble at him, but Jack's attention was riveted on Lyla. She looked like a doll—her eyes open but sightless, her face an expressionless mask.

And then she was back! Instantly alive. In his mind's eye, he saw a little white switch.

Flip it up, Lyla lived. Flip it down…

His heart swelled with joy—demented joy. Unnatural. Then her voice—it wasn't quite right—spoke aloud the accusations he had hurled at himself for years, the ones that screamed in his head and woke him in the midnight dark.

She told him it was his fault, that if he'd let her go to her doctor's appointment that morning, she'd be alive.

She was right, of course. Lyla was dead because of him. His eyes were drawn unbidden down her body—he did this to her.

"Lyla…baby…" His voice broke and he could barely finish. "I'm so sorry!"

Crock had gotten up off the floor when Lyla'd started speaking. He grabbed Jack and yanked him around so he was looking full into Crock's face.

"That's not Lyla, Jack. Remember what the angel said—he serves the Father of Lies."

Then the cloud spoke again, but not in a gravel-in-a-blender roar. This time, its voice was smooth and melodious—the kind, reasonable voice of James Earl Jones.

"It's no lie, Jack. You watched her fall."

The limp arm dangling to the floor from the hand Lyla held suddenly came to life. It rose as if it were attached to the shoulder of an invisible man. The cloud spoke again, but Crock held Jack firm, wouldn't let him turn and face Lyla and the cloud.

"She died holding a man's hand, but it wasn't some random man, Jack." The voice paused and then whispered the rest, "He was her lover!"

No! Lyla wouldn't…

"Those times she told you she was at her sister's house

—she was rolling around in bed with him, making that special groaning sound you thought she only made when you pleased her."

Jack gasped and Crock yelled in his face, said what Jack knew to be true. That this Lyla was a fake, a reproduction. Then there were more Lylas all around him, each one… did he do that to her? That was how she looked in the grave. He killed her and that was how she—

Crock shouted at him, telling him not to look at the swarm of Lylas.

"She went to him because you wouldn't give her what she needed," the cloud said. Then a sound like a dog's snarl twisted and distorted the melodious voice. "She was carrying his baby, Jack, their love child—because you hate children!"

"I'm real," Crock said, not shouting but in a deep, intense whisper. "They're not!" He gestured toward the pack of jackal Lylas. "They're evil in human-being suits. I'm your friend. Look at me."

The black cloud bellowed in a rumbling, inhuman roar. "Your turn, fat man!"

Crock didn't cringe or cower, though, just ignored the words and focused all his attention on Jack.

But when a form materialized next to Crock, he let go of Jack and turned toward it.

IT WAS clear to Crock that Jack was losing it. Why would God send a man like him on such a mission? He was broken, had known so much pain, had lost his wife and thirty-one friends, every man he served with, survived when they all died in a rumbling roar heard around the world. Why Jack? Then it occurred to Crock in a flash of thought that was there and then gone as fast as it had come. Maybe Jack hadn't been sent here to expel this demon but to exorcise demons of his own. Maybe he'd been sent to heal his own soul.

Crock felt the percussion again and saw Andi cringe closer to the angel's side. The voice must be bellowing. Likely at him. He probably ought to look at the cloud, pretend to listen, but not looking was working for him right now, and until there was a compelling reason to do so, he didn't intend to change that strategy.

Then Billy Bickerstaff was standing beside him. Empty air one second; Billy Bickerstaff the next. He let go of Jack's shoulder and turned reluctantly toward the boy with blood all over the front of his shirt and leaking from the corners of his mouth.

When Crock had taken his own fearless moral inventory—brief though it had been given that he didn't find out he was going on this little expedition until a couple of hours ago—he'd known Billy would eventually show up. Had to. Rookie cop, chasing a guy who'd just held up a liquor store through yards and alleys in a suburban neighborhood, gets him cornered and...

The little boy was about ten years old, red hair and freckles and a hint of buck teeth. He'd stepped out of nowhere in an alley with a gun trained on Crock, and Crock'd fired. It was self-defense, of course...or would have been if the kid hadn't been holding a water pistol.

True, the statute regarding the use of deadly force required only that you had "reason to believe that your life was in danger." It didn't require that you actually were in danger. Internal affairs cleared him and gave him back his gun and his shield. And every few months since then, Billy Bickerstaff paid him a visit as he slept. Just to talk over old times.

The little boy with the gaping bullet wound in his chest was talking to Crock, who did the best he could to act like he heard and understood what the child was saying. Apparently, the result was not pleasing the big dude in the black cloud because there was more percussive yelling and more of Crock's "victims" appeared. One by one.

The crazy old woman who'd wrenched herself out of his grasp and raced into her burning house to save her cat. Only enough of her revealed on the charred body for him to recognize her.

And Bonnie. Of course, Bonnie. His sister was fifteen years older than he was, got married when he was three and moved to England. He hardly knew her. But when he was a junior in high school, she divorced and moved back home, and by the time he was a freshman in college, she was a raging alcoholic with a thousand-dollar-a-day crack habit she supported by stealing, shoplifting and engaging in the world's oldest profession.

About once a month, she called his dorm room in the middle of the night, drunk, high and threatening to kill herself. It would take him until dawn to talk her off the ledge—sometimes literally as well as metaphorically. He stood it for six months, then announced to family and friends alike that his grades were in the tank from too many late nights and he would no longer answer the phone after ten o'clock. No exceptions. Three weeks later, the phone woke him at midnight. It rang again and again—and he sat looking at it, doing nothing.

Crock was the one who found her body, went to her sleazy apartment to check on her because their mother begged him to. Bonnie was lying naked in a bathtub full of bloody water, both wrists slashed to the bone. She'd been dead several days, her face was black and distorted, her body bloated. He'd heaved for hours from the stink. The sight of her here in front of him shook him to the core—didn't even matter that he couldn't hear what she was saying.

Enough!

"Hey, you!" He addressed the black cloud that bubbled and boiled in the air in the back of the cavern. "Why don't you take your monstrosity circus on the road. Clowns and elephants are way more entertaining. Or jugglers. You got any jugglers?"

He spoke with more sassiness than he felt. His knees were Jell-O and he couldn't feel his legs below them at all. It had taken every sinew of his determination, every morsel of his will to get the sarcastic remark out past his lips, and if he were called upon for any more heroic deed here this day than just being a smart-ass, he was definitely not man enough for the job.

The black cloud was not pleased with his response, and in the blink of an eye everything in the cavern changed. The walls, floor and ceiling were no longer milky swirls of rock, polished and shiny. The cavern was black, dirty and sooty and smelled like burned flesh. The room was no longer filled with flickering red light from candles on the walls. It was lit by the flames of a burning lake that extended away into the distance as far as the eye could see.

ANDI COULDN'T BREATHE. Not at all. Couldn't draw in a single breath. But she had to be breathing, didn't she? You'd pass out or die or something if you didn't breathe. She wasn't, though.

She held onto the angel's hand with both of hers, was huddled up against the angel's body—would have hidden in the angel's skirts if she'd been dressed as Princess Buttercup instead of wearing jeans.

The angel was warm and Andi could feel the steady thump, thump, thump of the angel's heart on her cheek. That was more comforting than the hand she clutched or the warmth she felt. The angel's heart wasn't pounding. Andi's was! It was hammering inside a gigantic hole in the middle of her, a hole in that place where scared lives. Scared was gone, had run away screaming. What she saw in front of her—what only she and the angel could see—had chased it away.

Demons. Everywhere. Every shape and color, hideous and angry—they all looked so angry!—so full of hatred for everything and everybody that she shrank back in horror and revulsion. All the monsters from a lifetime of nightmares were collected in this chamber, making horrible growling sounds she didn't know if the others could hear or not, and fighting in vicious tangles of violence. Creatures rolled around on the charred rocks, tearing at each other with claws, biting with horrible jagged teeth, trying to rip each other apart for no reason that Andi could see.

She recognized some of the monsters—the one made out of wasps that had killed Miss Lunde and Mr. Bishop that day at school, so long ago it might have happened in another lifetime. The lizard-faced demon with tentacles and red eyes with no black spots who rode the back of the man who shot Mommy. The green demon with oozing red blotches she and the angel had driven out of Ariel Murphy and the small, sticky-looking one with legs all up and down its sides that had ridden Ossy across the street and made him attack her.

And she could tell how they must look to the others because some of them wore a filmy, gauzy, see-through shape like a mask, only as big as a person. The demon who'd killed Mommy wore the shape of a pretty black woman who was torn up like she'd been run over by a bulldozer. The monster made of flies from the school wore the body mask of a little boy with freckles who yelled at Mr. Crock that the officer had "murdered an innocent."

But the black cloud that boiled and bubbled and filled the whole top and back of the cavern cloaked something Andi couldn't see. The voice out of it hurt her ears and she wanted to put her fingers in her ears so she couldn't hear it. But to do that she'd have to let go of the angel's hand and she feared if she did let go, all the ugly evil she could see would swallow her up.

Then Mr. Crock said something about clowns and elephants and the cloud vanished and Andi could tell that the others could see now what the cavern really looked like. A lake of fire where masses of demons sat on the burned shore.

But when the black cloud went away, she could see what had been hiding in it, the thing in the lake.

It roared and Andi screamed.

DANIEL HEARD the echo of a rumble from the cave on the other side of the crevice, a roar, something like the sound of the lion before an MGM movie, only louder, meaner and angrier. The roar was followed by a scream, the voice of a child. That scream sliced open his heart and laid his soul bare. It was a little girl's scream.

It was Andi!

There was no way he could know that, but he did. It could have been any child, maybe even a little boy. There was no voice in a shriek to recognize. But he knew it was her all the same. At the sound, something had thrummed in Daniel's chest like a bowstring releasing an arrow. It was Andi, and Andi was terrified.

His fingers went numb and the scimitar he was holding dropped to the cavern floor, bounced once and then plunged into the black depths of the crevice.

It had freaked him out just to touch the blade when he'd used it to saw through the layers of duct tape that bound him. He'd gotten a pretty nasty cut on his arm from its razor edge and had been terrified for a moment when he saw the blood dripping onto the stone floor. But he hadn't been murdered. Neither had Jeff. He'd given his life —for Daniel.

And someday, he would think about that. He'd puzzle it through in his head, figure out how he felt about it, what it said about Jeff and about the nature of a God who worked things out in ways no one would ever dream. And he'd think about battery acid and concrete and how Jeff had figured out you could destroy the base of Billy Ray's gate and escape.

Later. He'd think about all that later. Right now, the whole universe was condensed into one little girl's voice.

Daniel's heart began to hammer blood through his veins in powerful bursts that rocked his whole body. He was gripped by a far greater terror than he'd felt at the prospect of getting his head chopped off.

How could Andi be—?

Had Chapman Whitworth kidnapped her like he had Daniel? Had he taken her to the efreet? To…kill her, some awful kind of sacrifice? But he didn't need her blood to summon efreets. He had Daniel's. And the additional pentagrams were in this cavern, not the other one.

Then it occurred to him that maybe Chapman Whitworth hadn't taken her to the cavern at all. Maybe Jack and Theresa and Becca had. Maybe the others had figured out that the efreet was in that cavern and had gone in after it. But why take Andi with them? She was a little girl, only ten years old. What possible reason could there be?

Still, that seemed a more likely explanation. But either way, the result was the same. His precious little girl was in the cavern on the other side of this crevice with a prince of demons. How she got there really didn't matter. She was there and he had to get her out.

Take good care of Emily's little girl.

But how could he possibly get to her across the crevice? At its narrowest point the crack in the cavern floor was still close to thirty feet wide. Maybe Chapman Whitworth could levitate over it, but he couldn't.

Rope!

Billy Ray had used rope to tie the lanterns around their necks and to tie the two of them to each other. None of the pieces of rope was long enough by itself to stretch across the chasm, but maybe he could tie them together, put the skill he'd learned as a Boy Scout to use.

He ran to the pile of discarded ropes, grateful that he hadn't mindlessly kicked the rope into the crevice in a frenzy of revulsion along with the duffle bag and all the artifacts Billy Ray'd set up on the pentagrams. The lantern ropes were only four feet long—too short. It would take the whole length of them just to make the proper knot. But the two longer ropes—the one Billy Ray had tied around their necks and the one he'd used as a lead rope—yes!

An overhead knot. No, a double fisherman's knot. If he tied it right, a double fisherman's knot would hold anything.

Swell, so he had rope. How could he use it to get across the crack?

The stalagmites. There was one very near the edge of the crevice on both sides! The one on this side was about ten inches in diameter and about four feet tall. The one on the other was shorter and smaller—six by three. If he could stretch the rope between them, he could—what? Hand over hand above a bottomless chasm? His mind recoiled from that prospect, the reflex of a finger on a hot stove. But desperation shoved fear aside. Dangle above a bottomless chasm or off the top of a skyscraper—it didn't matter. He would do whatever he had to do to get to Andi.

He tied the pieces of rope together carefully. Untying them and then retying them to make sure he had the knot right. The combined ropes stretched maybe thirty-five feet. It'd be close. He made a noose in one end of the rope, stood on the edge of the chasm and pitched it across, trying to lasso the stalagmite on the other side. It fell short and dropped into the darkness. He pulled it back up and tried again. And again. Over and over. It was like pitching a ring at a milk bottle in a carnival—looks easy, but isn't.

And then the rope finally looped over the top of the stalagmite and hung there. He shook it a couple of times, working the noose farther down on the column of limestone it'd taken a hundred thousand years to create, one drip of water at a time.

He pulled the rope taut and the bottom fell out of his stomach. There wasn't enough rope. It was long enough to reach the stalagmite on this side of the crevice but not long enough to wrap around it and tie.

Chapter Thirty-One

Theresa leaned over and examined the keyhole beneath the red elevator button. It wasn't for no ordinary key. It was for one of them special round keys like opened a soft drink machine. Who had a key that fit? Darth Vader, maybe? And how could she talk/con him into letting her borrow it for just a little while?

"There are other elevators in the atrium," Becca said.

"Them's for guests. Don't none of them go all the way to the top. This is the only one that does."

Becca pointed to a lighted exit sign above a nearby door. "There are stairs," she said.

"Haul these rats up sixteen flights—?"

"No, ride an elevator as high as it goes and then take the stairs."

Theresa pushed the wheeled laundry hamper into the elevator and looked out the glass wall in the back into the atrium of the building as it ascended to the sixteenth floor. The door swished open and she and Becca hurried through hallways to the back of the building, where they found the keyed service elevator beside an exit sign and a stairway door. Inside the stairwell, they found steps leading down on the left. But a door on their right barred the way to the stairs leading upward. A red sign on it proclaimed Employees Only. It was a heavy metal fire door. Theresa tried the knob. It was locked.

"Theresa, help me take my tail off," Becca said. Theresa turned to see her twisted around trying to get to the spot where the forked tail was affixed to the fabric of the red tights. "I can't bend it." She indicated her mashed finger with a black nail.

Theresa lifted the tail, found two big safety pins that held it to the red tights, unhooked it and dropped the tail on the floor. She gave the pins to Becca, who promptly bent the pointed ends out straight, dropped to her knees in front of the door, stuck the pointed ends of both pins into the lock and began moving them around.

"Spend time on the street and you learn all kinds of useful life hacks."

Theresa didn't have no idea what a life hack was.

Becca had her ear close to the doorknob, listenin'. "A deadbolt would be hard to pick with something as flimsy as these pins, but a doorknob…" She continued to wiggle the pins around in the lock. "I'd have frozen to death in Buffalo in a blizzard once if I—"

There was a little clicking sound and Becca turned the knob.

Theresa stood and held the door open while Becca went back out into the hallway and shoved the rolling laundry cart into the stairwell. Each of them grabbed a bag full of rats out of it and started up the concrete steps.

Them rats was heavier than you'd think they'd be. They was big 'uns, some of them was way bigger than cats. Musta been well fed. Theresa didn't let herself wonder what they ate when they wasn't having her for dinner.

They come to another landing, then another flight of stairs, and at the top was another door marked Employees Only. But it led into the building on the seventeenth floor and the stairs continued to climb. They was goin' all the way to the top.

By the time they got to the next landing, where the stairs switched back and led higher still, Theresa was panting and her head was spinning.

Lord, if you's planning on giving me a heart attack, right now might not be the best time to do it.

"Hold up, Theresa," Becca said. "I need to catch my breath."

Shoot, that girl hadn't even broke a sweat. It was Theresa's breath she was worried about.

"Set your sack down and…" This time it was Becca trying to do the distractin'. She wasn't no babbler like Theresa was, though, and struggled to come up with something to say. "Uh…tell me how balloon drops work," she finally blurted out.

Theresa held onto her bag and squared her shoulders. "I can walk and chew gum at the same time, child," she said and slowly lifted her foot up onto the step in front of her. "For a balloon drop they stretch a big ole net…across that roof opening…and toss balloons into it," she said.

Up onto the step. She lifted her foot to the next one.

"Them balloons…is filled with air…not helium…so they won't float."

Another step up. And another.

"The switch in the 'lectronics room releases one side of the net and…"

The metal door at the top of the steps came into view. Becca dropped her rat sack on the steps and hurried past Theresa to it.

God, you wouldn't let this one be locked, too, would you?

Becca tried the knob, then dropped to her knees and went to work with the safety pins while Theresa ponderously climbed the final steps, noting at the top that the nearby service elevator didn't require a key here on the top floor. Figured. How long would that monster wait before he set off his bomb? She'd read that they was a big awards ceremony—when they'd give out a whole bunch of plaques along with the gold-plated manhole cover—and that each one of the candidates was going to speak for five minutes. She'd never yet heard a political candidate speak for only five minutes. Whitworth would have to wait at least until his turn to speak was over. She hoped he came dead last.

Becca continued to work on the door; Theresa continued to fidget.

"I bent the pin on the first door," Becca said without moving her ear from the knob. Now I can't seem to—"

The knob clicked and then turned. Becca got to her feet and eased the door inward. She stuck her head in and looked around. Then she reached down and picked up her rat sack and stepped through the doorway with Theresa on her heels, closing the door as she entered.

They could see no one. No lights were on in the cavernous room, an empty attic-like space between the ceiling of the Balloon Ballroom below and the roof of the building. But light shone up through the mountain of balloons lying on the netting stretched across the gigantic opening extending the whole length and width of the room. There was a ten-foot-wide catwalk between the opening and the walls, and the rails around the catwalk formed a bowl into which workers had placed thousands of colored balloons. From above, red, orange, blue and green light flickered from the neon balloons at the four corners of the outside of the building, visible because the domed roof of the building had been rolled back tonight to reveal open sky above. Only there was no sky. There was just that odd gray fog, turning the neon balloons into colorful blurs.

"Theresa...do you see it?" Becca's voice was small and hushed. "The fog. Do you see how it's coming up from below?"

"No, sugar, I don't see that part. I just see the fog."

"It's coming up through the pile of balloons and leaking out into the world, dirty mist, ugly gray vapor. It's so...cold." She hugged her arms to her body and began to shake.

Theresa picked up her rat sack. "You go around that side and I'll go around this way," she said. "Toss them rats out into the balloons spaced out even as you can 'cause we want to give everybody an equal opportunity to get a dead rat dropped on they heads."

But as Theresa walked along the railing, pitching rats out into the pile of balloons like she was throwing feed to chickens, the fear grew in her belly. She'd told that Darth Vader fella them things was rubber rats—and he'd believed it 'thout a second's hesitation! What if all them people down below thought they was rubber rats, too, that it was part of the Halloween festivities—balloons and rubber rats?

What if they thought it was a joke and nobody got scared?

What if nobody left?

They'd all die. She and Becca would die right along with 'em.

❧

SEBASTIAN COULD SEE nothing but fuzzy white blurs of lights in the dense fog as the barge began to pass into the outer suburbs of Cincinnati. He pulled the burner cell phone from his pocket, the old flip-top kind, and checked to make sure the number was already dialed in. When he caught first sight of the target, he would call the number and let it ring one time. It would be set to vibrate, of course, and that instant of vibration in his pocket would tell the Boss that he had exactly nine minutes to get out of the top floor of the building.

Getting to his knees, Sebastian lifted the missile launcher onto his right shoulder. When he lowered his face to the sight, the blurry shoreline leapt into focus. Few details, but the outlines of buildings, trees and cars were plainly visible where looking through the fog had revealed nothing but blur.

He had fired a Javelin twice before, so he knew what to expect. There would be a blast of fire out the back of the launcher as it propelled the missile twenty feet or so out into the air, where the propulsion unit on the missile itself would fire and the guidance system would direct the payload to the target.

Sebastian had scouted the target several times. The phalanx of doors along the ballroom walls that opened into the gigantic lobby/atrium were fire doors set in steel casings. The two small doors for staff at the back of the ballroom were not. The steel-casing doors would likely hold, containing the blast so that inside the ballroom the damage would be catastrophic.

When the ballroom exploded, Sebastian's job would be done and his operatives' jobs would begin. After the blast, the Boss would send out a wordless group text. The incoming text would vibrate in the pocket phones of one operative on each team. That would be their signal to "fire at will" on the targets that'd been picked out.

Sebastian's falling domino would knock over other dominos in California, New York, Illinois and Louisiana. He couldn't imagine what the total death toll might be. The parade in Los Angeles boasted half a million spectators, the Halloween celebration in New York City billed itself as the biggest block party in the world. The buildings close around the blast sites would concentrate the explosive power and make them more deadly.

He watched the lighted buildings glide by in the gloom, visible only through the Javelin sight.

Then the Bank of Ohio building burst into view! He tensed, shifting his weight a little because kneeling with the heavy weapon on his shoulder had cut the circulation to his right leg and he couldn't feel his right—

There!

Fuzzy red, orange, green and blue orbs suddenly materialized, glowing like bright marbles inside a cotton ball. Through the sight they were clear. Balloons.

Without moving the launcher off his shoulder, he reached his left hand into his right breast pocket, retrieved the phone and flipped it open. He punched "call," heard the phone ring once, killed the call and hurled the phone out into the river. Then he started the timer on his wristwatch.

The Boss's meter was now running. When the digital readout on Sebastian's watch blinked 00:00 precisely nine minutes from now, he would fire. If the Boss wasn't safely out of harm's way by then…that was not Sebastian's problem. He'd already collected his fee—in solid gold bars.

❧

CROCK HAD SOMEHOW GOTTEN it into his head that he might just make it out of this alive.

Riiiiiiight.

After all, he didn't fold when bloody, dismembered, rotting burned/shot/strangled corpses were paraded in front of him; he'd stood up to the freak show in the Efreet's Carnival of Monstrosities.

Step right up, ladies and gentlemen, and see the aberrations of nature gathered from the jungles of Borneo to the slopes of the Himalayas. Hur-ray, hur-ray, hur-ray.

But he couldn't hear the blame and accusations—the lies hurled at him. He wouldn't collapse under an intolerable burden of guilt, shame and remorse. He'd found a way out. He was going to make it.

Then he'd ticked off the Smoke that Spoke. Note to self: never yank a tail that might have a dragon attached to the other end.

He'd made a smart remark and the world had exploded. The cavern he thought was reality—hard, stone reality—dissolved in an instant and was replaced by a scene from hell. Literally. A sea of flames washed up against a charred, desolate beach not twenty feet away, and stretched out as far as he could see beneath a sky of molten tar. Creatures from the worst animated horror show Hollywood had ever produced climbed over the burnt rocks and ashy boulders on the shore, swarms of them like locusts, big and small, each an individual abomination—all of them vicious and angry, attacking each other, brawling in tangles of rage.

The air was no longer the constant-temperature cool of a cave. It was hot and dry and the stench was...staggering, overwhelming. Was this what Theresa could smell when a demon came near? It was the reek of rot and decay, excrement and vomit and moldering corpses, all mixed up with the singed hair stink that had emanated on sultry summer days from the back door of the crematorium down the street from his grandmother's house. The air was somehow thick, too, like it wasn't air at all but some substance more like water—the squalid water of a pigsty or the stagnant pool where the bloated corpse of a dead dog floated.

Then the cloud was gone, and the thick air was no longer why he was having trouble breathing. He couldn't pull air into his lungs because what he saw hammered the air out of him. The horror of it filled his head with a boiling black ugliness that burned away thought and desire, past, present and future. Purpose and intent turned to ash. Who Charles Crocker had been when he stepped into that cavern popped out of existence like a fly hitting an electric bug killer; his mind was consumed by that lone image.

The creature obscured by the boiling black clouds—that had lurked unseen in the pillar of smoke in the painting in Bishop's office—stepped into the light. Towering fifty feet above them, a monster stood in the inferno of the burning red sea. It was the color of the flames that licked off its body—black and red and orange. The muscles bulging from its arms, shoulders and chest were so enormous they stretched taut the scaly, scorched red-yellow skin that glistened with a thin sheen of—not sweat, it was red. Blood? Fire danced on the razor tips of claws—there were too many fingers, eight, ten, maybe more. Horns grew out of its head, six sets of them: four from the sides and back and two black curling ones on top, their tips as sharp as ice picks. Two more huge horns like a bull's, except bright red, protruded from either side of its forehead. Its ears were large and pendulous with dangling gold earrings gleaming in the flickering light. When it unfurled its black bat wings, they rose twenty feet above it to form a canopy lined with dagger-sharp spikes. Flames leapt from the edges of the wings like tongues of fire off the charred remains of a log. Below the wings, a tail twitched back and forth, flinging thick green venom from the sharpened spike that stuck out from a scorpion stinger as big around as a basketball.

One hand clutched a scimitar that glowed red hot, as if it'd just been yanked from a forge. The other arm ended in a stump below the elbow.

But it was the face. The face…

Where its eyes should be were sockets with fire in the center, blazing up off unseen eyeballs. Or maybe it had no eyes, maybe it saw with flames. Its features were irregular and boney, with nubs on one cheek and a jagged slash that bled flames down the other. The look on the face was utter loathing. The thing hated. No, it didn't merely hate. It was hate. It wasn't filled with evil, it was made of evil. It was a life form devoid of all goodness in the grip of a rage so pure it consumed the ugly features. It twisted and contorted them in such maniacal intensity the body could not contain it and the creature threw its head back and opened a mouth full of three rows of broken, jagged teeth curved inward. And it roared.

Even through his deaf ears, Crock heard the roar—with his bones and his skin and his blood. The roar was more than sound, it was a single corrupt thing that would have shattered glass, clear and horrible beyond description. It was the sound of pure, consummate evil, and to hear it was to die.

Crock's legs folded out from under him and he dropped to his knees, unable to look away from the horror and knowing that every second he continued to look at it, to see it, to countenance its presence in reality stripped him of some essential element of his humanity that he'd never recover.

There was another sound, too, closer—a whining, moaning groan of fear and submission. He could hear it clearly because he was making it.

Jack had fallen to his knees at some point, too, and was rocking back and forth, tears streaming down his cheeks. "Lyla" had transformed into a hideous creature with a lizard's face and red eyes. And Jack was mouthing her name, mourning the loss of his wife again as if she'd just jumped out a window a hundred stories high and plunged in her red dress to her death.

Only the angel was unmoved by the spectacle. Andi clutched her, arms around her waist, trying to bury her face in her side. But the creature leaned toward Andi, halted only five feet away, and said something Crock couldn't hear. The little girl peeked out at it. Then slowly lifted her face, so pale it reflected the glow of the monster as if she had a sunburn.

She shook her head. Back and forth.

The monster said something else and Andi screamed, "Nooooo!" a cry of raw, jagged desolation, and then she slid down the angel's body to the floor and lay there sobbing.

~

"NOOOOOO!"

There was no mistaking Andi's voice this time! Daniel's little girl was in danger, in pain. She needed her daddy!

Daniel seldom swore, but he cursed then, yanking on the rope wrapped around the stalagmite on the other side of the chasm to pull out all the slack. Like there was slack!

It was too short and all the pulling in the world wasn't going to stretch it out far enough.

He began to cry, not sob. It hurt far too bad for something as simple and cleansing as tears. His body merely shook slightly, his face a mask of grief, and tears streamed down his face.

He sank to his knees on the cavern floor.

God, please. Help me.

He spoke the words aloud, without enough volume to echo, but there was a soft repetition of the sound off the surfaces in the cavern all the same.

Help. Help. Help.

Then silence.

He wiped his eyes on the sleeve of—

His shirt.

He didn't stop to unbutton it, just yanked it open, sending buttons pinging off the floor and nearby stalagmites like ricocheting bullets. He ripped it off his body and with shaking hands tied one of the long sleeves to the end of the piece of rope, then stretched the rope tight across the chasm, wrapped the shirt around the stalagmite on this side and tied the other sleeve to the rope.

There was not enough fabric for anything but simple square knots. He tied three of them and pulled the knots as tight as he could, then sat for a moment, looking at what he'd done. Could his simple cotton shirt hold his weight without ripping? Would the knots hold?

There was only one way to find out.

He stepped to the edge of the crevice next to the rope, sat down and dangled his feet into the hole. Yeah, he could hand-over-hand it…macho style…if his grip held. No, it'd be safer to shinny across the expanse of open air dangling beneath the rope, holding on with his hands and locking his feet together above the rope.

It took him a few moments to figure out how to get into the right position. Then he kicked off his shoes and they vanished soundlessly into the black chasm.

After that, he didn't hesitate. Straddling the rope, he inched out onto it, gradually letting it hold his weight. He looked back over his shoulder. The knots had pulled tight but were holding. Then he lowered himself beneath the rope and began to inch across it to the other side.

Air lifted out of the crevice beneath him, the cold breath of a tomb. A breeze ruffled his hair, and it occurred to him that there might be a way out of the caves down there at the bottom, not that Billy Ray or Jeff were in any condition to find the opening.

Daniel was halfway across the chasm, right in the middle, when the knots he'd tied in his shirt let go.

Chapter Thirty-Two

Maybe it was the bright light that suddenly shone through a crack in Jack's darkness that lit the way out. He could see its brilliance even with his eyes closed. It had been dark— all ashes and burned air. And then Andi screamed, "Nooooo!" and a brilliant light appeared that lit up his whole mind even though he couldn't see it.

Maybe that light had awakened who Jack was, shook him by the shoulder, brought him back.

Jack had been searching for himself in a dream, in a world where doors opened onto long hallways with more doors and more hallways and it was all gray and misty.

He'd gotten lost somewhere inside himself. Came unhooked from reality. No, actually he had hooked up to reality for the first time in a long while and his psyche flat out didn't like what it saw. Reality was that his beautiful Lyla was dead—like the three thousand three hundred other people who died that day. She'd died at the hands of terrorists who would one day stand before God and have to give an accounting of their lives. Jack wouldn't want to be in their shoes when they did. Thirty-three virgins—good luck with that, pal!

Militant monsters had killed Lyla. Jack had not. It wasn't his fault.

And perhaps he had to hear that accusation out of the mouth of evil itself to see it for the lie it was. He'd spent a good many years whispering that lie into his own ears. He was done with that. And he was done with running, cowering here inside himself. Becca had gotten lost in the same place, chased up and down the corridors of her mind by monsters too hideous to describe. He might have come very close to going over the edge into that lost world himself, but he'd been brought back just in time. By the brilliant light. No, before that—he'd been brought back by Andi's scream.

Andi.

You killed me because you hate children.

Now there was a lie that smelled like sulphur because it had sprung from the very bowels of hell itself. He couldn't have loved Andi more if she had been his own flesh and blood. She had come back from death when he'd called out to her—because he needed her. Now, she needed him.

It took all the strength he had to force his eyelids upward. He peeked out, then opened his eyes wide to see a brilliant, shining creature made of a light with a shadow-less radiance, a light you could look full into without squinting. The beauty took his breath away.

Where the angel in jeans and a denim jacket over a T-shirt had been only moments—hours? minutes? days?—ago now stood a being whose beauty was the perfect counterpart to the ugliness of the blackened creature in the fiery lake. Standing fifty feet tall, she towered over them. Her robe—was it a robe? a gown?—shimmered with light, maybe was actually made out of millions of points of perfect light—like fiber-optics. Each crystal reflected and refracted the light from the one next to it so there was an illusion of movement even in stillness. The light spread out from the angel in all directions, a brilliance that somehow seemed to have substance, like you could touch it, and if you did, it would feel soft, like a baby's blanket. It lit every crack, every crevice in the chamber, flowing around corners like bright warm honey—except within the pentagram marked out in black chalk on the floor, where there were swirling shadows, lit only by an ever-shifting ugly red glow.

Jack was certain that the angel's light shone out into every corner of the whole cave—of all the caves, every cavern and tunnel, all the thousands of miles of them that lay beneath the county—and that great streaks of brilliance radiated out into the world beyond the caves from beneath rocks or cracks on the hillsides. He could envision the rolling Kentucky countryside lit from within by an unfathomable brilliance, and streaks of bright illumination shooting up into the sky to connect to the twinkling stars. Everything and everybody touched by that light was safe from all harm, guarded from all evil.

Though the angel in jeans was clearly female, this being could have been either sex or none at all. Blond hair so pale it was almost colorless flowed in waves over her shoulders and down her back. The features were strong—straight nose, eyes a shade of gray so light as to be almost translucent, high forehead and a mouth set in a firm, determined line. Rising up behind the angel were great wings the downy white of a baby duck's bottom, that moved gently back and forth, creating a slight breeze that smelled of sunshine and honeysuckle. It appeared there was more than one set of wings—Jack couldn't tell for sure. What he could see clearly was what lay in the angel's hand

—a sword of burnished silver, a flawless weapon both brand new and unutterably ancient at the same time. The angel held it with an easy confidence.

"You cannot harm them," the angel said. The voice was as low and vibrant as the tolling of a cathedral bell.

"And you cannot save them," the beast snarled back. "They stand or fall on their own."

Jack had a flash, a vision of this angel and the beast in the fiery lake engaged in combat, sword against scimitar, light against darkness, a scene from a world of spirits. But they wouldn't do battle here, not like that. Theresa'd said that in this world, occupied by the enemy, under the rule of the Father of Darkness for a time it had been given to men—not angels—the task of standing against evil.

He wasn't sure he could stand, that his legs would bear his weight. So he simply crawled the few feet across the polished floor of the cavern to the spot where sweet Andi lay curled in a ball, sobbing. He reached out and gathered the little girl into his arms.

THERESA SPOTTED him soon as she and Becca stepped out of the service elevator. The wide hallway behind the ballroom was empty now because the ball was still goin' on and all the people was inside.

All except Chapman Whitworth.

Dressed in a suit and tie instead of in some Halloween getup, Whitworth had obviously just left the ballroom by one of the two small back doors because he was striding purposefully down the back hall toward the atrium around the corner and the bank of guest elevators.

He's sneaked out. The fireworks is about to start.

Lord, we ain't ready!

"Hey you, efreet," Becca called out in a firm, clear voice. "I want to talk to you."

Whitworth was only a short distance down the hallway. He turned in their direction and the little red tailless demon set out across the expanse of empty tile flooring between them, leaving Theresa to slip through a doorway just down from the service elevator on the wall opposite the ballroom. The 'lectronics room was at the end of a short hall at the top of a small flight of stairs.

What was that child gone do? Theresa couldn't begin to imagine.

Keep him occupied for a couple minutes.

Don't need but a couple. Surely, won't nothing blow up long's he's still here.

Theresa snatched a serving tray with a water pitcher off a cart sitting in the hallway and balanced it on the palm of one hand as she plowed up the steps to a door marked Employees Only.

Don't let it be locked, please!

The knob turned and she used her considerable backside to shove open the door. A man sat in a dark room next to an empty chair in front of a huge control board with more buttons, dials and switches on it than the cockpit of a 747—not that Theresa'd ever seen the cockpit of a 747. He was looking at a big monitor, where the image was divided into six sections that showed views of the ballroom from the front, both sides and the back—some close-up, some wide-angle. The monitor screen provided the only light in the room.

The man didn't turn around when he heard Theresa come in, just said, "You told them mustard, not mayo, right?"

Theresa didn't even break stride, merely stepped out of

the shadows and launched the full pitcher of water out onto the control board.

The board exploded in a hail of sparks and the man leapt to his feet, sputtering and cursing. The lights on one side of the ballroom flickered and blinked out, and the screen with a wide-angle view of that side went black, blinked back on, went black again, then flickered.

The man turned around, squinting into the gloom. He'd been staring at the lighted screen and could make out nothing more than her shape in the shadows.

He took a menacing step in her general direction, looking around for her.

"What do you think you're—"

Theresa elbowed him out of the way. He fell backward, tripped over the chair and sprawled on his back on the floor. Good thing he was a little scrawny fella. Her eyes raked over the steaming, sputtering board, looking for… There it was! The switch the bellhop had showed Nyree on the wall above the board on the left side of the monitor. A normal light switch except the toggle was red. It wasn't identified in any way, though. If she wasn't rememberin' right or that bellhop was just blowin' smoke…

She leaned over and flipped the switch.

DANIEL DROPPED INTO BLACK NOTHING, plunging toward the depths of a bottomless abyss.

He didn't know the knot in his shirt sleeve had let go until he was falling.

A second, maybe two to respond.

He clutched with all his strength at a rope that was no longer attached at one end and banged into the wall on the far side of the crevice, smacking into the rocks with brutal force. His head whacked so hard his vision blurred and the rope was almost yanked out of his grasp. He didn't let go, though, and hung on with the strength of desperation, dangling at the end of a thirty-foot stretch of rope held together with a double fisherman's knot and attached now to a lone stalagmite on the cavern floor above.

Using his foot to swing himself around so he was facing the rock wall, he felt around on it with his toes, searching for any kind of outcrop or ledge or just a lump where he could rest his weight. He figured he had less than five minutes before his fingers could no longer grip the rope.

Nothing. The rock face was smooth. His toes scoured the stone, searching for any—

There!

His right toe found a bump on the rock face. Hardly a ledge, it extended out about an inch, but he was able to step onto it, balancing with the rope, and allow the rock to bear the majority of his weight. He sucked in big gulps of air and tried to still his hammering heart, set into overdrive by the drop into nothingness. Then he felt around with his left foot higher up on the rock and his toes found a small crack. Jamming as much of his foot as he could into the crack, he shifted his weight onto it, then lifted his right foot off the mini ledge and felt around with his toes for something higher than the crack. Nothing protruded, but he discovered that the crack where he'd jammed his left foot extended at an angle up the rock face, getting wider as it went. Daniel shoved his right foot into the crack above his left, pulled his weight up onto it with the rope and rose higher on the wall.

He inched his way up the widening crack, feeling for footholds, pulling his weight with the rope again and again. But his arms were tiring rapidly. By the time he pulled himself up high enough that his head cleared the rim of the crevice, his arms had begun to tremble.

Just a little more. Please. A little more strength.

He felt with his left foot in the crack and found a slanting surface where he could place the whole length of his foot. He stepped onto the surface, pulled with all his strength on the rope and lifted his body up another twelve inches or so.

One more pull. He'd have to make it in one more because his arms were shaking badly and his fingers had begun to cramp. He felt above his left foot with his right. Nothing. The crack he was climbing widened there to about three feet, too wide to jam his foot into. As he felt frantically for a hold with his right foot, his right knee slipped onto a ledge. He pulled hard to get his knee firmly up onto the ledge, straightened, then held tight while he replaced his knee on the ledge with his left foot. When he pushed upward with that foot, the upper part of his body rose above the rim of the crevice.

Time was running out. The image of an hourglass with only a few grains of sand left to fall filled his mind. His fingers were cramping and his arms were shaking violently.

He was losing his grip on the rope. Crouching with his weight on his left foot on the ledge, he lunged upward, throwing his body forward. His chest flopped over onto the cavern floor; he pulled the rope tight and used the last of his strength to drag the rest of his body out of the crevice.

Scooting forward on his belly away from the edge, he let go of the rope and collapsed, fighting a sudden nausea from the exertion. He rolled over onto his back, gasping. He flexed his cramped fingers and shook his trembling arms, trying to still the shaking. Then he lurched to his feet, his knees quaking, and staggered toward the cave opening illuminated only by an ugly red glow.

Chapter Thirty-Three

Andi felt warm arms gather her up off the ground, where she lay sobbing with her eyes squeezed tight shut. She smelled the comforting aroma of Uncle Jack's Old Spice aftershave and his coffee breath.

"Shhhh, baby girl," he crooned. He sat back with her in his lap, rocking slowly back and forth. "Shhh."

He didn't tell her not to be afraid. Or that everything would be all right. He just held her close and whispered, "Shhhhh," into her hair.

She continued to sob, grateful for the arms around her and the comforting lap, but so desolate none of that mattered. Nothing mattered anymore. Daddy was dead.

The demon had demanded that she look at him. She had been way too scared of him to defy him, so she had peeked out from where she had her head buried in the angel's T-shirt. His voice had not roared then, it had rumbled, making a grating sound like she imagined would come from a disposal if you put rocks into it.

He'd leaned close and rasped, "When they chopped

your daddy's head off, it dropped on the ground and rolled away like a soccer ball with a bloody stump."

She'd shaken her head slowly. Back and forth. Back and forth. It couldn't be.

"His eyes were open and they filled up with dirt. And blood squirted out all over everywhere. Spewed out—you should have seen it! Bright red and sticky."

She'd screamed then, let go of her terror and grief in a shriek of desolation.

"Noooooo!"

Daddy was gone.

The demon had spoken again after that and she'd heard another voice, too, stronger and more gentle. But she had not listened to what either of them said. She'd been crying so hard she'd heard none of it.

"Andi, honey, open your eyes," Uncle Jack said, his voice kind and tender. "Open your eyes and see the angel."

She didn't want to open her eyes, angel or no angel. She didn't want anything except to be left alone so she could cry and cry until she died. Mommy was dead and now Daddy was dead, too. Andi wanted to go with them. To be with them in Heaven. She didn't care about angels or demons or anything at all anymore. She only wanted to die.

"Mr. Crocker and I...we need you," Uncle Jack said. "We can't do this without you. Please, will you help?"

Help.

The word she'd heard in her head: help. Help them make the demon go away. The demon that had sent that man to shoot Miss Lunde and Mr. Bishop in school that day. The demon who had killed Mommy. And now...Daddy.

Yes! She would help them if she could!

Mommy and Daddy would want her to help. She

would make that demon sorry he'd killed them. There'd be time after…She could wait until later to die.

She made herself stop crying, sniffled, but her breath still hitched in and out of her throat, sounding ragged, like that time she had the croup and Mommy made a croup tent in the living room out of plastic trash bags and chairs and a humidifier. It was nasty in there and she hated it, everything was wet. But Daddy had crawled in with her to keep her company, curled up tight because it was such a small place. He had read her stories.

Daddy.

She sucked in a shuddering breath and opened her eyes. When she saw the huge white angel standing there with a sword, she was glad she wasn't dead yet because it was so beautiful. Of course, there'd be dozens—no, thousands—of angels in Heaven. She hoped they wouldn't be mad at her when she got there and told them she'd cried herself to death. She wondered if God would be mad.

Uncle Jack leaned over and kissed her lightly on the forehead.

HE WAS OUTLINED IN RED, glowing. But as Becca approached, the red outline grew, expanding out from the scar-faced man in the business suit, and began to stretch up from him toward the ceiling.

Becca sucked in a gasp and tensed for the blow to her soul, the hammer strike of her own fear that would grow faster and larger and fiercer than the red monster forming before her. Terror was the wallpaper of her life, the canvas on which every day had been painted. Horror had held her hostage since the day she'd cowered with McDougal in a mulberry bush beside a river.

Did you ever pull the wings off a fly?

This time it would kill her—fear or the monster—one or the other. Why had she been so foolish as to think she wouldn't have to face the creature? Their meeting had been carved in the foundation of the universe, its imprint stamped into the wet cement of reality, and the efreet was here to keep that appointment.

Theresa had said an efreet could be in two places at once. It was in a cave somewhere in Caverna County, but it was here, too. Chapman Whitworth was here and the efreet was with him. In him. Not some avatar of the demon she'd conjured up in her head, but the real monster.

She should have known it would end this way. She was too tangled up in all that had happened to escape the final confrontation. Becca Hawkins and the efreet. Just like before when a twelve-year-old girl had collapsed on the floor in a cave in front of the lake of fire. Alone, this time, though. No Jack. No Daniel. Only Becca. She would face the efreet and he would kill her. And she greeted the prospect of death with something approaching delight. It was going to end now. In a few minutes it would be over.

The red outline grew into the creature she had seen the day twenty-six years ago when it had shattered her psyche, destroyed her sense of self and stolen her future. It rose up blood red out of a lake of fire—that only one with the knowing could see—and spread out over the tiles of the hallway behind the hotel ballroom. Horns on its head, rows of teeth, and a face that was the definition of hatred and evil.

She had to endure his presence, could not go running away into mental illness this time, though. She had to stall him, delay him long enough for—

"What have you done with Daniel and Jeff?" she said

in a voice loud enough to carry over the space between them, said the words with the last bit of air in her lungs and knew she would not live long enough to draw in another breath to say more.

"I burned them!" the monster roared. "Dangled them over a flame while they twisted and screamed; watched their eyes melt and run down their faces."

The words struck a blow that drove Becca to her knees. All sense went out of her mind, all thought was blasted from her head. The voice burst her eardrums and stole all sound from the world. Her whole being, every molecule was about terror and revulsion.

"I fried them."

"No, you didn't," said a calm voice from only a few feet away.

Becca turned to look. Standing beside her was a black-haired woman in a Halloween costume.

She was dressed as the Cat in the Hat.

ALL FOUR OF the neon balloons atop the Rivergate Hotel's Balloon Ballroom were visible now through the sight of the Javelin missile launcher. The coal barge bearing Sebastian Nemo and his antitank weapon slowly downstream through Cincinnati was now directly opposite the hotel.

The fog had been his friend since it had first settled around him, and Sebastian didn't stop to consider that it was at least an odd coincidence—if nothing more—that the fog had appeared out of nowhere in a city not given to fog at just the right time to cloak his mission in a fuzzy gray blanket.

He couldn't help noticing that the fog itself was odd.

Fog was mist, after all, a cloud on the ground. Damp and cool. This fog was neither. If he'd seen it from a distance, he would have assumed it was smoke—perhaps from a garbage dump full of old car tires. It was that color gray, the shade of a ten-penny nail. In such thick fog, he'd expect to see a thin sheen of moisture on everything—the metal of the barge and the missile launcher. There was no moisture. The fog wasn't just cool, either. It was cold, a cold so fierce it bit into his exposed skin. So cold he couldn't understand why there wasn't a sheen of ice instead of moisture on the surfaces around him.

But Sebastian Nemo was not a man given to looking gift horses in the mouth. The fog had made his job easier and safer. It kept the deckhands off the barges, and the tug captain had slowed down to a crawl...though the normal speed of a barge and tow was little in excess of a leisurely walk.

He thought to wonder, briefly, before he dismissed the thought, if his operatives in the other cities were shrouded in an odd gray mist as he was.

He ticked off in his mind the locations—the rooftop overlooking Sixth Avenue, where the vibration from the Boss's incoming text would send a Javelin missile down into a crowd numbering in the thousands. Was there fog there, too—to make noticing one man carrying a base guitar case in the resulting pandemonium even more unlikely?

New Orleans, maybe? At least, it was a city prone to fog. The mortar launch site positioned behind two huge dumpsters could benefit from a little shrouding. He'd put Ahmad and Tareq there, because that position was the most vulnerable and therefore they were the most likely to be caught. Ahmad would definitely not let them take him alive. He'd see to it Tareq didn't either.

Dressed in Halloween garb, Sulalman and Mukhtar in

Los Angeles would blend into the hysterical crowd after the blast. They were costumed as a horse, Sulalman in the front and Mukhtar leaned over as the horse's rear, with the mortar in the "body of the horse" between them.

Sebastian was not an impatient man. If his line of work had taught him anything, it was the value of calm equanimity. If you can keep your head when all about you are losing theirs…you'll live and they'll die. He sat quietly, watching the digital numbers blink from one to the next. The cramp in his shoulder and his numb left foot barely penetrated his shifting concentration—from the watch to the images made visible by the sight. Back and forth.

Dropping a Javelin missile down the chute formed by four gigantic neon balloons was as easy as landing a plane on a lighted runway.

He was in perfect position. 00:07…00:06…He drew in a cleansing breath and let it out slowly, steadied the heavy launcher on his shoulder. 00:02…00:01…00:00.

Sebastian fired.

WHEN ANDI'D SCREAMED, "NO," Crock had checked out. Too much. Overload. Fried circuits. The man who was Charles Crocker had turned away from it all, put reality firmly behind him and selected a corridor in his mind that led to the deepest part of himself. Yeah, it was time to pay a visit to the subbasement, take a look at the HVAC unit there.

From the safety of his deepest self, Crock considered a question: what happened to you when you went up against a demon and lost? What would come next?

Dying would come next. Duh!

He hoped it wouldn't be a brutal death. A man should

be allowed to die with some dignity—as much as the situation allowed, anyway. He was in for dying, but he didn't want to plead, to beg.

Of course, it was possible death wasn't the only option. The monster hadn't killed Jack, Daniel and Becca twenty-six years ago. Their minds had been wiped clean of all memories of it, which was, in Crock's humble opinion, a reeeeeeally good thing. To remember was to be dead in a way. Some essential part of your humanness died in the presence of such consummate evil.

So that was it? They'd walk out of here—pass that thing and slap hands with it like opposing teams after a baseball game?

What about Whitworth? Theresa'd said that when Bishop was in Vietnam, he'd seen a demon inside the leader of the Cambodian Khmer Rouge. Look what Pol Pot had done—two million people massacred. And he'd just been the petty dictator of a wide spot in the road in Southeast Asia. What evil could the most powerful man in the world perpetrate on mankind?

Then bright white light settled over Crock like a shroud, pure and perfect, sparkling even through his eyelids. He was on his knees, bent over in something resembling a Muslim prayer position, and when he opened his eyes, he was looking at the limestone floor of the cavern. And at light that somehow didn't...his body cast no shadow on the rock floor. The glow around the angel in jeans had cast no shadow, either.

He didn't want to look up, though. Absolutely was not curious enough to risk drawing any attention to himself from the monster. A real, live, not-Hollywood-special-effects monster. Right here. That was crazy, but it was also true.

His mind flicked briefly back to that day in his office with Jack.

There are some things in life you're better off not knowing.

You got that right, pal!

Then a voice spoke, a voice made out of honey—so pure and sweet it warmed his ears to hear it. Wait a minute —hear it...he could hear it.

"You cannot harm them," the voice said. Then Crock felt the wall of percussive energy he had come to recognize as the monster's speech, only it wasn't shouting this time, so there was only a vibration in the air.

You cannot harm them.

He dared to look up then, stared right into the light, and it was like the illumination alone turned all the ugliness in his life—the horrors the monster had shown to him —into ashes and blew it all away. Crock merely sat back on his heels, couldn't drag his eyes off the beauty of the apparition in front of him. The monster was still there, of course, right outside the edge of his vision. But he couldn't even smell the acrid stench of it anymore. The air smelled of the lilacs that grew beside his grandmother's porch when he was a little boy.

Jack sat on the floor a few feet away, cradling Andi in his lap, speaking softly to her.

So other than the angel in the room, things were pretty much as Crock had left them when he checked out.

Now, he checked back in.

"What are we supposed to do, Jack?" he asked— croaked. His throat was so dry he could barely speak.

The monster rumbled at his question and Crock thought for the thousandth time today how grateful he was that he could not hear its words.

"Put a sock in it," he said to the beast. "I'm not talking to you."

Without looking at it, he tensed for the percussion of its anger. There was no response, but Crock wasn't stupid enough to look that way. He just got unsteadily to his feet and went to Jack, who was helping Andi up off the floor.

"Now what?" Crock asked.

"We stand," Jack said simply, and turned slowly around to face the beast.

Crock drew in a deep, shaky breath. Right. Don't just do something, stand there. Then he, too, turned to face the monster.

DANIEL STAGGERED toward the cave entrance filled with ugly red light. He hadn't gone ten feet away from the edge of the chasm when he saw it. There in front of him lay the horror that had assaulted him in nightmares for more than a quarter of a century. His mind skipped right over denial, didn't even bother to try to convince him it couldn't be real.

Flowing in a deadly tide out the cave entrance and across the stone floor toward him was a solid carpet of snakes and spiders, thousands of them, black widows, water moccasins, brown recluse, rattlesnakes, crawling all over each other in a tangle of death. They were making that scuttling, rustling sound he couldn't possibly hear but did.

What Comes Behind.

Daniel had known they'd show up eventually. Had to. But he had refused to let himself think about it. He had to get to Andi. There had to be a way through them or around them and he would find it! The reality showed him how pathetically foolish he'd been even to countenance such a possibility.

Like the tide coming in on a beach, the slithering tangle of poisonous evil glided toward him. He backed up. And backed up. They were less than twenty-five feet away now—they moved so fast!—and he couldn't escape them. He couldn't climb the walls. He couldn't jump the crevice.

Daniel was trapped.

Andi. No…please!

He wouldn't find her now. He couldn't save her. His own death was only seconds away, but he would not die as Marianne had died—gasping for breath, writhing in agonizing convulsions.

He would not let What Comes Behind take him!

Standing with his heels on the edge of the crevice, Daniel felt the cool breeze waft up to him from its black depths. He would die on his own terms, choose his own end as Jeff had done.

What Comes Behind was right in front of him.

"I'm sorry, Andi," he cried.

He wanted her name to be the last word he ever spoke. Then he lifted his foot to step backward into eternity.

Chapter Thirty-Four

Nothing happened for a heartbeat after Theresa flipped the red switch. There was a man at the podium speaking about "...service to society..."

Then one side of the gigantic net in the ceiling of the Balloon Ballroom fell away and what was in it rained down into the room.

Dead rats. They were heavier than the balloons and fell like sacks of sand, splatting down all around the ballroom with the balloons floating down gently behind.

At a table shown on the monitor that provided the back-of-the-room view, a man dressed in a furry pink suit and rabbit ears with the Energizer Bunny drum hangin' around his neck was seated beside an orange-haired, white-faced clown. The couple seated across from them were decked out in matching baggy brown outfits with Mr. and Mrs. Potato Head faces affixed to the front. A dead rat landed with a splat in the middle of the celebration mini-cake in the center of their table, flinging white icing, yellow cake and a smattering of recently defrosted rat blood in their faces.

There was an instant of stunned surprise.

Then Mrs. Potato Head let out a piercing scream and leapt to her feet, knocking over her chair. It collided with the falling chair of the zombie seated behind her, who had jumped up when a rat landed on the head of Gandalf seated across the table from her. The rat slid down off the pointed gray hat, leavin' a bloody snail trail behind it, and dropped into the wizard's plate, knockin' over Harry Potter's water glass and sendin' the green mermaid beside him into hysterics.

A few tables away a rat landed in Glinda the Good Witch's lap. She batted at it to shove it off, but its claws caught in the netting of her pink skirt and hung there. She jumped to her feet, tryin' to shake it off, shrieking, backing away and crashing into other people who'd also leapt up to escape the creatures raining down on them.

Theresa felt a wave of sympathy for Glenda. Wasn't nothing in the world worse'n havin' a rat on you and you can't get it off.

The front-of-the-room monitor showed a rat scattering Thing One and Thing Two, a carrot and Michael Jackson. In the growing chaos on all the monitors, Minions bumped into Egyptian princesses and Vikings, nuns, Chewbacca and Pippi Longstocking.

It was like popcorn then.

Theresa watched, holding her breath. The man she'd knocked aside got to his feet and never cast so much as a glance at her, just gawked at the spectacle on the monitors. Pandemonium had erupted in the ballroom and it was impossible to tell exactly what was going on in the rain of fist-sized balloons from the ceiling.

Where the rats landed, there was instant hysteria. At the tables not fortunate enough to get a rodent visitation, however, folks was just confused. With balloons falling as well, it was hard to see. Unless they was seated at a victim table, people wasn't really certain what was going on. There was more than two hundred fifty four-person tables in the room. Six dozen rats was spread pretty thin among them.

Theresa felt sick. It was happening just as she was afraid it would. People was confused, upset, angry, freaked out, revolted and horrified.

But they wasn't scared.

And they wasn't runnin' out of the room.

A man in a red- and white-striped shirt and hat who was either a barber pole or Where's Waldo, leapt up onto a table and called out for calm, telling people to sit back down.

Theresa bowed her head. The tear that rolled down her cheek added one more drip of moisture to the deluge that had fried the control board.

God, please…

THE JAVELIN MISSILE was propelled from the launcher resting on Sebastian Nemo's shoulder by a charge that hurled it twenty feet or so out over the water beyond the barge. It hung there, suspended, for an instant. Then its own navigation and propulsion systems took over.

Sebastian watched in what seemed like slow motion as the nose of the long tube lifted until it was pointed straight up. A blast of red-orange fire ignited its tail and the force launched the cylinder up into the sky like it'd lifted off from a pad at Cape Canaveral. It was visible for only a second before the fog gobbled it up.

Even its small trail of smoke dissolved in the fog. There

was no sound but the rumble of the tug's engines far behind.

In his mind's eye, Sebastian followed the missile's progress.

The white cylinder rocketed up into the invisible sky.

It reached the apogee of its upward arc.

It paused, hung suspended, then turned and hurled down on a target lit at the four corners with colored balls of light.

THE CAVERN suddenly turned dazzling white, like a flashbulb going off in Daniel's face. The ugly red glow coming from the cave entrance was replaced by a sparkling brilliance, radiant, a bright warm illumination that lit the tops and bottoms and every angle of every surface it touched. And left no shadows.

Daniel stood with his foot raised to step backward into the chasm. What Comes Behind filled the whole cavern in front of him, all around him, the black tide was inches from his toes.

But the instant the light touched the tangle of horror, What Comes Behind disintegrated. The solid mass of snakes and spiders scattered, backing up from the light, scrambling into cracks and crevices in the walls and ceiling, tumbling on top of each other in their haste. It was as if the light burned them, somehow. And maybe it did, a heat that sent them running more frantically than roaches across a kitchen floor when you turned on a light in the middle of the night.

Roaches.

Jeff covered in roaches.

Jeff was dead, had given his life for Daniel.

Not now, no time to think about that now. Andi was up ahead and she was in danger.

In the bright white glow, the walls and floor of the cavern were bare and smooth and Daniel could see so well he began to run—barefoot, his right big toe bleeding from where he had jammed it so hard into the crack in the rock wall of the crevice. He felt no pain from it though or from a dozen other wounds as he sprinted as fast as he could toward the white light. And Andi.

A SINGLE HORRIFIED shriek silenced all other sound in the ballroom. For a heartbeat after, there was silence, then an instantaneous, panicked hysteria exploded.

Theresa's bowed head jerked up. On the monitor screen that filled all her vision a huge black rat bounded across the table and began to climb up Where's Waldo's leg.

A brown one leapt on the shoulder of the Raggedy Ann doll seated at the same table. When it stuck its hideous face up next to the woman's rosy cheek, she totally lost her mind.

All over the room, rats—dozens of rats, hundreds of rats, no, thousands of rats were runnin' across tabletops, jumpin' up on people, swarmin' over some of them two or three rats at a time in a frenzy that instilled instant panic in the crowd.

Theresa stared at the scene, stupefied. The rats she'd brought here in a garbage bag in the trunk of her car, the ones she liked to a'had a heart attack hauling up two flights of stairs, the rats she and Becca had tossed into that net above the ceiling was dead. Not just dead, half frozen.

These here rats was alive!

The stampede toward the doors was brutal. People couldn't get out of the ballroom fast enough. They knocked over chairs and tables and each other and trampled the slower among them in mindless flight.

Theresa's mind flashed back to that day in the funeral home, snakes everywhere and the only exit blocked. But the back and one side wall of the ballroom were lined with doors, side by side, maybe two dozen of them, heavy fire doors, all of them functioning. There was no backup, no bottleneck of panicked people at a lone exit. The crowd simply leapt up and raced out of the room. It emptied in seconds.

The big doors had closed behind the panicked crowd when they rushed out and it was suddenly eerily quiet. Balloons still bobbed up and down in the air from the motion of the moving bodies, but that was all. Nothing else moved. The crazed rats, running around in a frenzy, jumpin' and climbin' and—

Theresa's mind stopped so dead in its tracks, her thoughts crashed into each other like cars in a pileup on the expressway.

Where was them rats?

The man she'd shoved out of the way to get to the switch found a voice and bleated, "What the…?"

The far left monitor screen showed a rat lying in the middle of one of the celebration cakes. It was dead. Clearly, unarguably dead—it was missing a head. The rats you could see scattered on tabletops all over the room lay motionless.

One of the close-up screens showed a table in the right corner of the room. A black rat was draped over the back of one chair at the table, blood dripping off its mouth onto the white tablecloth.

A gray rat lay on a plate on the other side of the table.

His head was crushed, smashed flat, looked like it'd been stomped.

These rats is dead! How—?

The thought was wiped out of Theresa's mind by a blinding white light on all the monitors. Then a rumbling roar ate up the world.

~

IT BEGAN THE MOMENT JACK, Crock and Andi turned to face the efreet. Their senses became confused. They could smell the foul language of the beast, see the offensive odor, hear the ugly red light and taste the cacophony of voices. The senses switched back and forth. Colors became sounds; tastes became light.

Three demons appeared, one in front of each of them. They were all grinning. Then their grinning faces were replaced by a human face with a similar grin. Then another. And another. At the speed of a juiced-up kaleidoscope, a succession of faces came and went, one flickering after the other. All had the same grin.

In the motorcade of faces that flashed before Jack, he saw every one of the officers in his New York City Police Department unit who had gone into the towers that day and never come out. He saw the faces of dope dealers and prostitutes, pimps and murderers, pornographers and thieves. He saw the victims as well as the criminals, men he served with in the military, soldiers he'd killed, women he'd loved. Faster and faster they went. Young, old, black, white, Asian, men, women and children. All grinning as maniacal laughter rose up behind them.

A procession of the great unwashed flashed before Crock. Fire victims with charred lips, murder victims with slashed throats, bloated bodies hauled out of the

Ohio. All their dead eyes were open and they were grinning.

Only two faces appeared before Andi. Her mother and father. One, then the other, back and forth. The grin remained, but somehow the faces looked sad, too, angry and hurt, annoyed and puzzled. Sometimes, the whole right side of her mother's head was missing and sometimes her father's face was on a head that wasn't attached to his body. Sometimes, they looked like they were in excruciating pain, pleading for it to stop, begging her to make it stop. Still grinning, though. Always grinning.

Faster and faster the faces went, dizzying, blurry, and behind it all the rumbling voice spoke with the sound of metal scraping against metal.

"What's real?" the mocking voice asked. "Death is real. Hate is real. Pain and desolation are real."

Then the beast began to spew out obscene accusations in a roar of words that was far more horrible than the images. The repulsive charges and disgusting recriminations hammered at Jack's soul, beat him down, filled him with growing hopelessness.

But Crock didn't react in any way to the monster's mockery. As far as Jack could tell, it had no effect on him at all. His face was expressionless.

Then a blackened, bloated face appeared before Crock with clotted blood clinging to its hair and he reflexively turned away toward Jack. He must have seen on Jack's face the effect the creature's screaming accusations were having on him because Crock's vacant expression disappeared. He engaged. He looked past the grinning faces to the roaring monster for a moment, then back at Jack. Suddenly, Crock grabbed Jack's shoulders and began to sing.

"Jingle bells, jingle bells, jingle all the way," he sang, in a pitifully off-key baritone. "Sing with me, Jack. Loud. As loud as you can! Oh, what fun it is to ride in a one-horse open sleigh, hey…"

Jack took up the song, pulled Andi into the circle with him, and Crock and she began to sing, too.

"Dashing through the snow, in a one-horse open sleigh. O'er the hills we go, laughing all the way. Ho, ho, ho. Bells on—"

Sudden silence filled the chamber. Not just the absence of sound but an entity of its own. A thing that gobbled up the words they were singing so no sound made it out into the cavern. It was like going instantly deaf.

The demon unfurled gigantic bat wings that stretched out twenty feet in each direction.

"I cannot harm you," it roared, "but the others aren't protected by—"

The demon didn't say the word angel. Instead, he snarled an epithet in another language, spitting out the unpronounceable syllables as if the taste of the word were foul.

"All your friends are dead," the efreet roared and the last word echoed through the cavern, reverberating, not growing softer and softer but louder and louder. "I burned them alive. They died screaming."

Dead, dead, dead bounced off the walls as the efreet leaned toward Andi and sneered at her. "Except your daddy. He couldn't scream because I chopped off his head."

"Her daddy's head is right where it's supposed to be," came a voice from the far left side of the cavern.

They all jerked toward it with the perfect unison of a chorus line; then Andi broke out of Jack's grasp and raced toward the barefoot man in a T-shirt, threw herself at him and almost bowled him over, crying in joy that rocked the walls of the cavern, "Daddy! Daddy!"

It was Daniel. Here. How? Jack had no idea. He shot a glance at the angel, her beauty so overwhelming it was hard for him to drag his gaze away. The angel was smiling.

～

BETWEEN ONE HEARTBEAT and the next, the Cat in the Hat was transformed into a light without shadows, the brilliance of the sun you could look into without blinking. And in the light, or made of the light—or maybe the light was made of her—was a being of breathtaking perfection. She towered above Becca as tall as the monster, white wings of down moving slowly back and forth, her black hair flowing down her back, her face so beautiful it made Becca want to weep. Perched on the top of her black hair was a red-and-white-striped hat. The hat she'd worn in Becca's closet all those years ago. The hat that had floated all by itself in the muddy water under a purple bridge.

Suddenly, the beast faltered, seemed uncertain. It turned toward the ballroom.

Its concentrated attention had been a blistering spotlight on Becca, like a kid using a magnifying glass to burn an ant. She only recognized the intensity of it when it was removed.

Then Chapman Whitworth cried out—not the beast, Whitworth. A single, strangled word: "No!"

Around the corner in the gigantic main atrium outside the ballroom two dozen doors flew open at once and a screaming crowd of people poured out, a thunderous stampede of terrified humanity that filled the huge silent space with the noise of their cries and running feet.

Whitworth turned back to her, limitless rage in his eyes. He held out his flip-top cellphone and snarled, "When I punch this button, thousands of other people will die and you can't rescue them with dead rats!"

His finger moved toward the text button on the phone —and then the world exploded. A percussive fist slammed into Becca and knocked her backward off her feet. A thunderbolt of sound, a reverberating boom, like standing next to an erupting volcano, crashed into her ears. The rumbling roar ate up the world. The ballroom door on the far end blew out and flew across the atrium, mowing down the crowd, a scythe through wheat. But the other doors held and the room contained the blast.

Whitworth stood in place with the red demon behind him and Becca knew that the monster would remain unscathed by a direct hit from whatever explosive device went off in that ballroom. Its diabolical force was unequaled by any weapon. The vile creature possessed the dark power of the universe—limitless and unknowable.

Now, it was the beast that was enraged. The monster jerked its hideous horned head back toward Becca and the light. He let out a roar fueled by consummate hatred and raised the scimitar above Becca's head.

"You cannot harm her," the angel told the red monster, her voice as pure as a note that would shatter crystal.

"And you cannot save her," the beast snarled back. "She stands or falls on her own."

WHEN DANIEL BURST out into the cavern filled with white light, he drank in the sight of its occupants. Jack, Andi and Crock were standing together. Had it been his imagination as he ran through the cavern—had he heard "Jingle Bells"?

His gaze gobbled up Andi. She was alive. Unharmed.

He almost collapsed on the spot from relief. After that, he allowed himself to pay attention to the rest of the scene and it took him a moment to adjust to what he saw, that it was, indeed, real and not some movie on an IMAX screen.

A horrific red demon towered fifty feet in the air, facing a transcendently beautiful being made of light. Darkness and light. The definition of good and evil.

Between the two stood Jack, Crock and Andi.

The words popped into his head so crisp and real he almost turned around to see if Clayton Abernathy, the church's elder board chairman, were standing behind him.

When you don't know what to do, you stand, Daniel. You hold your head up and you stand.

The demon leaned toward Andi and spit into her face that he had beheaded her father.

"Her daddy's head is right where it's supposed to be," Daniel said.

Andi snapped around toward him, her face broke into the most beautiful smile he'd ever seen, and she came running. "Daddy, Daddy!"

He knelt and caught her in his arms, staggered back from the collision and held her close, smelling the little girl smell, feeling her warmth. Then she whispered into his ear, took his hand and led him back to the others.

Jack grabbed him in a bear hug. Crock nodded.

"Liar!" Andi cried at the demon, squeezing her father's hand tight. "You're scary and I'm afraid of you, but you're a liar."

Jack reached over and took Daniel's other hand, then turned to Crock and took his, too. The four of them stood facing the monstrosity.

"You don't belong here," Daniel said.

"Go back where you came from," Jack said.

"Don't let the door hit you on the backside on your way out," Crock said.

Before Andi could speak, the boiling, bubbling cloud that had concealed the efreet earlier exploded into the whole chamber, unleashing a storm as powerful as a hurricane making landfall right there in front of them. Suddenly, a brutal wind assaulted them—it was black, how could wind be black? It hurled raindrops at them like shrapnel. The rain was black, too, as if it had dissolved the night sky, sucking ink drops of darkness from the universe beyond.

Hammer blows of surf detonated on the desolate, rocky shore, spawning chaos on the ashy rocks, an explosion of deranged movement and sound. The host of demons scrambled for cover in an insectile frenzy, screeching shrill slaughterhouse grunts and squeals. The larger ones pushed the smaller aside, attacking in vicious fury with jagged claws and rows of razor-edged teeth.

Daniel pushed Andi to the floor and covered her with his body to protect her. Crock and Jack huddled close. Thunder boomed like faraway cannons. Pulses of lightning strobed a sea that roiled and heaved beneath bubbling black clouds. The jagged fragments of light illuminated what was forming far from shore. Daniel watched in breathless horror as a greenish-black tornado, a leviathan vortex, snaked down out of the tumult, writhing and twisting, sucking up the shadows and fire to become a swirling torch of flames with a center as dark as the far side of the moon.

As the tornado hurled across the sea at them, the beast began an odd babble. Roaring above the sound of the wind, it pronounced the first few syllables of words slowly, like a tape on half speed, a totally alien sound. But Daniel's mind couldn't help trying to understand the words. Every syllable echoed, though, and the echoes blended together. All the previous sounds hit his ear at the exact instant that the beast went on to the next syllable, which Daniel's mind tried to process amid the echoes of the first.

The twister was closing on them, the wind battering them as they huddled drenched on the floor. Daniel felt dizzy, light-headed, his mind whirling and spinning. He couldn't think with pieces of words bouncing around, lighting the inside of his skull like a pinball machine.

Theresa's voice spoke clearly in his head.

"He'll do anything to distract you from what you's there to do. That beast will bewilder and confound you, keep you tied in knots—upset, scared, confused—so you won't have no strength to use against him."

With jaw-clenching will, Daniel clamped down the cacophony in his head and silenced it. He refused to look at the twister bearing down on them, ignored the storm.

Then he got slowly to his knees. When he did, rain and wind pelted Andi and she curled into a ball on the cavern floor, squeezing her eyes tight shut and cringing away from the drenching gale. Daniel reached out and lifted her face and she squinted up at him through the torrent of rain. Then he put his hands tight over her ears, muffling sound. He leaned close and looked deep into her frightened, bewildered eyes—sea green, the same color as Emily's.

There was Andi. Only Andi. He gently kissed her forehead, both cheeks, the tip of her nose and her chin. He mouthed, "I love you!"

At the end of all things that was what mattered. Love.

Andi's face relaxed. The terror drained out of her eyes, replaced by—what? Peace. Then a spark flickered there. Not peace, anger. She staggered up, leaning into the wind, and faced the beast. Daniel noticed for the first time that the angel stood untouched in the tempest.

Andi cried out at the efreet, her little-girl voice somehow loud enough to carry over the din of the storm raging around them and the beast's growling words.

"Stop it!"

The beast instantly silenced. The wind stilled. The tornado sank down into the flaming sea. The rain stopped. Echoes of thunder died away and it was eerily quiet. Jack stood, put out his hand and helped Crock to his feet. Then they linked hands again.

An endless lake of fire still boiled within the pentagram Chapman Whitworth had drawn in black chalk on the rock floor twenty-six years ago. The efreet he had summoned from hell towered there, fifty feet tall, with black batwings raised in a canopy above it.

The creature snarled at them in defiance. Or was that…fear?

Andi reached up with the hand not clutching Daniel's and lifted the cross that hung on a silver chain around her neck. It had been her mother's necklace. At Emily's funeral, his wrist in a cast, Daniel had handed the necklace to Jack and watched him fasten it on Andi. As far as Daniel knew, Andi had not taken it off since.

The little brown-haired girl held the small cross out toward a creature that had stepped into time from forever.

"It's not just us," Andi whispered in the silent stillness. "God doesn't want you here, either."

She squared her shoulders.

"Get out of our world," she said. When Andi spoke again, her tiny voice reverberated through the chamber as if it were echoing down through the centuries, through the millennia.

"Go!"

The beast vanished.

Andi, Daniel, Jack and Crock stood together in an

empty cave warmed by a brilliant light that cast no shadows.

~

BECCA GOT to her feet slowly, reached out and took the angel's hand. And stood.

"This isn't your world," Becca said, her voice a whisper on a breath. "Go away and leave us alone. Go!"

The red form that had risen up around Whitworth was suddenly gone. Like the flame of a candle, it left a little puff of smoke in the air to mark its passing.

The light was suddenly gone, too. The shadowless glow instantly became a little sparkle like a soap bubble.

Chapman Whitworth fell to the floor, a glove with the hand suddenly removed. His energy, his life force gone, he lay on his back, stunned and disoriented. Becca walked slowly over to the man—and he was just a man—and looked down at him. The hatred that transformed his features when he looked up at her was not the glare of a demon from hell. His was the rage of a man who had everything he wanted within his grasp...and then had it snatched away.

"You..." he growled menacingly and struggled to get to his knees. Becca put out her foot and shoved him and he collapsed onto his back again. Then she leaned over and picked up the cell phone that had flown out of his grasp when he fell. She flipped open the cover.

"Did you ever pull the wings off a fly?" she asked him.

He looked at her, uncomprehending.

She held out the phone and snapped it in two. Then she dropped the two pieces on the tile floor and stomped them. Again and again. Just like she had the rats.

Chapter Thirty-Five

They'd up and gotten Theresa a puppy for her birthday! She hadn't seen it comin', neither, or she would have headed them off. Last thing in the world Theresa Washington needed was another dog! Them critters didn't do nothin' but eat and pee on lampposts. And this one was just a baby—caught it chewing on her slippers the other day and she liked to whopped it…

Oh, who do I think I'm foolin', Lord. This here little mutt is the lovinest creature I ever did see.

Theresa scratched behind the ear of the little golden retriever puppy lying contentedly in her lap. She'd named it Cornbread—'cause it was the color of cornbread, and 'cause ever time she called out that name it put her in mind of the other dog called Biscuit that had saved her from the rats and Becca from the snake. That dog was buried under the snow in the backyard beside the rose trellis.

Theresa breathed deep and smelled the turkey roasting in the oven. She'd always liked Thanksgiving. She and Bishop usually went to her sister's house to celebrate with her big family. They'd always planned on having a bunch of kids of they own, but the Lord had only blessed them with Isaac, and they'd lost him twenty-six years ago. She looked around the room and smiled. Now, it appeared the Lord had done blessed her with three other children that'd been "lost" twenty-six years ago, too—Jack, Daniel and Becca. Them and the others made a family good as anybody else's.

She smoothed Cornbread's shiny coat and looked out the window. It had actually snowed the day before Thanksgiving, and a delighted Andi'd talked the grownups into waging a snowball war.

Jack, Crock and Becca were taking on Andi, Daniel and Sheriff Lincoln. Surely to goodness that man had a first name other than sheriff, but if he did, Theresa hadn't heard it. He'd had business with the US Attorney's office, and when the snowstorm stranded him in Cincinnati—it'd snowed three feet in Caverna County and wasn't a single road passable—Daniel had played host to him last night and she'd insisted he come to dinner today. The sheriff had brought along an old yearbook for Jack, Becca and Daniel to look at. His uncle had been Jack and Daniel's shop teacher when they was in junior high school.

Nice man, that. Helped out best as he could when the federal authorities come buzzing around like flies on road-kill. They all knew wasn't no way in the world anybody'd believe Chapman Whitworth was behind all that'd happened—that man was slick as Teflon. So they'd had to come up with some kinda plausible explanation of they own to explain it else they woulda spent the rest of they lives tangled up in legal trouble.

The sheriff had backed up Daniel's version of the Bradford's Ridge end of it, had reminded them out-of-town fellas that Billy Ray Hawkins mighta looked like some dumb hillbilly, but he'd been smart enough to run a marijuana business that made him a millionaire twice over, and smart enough to stash two million dollars in gold bullion for twenty years in a boxcar that didn't exist! It didn't surprise the sheriff none a'tall that a man like that could come up with a creative scheme to get away with murder.

Daniel told 'em Billy Ray'd bragged about how he was gonna outsmart all them Suit-and-Tie Men. He said he'd made up an elaborate story about a terrorist group called the Maelstrom, got the inspiration from them bombings in Minnesota and Phoenix. He'd hired somebody to send out an e-mail about "coordinated terrorist attacks"—that never happened, by the way!—and come up with that beheading nonsense—all so's he could get his revenge on Jeff and Daniel and wouldn't nobody ever come sniffing 'round his door.

He'd promised they'd regret crossing Billy Ray Hawkins one day, and Billy Ray always kept his word.

'Sides, wasn't no way to tie Billy Ray to any real terrorists, and wasn't no reason for him to go around blowing people up all over the country when he had a boxcar full of gold pushing up daisies in a field in Kentucky.

Billy Ray would have got away with the whole scheme, too, just like he done with the boxcar, if Jeff hadn't knocked him into the crevice. Jeff had saved Daniel's life. He'd been a hero. That much, at least, was true. As was the part about Daniel crossing the crevice to find a way out of the cave since Billy Ray'd locked up his end and put the key in his pocket.

They didn't never find that key—'cause they didn't never find Billy Ray and Jeff. Truth was, they didn't look real hard. They shone the biggest light they could find down into the crack in the floor of that cavern and still couldn't see the bottom. But that light did show shafts in the black walls of the crevice, dozens of 'em, leading back who knew where. A honeycomb of caverns like was under the whole of Caverna County. Wasn't safe to go poking around in a place like that. Floor could collapse out from under you or the roof fall down on your head. Didn't make sense to risk live men looking for dead ones.

And didn't nothing come out that connected them three possessed children to that cavern because the sheriff seen to it that nothing did. Theresa sighed and shook her head. Them poor babies as was took over by demons—it'd be a long time before they healed up, if they ever did.

Either God or they own minds had wiped out all Cassidy Davenport's and Russell Willis's memories. Like what happened to Jack, Daniel and Becca...except the Three Musketeers hadn't had to face the consequences of things they bodies done that they didn't have no say over. Rusty had killed a police officer. Cassidy had killed a nurse. Wouldn't be no legal ramifications, though, because they was just eight years old and obviously hadn't been in they right minds when they done what they done. Still, both of them was gone have to live the rest of they lives with them terrible crimes hanging over their heads. It would take years of plastic surgery and dental work to repair the damage that somebody had done to Cassidy's face. Rusty had an easier road. He'd woke up in a psychiatric hospital with no memory of anything that'd happened to him after the day he, Cassidy and Ariel Murphy had kicked around a soccer ball in the field next to Milkstone.

Ariel Murphy remembered kicking that soccer ball— and all the rest of it, too. Maybe she'd be okay with that since she seen the Lady of Light. Might be Andi and the angel helped heal up that child's soul. Ariel and Andi had become friends—talked on the phone, texted each other every three seconds, emailed, and were planning sleepovers as soon as Ariel got the cast off her leg. Theresa suspected they'd be special friends for the rest of they lives. What they had shared wouldn't nobody else in the world ever understand.

Them men from the Treasury Department might have been so starry-eyed 'bout finding and confiscating two million dollars in gold bullion in Caverna County that they wasn't inclined to poke too hard at the rest of what'd gone on there, but the Cincinnati police wasn't distracted by the gold in a dope grower's buried boxcar. They was investigating a terrorist attack. Somebody'd fired an antitank missile, a state-of-the-art military weapon, at a hotel in Ohio, for crying out loud! And the gub'mint had hauled out all they big guns to find out how that'd happened.

Homeland Security. FBI. CIA. ATF.

After all, it was obvious that somebody with a political agenda had been trying to take out all the candidates for the Democratic presidential nomination. That explosion coulda killed hundreds of other people, too, would have been a big bad thing...except they wasn't nobody in that room when the blast went off there.

And why was that?

Well...

There'd been more than a thousand people at the Better Day Society costume ball and seemed like ever last one of 'em had a different story 'bout what'd happened that night.

The only thing they all agreed on was that they was rats mixed in with the balloons that fell on they heads. Some of them swore the rats was alive. Others said they was dead. And others said they started out dead and then came to life. The herky-jerky footage from the only security camera that was still working after the 'lectricity went all wonky right before the blast appeared to back up the "dead" version. The only rats visible on it was just lying where they fell, not moving. They done autopsies on all the rat carcasses they could find and turned out they wasn't just dead—they'd been froze solid and then thawed back out.

Them investigators figured must be them folks who'd said the rats was alive had got hysterical and was hallucinating. They'd probably have kept right on thinking that if it hadn't been for a video a teenage girl posted on YouTube. Her boyfriend had been a busboy at the Rivergate that night, had pulled out his phone and captured twenty, maybe thirty seconds of what had gone on in the ballroom. Not much, but enough to show live rats, dozens of them, hundreds of them, a sea of them crawling all over chairs and tables and people.

Where'd them rats come from?

What was they doing there?

And where'd they go?

Theresa knew it was real likely the police was gone come knocking on her door one day. After all, she couldn't hide the fact that she'd been hospitalized after a rat attack three days before the Rivergate was all broke out with 'em. A coincidence like that was hard to ignore. And she definitely coulda been the "Big" Red Riding Hood Darth Vader'd seen with a rat in a laundry basket that night. Of course, that particular rat wasn't neither live nor dead—it was rubber! The concierge guy had picked it up and examined it thoroughly, he said, it being his responsibility to look after the welfare of the hotel's guests and all. He was prepared to swear on a stack of Bibles that thing was a toy.

The poor man in that control booth didn't see nothing but a big black shadow, and if they questioned Red Riding Hood's little demon sidekick...well, poor Becca wasn't right in the head, you know, had been in and out of mental institutions her whole life, had had screaming wall-eyed psychotic episodes in front of dozens of people over the years—you could check. And she didn't remember nothing 'bout the night of the Better Day Society ball. Not one thing.

The authorities wasn't likely to buy their stories. They was smart fellas. They'd find Becca's tail lying in that stairwell and they'd check costume rental places. But wasn't a whole lot they could do since the police didn't have no actual proof. Oh, some security camera somewhere probably took they pictures, but you couldn't see Theresa's face at all under that hood, Becca's mask hid everything but her chin, and them gloves had been a real good idea.

Bottom line was that until them officers could figure out how a volunteer elementary school crossing guard like Theresa Washington had known somebody was gonna fire an antitank missile at the Rivergate Hotel on Halloween, how she'd managed to come by thousands of live rats, how she'd fit the whole herd of them into a single rolling laundry hamper and kept 'em there, how she'd got 'em up to the top floor with the elevator and stairway doors locked, and what possible motive she'd have to do any of it, they wouldn't be locking her up anytime soon. That was a good thing, too, since she didn't have Jeff around no more to get her out.

"You sneaked up on me!" Crock called out when Andi's snowball caught him in the back of the neck. "That's against International Snowball War Law and violates the Frosty the Snowman Treaty."

"Does not!" Andi cried and lobbed another one that caught him on the shoulder.

"I am a sworn law enforcement officer," Crock said. "If I say it's illegal, it's illegal." He threw a snowball at her that missed by three feet and she landed another on his chest. "You need to learn to respect your elders, little girl."

Becca looked good, Theresa thought. She had a little meat on her bones now. Not as much as she needed, but some. More important, the haunted look had left her eyes; she didn't cringe like she was expectin' a blow anymore neither. She was getting well.

They all were.

Becca ducked the sheriff's snowball and tried to smash one into Daniel's face. They fell together and lay in a laughing tangle in the snow, then rolled over on their backs and started making angels. Theresa shot a glance at Jack, who had no expression of any kind on his face. One or the other of them boys was likely to claim that girl one of these days, though which one it'd be was anybody's guess. And what that would mean to the one who didn't, well...

The snowball war became a snowman-building contest before they all came inside with red noses and numb fingers. A few minutes later, Andi came out of the kitchen, carrying a tray of hot chocolate and it was déjà vu all over again. She'd come into the room carrying a tray of brownies the night they saw Chapman Whitworth's face on television when he accepted the president's nomination to the supreme court. Andi'd screamed, terrified by the demon presence she could see all around him, and what had happened after that had wounded each of them in a different way. Left its mark on them. None would ever be the same.

Not the least of which was Chapman Whitworth.

Theresa chuckled out loud and Crock looked up from the cinnamon toothpick he'd just pulled out of a vial of them in his hand.

"Private joke?"

"Oh, I was just thinkin' 'bout our mutual friend's interview on The Today Show."

Crock grinned. "They replayed that clip like it was the winning touchdown in the Super Bowl."

Chapman Whitworth had been invited to discuss his unproven but unshakeable belief that the terrorist attacks were homegrown. And he'd shown up. The man, sans demon. Not impressive. So dull, in fact, that they'd used the second half of the show for footage of a blizzard in the Rockies instead of the remainder of his interview. The next day, he'd withdrawn from the nomination race.

Andi set the tray of hot chocolate down on the table beside Theresa, then poured her a cup.

"It's just milk with powdered chocolate stirred up in it and heated in the microwave," she said. "That's the only kind I know how to make. Do you like it?"

There was so much powdered chocolate floating on the top of that cup you could have trotted a mouse across it. Theresa took a sip and gasped. "It's fine, real good."

"Jack!" Becca called out. There was alarm in her voice and it instantly yanked a knot of fear into the pit of Theresa's stomach. "Come here. Look at this!"

Jack crossed to where Becca and Daniel were seated on the couch, looking at the 1985 Bradford's Ridge Junior High School yearbook Sheriff Lincoln had brought. The rest gathered around, too.

Becca held out the book so Jack and the others could see and pointed to a picture in the upper left corner of the page beneath the heading "Award-winning projects, Steve Tulley's shop class, 1985."

The photo grabbed a moment from the past and dragged it into the present. Two boys were grinning off the page—Jack and Daniel! Theresa's eyes filled with tears at the sight of them as the boys they used to be.

"The picka-nick basket, Jack," Becca cried. "I remembered it when all the other memories came back to me, but I couldn't picture it in my mind. Do you remember it? You and Daniel made it for me in shop class—for my birthday, to replace the big yellow one that fell off the back of your bike and scattered our lunch all over the street."

"Picka-nick basket...?" Jack was thoughtful. "I sort of—"

"Whether you remember it or not, look at it! Just look!"

They all leaned forward. The picture showed two smiling boys standing beside a table. On the table was a shiny can with the top cut off and reattached as a lid with hinges and a catch. The lid was open and the inside of the can was visible, lined with something yellow—felt, maybe. Jack gasped and Theresa figured it out a second later.

The can was a five-gallon gasoline can.

"I do remember," he sputtered. "We thought and thought, trying to figure out what we could make that wouldn't break apart and spill everything if it came off the back of one of the bikes and—"

"We took it everywhere we went," Daniel put in, wonder dawning on his face with the memory. "I was carrying it that day in the woods when the Bad Kids..."

"We had it with us the day we went up into the top of the furniture store. The day we—" Becca began.

"It was on the back of your bike that day, Jack," Daniel said. "I was riding behind Becca because my bike had a flat tire."

"You rode away with it when you—" Becca began.

"When I went after the Bad Kids."

"And it wasn't on your bike when we found it later in the woods," she continued. "I never thought about that until just now."

"Which means you—" Daniel began.

"Which means I must have taken it with me into the nursing home. I have no memory of...I must have been hungry, I guess, and—"

"That's what the security camera caught, Jack," Becca said. She jumped up and threw her arms around him. "You weren't hauling a can of gasoline into the nursing home. You were carrying a picnic basket full of peanut-butter-and-jelly sandwiches."

The smiles on Crock's and the sheriff's faces would have melted frost off a windowpane.

The relief on Jack's took ten years off his age.

Then they were babbling, piecing together fragments of memory, recalling things they hadn't thought in a quarter of a century. Not horror thoughts, monster thoughts—just picnics and baseball practice, catching tadpoles and chasing fireflies, children growing up best friends. The Three Musketeers.

Theresa picked up Cornbread, snapped his leash on his collar and stepped out into the cold air on the back deck. She set him down to go potty in the backyard, then stood watching the puppy play in the snow.

She'd been afraid Jack's life was gone be permanently ruined by the video Chapman Whitworth had dug up of him hauling gasoline into the Twin Oaks Nursing Home right before it burned down. Now, that part'd been worked out, too.

I know you ain't s'posed to talk to dead people, Lord, so could you give Bishop a message from me? Tell him...

She stopped and started over.

Bishop, honey, I needed you here to hold my hand and cry with me when Daniel told me 'bout Billy Ray killin' Isaac. That hurt my whole soul. Daniel said there was details I didn't want to know and I didn't ask what they was. What difference does it make now.

She stopped again and sighed.

You reckon I'm ever gonna get used to you not being here to talk to? I don't think so. Jack said that maybe the more my life's filled up with live people, the less I'll think about the ones that's dead.

She made a humph sound in her throat.

I told him that was a load of crap.

THE END

The Series Continues

Loved reading *The Reckoning* and want more Ninie Hammon right now? You're in luck! The series continues with *The Fault*.

Click here to get The Fault.

A Note From The Author

Thank you for reading *The Reckoning*.

If you enjoyed this book, would you please consider writing a review on your favorite bookseller site so other readers might enjoy it too? Just a couple of sentences. That would mean a lot to me.

Thank you!

Ninie Hammon

About the Author

Ninie Hammon (rhymes with shiny, not skinny) grew up in Muleshoe, Texas, got a BA in English and theatre from Texas Tech University and snagged a job as a newspaper reporter. She didn't know a thing about journalism, but her editor said if she could write he could teach her the rest of it and if she couldn't write the rest of it didn't matter. She hung in there for a 25-year career as a journalist. As soon as she figured out that making up the facts was a whole lot more fun than reporting them, she turned to fiction and never looked back.

Ninie now writes suspense--every flavor except pistachio: psychological suspense, inspirational suspense, suspense thrillers, paranormal suspense, suspense mysteries.

In every book she keeps this promise to her Loyal Reader: "I will tell you a story in a distinctive voice you'll always recognize, about people as ordinary as you are--people who have been slammed by something they didn't sign on for, and now they must fight for their lives. Then smack in the middle of their everyday worlds, those people encounter the unexplainable--and it's always the game-changer."

Also By Ninie Hammon

Cornbread Mafia

Fire In The Hole

Blown' Up A Storm

Ridin' For A Fall

Nowhere, USA

The Jabberwock

Mad Dog

Trapped

The Hanging Judge

The Witch of Gideon

Blown Away

Nowhere People

Through The Canvas Series

Black Water

Red Web

Gold Promise

Blue Tears

The Taken Saga

The Taken

The Changed

The Hidden

The Saved

The Unexplainable Collection

Five Days in May

Black Sunshine

The Based on True Stories Collection

Home Grown

Sudan

When Butterflies Cry

The Knowing Series

The Knowing

The Deceiving

The Reckoning

The Fault

Stand-alone Psychological Thrillers

The Memory Closet

The Last Safe Place